GOD HELP US

GOD HELP US

ARTHUR (MAC) MC CAFFRY

TATE PUBLISHING
AND **ENTERPRISES,** LLC

God Help Us
Copyright © 2016 by Arthur (Mac) Mc Caffry. All rights reserved.

No part of this publication may be reproduced, stored in a retrieval system or transmitted in any way by any means, electronic, mechanical, photocopy, recording or otherwise without the prior permission of the author except as provided by USA copyright law.

Scripture quotations, unless otherwise indicated, are taken from the *Holy Bible, King James Version,* Cambridge, 1769. Used by permission. All rights reserved.

This novel is a work of fiction. Names, descriptions, entities, and incidents included in the story are products of the author's imagination. Any resemblance to actual persons, events, and entities is entirely coincidental.

The opinions expressed by the author are not necessarily those of Tate Publishing, LLC.

Published by Tate Publishing & Enterprises, LLC
127 E. Trade Center Terrace | Mustang, Oklahoma 73064 USA
1.888.361.9473 | www.tatepublishing.com

Tate Publishing is committed to excellence in the publishing industry. The company reflects the philosophy established by the founders, based on Psalm 68:11,
"The Lord gave the word and great was the company of those who published it."

Book design copyright © 2016 by Tate Publishing, LLC. All rights reserved.
Cover design by Joana Quilantang
Interior design by Mary Jean Archival

Published in the United States of America

ISBN: 978-1-68164-224-6
Fiction / Christian / Fantasy
15.10.29

Acknowledgments

I humbly dedicate this novel to my good friend, Ethel Hamilton, now deceased at the age of one hundred and one. She introduced me back into the Lord's grace after years of absence. My disregard toward the church has been erased, and through her love, patience, and devotion, I'm finally able to forgive my enemies as Christ forgives me. My appreciation and love of her is never ending.

I dedicate the same to my wonderful Uncle Joe, a poor man with riches beyond imagination awaiting him in heaven.

Thanks to long-time friends Phyllis Gurganus, Kathy Tuley, and my brother Randy for their support and wisdom.

And I have never-ending thanks to the four most notable persons affecting my personal life: Billy Graham, John Hagee, Dr. David Jeremiah, and Greg Laurie. Their message of dwelling with the Lord throughout eternity has given me faith and understanding beyond my wildest dreams. But most important, their words of love and forgiveness never runs dry, even for a sinner saved by the grace of God, *like me.*

God bless you my publisher; may our Lord and Savior
look down upon you favorably.

—Mac Mc Caffry

Author's Prediction for Tomorrow's Headlines

I predict there will be a treaty drawn for a period of seven years, supported by both the Israeli prime minister and President Obama before he leaves office at the end of 2016. I predict the selling of the treaty will include most of the provisions stated in the 1995 Oslo 11 Accord between President Clinton, Yitzhak Rabin, and Yasser Arafat. And I predict the authors of this treaty will be exalted with legacies never to be forgotten.

The author includes his prediction as part of his fiction novel *God Help Us*, but his true motive for this novel is to make people aware the rapture of the church is near; before a bugle sounds high in the heavens with our Lord Jesus appearing to gather His church, the ones the Bible calls *the elect*.

PREACHER AT 5

ALTHOUGH only old enough to be in kindergarten, Arthur McCaffrey Jr., 5, above, is telling amazed adults what a sinful world we live in. He recently made his debut as an evangelist before a large gathering at Evansville, Ind. He knows 600 Biblical quotations and his favorite is "Repent, for the kingdom of God is at hand."

Contents

Introduction 11

Prelude 13

1   Awakening 15

2   Walk with an Angel 18

3   The Chosen 30

4   And There's Angels 39

5   Trouble Within 44

6   Setting the Future 51

7   Everything Is Beautiful 61

8   Daddy Keith 71

9   Homecoming 76

10   Something to Worry About 85

11   Assignment Unknown 94

12   Setting the Stage 101

13   Preparing for Battle 106

14   No Way Out 112

15   Farewell, Oh My Captain 118

16   Someone for Rosy 124

17   Person of Interest 129

18   Someone to Think About 138

19   Thirty-Nine Steps to the Upper Room 152

20	Finals	160
21	And Then, There's Grace	167
22	Ready to Roll	172
23	Berchtesgaden: A Place in History	176
24	Halloween	182
25	Why, Oh, Why, Lord?	192
26	To Hell and Back	202
27	A Place of Torment	207
28	Decision Time	215
29	Looking Ahead	221
30	Help Us, Lord—Help US	232
31	A Stranger from Nowhere	242
32	Welcome Aboard, Marla	248
33	Strangers in Paradise	256
34	Celebration	264
35	A New Player	270
36	Changing Plans	284
37	A Time to Heal	294
38	A Time to Pray	306
39	A Stranger in Paradise	318
40	A Plan for All	327
41	Looking Ahead	335
42	The Reception	343
43	Predestination	354
44	A Man to Remember	365

Introduction

A couple of years ago, I read Thomas Friedman's book, *The World Is Flat*, and I began to realize he might be writing something yet to come—something in line with biblical prophecy. And I'm beginning to wonder what's next for us to see in this brave new world filled with knowledge beyond imagination.

Recently, great tragedy struck the United States, and suddenly, all peace-loving persons on earth were shocked; twenty of our most loved were brutally murdered, along with six of their protectors at a school in Connecticut.

And I thought of other places the same took place: a movie theatre in Colorado, where six innocent persons met death by one of the same. And yet another where Congresswoman Gabrielle Gifford was shot without reason except maybe someone with a troubled mind, beady-looking eyes, demonic, devil possessed.

The world seemed to stop, searching for a reason. And I began to realize this isn't new; it has happened before. And I asked myself the age-old question: who in their right mind could commit such atrocities? And the answer always comes up the same: Satan and his demonic possessed followers here on earth.

And again, I ask myself, "Who reaps benefits of these sick characters with the beady-eyes, weirdo personalities, filled with an unending desire to destroy the ones God loves the most?

Arthur (Mac) Mc Caffry

Is it the NRA, the ones who like to hunt, the ones who like to protect themselves from thieves or murderers, or could it be demonic forces taking over the hearts and minds of people here on earth?

—⚡—

I have a decision to make! I'm eighty-eight years of age, attempting to write something so great and wonderful upon my simple mind since childhood: Jesus, our Lord and Savior, returning to gather His church just before Armageddon. It's challenging for sure, but with His help, I'll do it!

Night after night, I lie in bed, remembering the words of Moses! The words he said when the Lord told him he would deliver his people out of Egypt, but I'm no Moses—that's for sure! But I just might be one of his chosen, perhaps the same as one of you. And the very thought of something so wonderful makes me think of my personal life, *my redemption*!

I guess I'm about like what the apostle Paul called the worst of the worst—a sinner saved by the grace of God, searching, but never recognizing His almighty power.

Again and again, I contemplate the seriousness of something dwelling within my heart and soul, the power of the enemy that I must face. And I recognize from the very beginning, I'm no match for him, the evil one, *the devil himself*, without help from above.

And I search without end, asking myself questions never dreamed before. And it always comes up the same: my help is in the hands of the Father, Son, and Holy Ghost.

Prelude

Mike, a Vietnam vet, returns home after two and a half years in and out of combat. His return is greeted by waiting protesters as he disembarks from a hospital ship in San Francisco. He's spat upon and cursed for serving in a war they refused to support. He's filled with bitterness, but decides to move on with life.

He begins raising a family under the guidance of a *very conservative church*. Life moves on year after year as Mike and his wife become part of accepted church life. Then it happened! His neighbors' daughter is sexually molested by a deacon in the church. Cover-up and denial from the church causes him to develop a never-lasting disregard for the church and all it stands for.

Friend, his guardian angel, guides his way back to the church where he meets Ailene Brooks, a fiery, fast-talking lady reporter for the *Indianapolis Star Newspaper*, along with Brad Carson, pastor of Morris Avenue Baptist Church. Their friendship proceeds as planned, and Brad describes Mike as "another John the Baptist, waiting in the wilderness for something from above to guide his life."

Mike's uncontrollable temper overcomes reason, and hearing the word "Vietnam" causes it to erupt. The appearance of a *satanic Bible*, terror plotting in the Middle-East, turmoil, and romance, all become part of an exciting story of Mike's new life within the church. His guardian angel reveals God's plan for the remainder of his days, but it's hard for him to understand. He considers himself a man without purpose, wandering in a strange new world looking for help till his guardian angel takes over, guiding him through a seemingly impossible mission.

But why he is one of the *Chosen* is beyond his wildest dreams.

The sudden appearance of a satanic Bible at the famous Eagle's Nest in the Bavarian Alps becomes his problem. He searches for an answer, why he, Mr. Nobody, is selected for operation, Un-Holy Ground.

> Be not forgetful to entertain strangers; for thereby
> some have entertained angels unawares."
>
> —Hebrews 13: 2

I ask myself the question, "Is it possible I've met an angel, maybe somewhere, sometime during my lifetime?"

And my answer always comes up the same, "But why not me? They're God's messengers among us."

1

Awakening

Have mercy upon me, Oh Lord, for I am in Trouble.

—Psalm 31:9

Mike Cutler rises from bed after another night of sleeplessness. Rolling and tossing throughout the night becomes his way of life. His four-bedroom home on the west side of Indianapolis has become his prison without promise of parole. He heads to the bathroom for his morning shave. Looking into the mirror isn't pleasant for a man once considered fairly handsome. His eyes are red and bleary, his beard dark and crusty. He looks in the mirror gazing at himself, turning away disgusted. Wife has been dead ten long years, children married and gone, grandchildren in college, while old friends depart for heaven or hell, never noticed.

He returns to the dining room, sipping coffee from a cup. He strolls across the dining room, opening a sliding door leading out to a large wooden deck. He gazes across the yard, remembering grandchildren romping with his two big golden retrievers, Barney and Fred.

And he stops, muttering to himself, "Oh, wonderful memories, please never leave me. How in the world do I find myself sixty-two, no wife, no kids, no friends, but lots of buddies? Has everyone deserted me? Why, oh, why, Lord, are you doing this to me?" Walking to the farthest part of the yard, he turns, gazing across the street noticing a building recently opened for business. He glances at the sign in front displaying the words, *Nancy's Child-Care Center*. Young women run in and out, unloading children to be cared for.

He walks inside, sitting in his favorite chair. The news he dreads, but for Mike, necessary. ABC news anchors are discussing a well-known politician cheating with numerous women. People express shock, want to forgive and forget, others condemn and punish. Some call it sex addiction, maybe a disease, incurable! He reads the newspaper, noticing a small article at the very bottom describing children dying by the thousands in places like Syria, Somalia, Kenya, the world over.

He turns away, disgusted; turning on the news again, he sees Christian men in Syria, standing before ISIS, about to be beheaded for putting their faith in Jesus!

Again, he switches channels, hoping for some good news. A government spokesman from the White House addresses the press. He announces they're dealing with persons in the Security Exchange Commission watching pornography while on duty. And a reporter asks, "What will happen to those guilty watching porno while our government heads into bankruptcy?"

The spokesman shrugs his shoulders, looks around the audience before replying, "We're dealing with it, sir, don't worry. We may need to conduct a study to see if there's wrongdoing. Conference over!"

He switches channels, and the president is speaking in Berlin. Thousands stand before him, shouting his praise as a new world leader. He promises a world of change coming soon. He tells the world, diplomacy is the answer to past American mistakes, his way of solving problems in the future. He mentions America's handling world affairs in the past, future problems negotiated.

Disgusted, he switches to NBC—more of the same. They show lawmakers and lobbyists walking from the White House smiling, pleased with their day's work, changing America overnight. But a few blocks away, they fail to show prostitutes walking the streets selling their bodies as pimps stand waiting to grab the money. This is the new America with a generation gap greater than ever.

Fox News shows youth gangs beating and killing a fellow student with two-by-fours in Chicago, murder capital of America. Politicians are on the scene, saying something needs to done, but no suggestions. Someone yells, "Call out the National Guard," and cheers ring out throughout the crowd. The high school principal appears, looking confused. He offers no statement for the killing till someone asks for an explanation. He gazes over the crowd announcing, "Parents are the problem, don't blame us." Nothing is accomplished and crime continues with prisons filled to the max. Disgustedly, he asks himself over and over, *"What, Lord, what is happening to my wonderful country? The country I love and adore is going to hell, and nobody cares."*

2

Walk with an Angel

And at the ninth hour I prayed in my house, and, behold, a man stood before me in bright clothing.

—Acts 10:30

Morning sun peeks through the clouds, and once again, Mike Cutler awakens to the sound of chirping birds outside his bedroom window. It's a new day, and for the first time in months, he's rested. He moves to the living room, listening to songs shared with his wife during days of wine and roses, dancing the night away.

Karen Carpenter sings, "We've Only Just Begun," followed with Eddie Arnold singing, "Make the World Go Away," beautiful, wonderful songs gone forever. His sixty-two years are beginning to show, romance of youth is fading, it's time to move on, but where?

He moves outside, walking to nowhere. His thoughts begin to ramble, thinking differently; today, this very day, things will change for the better. Houses appear unnoticed before and he wonders. His thoughts run deep, searching for important lovely things from yesteryears. He wonders if time remains on his side, what to do if it isn't. It's like being in a dream world for no reason.

God Help Us

Life for Mike has been interesting: real-estate, oil exploration, business ventures. Vietnam, come and gone, memories forever. His once blond hair turned silver and his six-foot frame has dwindled. He struggles with his wife's absence, remembering her final words, "I love you, darling. We'll meet again tomorrow." And he's mumbling to himself, "What's going on in my miserable life? Where are my friends? Who can help a guy like me? *Why! Oh, why was I ever born? Oh, Lord, help me, show me the way...I need you...oh, how I need you.*"

Memories run wild, flooding his mind as if it was only yesterday. He thinks of neighborhood friends, the Indy Five Hundred. And he wonders if ever again children in school will have the privilege of singing *"Amazing Grace" or "The Star-Spangled Banner."*

And he stops abruptly, wondering if this is same place he was once proud to call America the Beautiful, home of the brave, land of the free.

Again, he begins walking, remembering how in grade school days he would stand in the hallway, pledging his allegiance *under God* before *Old Glory. And he remembers how he would look again, seeing* the *Ten Commandments* hanging beside it. *And he's sad, disappointed again.*

He stands gazing upward into nowhere, barely muttering, "Where is the answer to my problems? Where, oh, where, Lord, can I find help? Is there a place of happiness for a guy like me...anywhere on God's green earth? Lead me, Lord, lead me wherever!"

And coming from out of nowhere, a basketball rolls down the sidewalk beside him. He's startled, glancing to his side where a tall young man stands beside him, dressed impeccably in a white

| 19 |

Arthur (Mac) Mc Caffry

linen suit. He looks him over, staring into eyes like never seen before—bright fiery-red—causing him to shudder.

He watches him pick up the ball, twirling it around his fingers with ease, and he's amazed, thinking, *One of the Pacers, no doubt.*

And the new friend moves close, speaking as someone from the past.

"Good morning, Mike. My name is Friend. Where are you headed?" he asks so pleasantly.

But Mike keeps walking, looking ahead, never looking back.

"What a lovely day…almost heavenly, Mike. I'll walk with you a while," he says, friendly, gazing upward.

And Mike turns, staring at him, wondering, *Who is this guy, and why is he so friendly? Nobody cares for me, nobody! Is it possible we've met before, but where or when?*

He's puzzled, wondering why some unknown guy has entered his life with only a smile, a bouncing basketball, eyes that sparkle, wanting to join him. He stops, looking around, thinking, *Odd indeed…whatever!*

"Probably nowhere, just walking, thinking 'bout things…you know, things gone by. I'm really not in the mood for conversation, didn't quite get your name."

"My name is Friend, Mike. Feeling sad for yourself, aren't you?"

And Mike hesitates, looking him over, thinking, *This new guy is different…his speech, his voice…all different.* He stops walking, trying to remember. He begins walking again, and suddenly, he remembers something secretive about himself: nobody truly knows Mike, but Mike only!

"Why shouldn't I be sad? I've no friends, maybe a few buddies."

Friend moves beside him. "But He will always love you. Mike. You remind me of Job. a guy my father knows."

And he hesitates, wondering if it's the same Job he read about thirty years ago when he followed the word of God, a Christian!

"Anyone who calls himself a Christian knows about Job," he says smartly.

"Not everyone, but you do, Mike!" he says, his eyes red as fire fixed upon him only.

And he's speechless! He's never met this guy, but somehow, the guy knows things, his secret things.

"Friends deserted Job, Mike, earthly treasures gone…"

And he's worried! Perspiration shows upon his forehead. "What does Job have to do with me?" he asks, probing.

Friend reaches out, stopping him. "He's haunting you, Mike… night and day…he's haunting you!" he says, startling him.

Mike moves, backing away, stunned! He's talking Bible talk, something he doesn't want to talk about.

"You gotta be joking! I've nothing left to fight over."

Friend moves even closer. "He wants your very heart…your very soul, Mike!"

And *bang*! Right out of the blue, Mike begins to realize this guy is different; he knows things! His head hangs low; his eyes show worry.

"What's his name, Friend?" he barely whispers.

"Satan, Mike!" he says, causing Mike to back away, shuddering.

His heart pounds, his memory runs rampant! This new guy talks about personal things, time to change the subject.

"Are you out for a morning stroll, Friend?" Mike asks, pleasantly.

"Business only, Mike."

"Business—"

"Yes, Mike! Business between you and me only!"

And Mike turns away, pretending to not be interested.

"What else is on your agenda, Friend?"

He stops, placing the ball under his arm, while his other hand rests upon Mike's shoulder.

"You're my agenda! Today! Tomorrow! Forever, Mike!"

And Mike is staring at him, speechless! This is a dream for sure! This never happens, he's telling himself, looking away, shaking his head unbelievingly.

"You're joking, of course!" he says frivolously, jesting.

Friend's eyes focus upon his, fiery red, blazing! "I don't joke, Mike! I've a message for you!"

Mike looks up again at him, standing before him, frozen! He wants to move away, forget he ever saw this guy, but it's useless.

"A message for me…" he barely can mutter.

Friend moves even closer, eyes sparkling as diamonds. "He heard your cry, Mike! He heard your loneliness!"

His heart skips a beat! He's in trouble, deep trouble, and he knows it.

"He…who is he?" he asks, groping, pretending.

And Friend reaches out pulling him closer against him, speaking, demanding, "Get serious, Mike! Don't forget to whom you speak…think again, Mike! Be sure how you answer!"

His hands tremble; he turns, gazing down at the concrete. "You mean Him?"

"Yes, Mike…Him! The one who will never leave you, never forsake you!"

And he's frightened again, turning away, mumbling, "I've heard those words a thousand times, Friend. I went all the way with Him. Take a good look at me, see what it got me!"

God Help Us

Friend's fiery eyes come alive, sparkling as diamonds, while Mike stands beside him, shuddering.

"We're talking about Jesus, I suppose," he barely mumbles.

"You know we are, Mike! We're talking about the Son of God, Jesus, the one who gave His life for you at Calvary!"

His hands tremble, his heart pumps faster! "My wife reminded me of Him till the day she died," he mutters, hanging his head, never looking up.

Friend moves even closer. "She did, Mike! It's time you come home and join her! The Lord our God…He needs you, Mike," he whispers, moving against him.

And his past flashes before him…thirty years past, when he swore he would never again listen to the words, "Jesus, our Lord…God." He's angry and it's showing.

"Get away from me! You remind me of the ones who betrayed me, the ones who sent me away, lied about me!" he says belligerently.

Friend moves up in his face, red eyes blazing. "But He hasn't forgotten you, Mike. Thirty years are nothing to Him!"

Wow! The very thought of it! Thirty long years ago, a time, a place…

His mind is spinning, wondering how to continue. The very thought of it…sorrowful memories never forgotten!

"I don't know why you're here, Friend, but it's over…gone forever! You know nothing of my past!"

Again, Friend stops, moving against him.

"Speak from your heart, Mike: I know you! I know what you're hiding! He sent me, Mike!"

And wham! Again he hits hard! He studies his words, beginning to smile.

"Do you really want me to explain why I left the church when my neighbor's six-year-old daughter was sexually abused by one of your deacons?"

"But He knows, Mike! It's written in the Book of Life, opened on Judgment Day."

And Mike turns, facing him, his anger raging!

"Stop it! No more of that Judgment Day stuff, stop the rhetoric!"

"But I'm here for you, Mike…I'm listening!"

"I'm glad you're listening! Maybe now we can talk about the real problem!"

"Tell me the real problem!"

And a smile appears! "Oh yes, I'll tell you! This is my best day ever…a day to remember!" he's shouting wildly.

"I'm listening, Mike."

"A six-year-old neighbor's daughter was molested by a Sunday school bus driver in broad daylight, and the church denied it, did nothing!" he says, up in his face, exploding.

"Mike! Mike! Calm yourself please," Friend says, taking his hand, calming him.

But Mike doesn't calm; he's shouting angrily, "Don't try and stop me, Friend…don't! I warn you again…don't try it!"

Friend stands beside him, listening to his on and on ranting. "But it was the same little girl's single mother, the one my wife and I invited to church, hoping to convert her! But it didn't work because of my wife and me, everyone was telling their friends and neighbors all over!"

Friend moves closer. "And the rest of it? Tell it all, Mike!"

"I was angry! I wanted to kill the miserable scumbag, but my wife and the mother thought differently, they wanted to do it the 'good old church' way. You know what I'm talking 'bout…

turn it over to the church, let them be the judge, let them be the jury!"

And he stops, gazing upon Friend differently, in a most compassionate way asking, "Why are you bothering me? I didn't ask for your advice. Get away from me, leave me alone, forget it."

Friend moves even closer. "But you asked for me, Mike! He heard your plea...He loves you!"

And Mike's head drops, gazing downward, worried! He's confused, wondering why Friend always brings in words like *He* or *Him*. Surely, it can't be *Him!*

Again, they walk side by side while Mike berates the church without end.

"My wife and neighbor insisted we bring the pervert before the deacons and elders, the good old church way. And I did, Friend, I really truly did. He confessed his sin before Richard Blake, an innocent young preacher, while I stood beside the pedophile, accusing him in utter contempt forever! But then it happened, the biggest mistake ever..."

"Tell me your biggest mistake ever, Mike!"

"I trusted the church, Friend! I assumed the matter was settled, but it wasn't! When it was over, my wife and I became victims, not the accusers! It was terrible, Friend, terrible! And the only excuse the pervert had to offer were the most despicable words ever!"

Friend comes to a halt, reaching out, placing his hand upon his shoulder.

"But that was yesterday, Mike, today is tomorrow!"

Again, his temper explodes, shouting full out, "But not over with me, Friend, it's never over with me! He simply looked at the preacher and with his filthy, dirty mouth, he said, 'I can't keep my hands off little girls, Preacher, I'm guilty!'"

Arthur (Mac) Mc Caffry

"Let it out, Mike...let it all out!" Friend says, moving against him.

Mike's head lowers even further. "He showed no remorse, Friend, none whatever!"

And Friend moves away, gazing upward.

Again nothing but silence till Mike explodes viscously. "Leave me! Get away from me! I hate the church and all the hypocrites within it!"

Again, nothing but silence! "Are you finished, Mike?" Friend asks, standing beside him, searching the heavens.

"No way I'm finished! Pastor Blake and I believed the case was over, time to send it to the deacons and elders. But boy, oh boy...was that ever a mistake?"

"Explain yourself, Mike."

"The church did nothing! We became the problem: my wife and I. All I could hear was *protect the church, think of the families...let it die...always ending with those famous old words—*"

"*Famous old words?*"

"*Oh yes! The Lord will take care of everything!* Over and over, they repeated the same while our hearts bled, never stopping. And yet today, I ask myself, 'But why, Lord, why haven't they asked forgiveness?'"

Friend moves against him facing him, fiery-red eyes blazing, "But you must forgive too, Mike, as God forgives you!"

And he's speechless again! He tries to hide the tears, but it's useless.

"But all I could feel was hatred, never-ending hatred! It filled my heart and soul always. They stood before me looking righteous as a bunch of Pharisees, gazing down upon Mary Magdalene! I couldn't handle it, Friend, I just couldn't handle it!"

And he stops, getting his breath, beginning again.

God Help Us

"*Don't cause dissension in the church,* they would say to me over and over. It was a nightmare never ending. I'm bitter, Friend, I can stand it no longer!"

Friend moves even closer, listening.

"I wanted to die, but revenge…I wanted more! I wanted to get even, make them suffer!"

Again Friend walks beside him silent, staring upward, searching the heavens.

"Preacher Blake and the pedophile knew the truth, but they said nothing! Night after night, I would lie awake, visualizing Pastor Blake standing at the pulpit preaching of sin, while my never-ending desire ran at its highest, wanting to grab him by the throat, choking him forever! And at the end of this sad painful story, my wife and I, we became the untouchables… turned away forever!"

Slowly, Friend moves ahead as Mike's anger continues on and on, never ending.

"Don't walk away! Listen to me, Friend! My wife and I went through living hell. They shunned us, looked upon us with contempt, enemies within!" he's yelling, never stopping.

And finally he stops. He moves close to Friend, grabbing his arm, looking up to him, shouting, "Stop, Friend, stop and listen!"

Friend turns, facing him, "I've never stopped listening, Mike."

"You're listening! Then quit looking at me as if I'm nothing!"

"But you're wrong, Mike! You're someone He loves dearly… you're His forever! He loves you, Mike!"

And Mike is worried. His head lowers further, thinking back to better days. Tears show, pitiful-looking tears, the kind he hopes Friend doesn't notice.

"But I'm tired of listening. This conversation is over!"

| 27 |

Friend reaches out, pulling him close beside him, "Over, Mike? It's just beginning!"

Mike looks up again at him, puzzled, pitiful like. "But I've had enough! I'm tired of listening to you pretending to be someone holy! And something else, Friend..."

"Yes, Mike?"

"You're no angel, not the kind of angel I've read about," he says, hatefully.

Again, moments of silence while Friend's eyes stare hard into Mike's eyes, blazing!

"But I am! *I'm your guardian angel, Mike! He sent me!*"

Mike's body runs numb, speechless again! He runs his hand across his brow, wiping sweat caught up in something holy, beyond imagination. His mind is reeling! And he's asking himself, *Can this be possible? Can this truly be an angel of God, standing before the sinner of all sinners...someone like me...nobody?*"

And he's panicking full out! He's thinking, *I need a plan, a plan to get rid of him outta my life forever! I'll talk him down, know who he really is. Nobody fools with Mike Cutler!*

He begins to smile, beckoning Friend closer. "But let me tell you the rest of my story, Friend."

"I'm waiting, Mike."

"The only person believing our story was Uncle Joe, a converted sinner, a person like Paul, the Apostle, the worst of the worst."

"He was, Mike, till he met Him!" Friend says, his eyes focusing upon his without emotion.

Again, Mike pauses, staring at Friend, wondering where, how to begin.

"But my uncle was an escaped convict from a Georgia chain gang, a bootlegger, a whoremonger among the best of them.

God Help Us

The guy did it all and I loved him...*oh, how I loved him!* He was saved from a life of sin, the greatest witness for Jesus I've ever met," Mike tries to explain, his voice changing, fighting back tears.

Friend moves even closer. "He was, Mike, a holy man, a believer in Christ...riches in heaven above many!"

And Mike is stunned again! He watches his every move as he bounces the ball, gazing up into the morning sun, never ending.

"Well...if ever I've met a saint, it was my *Uncle Joe!*"

And Friend's eyes dance in all their glory, bright as diamonds. He stops, reaching out pulling Mike beside him, placing his finger over his lips without warning.

"Quiet!" he barely mutters. "My Father has a message for you, Mike!"

And he's motionless, frightened again.

"Message from your father?"

"Today's the day, Mike, time to pay your debt!

Again, he's speechless! Friend knows everything, all the way to the sad, dirty ending.

| 29 |

3

The Chosen

Because God has from the beginning
chosen you to salvation thru sanctification
of the Spirit and belief of the truth.

—2 Thessalonians 2:13

Mike turns away, looking into the street where traffic increases. He's afraid...no desire to talk about other events.

"I'm talking about today, nothing else, Friend. I'm fed up listening to evangelists tell me all about the facts of life. I've tried their way...believe me, I have. All it gave me was a bigger desire to hate the hypocrites...the so-called pure and sanctified Christians," Mike shouts, out of control again.

Friend places the basketball in Mike's hand, walking to the edge of the sidewalk, bowing down upon his knees. His arms raise upward, speaking words without meaning.

And silence takes over, except for the sound of a few passing cars heading to work unnoticed. Friend slowly rises, standing before him, fiery eyes blazing. He reaches out grabbing Mike's hands, and he's helpless, left wondering.

"Take a deep breath, Mike, stop and listen, Mike! From this day forward, I'll guide you into eternity! You've a debt to pay...a debt everyone must pay to enter His kingdom!"

God Help Us

His heart pounds, fear overtakes him. "But this debt, Friend... where...when...?" he asks, breathless, arms and legs shaking.

"Ashamed, aren't you, Mike! You know the answer better than anyone! You've been there, Mike! You've been there!"

And he's searching everywhere for an answer, but there is none. He's helpless, looking up at Friend, pleading, "I'm tired, Friend! You win! I can't go on with this torture; tell me my debt, Friend!"

Friend moves closer, barely announcing, "But you've always known, Mike, everything begins and ends at Calvary!"

"Wow. Calvary!" A place, a time he'll never forget! His memory explodes, peaceful, happy days, all from the past!

"Leave me alone, Friend...I've had it! I need nobody, nobody needs me!" he can barely shout, out of control again.

Friend reaches out, grabbing his hand bringing him to attention! "But, Mike, everyone needs someone sometime!" he says nicely, pleasantly.

Frustrated and exhausted, he looks up at Friend while a couple of tears drip slowly downward. He's thinking of a beautiful song he heard long ago, "He Touched Me." And his thoughts go back to another time, another place, the time he first met Jesus.

Friend's eyes show their color, sparkling as diamonds.

"I touched you, Mike! And from this moment forward, you will never forget the way I touched you, never again, Mike... never!"

And he's helpless, afraid to speak freely!

"Ashamed, aren't you? You've been there, you know better than all, Mike."

And again, he's looking up at him pitiful-like, asking, "Now... what are you talking about? Just let me be left alone. Take your ball and go away, you're torturing me, Friend!"

"But I touched you, Mike! And from this moment forward, you will never forget the way I touched you!"

And his head drops, humbled again, staring at Friend, helplessly.

"Have mercy, please, Friend, have mercy. Help me or leave me...please..." he's begging.

Friend moves beside him, eyes filled with pity. "I'll never leave you, Mike...never have...never will! Think back, Mike, back to a time of war...a filthy, bloody, unforgiving war!"

And he's aroused, coming alive! He's wondering where, when. And suddenly, it hits him! "No! No! It can't be...it can't be!"

Friend moves against him, touching him. "Yes, Mike, war in faraway places! Ruthless, never-ending war! War at its best unforgiving glory! I stood beside you in a rice paddy while you lay helpless on your back praying. Your buddies! Your enemies, dead and wounded, covering the ground around you. Think, Mike! Think!"

His heart pounds, his feet and hands, numb top to bottom. He can't remember his face, but oh! That magic touch...so comforting, overwhelming!

"But where does this guy come from?" he asks, himself over and over. And without warning, his face turns pale, remembering the bloody, bloody days and nights in the killing fields of Vietnam all over!

He moves away, standing alone, wracking his brain over and over.

"And the landing strip, the Colonel! You were with me at *Phu Bai?" he barely mutters.*

"I was, Mike! I was with you at Phu Bai, Mike."

"And the killing, the cursing...the yelling...the screaming..."

God Help Us

"That too, Mike!"

Mike lowers his head, thinking endlessly. "And the kid, the kid with his leg blown to bits?"

"Joey…a farm boy from Indiana…Second Marines… Charley Company."

"And the crazy colonel from the 101st Airborne?"

"I watched a chopper take off through a hail of bullets on a rainy blood-soaked runway. I observed the one you call the crazy colonel as he dragged you and another marine inside a chopper. And I listened to your cursing while the young marine was telling you, 'Shut your stupid mouth, Mike. I'm going home…forget it!'"

He lowers his head, wanting to cry, but can't. Memories, unforgettable memories, the screaming! The shouting, "Corpsman! Corpsman!" On and on throughout the night, never ending! All in a hellhole far away, Nam! A place called hell in the rice fields…over and over!

"I've never deserted anyone, Friend. If only I could have moved, I would have crawled on my belly to be with my buddies. I felt paralyzed, wished I could die, but didn't. What else can you possibly ask of me?" he's pleading over and over!

Friend comes to halt, grasping his hand stopping him! "But Joey didn't complain, Mike! He suffered terribly, accepted war and death as a marine; a marine he was proud to be. He asked for your Bible, the one you held in your hand offering freely! You remember, Mike! You remember the day, the time, you remember it as only yesterday!"

"Shut up! I don't want to hear anymore, I've heard enough, Friend!"

"But it wasn't your friends you deserted, Mike, it was Jesus. You needed Him…you called his name…He heard your prayer, Mike!"

Friend reaches for his hand, but he draws away, frightened. "Don't touch me, Friend! But don't believe I haven't wanted to be home with Jesus. He's all I can think of…my life is miserable!" Mike barely utters, tearfully.

Again, Friend's fiery eyes focus upon him, sparkling as diamonds. "But…you're worthy…all are worthy unto Him, Mike!"

And he's puzzled again…left wondering! He wonders why he is so loving, why he is so compassionate? He remembers the day like yesterday, the time and the place, all pleading for help, dying beside him. But it was their secret, Jesus and him alone… together forever!

Again, he looks up at Friend, watching eyes of fire turn sparkling blue! And out from nowhere, he can hear a message filling his mind and soul; Friend knows it all and then some!

"Guilty as charged, Friend! I'm lost, nowhere to turn, help me, Friend, please help me," he's pleading, dabbing at never-ending tears.

Friend moves closer, placing his hand gently upon his shoulder. "I'm here for you, Mike! I'll guide you into a future beyond your wildest dreams and then some…"

And quickly, he asks, "My wildest dreams and then some…?"

He moves next to his side, holds his hand, looking deep into his eyes, announcing, "All the way, Mike! From here to eternity…wherever!"

God Help Us

Again, a powerful statement, words filled with meaning, words like…from here into eternity. "But what does it mean?" he asks himself, over and over.

And he's smiling! Friend, this new guy, has to be his guardian angel; there's none other to satisfy him.

Mike glances at his watch, noting they've been walking and talking for an hour. "Your Father, the Lord, I assume."

Friend turns, facing him. "He is, Mike, the one you once served. My Father knew you before you were born, before you lay in your mother's womb. I was there when your mother and father placed you upon the altar of God. I was there while Pastor Jeffrey stood before the altar anointing you with oil, dedicating your life and service to Him. You're one of the few, Mike, you're *one of the Chosen!*"

Mike stops, looking again at him, bewildered! "But this is impossible! I'm the most miserable person on God's green earth…"

"I believe you. But it's over, Mike! My Father wants your consecration to Him alone!"

His face turns pale, shocked again! He walks beside Friend, never speaking, his words he takes seriously. His thoughts wander back to childhood, another time, different places. And now, his thinking is different; he's thinking, *But just maybe…I am one of His Chosen.*

Friend moves beside him getting his attention. "He loves you, Mike. He shows His mercy unto you," he barely whispers.

"I know he loves me, Friend. I know his power! I tremble, thinking about it!"

"You're learning, Mike, tell me of His greatness!"

Mike stops, wondering how to say the words, "His power is unthinkable! His grace is forever! He's my God...there's none other!"

And his eyes sparkle as diamonds! "Wonderful, Mike... He heard you! Your future is planned, Mike. His plans for you are priceless!"

Friend gazes upward, looking into the unknown. "Tell me about your name, Mike!"

"My name..."

"Yes, Mike...your name!"

And Mike is thinking hard! He's remembering something his mother whispered to him at the altar. And suddenly, he's smiling as never before.

"My name is written in the Lamb's Book of Life, Friend... His book...the greatest book ever!"

Friend stops, looking at him surprised! "Well said, Mike! He heard you!"

Excitement runs high, but still he worries!

"But why...why do I feel doomed forever...nothing but misery? Help me, Friend...please help me," he's pleading over and over.

Friend reaches out grabbing his arm, pulling him closer... facing him. "But the past belongs to yesterday, Mike! Your future is tomorrow!"

And he's traumatized! Wondering if Friend is aware what's going through his mind, hating every word of it. He continues on and on, walking, wondering!

"Can this be real?" he asks himself over and over. He pinches his arm till it hurts and slaps his face in disgust. And he stops, staring at Friend, not speaking.

"Is something bothering you, Mike?" Friend asks casually.

God Help Us

"There is, Friend! I've been there before, you know the story. I know all about the Lamb's Book of Life, Jesus, Judgment Day...and then some. I hate myself more than my enemies. But when I think of those thirty miserable years of remorse...I don't understand, I cannot understand! And when I'm finished, I ask myself again, 'Why? Why...in all those years...someone from the church didn't step up...confess they were wrong, but never an answer...'"

Friend comes to a halt, staring hard at him. "But you forgot to ask another, Mike!"

"Another?"

"Lucifer, son of the morning, ask him, Mike, only he knows the answer!"

Mike moves back and away from Friend frightened. Friend isn't the gentle, kind, forgiving one as before.

"I've dreaded this moment, Friend! But always within...I knew this day would come, my most dreaded day ever!"

Friend reaches out, grabbing his hand forcefully, surprising him. "He's waiting, Mike! Today's the day, Mike!" he announces loudly.

And he's startled, looking up at him, feeling broken.

"It all started late one cold winter night. I was driving home from a poker game with some buddies. I was tired, burned-out! Tired of living! I turned on the radio to keep me awake. And suddenly, I was like in a trance, listening to a song from happier days, unforgettable days, days filled with love for Jesus. And I loved it, Friend. Oh, how I loved it!"

"But the song, Mike, tell me the song. It's important, Mike!"

"Everyone knows 'Amazing Grace,' Friend. You probably know the guy who wrote it. I listen to the words endlessly. I'm humbled! I want to die, but can't! I go to bed feeling guilty...

Arthur (Mac) Mc Caffry

waking up feeling guilty! And when it's over, I fall on my knees, crying like a baby!"

And he stops, wringing his hands, looking up pleading, "Help me, Friend…help me!"

Friend looks away and back again. "But the words, Mike, tell me the words."

And pitiful-like, Mike stares down to the concrete, waiting, afraid to say the words he's been dreading to say. His voice quivers, he's mumbling faintly, "A wretch like me, Friend, for someone like me…it would to be a miracle!"

"A miracle!"

"Yes, Friend…nothing but a miracle!" he says, staring downward.

Friend moves beside him, touching his arm, getting attention, "Is forgiving worth your soul in hell, Mike? Think of John! Think how John, the slave trader, felt!"

And his memory goes blank! He's never heard of a guy called John, except maybe the one he's talking about, a slave trader a couple hundred years ago.

Again, Friend places his hand upon Mike's shoulder. "Search no more, Mike. His name is *John, John Newton,* author of *'Amazing Grace,' my father's song!*"

And again, Mike is shaking his head, bewildered. Friend reads his mind, no doubt about it.

4

And There's Angels

For he shall give his angels charge over
thee, to keep thee in all thy ways.

—Psalm 91:11

Mike is ready to listen. He wants to be part of whatever, but how do you explain the past to an angel, someone holy?"

"Oh yes, I remember reading about John Newton, the life he lived, sailing over the ocean three hundred years ago in the slave trade."

Friend stops staring at Mike. "John was like you, Mike!"

Mike moves close to him searching for his meaning, confused again. "John, the slave trader, like me?"

"John found a cure for his sin, Mike."

And he's puzzled again. "You're losing me, Friend. I'm not good solving riddles."

"But you are, you're one of the best, Mike! Think back to pleasant days, something you lost…something most precious!"

And his face turns pale. "You mean…His…?"

"Yes, Mike, His grace…the most precious thing ever!"

He turns, staring into empty space, tears falling, unrestrained.

"You know about my promise to God, the kid, the Colonel, at the rice paddy?"

"I do…I know it all, Mike!"

| 39 |

And his head drops, afraid to look, worried.

"Are you talking about the Lamb's Book of Life again?"

"I'm talking about the Bible, Mike, the book your uncle gave you before heading for Nam.

"Yes! Yes! Now I remember!"

"I've a message for you, Mike."

Mike stops his walking, staring at Friend, wondering.

"A message…about what?"

Friend stops suddenly. His eyes show fiery red, he's up in his face, shouting, "There's a showdown coming, Mike!"

And quickly he steps back, looking again at him, surprised! "There's a showdown about what, Friend?"

"He has a plan for you, Mike! You will do His will as He pleases, not what pleases you. When finished, your reward will be great, your needs satisfied, your long-sought question answered!"

His eyes focus down to the concrete, feeling busted! Nobody fools with Him and he knows it. And again, he's wondering if he's dreaming. Some guy out of nowhere threatens his future.

"Hold it a minute, Friend! Use words I understand…plain words, simple words."

Again his eyes burn as fire, his speech demanding. "My Father has plans for you, Mike!" You were anointed upon the altar of God as a baby, you belong to Him! None other! You're blessed from above…beyond all others!"

And Mike's body trembles as never before, frightened as never, turning away wondering.

"But I'm nothing! I'm nobody, Friend. Leave me alone… leave me please…"

Friend stands motionless, waiting.

And Mike panics! He's lost, searching his past, finding nothing. But Friend is serious, and he knows it. But there's

God Help Us

something else he does remember: his grandmother telling him the same, his dedication as a baby upon the altar of God.

Friend points his finger at Mike, eyes blazing fire, demanding. "But little you know, Mike Cutler!" he exclaims, causing Mike to wonder the meaning.

Again, he's lost! He searches for a meaning, but it's useless. He feels threatened, wants to move on, but there's no way out. Friend controls him, controls his future, but he can't stop wondering.

"You read my mind, didn't you, Friend!"

A big heavenly smile and, "Time out, Mike! Console yourself! Think again!"

And he's cornered! Nowhere to turn suddenly.

His head bows…looking downward. Bending further, he drops upon his knees, looking upward, reminiscing. And at last, a humbling smile, something different.

"I don't know why, but I believe! I truly believe, Friend…I do!"

Friend reaches out placing his hand upon his shoulder, soothing his mind, his body throughout.

"It's important you believe, Mike. Your life is about to change, greater than anything you might ever imagine!"

But he's confused. He wonders how in just moments, his life is changing, he can feel it. He wants to wake up and know it's nothing. But it's impossible; the guy is real, a real live angel talking to him, Mr. Nobody. And words he hates most flash before him: it's reality time, time to start over.

"Where are you headed, Friend?" he asks, looking away, complacently.

"Morris Avenue Baptist Church, Mike."

Again memories flash before him, *hard-to-forget memories.*

"Oh yes, my wife Joyce went there."

"I know, Mike."

Mike moves closer, wants to be near him, the guy who knows it all. It's time to be a "nice guy...a nice friendly guy."

"Our meeting, Friend, quite a coincidence..."

"But not a coincidence, Mike."

Mike stops again, turning, facing him. "I've made a decision, Friend, a once and forever decision."

Friend looks hard into his eyes, fiery eyes blazing. "And your decision is..."

And quickly, his head bows low, he mutters pitifully, "Whatever He wants...I'll do, Friend...whatever He wants!"

"But the rest of it, Mike... the rest of it!"

Again, he wracks his brain, searching.

"For Him, Friend, God alone," he says, gazing up into Friend's sparkling eyes proudly.

And his face glows brightly...his eyes sparkle as diamonds.

"Good! And now...something for you, Mike..."

"For me..."

"You only, Mike. From this day forward, I'll be near you, protect you...guide you into His presence!"

Again, he's lost, searching for a meaning, but there is none. But still, there's a terrible yearning within, a yearning to be a part of something great, something everlasting.

And finally, a slow drawn-out voice utters, "When, Friend... when do I begin?"

He reaches out grasping his hand, squeezing it hard. "Today, Mike! This very day, you begin!" he says, bringing him alive.

God Help Us

Again, he's shocked! All this happening in moments, unbelievable moments, with an angel.

And his head rises to face Friend full-out. "But tell me again, how do I find Morris Avenue Baptist Church, you know, the church my wife belonged?"

Friend's eyes run wild, sparkling as ever. "Simple, Mike...go three blocks down, two blocks to the right, and just 'round the corner," he shouts, moving away, drifting out into nowhere.

Mike doesn't wait. He's walking away satisfied, humming a tune from childhood past.

"And he walks with me, and he talks with me, and he tells me I am his own...and the joy we share, as we tarry there...none other has ever known."

5

Trouble Within

God is our refuge and strength, a
very present help in trouble.

—Psalm 46:1

Hurriedly, he returns home dressing in his best attire, and soon, he's walking down Morris Avenue. He travels three blocks, stops, looking, no Friend. He turns right two blocks and just 'round the corner is a big white building: a church with a belfry, a bell, and a cross at the top.

And quickly, his memory reflects to the past. In this building, his wife spent her life with Friend and his Father. And again, he's wondering why Friend said something from the past, bringing his attention: dedicated, anointed when a baby.

His mind runs rampant! Maybe this could be the day he has waited for, his day of redemption. Excitement builds; his pace grows faster, and now he's running to the building with a belfry and a bell at the top.

He stands outside gazing around; it has been a while, a very sorrowful long and dreary while. But this is a new day, perhaps even a new beginning. He thinks of another time, another church, when he and his wife worshiped together before all went wrong…so very, very wrong.

God Help Us

And he thinks about Friend and whom he serves. Sweat appears upon his brow and he begins to wonder, "Can this be a day of reckoning? Surely...surely this new guy has to be my guardian angel, the guy with answers about tomorrow," he mutters to himself. Life is changing fast...maybe too fast!

Slowly, he opens the door, glancing around, wondering if anyone recognizes him. It's the church, but where are all the people? He hesitates, looking over the small group of persons: no youth whatever, maybe thirty or forty elderly throughout.

And he stands pondering, asking himself, *Can this be Morris Avenue Baptist Church, the church where my wife went? What in the world has happened? It's nearly empty, but it does have a belfry with a bell at the top!*

From the front of the church comes an old but spritely looking lady dressed impeccably in latest fashions. She's small in height, thin, head full of beautiful silver hair, a heavenly smile ready to greet him. And he pauses to look again; there's a certain little twinkle in her eyes that catches his attention. It's one of those good old mischievous twinkles, the kind he likes, twinkling brightly.

"Hi, Mike...I'm Ethel. You've been taking your time getting here!" she says, extending her hand, greeting him.

"We've...met?" he asks, glancing again at her.

She looks up at him, surprised! "Sure, Mike, you remember me, you know, your wife's friend, me...Ethel. I've watched you drop her off here on Sunday morning a hundred times over!"

He doesn't recall the happening, but remembers Joyce did mention the name frequently. She would smile and say, "Darling, when you go to church, and someday you will, look for the one who giggles and laughs a lot: the one with twinkling eyes, always making you happy!"

"Oh, yes! She spoke of you many times, Ethel."

And her eyes light up, a smile appears, displaying her pleasure.

"I'm sure she did! A hundred times she told me you would be getting here…*when the time is right!* And over and over, I asked, 'But when will the time be right, Joyce?'"

"And?"

Ethel turns her head to the side, giggling. "Always she would answer the same…when he gets ready to forgive, but only Mike would understand."

Mike hesitates, wondering what else she might know. Everything is happening so very fast! First it was Friend, the guy whose eyes look straight into your heart. And here's another gazing at you, giggling, with twinkling eyes, making you wonder.

She reaches out, grasping his hand, guiding him forward. "Come with me, Mike, we'll sit up front so I can hear," she says sharply.

Mike turns, facing her. "You have a hearing problem, Ethel?" he asks, but wishes he didn't.

She stops, staring at him, surprised! "Maybe I do, but only slightly! I've two hearing aids, but neither work. Does it bother you, Mike?" she asks, firing back quickly.

He looks again at her, wanting to apologize, but how?

"But you're getting up in years, Ethel, it's expected," Mike says, but again, wishes he hadn't.

And she's peeved! "But remember this, Mikey boy, I'm old in years, but young at heart. I've been there, I've done that. Eighty-four years, and I've never felt better! I'm what some call elderly, others call me feisty. And I'm…"

"And what, Ethel?" Mike asks, reaching out, stopping her.

She looks at him hard! "I know what life is all about, sonny boy, learned it the hard way!" she says defiantly.

And he likes her! He likes the way she tells things, right to the point with no holds barred. She's proud, making him liking her even more.

She pauses, pretending to be unconcerned. And suddenly, she turns staring up at him, explaining, "But I kinda figure everyone will have to answer for themselves when they stand before Jesus," she says, so sweet, so pleasantly.

Again, he looks down upon her, grinning, wondering if Joyce might have put her up to this moment, thinking, *Oh yes! Joyce definitely would have put her up to this moment!*

A small choir begins to sing *"Amazing Grace,"* the song that brings the tears. And they come to the words Mike fears most, *"A wretch like me." And it's hard for him to think of his past, their times together: days of love, wine, and roses. And his head drops low…reminiscing.*

From the corner of her eyes, Ethel watches him cringe, thinking hard, looking desperate! She remembers what Joyce said ten long years ago; it's here, it's finally here! And she's smiling as never before, loving the moment.

Mike's head drops even further, seeing the cross hanging beyond the podium; more songs praising Jesus and an offering is given. He dabs his handkerchief, wiping away tears.

An elderly gentleman, hair silver, stands tall in the pulpit announcing his sermon.

Ethel moves next to Mike. "His name is *Brad Carson*, once a pastor and missionary, but now retired."

And she stops, thinking.

"Something wrong, Ethel?"

"There is something else I admire about Brad..."

Again he waits, left hanging.

"Admire him for what, Ethel?"

"He tells it like it is, Mike, no hedging around with Brad! I can't stand these modern-day Peter Pan preachers," she says, feisty.

"Peter Pan preachers?"

She looks up at him, surprised. "You know what I mean... sure you do, the ones pretending there's no hell, always a place in heaven for everyone. Oh yes, that's how it is in today's theology: everyone goes to heaven, nobody goes to hell!"

Mike would love to burst out chuckling, but never in church.

"But you said he was retired..."

"He was, Mike! He wasn't busy preaching, so we asked him to come home, do some preaching here."

Pastor Carson stands tall behind the podium, glancing down upon his small crowd of worshipers; frustration shows, and finally, he's speaking.

"This is amazing! For the first time in my career as a minister, I stand in bewilderment! Why...I don't know! I simply don't know!"

Quietness reigns throughout while perspiration covers his forehead.

"But as I stand gazing out among you, something is different! There has to be. Someone here today is faced with a situation as the prodigal son once faced, but nothing in comparison! I'm talking to someone in trouble, believing he or she stands at the gates of hell, nowhere to turn, lost forever!"

God Help Us

Stopping only to get his breath, Brad gazes out over the audience, asking, "Is that person you, my friend...is that person you?" he shouts, pointing his finger.

Quickly, an eerie feeling settles over the congregation. Something is different, someone is in trouble, and his audience knows it.

He stops, peering over his audience. His arms rise up-ward, shouting, "Are you our prodigal son, my unknown friend?"

And stone-cold expressions run throughout.

But sitting next to Ethel, Mike is different. He moves away slowly. His head bows low; his eyes show tears.

Ethel reaches over, punching his side as her blue eyes begin to twinkle! She grasps his hand, whispering, "Now, you're about to see what it's all about, sonny boy."

And she turns, seeing Friend standing just inside the church watching his every move, his fiery eyes blazing.

It's invitation time! The pianist begins to play an old-time favorite: *"At the Cross," a never to be forgotten song from the past.*

And Mike rises, moving to where Brad stands ready to greet him; it's confession time, time to face reality!

And Mike's broken voice begins, "Never in thirty years did I dream I would be standing before you asking God to forgive my sins. I'm a sinner, I'm lost, I'm miserable. *I'm the worst of the worst.* I've read scripture from one end of the Bible to the other. But today, I'm different! I stand before you asking God to forgive me!"

And Morris Avenue Church comes alive! They remember his wife's words, "When he's ready to forgive, he will be here, Ethel." Suddenly, all eyes turn, gazing upon the cross, the place Friend calls Calvary.

Arthur (Mac) Mc Caffry

Ethel moves beside him, her blue eyes twinkling. "You did good, Mike! Real good! I'm proud of you...*you old-dirty-good-for-nothing scoundrel,*" she whispers.

Mike turns, looking up at the cross; he's smiling, thinking about tomorrow!

6

Setting the Future

And when these things begin to come to pass, then look up,
and lift up your heads; for your redemption draweth nigh.

—Luke 21:28

Mike's life is changing. He studies Bible scripture day and
night, refreshing memories. He can't forget Friend's
startling remark: "*anointed, dedicated* at the altar of God." He
wonders if he's capable, what's in store for his future.

He tries explaining his new life to old friends, conversations
cease immediately! It's a different life, different friends, and
Mike is deadly serious.

It's Sunday morning and he's headed for Morris Avenue
Baptist Church. Fellowship with new friends becomes the love
of his life. Brad's preaching stirs his lonely heart with a never-
ending desire to learn about the Lord's return, it's overwhelming!

He returns home, opening his Bible. He reads the book
of Daniel, going forward to the book of Ezekiel, ending with
the book of Revelation. And he's thinking hard, comparing it
with daily news: it's frightening to even think about! Things are
changing fast; knowledge grows daily while gloom and doom
spreads like wildfire.

Mike remembers *Pastor Jeffry's words from back long ago,*
words about the second coming of the Lord, and it matches!

| 51 |

"The world will be in great tribulation: we must be ready to meet the Lord…any time, any place, anywhere." He remembers him shouting to his brothers and sisters in Christ, "*You think World War II was bad…you ain't seen nothing yet!*"

He settles at his desk, reading Bible scripture. He reads Mathew, Mark, and John. And when he's finished, he gazes around the room, asking himself, "Was it this way before the flood during the time of Noah; when sexual depravity, drunkenness, and nothing but sin ruled the earth? Was it this way before Sodom and Gomorrah?"

He reads and reads, eyes grow tired, but never quitting. He's convinced the world is in trouble. But there's good news along with bad: it's time to look up. Jesus, our Lord and Savior, is coming!

He heads to his library searching for the Bible, a certain Bible with some history, his history. And at the bottom of the closet, there it is, the Bible Friend reminded him about. He remembers how his uncle placed it in his hands just before heading out to war, telling him how holy it was. He removes dust, noting pages marked in red. And out from old pages falls an old crinkled note.

Dear Nephew,

I leave you no money, but knowledge without end. This Bible is precious…precious above all else. Use it well, search the scriptures, and understand. It's your passport to heaven with life never ending.

And that's what it's all about, Mike: *a time to be born, a time to live, a time to die.*

Your loving uncle,
Joe

P. S. And don't miss this Mike…whatever…

> For what has a man profited, if he shall gain the whole world, and lose his own soul? Or what shall a man give in exchange for his soul? (Matthew 16:26)

He walks out on to the deck, looking up, wondering. "But why! Why underline certain scripture in red? Is it possible he thought I might witness the Lord's return?"

And his mood changes; troubling questions remain he's not sure of. It's time to call Brad, the guy with some answers.

Pastor Carson greets him at the door, seeing his troubled eyes blinking. "Tell me what brings you here, Mike…some kind of problem?" he asks jovially.

Mike is speechless, standing before him wondering where to begin.

"I'm confused, Brad, more than confused would be a better term!"

Brad begins to grin. "That's nothing new, Mike, the whole world is confused. Sit down here at the table with Mary and I… we'll have some coffee. And maybe, before we're finished, the both of us just might learn something," he says, grinning pleasantly.

Mike sits across from Brad, reminiscing how he got here. He thinks of his conversion, his hunger to learn more. But most of all, his never-ending desire to think about His coming!

And there's speechless moments, moving books from one end of the table to the other, talking about things yet to come.

Brad moves closer, placing his drink down, looking up at him, asking, "Now tell me what we're talking about, Mike…this could become interesting!"

Mike looks up at him again, wondering where to begin.

"I'm in over my head, Brad, way over my head! I can't think of anything but the return of Jesus, our Lord and Savior. I'm beginning to wonder if I'm the only one believing Jesus is about to return...or is it just me?"

Brad looks again at him surprised. "You're only one of millions, Mike. We're all wondering the same! Tell me the rest of your thoughts and wonders, you're beginning to interest me!"

Mike turns away, afraid to answer 'til, "Call it what you want, but it seems like the world is turning upside down, going crazy over the weird and filthy things! It's getting to me big-time, Brad: I don't know how to stop it!"

And Brad looks again at him, smiling. "This isn't news, Mike...we're all having the same problem! Sit back, take a good breath, and tell me the rest of your worries."

Mike rises from his chair, walks around the table and back to Brad, confronting him.

"But I'm desperate, Brad! And I don't know the reason! For the first time in my life, I'm truly desperate!"

Brad takes his time, trying to read in between his words. "And just what does desperate mean, Mike? Tell me about it!"

"I'm worried about the ones who are going to be left behind! I'm talking about my friends, the ones who can't see it!" he says, growing louder by the moment.

Brad rubs his forehead, wondering where to begin. "You're desire is admirable, Mike. It's great, but sometimes, I worry about you," he says, jolting his mind-set, causing him to look again at him surprised, asking, "Now, what are you trying to tell me, Brad?"

"I love you like a son, but sometimes, you don't know how to quit, partner!"

God Help Us

And he's grinning, thinking back, "I've been told the same a hundred times, Brad, believe me I have! But never in my lifetime have I experienced the feeling I have, never anything like this!"

"But tell me what your real reason is for this sudden interest in prophesy, and why it keeps bothering you!"

Mike looks hard at him, never blinking. "It's because everything I read in the Bible shows up in newspaper headlines day after day and people can't see it! I've been in churches where they don't talk about it! They're more interested in the next basketball game, the next social affair! And in the meantime, I'm beginning to panic, wondering why they can't see the Lord is just around the corner!"

Brad reaches out, taking his hand. "But calm yourself, Mike, we all wonder why they can't see it!"

And he slows, looking across the table hearing Mike sighing.

"Good! But my interest in prophesy...it's never ending! I read the Bible hours upon hours, watching the signs He gave us come true. I want to shout it to the world, but I'm not sure about...when!"

"But it's about to end, Mike! Things are happening faster than ever before, knowledge increases daily, sexual depravity... wars and rumors of wars. It's all here, Mike! Now tell me your greatest desire, something that would make you stand up and shout His name before thousands!"

And his eyes light up immediately! "I would like to show people the things I think about. I would like them feel the way I feel. I would let them hear the sound of a trumpet, watch dead people rise from their graves, all of us ready to meet the Lord in the air."

Again, Brad looks him over, turning away impressed. "You're talking rapture, right, Mike?"

Mike's face glows even brighter. "I am, Brad...all the way and then some! But the big question, the one everyone wants to know..."

"Yes, Mike?"

"Tell me about the church, the ones the Bible calls *the elect*! Will they be raptured before the battle of all battles, Armageddon?"

Brad turns, looking away searching for Mary. She stands at the kitchen table shaking her head; *no, not me*! He walks behind Mike, removing his Bible from a shelf, placing it before him.

"Let's read His words, Mike...no better place than the Bible!"

> For the Lord him-self shall descend from Heaven with a shout, and with the voice of the archangel, and with the trumpet of God; and the dead in Christ shall rise first;
>
> Then we which are alive and remain shall be caught up together with them in the clouds, to meet the Lord in the air; and so shall we ever be with the Lord. (1 Thessalonians 4:16–17)
>
> And except those days should be shortened, there should no flesh be saved: but for the elect's sake those days shall be shortened. (Matthew 24:22)

"Does this satisfy you, Mike?" he asks.

Mike sits thinking, still worried. "It does! I do believe *the church* will be gone before the tribulation period begins. But there's something else..."

"Tell me about it."

"My question remains, when will Jesus return? His Second Coming, you know what I'm talking about; when he actually plants His feet on solid ground in Jerusalem," he tries to explain.

God Help Us

Brad rises from his chair, amazed! His new convert knows the Bible: he's smart, he knows the answers. And from out of nowhere, a thought of mischief, something to make him think!

"You want an opinion…great! Move over here and take my seat, friend, it's time for your opinion! Tell me the time of His second coming!"

Mike turns his head looking away, concentrating, reflecting back to Bible days, never to be forgotten Bible days. His mind is reeling, thinking of friends, and he's suddenly remembering preachers he will never forget. And he's suddenly remembering something Reverend Jeffers said just as he was about to go to sleep on a cold winter night sitting next to his grandma, something Jesus said, something he said to His disciples.

"I believe this, Brad. I believe His second coming is soon, but only the Father in heaven knows the hour and day. But let's read the book of Matthew, everything we need but the day and the hour."

> Immediately after the tribulation of those days, shall the sun be darkened, and the moon shall not give her light, and the stars shall fall from heaven, and the power of the heavens shall be shaken.
>
> And then shall appear the sign of the Son of man coming in the clouds of heaven with power and great glory. (Matthew 24:29–30)

"It's his second coming, Brad…it has to be! Jesus tells us plain and simple, his second coming is after the tribulation, not before! But a lot can take place in the meantime. Think about the signs Jesus gave to his followers foretelling His second coming. Many have come and gone, except maybe preaching the gospel to all nations. And the fig-tree parable: a generation of Jews returning to Jerusalem before His coming."

> Now learn a parable of the fig tree; When his branch is yet tender, and putteth forth leaves, yea know that summer is nigh
>
> So likewise yea, when ye shall see all these things, know that it is near, even at the doors.
>
> Verily I say unto you, This generation shall not pass, till all these things be fulfilled. (Matthew 24:32–34)

Again, Brad is staring at him speechless!

"You're right, Mike. The handwriting is on the wall. Israel became a nation recognized by the United Nations in 1948. Count the years from 1948 till now, and when you're finished…"

"But then what, Brad?"

Brad takes his time, gazing at Mike cautiously. "We'll be near the end of the generation, Mike, the generation Jesus told us about. It's time to look up, my friend. We're going home…no doubt about it!"

"You mean…"

"I do, Mike! Soon the sky will open, a trumpet will sound, and the Lord with a host of angels will appear in the heavens."

And unexpectedly, his smile is no more!

"But why the worried look, Brad? You've changed, the smile upon your face…what happened?"

Tears show without reason! "It's the time element: time is running out, Mike! It's here and people can't see it! But it's here, Mike! It's finally here!" he keeps shouting, shaking his head, looking downward.

"But what can we do, Brad? We can't make them repent!"

God Help Us

And his face turns pale, remembering a sermon. "I think about a guy called Noah building an ark. He was preaching to them a hundred years out in the desert. They didn't listen to Noah, Mike, why listen to us?"

"That bad, huh?"

"It is, Mike! But we can try, it's our duty to warn them!"

And he's worried! "But then what...then what, Brad?"

Brad is motionless, struggling to say the words. He reaches out, joining hands. "Tell them this, Mike. When it happens, and it will happen: all hell will break loose on this place called earth!"

"And then, Brad...then what?"

"Tell them this too, Mike! When the time has come...run for the hills! The Lord is coming to gather His church! And tell them this too, Mike..."

"Yes, Brad...yes..."

"Tell them the truth, Mike. Make them understand if they're not one of His...they'll be left behind! But there's something else...tell them this, Mike: now is the time to repent!" he's shouting.

"You really believe it, don't you, Brad?"

And a smile covers his face, announcing, "With all my heart, Mike...with all my soul, I believe it!" he says, pulling Mike next to him, handing him a couple of envelopes before leaving.

Twenty minutes later, Mike is home. From outside, he hears the usual roar of motors and blowing of horns, no longer a problem.

"But what if I'm wrong?" he asks himself, over and over.

He glances at a picture hanging on his office wall, showing Jesus praying in the Garden of Gethsemane. His heart is touched, thinking how Jesus must have felt, knowing his time here on earth was about to end. He kneels to the floor, uttering his heartfelt prayer, "Come quickly, oh Lord…come quickly…I await you!"

He's tired, heading for the bedroom, but there's something else to think about…something else he must do. The envelopes Brad handed him just before leaving.

He opens the first, displaying a note showing only the word *immediately*; it bothers him. He opens his dictionary, and there it is spread out before him: *immediately…at once!*

He sits in silence, thinking back to life before Friend. He's not the same Mike; his life is changing fast, and he loves it.

And the other envelope Brad handed him, another message from Brad.

> But thou, O Daniel, shut up the words, and seal the book, even to the time of the end; many shall run to and fro, and knowledge shall be increased. (Daniel 12:4)

And the mystery of all mysteries, it's over! Jesus is coming; time to get ready!

7

Everything Is Beautiful

Be pleased O Lord to deliver me: make haste to help me.

—Psalm 40:13

Mike is awakened from a sound sleep early the following morning by the ringing of the phone. He recognizes the voice, but it's different: it's hoarse and weak, sounding as Keith's voice.

"Mike, I haven't seen you around lately. What's going on, partner?"

He's surprised, but pleased.

"I've been busy, but there's a noise in the background, Keith, what's going on?"

"There's a noise for sure! I'm calling from one of our wells near Utica, Kentucky. We had some problems last night... serious problems. Ashland Oil called about midnight, wanting me down here immediately, so here I am."

"How serious, Keith?" Mike asks, yawning.

"Bad! Real bad, Mike! One of the lines leaked spilling oil into a nearby lake. And as usual, I was looking for you."

"I understand."

"But, Mike, there's another reason I called."

"Yes, Keith."

"I'm hearing some crazy reports about you lately, Mike, something going on I need to know about?"

"Nothing you might be interested in, Keith."

"You're probably right, but someone said you might be in love, true or false, buddy boy?"

Mike's tired and sleepy, no time for jokes.

"Maybe…"

"Now come on, Mike, spill it out, tell me the change…what's going on in your new secret life?"

Mike pauses, thinking it's too early in the morning to start a long conversation, but this is Keith, his friend; not just any friend, *his real good friend.*

"There's a lot going on, Keith. I'm no longer in the oil business, sold my interest and made some changes."

But Keith isn't surprised. Rumors about Mike come and go, but why get away from something he loves doesn't make sense; he keeps thinking.

"Why now, Mike? We're making some dough, gettin' ready to drill again!"

"Not interested, Keith," he barely mutters, tired and sleepy.

"But this one is different, Mike. It's gonna make money, big-time money!" he says, persisting.

"Forget it, Keith!"

"I'll never understand you, Mike, but there's always a piece for you…anytime."

Mike grows tired, wanting to end it. "Thanks for the invitation, but my life is changing."

A long pause. "Changing! And how is it changing?"

God Help Us

Mike doesn't hesitate. "I've become a Christian…one of those down and out Christians…a Jesus worshiper! You know, one of those persons you're always laughing about!"

Long silence. "But, Mike…Mike—"

Mike interrupts, "I know what you're thinking, Keith, but you're wrong, dead wrong!"

Another long pause. "I don't know what to say, Mike, except good luck, wish you the best!"

"I knew this would surprise you, Keith, but I'll always remember…"

"Yes, Mike…"

"I'll remember the good times! We both will!"

Keith is suddenly searching for words. "I know I'm confused, but I believe I heard you say you're a Christian!" he mutters weakly.

And Mike begins to recognize something is different. Something isn't normal; he wouldn't stop laughing, if only he could.

"One more time, Keith. I'm going to church…I love it!"

A long pause. "You gotta be outta your cotton-picking mind," he barely mumbles.

"But not this time, Keith!"

"Mike Cutler a Christian! Never in my wildest dreams…" Keith is muttering, endlessly.

Mike takes his time responding, "I've heard the same before, Keith…it's my life, my decision, guess what, pal."

"You tell me what," a weak voice barely mumbles.

"I love it, Keith! I really and truly love it!"

Keith is struggling, breathing intermittingly. "My breathing isn't like it used to be, Mike."

"I can tell it isn't, Keith."

Another long pause. "But Mike Cutler gettin' religion, whatta shocker that is! But there's something else you should know, Mike."

"Now, what should I know, something you've been holding back on me, maybe a secret?"

"It's a secret for sure, Mike, but not to you!"

"That's good news for everyone, tell me you're joking."

"But it's not a joke! I've a problem...a big problem!"

And Mike sits straight up, taking him seriously. "I'm beginning to believe you're serious...really and truly serious!"

"I'm as serious as I can get, Mike!"

"I'm listening, Keith, tell me about it!"

"It's my left carotid artery, the big one leading up from the back of my neck to the brain. My doctor said I could lose my voice...whatever. It troubles me even to think about it!"

And Mike is shocked! "Another time around, Keith, it better be the truth."

"Yes, Mike."

"Are you putting me on...or is it the truth?"

A long pause. "I'm not putting you on, Mike. It's true! I know what you're thinking! You're thinking I've lost my mind, maybe I have...time I own up..."

"Own up to what, Keith?"

"Cigarettes, booze, pot, wild women, and all the rest, just name it...I'm guilty!" he says, struggling. "Life has caught up with me, Mike, nothing I can do about it!"

Mike's head drops, staring at the floor remorsefully.

"But there's a way out...there's always a way out, Keith!"

His breathing grows even harder. "Not this time, pal! I only want to ease the pain, forget about things...take things easy!"

God Help Us

"Tell me the rest of it...what am I missing?"

"You wouldn't understand, Mike. My life has been a game you've never played before!"

"Just try me!"

"Most days, Rosy and I smoke some weed, get a little high, do things our way, whatever."

"And whatever, tell me about it."

"After being in the woods most of the day, she shows up over at the lake at my place covered with chiggers, raring to go. It's playtime for the both of us!"

Mike tries holding back, but his temper is rising.

"And then what?"

"Oh! The usual! I put her in the tub, stick a joint between her lips, and she's happy...real happy! A couple of hours later, she's feeling good; wanting to sing some songs from yesterday, the kind that blows my head away!"

"I'll bet it does! And then what?" Mike asks, angry again.

"Oh! You know, Mike, some of the old stuff like 'Where Have All the Flowers Gone' by Peter, Paul, and Mary."

"Oh, yeah, I remember...Peter, Paul, and Mary! How in the hell could I ever forget Peter, Paul, and Mary?"

A long wait. "Don't start it, Mike, it's insulting. Rosy wasn't part of the sixties and seventies."

"You're right, pal; she was only a baby...you idiot!" Mike says, angrier by the moment.

Long painful silence. "Now hold it, Mike: time we get serious!"

"I don't know what you're talking about, but I'm serious as I'll ever be, Keith. Maybe it's time for you to get serious! Think about it, pal!"

"But there's something more, something you gotta know about Rosy, something between you and me alone, Mike…"

"Then quit fooling around, tell me about Rosy!"

Another long pause, wheezing and coughing. "Well…it's like this Mike. She's twenty years younger than me, easy to get along with, and always there waiting."

Mike studies, hesitating to answer. "Great, Keith! She's the perfect woman for you. What else?"

Again, he's struggling. "I worry about her, Mike! I worry about what might happen to Rosy if I wasn't around, you know…just in case. She has no education, except what life has taught her. She's had life the hard way. Parents were divorced when she was six. From that day forward, she was like a piece of worn-out furniture, passed from family to family! She's helpless, Mike, without a friend…except me!"

And Mike's heart begins to melt. "Sounds pitiful, Keith. Now maybe, you can tell me how you came into her life."

His voice grows still weaker. "I met her at a restaurant, waiting tables, been with her since. Sure! I've feelings for her, but not love…you understand, Mike!"

"Sure I do, but it doesn't make sense. Where do I come into her life?"

Keith grows more faint, struggling to explain.

"Well, she just might need some help, Mike! And I was thinking…maybe…if I'm not around…she might need someone like you to look out for her! You know what I mean, someone to give her advice…make her feel wanted."

And Mike is taken again, feeling sorry for Rosy.

"I understand! I've met Rosy a couple of times, maybe a little wacky, but she a good person," he adds reluctantly.

God Help Us

"She is, Mike! She really is! She's the kind of person you can't help feeling sorry for…a heart of gold, always there when you need her. You know what I'm talking about, you been around like me, Mike. All I want you to do is—"

"Is what, Keith?" Mike interrupts.

Another long pause. "Do what's gotta be done, Mike…that's all I can ask."

And Mike begins to realize something's pressing Keith, something to worry about, something he can't handle.

"Whatever, Keith…anything for an old friend! But there's something else to talk about…"

"About what?"

"Drugs, Keith! Mind breakers! Everything I hate!"

Keith sits alone, wondering how to reply. "I know how you feel about drugs, Mike, but the stuff works for me!"

Wham! Mike's temper explodes.

"It works! Are you nuts or just plain stupid?" he shouts, going berserk!

Wheezing, some choking. "Maybe both, Mike," a weak broken voice mutters pitifully.

And Mike's anger is no more, turning to forgiveness. "But what's next, Keith? Tried quitting?"

"A thousand times, Mike! But this is different…a different ball game, my friend."

And Mike pauses again, worried! He wants to console him, wants to save him, the way Friend saved him.

"It's never too late, Keith…believe it isn't."

"But it is for me, Mike! Time has run out. I can barely breathe," a weak voice barely can utter.

"I understand…I've been there! But it's time to get serious!"

"You're talking Bible stuff, going to church, right?"

"Nothing but Bible stuff. It works, Keith…believe me it works!"

More gasping, wheezing. "I've tried everything, why not the church? Maybe I'm just one of those doped-up happy persons from the sixties and seventies, you know what I'm talking about…*the hippie generation!*"

And his words strike a sore spot with Mike, something that never goes away. Vietnam, demonstrations in the streets back home, while other young Americans gave their all, dying in rice paddies a thousand miles away.

"Don't try being funny, Keith! I still remember a gang of flower children spitting in my face for fighting a war they refused to fight. I remember more than sixty thousand brave Americans fighting, dying in a land far away while your doped-up friends with faces painted like scarecrows paraded down the streets of San Francisco! Oh yes! It bothers me! It bothers me a helluva lot!"

Again, long silence. "But it's over, Mike! Vietnam is over…a thing of the past!"

And Mike is tested to the core! He wants to throw the phone at Keith, spit in his face like his friends did to him, but something's different; he's changed, by the grace of God, he's changed. And he knows it!

"Yesterday, I would be cursing you, Keith. But today, I'll be praying for you. I'll be praying that somehow, someday, you meet a guy like I did, a guy named Friend, someone who cared for me, introducing me to his father," he tries to explain, almost crying, thinking about it.

Another long pause, a faint muttering of scrabbled words and Keith says, "Praying for me! Is that what you said, Mike?" he barely can mutter.

God Help Us

"That's what I said, Keith…praying for you. I've been in your shoes, felt the pain, hated every moment!"

"But life is over, Mike! I've nothing left, what's a guy to do?"

Mike knows the feeling: hatred, shame, life in shambles, all gone till Christ took over.

"It's never over, my friend! I've been there, did that. Believe me, it isn't!"

"But I'm hooked, Mike! I'm hooked for the rest of my miserable life…no way out!" Keith is barely able to mutter as his voice drifts away into nothing.

"Are you all right, Keith?"

"I suppose…what else is there for a guy like me to do?" he barely can whisper.

And Mike is thinking back to a time when he felt the same.

"It's called repentance, Keith. It's what life is all about for all of us!"

"But I've other problems…insurmountable problems," Keith barely is able to mumble.

"You're putting me on, right!"

"Not today, Mike! I'm serious as I'll ever be…"

"Tell me about it!"

And he's struggling. "I'll try, Mike…I'll tell you…the only way I know how to tell you."

Mike is worried; it's hard to respond, but he has to. "I'm listening, Keith."

A never-ending pause. *"The party is over, Mike! It's half-past midnight…time to go home! Need I say more?"*

Boom! It resounds like a death sentence! Keith is desperate; he's got nowhere to turn.

"Use your breathing apparatus, Keith…you're struggling!"

Arthur (Mac) Mc Caffry

"I'm trying, Mike...really I am! I need more time. We need to talk, get down to serious business!" he barely mumbles, leaving him guessing.

And Mike sits alone, worried again. "Serious business! What's he talking about?" he mutters to himself, settling back against the headboard, waiting.

8

Daddy Keith

For mine iniquities are gone over mine head: as
an heavy burden they are too heavy for me.

—Psalm 38:4

Almost two hours since Keith called promising to call back, and Mike's concerned. A moment to remember back when—and the phone rings, it's Keith.

"Sorry for the delay, Mike, but back to Nam. I've often wished I could go back and apologize to some of your friends, but it's impossible!"

"It's a problem for everyone, Keith!"

Painfully long silence and Keith barely mutters, "I don't know what's happening to me, Mike, for the first time in my life, I don't have an answer for anything. It's as if I don't care."

Again, Mike is concerned, wanting to help him.

"It happens to all of us sometime during our life, don't worry about it," Mike tries to explain.

Conversation continues; good times, bad times till Keith ends the conversation with a single sentence.

"But for me…it's different, my friend!"

"Now, what are talking about, Keith?"

An extra-long time to say the words and said, "Time has run out, there's no tomorrow for me, Mike!" he can barely utter.

Again, Mike struggles, searching for words. Keith, his icon, his best friend ever, he's in trouble facing reality.

"But you're different, Keith, you've something going for you."

"I do!" he barely mumbles.

"Sure you do! I'll always be there for you...always have and always will; that's my promise, partner!"

A lot of gasping, wheezing. "I've always known it, Mike, it's time you hear my confession!"

And Mike sits straight up in bed, coming alive.

"Maybe I'm hearing things, did you say confession?"

"I did...my last and only confession! Everyone has something to confess when there's no way out, Mike."

Mike pauses, thinking back. "You're right Keith, we all do. Take your time, get your breath, and tell me about it."

And Keith breathes easy. "I was in England a month ago with my daughter, had the time of my life. It was heaven, Mike... heaven on earth!"

Mike interrupts quickly. "Am I dreaming, or did I hear you say *daughter*?"

"You're not dreaming, this is part of my secret life."

And he's afraid to ask. "Tell me about your secret life, Keith, it's beginning to sound interesting!"

He breathes hard, but doesn't hesitate. "I've a daughter, Mike...a beautiful, wonderful blue-eyed daughter! I was married thirty years ago in London to a well-known socialite. She had class! I had nothing but the good times! She had it all: wealth, beauty, everything a guy could want. She was way outta my class and then some!" he barely can mutter.

God Help Us

And he's struggling again!

"Take your time, Keith."

"I'm trying, Mike, really I am. The marriage went down in about a year, but I've always loved them…the both of them dearly. My daughter's name is Brittany Ann Lincoln, she's done well pursuing her ambition."

"Her ambition is what, Keith?" Mike asks, probing.

His voice grows weaker by the moment, continuing.

"She's big-time: a supermodel…pretty as her mother. And that really means something, Mike!"

And Mike wonders suspiciously. "But I don't understand, Keith, why tell me?"

A long pause. "Who else, Mike? You're my friend, I trust you! Brittany knows our friendship, she knows how I depend upon you!"

Again, he's puzzled. "But you're the father, Keith!"

Another long pause. "You're right about that, pal, but I just might not be able to be there!" And Mike wonders suspiciously!

"But what are you trying to tell me, Keith?"

A long pause. "It means I might not be around very much longer, Mike," a low shaky voice finally answers.

And Mike's beginning to get the message: Keith's in trouble with no way out!

"Stop it, Keith! Quit talking that way!" Mike shouts, hoping to bring him alive, fighting.

Keith's voice grows weaker and weaker.

"But I need you, Mike, I really need you!" his struggling voice is barely able to mutter.

Mike's head lowers, wanting to console him. "I'll be there for you, Keith, you know I will!"

Another long pause. "Having some trouble, Keith? Don't worry about it, we'll talk again later."

And finally, a weak voice says, "Hang with me, partner, please…just a few more moments…please, Mike."

"You know I will."

"After you meet her, tell her about the wells, the fun we had, but more than all…tell her how much I've always loved her. And tell her how I've missed her, always wishing things had been different. And tell her to inform her mother, I always loved her too, missed her terribly."

It's painful, hard to reply, but he does. "I'll do it, Keith, I promise you I will."

"Tell Brittany the lake and house you sold me; along with everything I own…it's hers, hers alone, Mike."

Mike's imagination runs wild. He can imagine a tear or two dropping down upon his pillow while he's trying desperately to stop the flow.

Pauses grow longer and Mike worries even more. He's putting pieces together, adding up to one big surprise: Keith's a daddy with a beautiful daughter living abroad; he's about to die, leaving her forever.

And the phone goes deathly silent! Mike sits alone, wondering how it all happened.

He remembers the good times, their week in New York watching the Broadway hit show, *Annie*. He remembers how they partied the night away, laughing, singing till dawn and then some! He leaves his bed, heading for his desk, searching for some old forgotten sheet music, a song from their night on Broadway watching *Annie*. And there it is, hidden away waiting for another day, this day, a day of confession!

God Help Us

Tomorrow
Oh! The sun—will come out tomorrow
Oh! I got to hang on till tomorrow—come what may!
Tomorrow, tomorrow, I love ye tomorrow,
You're always a day away—
The tomorrow—tomorrow
Only!—tomorrow.

He wants to cry but can't. It's reality time, and Keith knows it.

9

Homecoming

He shall call upon me, and I will answer Him: I will be
with him in trouble; I will deliver him, and honour him.

—Psalms 91:15

Early the next morning, Mike sits having morning
coffee and the phone rings, bringing a very familiar
voice.

"Uncle Mike, this is Doug, your nephew," he says, causing
Mike to come alive.

"You remember me! You actually remember me!"

"I'll always remember you, Uncle Mike…you know I will.
Martha and I just arrived at the airport and we'll be on our way
to your place right away. We're here on business, one day only."

"But one day…why?"

"I'll explain later. Right now, Martha's putting luggage in the
cab, and if I don't get moving, she'll leave me for sure. Be there
right away, Uncle Mike."

And wham! The phone is dead.

Twenty minutes later, a cab arrives in front of Mike's house,
and out jumps the two most important people in his life. He
watches their every movement, looking again and again. And
wow! How they've changed! No longer kids, they're young
ambitious members of America's future, nothing like the same

God Help Us

newlyweds six years back, ready to conquer the world and then some!

Martha's no longer the tall, blond, statuesque, blue-eyed beauty he remembers strolling down the aisle at Trinity Methodist. She's a beautiful business-like young lady, holding on to a briefcase, moving toward him swiftly.

Doug, too, has changed, shoulders wide as the front door, six-foot-two tall and handsome; no longer the little freckle-faced kid running around in his backyard, chasing Fred and Barney.

They head for the nearest bedroom with luggage in hand; moments later they're back, ready to become acquainted again.

Doug stands beside Martha, gazing out toward the large backyard, reminiscing. He's thinking of Joyce, his aunt, and the stories she put into his mind, all about Jesus coming back to earth when the time is right!

His head bows low and back up again, looking toward heaven, mumbling words only he and she would understand. A few moments later, he's finished, walking away, smiling satisfied.

Mike sits, anxious to explain something always bothering him.

"But before we begin, there's something you must know about me."

Martha watches Doug smiling back at her. "And just what might that be, Mike?" she asks.

His face brightens! He wants them to know he's not the same old Mike a couple years back, all mixed up, filled with hatred toward the church.

"I've changed, Martha! It's hard to explain, but true. My desire to get even with the church, it's over! I'm back where I started thirty years ago, serving the Lord, loving every moment of it!" he tries to explain.

"We know, Mike—believe me, we know!" Martha says, looking over at Doug grinning.

Mike isn't satisfied. "But there's something else, Martha."

"Yes, Mike."

"Things are happening in my life, impossible, wonderful, exciting things."

Again, she hesitates. "And what does 'wonderful, exciting things' mean, Mike? Tell me about it."

And he's looking down, searching. "It's hard to believe things, things I try to explain…never finding an answer!"

"But try again, Mike…try again! We've business to handle, important business…we're waiting, Mike!"

And he stops, lost again, staring at her, thinking. "I wish I could, but I can't, Martha! It's something never ending, something I can't get away from. Maybe I'll never find the answer."

She moves beside him, looking up at him. "Your worries are over, Mike! We've enough excitement to last you forever and then some!"

And Doug moves beside them, interrupting, "Martha's telling you straight, Mike. We're here to talk about the future, your future! We would love to stay a week, do nothing but talk about the good times… but this trip is different…it isn't possible!"

His eagerness turns sour. "Then what are you here for?" he asks, worried.

Doug takes his time, searching his thoughts, wondering how to explain it.

"Something radically different is about to take place in your life, Mike. Believe me, it's different! For some unexplainable reason, your future is being planned for you, planned by someone unknown, someone with clout! It's far beyond the two of us,

God Help Us

hard to believe, but true! That's the best way I know how to explain it, Mike... it bothers the both of us."

Mike moves closer. "Quit your worrying, nephew. Begin from the beginning...just tell me the facts!"

Doug moves next to him, beginning, "It's hard to explain, Mike, but somehow, some way, you're about to be a major player in something big! Your destiny is set with no explanation. And the sad part is—"

Mike reaches out, cutting him off. "The sad part is what, nephew?"

"I don't know why, Mike, but there's nothing you can do about it!" he says, wiping his brow, waiting.

And Mike can't wait! He's chuckling uncontrollably!

"Me! A major player! You gotta be kidding!"

Doug reaches out grabbing his hand, getting his attention! "But you're wrong, Mike! We're here strictly for business! I'm talking about business you've never heard anything like before, beyond your and my imagination! It's serious, Mike, grab hold of yourself and listen!" Doug says up in his face, suddenly a different kind of nephew, one he's never met before.

And Mike doesn't like the way he's talking, looking again at him, angry. "You better start thinking about someone else, nephew! I'm a candidate for nothing! I'm one of those over-the-hill guys, been there, did it all, but a major player...never in a lifetime!"

Doug is moved. Suddenly, he's angry, moving toward Mike even closer, eyes showing fire!

"I told you before, Mike, we don't have a lot of time. I'll tell you one more time, so listen good...take me seriously!" Doug says, threatening!

And a bitter demanding voice barks back at him, "I'm waiting, nephew! Let it all hang out!"

Doug remains calm. "We want your service for something beyond your wildest imagination! We want your soul, your mind, your heart…everything that goes with it!" he says strong and powerful, leaving him wondering.

Mike lowers his head, dumbfounded! Out of the blue, they come, saying things fast and furious, crazy things, things he knows nothing about. But they're his people, the ones he loves dearly.

"I'm listening, Doug, what else can I do?" a broken voice barely mutters.

"Good! Now we understand one another! Get your breath, sit back, and listen!"

Mike sits, looking Doug over and over again, wondering. He's wondering, *Whatever happened to that little kid I once saw running wild in the backyard a few years ago? This can't be real, this isn't happening! Why would anyone want me for anything? Impossible! It has to be—*

Martha moves beside him. She holds his hand, looking up into his tired-looking eyes, hoping. "There's a lot to talk about, Mike…maybe hard to sell you, but there's one thing you can be sure of…"

And he looks up, hesitant to go further. "Sure of what, Martha?"

"You're the one we came for, Mike…no doubt about it!"

His head drops. His face shows strain, looking up at her. "But of all the people in the world, why me, Martha? I'm nobody!"

Doug moves beside him. "You're going on a journey, Mike…a journey greater than anything you've ever dreamed about, beyond human imagination!"

God Help Us

Again, Mike is shaking his head, pleading.

"You've lost me, Doug! Stop it please. I don't wanna hear it!"

Doug moves even closer. "I've told you straight out, we're here on business! We might need the entire night getting through to you, but we will, Mike, bank on it!"

Mike's temper builds higher and higher. "I've listened to this crazy talk long enough, now out with it!"

Martha moves forward standing before him, threatening, "You're either in or out, Mike, all the way or nothing!"

Wham! Right to the point! Wild, crazy thoughts cloud his mind. He looks hard at her, holding his temper!

"I trust the two of you more than anyone, more than you'll ever know. But it's time we get something straight!" Mike says, demanding.

And Martha is right back at him, shouting, "Then go ahead, Mike…let it out! Let it all out!"

"It's time the two of you get it in your head I'm no five-year-old kid you can play with! I'm the same guy you met the last time, but a little bit smarter. Tell me the real purpose you're being here!" he barks viciously.

But Doug isn't surprised, remembering his history! He's shaking his head, wondering for his future.

"You're right, Mike! It's time you know the whole story, a story like none before…changing your life forever!"

"You've said the same before, Doug…now out with it, get it over with."

"We're here because of you, Mike! We're here to set the stage for the return of Jesus Christ! It's important! More important than anything…ever…"

Mike looks up at him, surprised. "What's more important than anything ever, nephew?"

"Jesus is coming! We're only the forerunners, preparing people to meet Him! Soon, a battle will begin with forces unimaginable. They're the devil's forces trying to stop us. It will be the war of all wars, the devil against Jesus; it's coming, Mike...get ready for it."

And Mike pauses, shaking his head, thinking, *This is my nephew, the little boy in the backyard, boy oh boy, whatta change... whatta surprise!*

Martha moves beside him ready for business. "But it's time we move on, Mike...time we tell you everything, the good, the bad...whatever! Are you ready for it, Mike?"

He looks up, afraid to answer. "Ready as I'll ever be, Martha," he mumbles suspiciously.

"But there's something else, Mike, something I forgot to mention!"

And he looks up at her, surprised again. "Yes, Martha?"

"Once you agree with our proposal, you're in for good, no backing out...agreed?"

And again, he looks hard at the both of them, barely murmuring, "Agreed! Now out with it!"

Doug moves beside him. "We want your participation in something out of your realm of thought, it's big time, Mike!"

He rubs his hand across his brow, worried. "But first, hear me out..."

And Martha moves beside him, interrupting, "We're waiting, Mike."

"From the moment you arrived, I felt something inside of me...something different, something I've never felt before! It was a wonderful feeling! It was as if you came for me...me alone, Martha!" he tries to explain, but it's useless.

And they rise, gazing at one another, wondering no longer.

God Help Us

"You're right, Mike, we are here for you," Martha says, pushing papers before him, ending the conversation.

A quick glance and Mike shoves the papers back, angry again!

"Now what's bothering you, Mike?" she asks disgustedly.

He doesn't wait, exploding again, "Bother me! Sure it bothers me! When I see the words *military intelligence*, I don't look twice, dearie, it bothers me bad...real bad!" he shouts back at her, heated!

Doug reaches out, placing his hand upon his shoulder. "But you're wrong, Mike...dead wrong! Sit back, hold your breath, and listen for a change!"

Mike looks up at him, barking angrily, "But just for the record, nephew, I've traveled this route before, and believe me, nephew...it wasn't pleasant!"

"I'm aware of it, Mike. I'm aware of a lot of things...including your history!"

Mike glances back at him, worried! "Then tell me about it, Doug...tell me all about my history!"

"I would love to, but this isn't the time or place. But rest assured, when we're done with you, Mike, you'll be changed forever...looking at things a world away differently!"

Again, Mike rubs his forehead, perspiration showing, sweating.

"Everything has a place with a purpose, Mike. But for the present, don't say a word... just sit quiet and listen!"

"I'm listening, nephew! Believe me, I'm listening!"

"I know you're listening, Mike. But there are matters you know nothing about. I've been ordered to come here and talk to you, that's what this trip is all about."

And Mike stops him. "Talk about what?"

"Some very important things we'll talk about later, things that will blow your head off and then some!"

Mike comes to attention, looking up at him differently. "Tell me about it! But just for the record, nephew, I don't give a crap who ordered you here!" he barks smartly.

"I know you don't, Mike, but maybe you just might be interested in knowing I'm with Military Intelligence, working along with the CIA wherever I go!" Doug says, bringing him alive, staring hard at him.

Wham! He's shaken again, left wondering, *Oh Lord...oh Lord...what have I done? What's next with this smart-looking, never-to-be-forgotten nephew of mine?*

Slowly, he rises from his chair, moving over to Doug, extending his hand. "I'm sorry, Doug...really sorry! I can only offer my apology...what else can I say?" he mutters, apologizing again.

"Sit back and take it easy, Mike. We're only beginning! I'll explain what we'll be doing here today. I'm only part of it, someone will be with you forever before this thing is over. Get ready for it, Mike, quit your arguing and join us."

"Continue, Doug..." he barely mutters, rubbing his brow, worried.

"But there's other news, Mike...important news!"

"Yes, Doug."

"I'll be leaving on a short vacation before heading for the Middle East, the hottest place in the universe...closer to hell than anywhere!" Doug says, causing Mike to come alive, speechless again.

10

Something to Worry About

Lord, make me to know mine end, and
the measure of my days, what it is.

—Psalm 39:4

And again, Mike wonders where to begin. He reaches out pulling the two close to him.

"And I'll be rooting for you, Doug. But when you talk about Military Intelligence, CIA, you're outta my class...something for me not to worry about."

Doug grasps his hand, squeezing it hard. "Stop, it Mike! No more of your excuses!"

And Mike moves closer, worried. "But what's the real reason you're here, Doug?"

"Our country is in trouble, Mike...big trouble! I go to bed every night, wondering if there's a way out."

"Tell me about it, Doug."

And Doug's face goes pale! "It's hard to explain, Mike. Night after night, I lay in bed wondering if it's me or my imagination."

"Wondering about what?"

And he turns, staring at him differently. "I'm sure, very sure, people in our own government work against us!"

"Wow!" Again, Mike is stunned, left wondering!

Arthur (Mac) Mc Caffry

"But working for whom, Doug? This is serious, more than serious, it's treason!"

His eyes stare downward, dreading to say the words. "I'm not positive...nobody is positive. But things are happening fast, hard to believe how fast they're happening! It's almost like Bible predictions coming to life right before us. It's scary, Mike—unbelievably scary!"

Mike looks up at him, puzzled again. "But there has to be someone, somewhere, knowing the answer to all of this, Doug...there has to be!"

"There's no doubt about it, Mike! But what we do in the meantime is the question! You're afraid of your friends, you know your enemies, but you don't know the traitors!"

"Are you positive about this, Doug? This is serious as it gets... treason at the highest places!"

"I'm only sure of one thing, Mike. The government is taking sides with people wanting to destroy us! The sad part is...people are going along with it, afraid to asks questions. I'm talking about fanatical Muslim terrorist groups wanting to change the world!"

"I believe I know what you're saying, Doug, to hell with your view, our way only! And that's bad, Doug...real bad!"

And Doug reaches out stopping him, beginning again.

"I'm beginning to feel as if I'm living in another world—a new world, not the world I knew only a couple of years ago. We're changing fast, Mike, people don't know where to turn and..."

Mike looks hard at Doug his face filled with anger. "There's only one way to say it, Doug."

"And what's that, Mike?"

"Call it whatever you wish to, Doug, but I sure as hell don't like it!"

God Help Us

Martha moves close to Mike, taking over. "But that's not everything, Mike! They're coming after Christians, the ones who are brave enough to stand up against them," she adds.

Doug moves close, placing his arms around her, kissing her tenderly.

And she looks up at him, smiling. "Thanks, darling, I needed something like a kiss or two to calm me," she says, nice and sweetly.

Again she's back at Mike, continuing, "But there's a bright side to everything, Mike! There's always something from the Bible telling the story better. It's something we can lean on, never forgetting where it's coming from."

And Mike's face brightens. "Tell me about it, Martha."

She reaches out, handing him a tract of paper. "It's straight from Jesus, Mike. Something he told us before he was crucified. Read it, contemplate the meaning. And when you're finished, think of someone powerful, professing to be Christians, but on the inside a world away different!"

Mike opens his Bible. A moment later, a huge smile crosses his satisfied face!

> Beware of false prophets, which come to you in sheep's clothing, but inwardly they are ravening wolves. Ye shall know them by their fruits. (Matthew 7:15–16)

"Ring a bell, Mike?" she asks.

"It does for sure. But I'm thinking about another one, one like, 'And then many shall be offended, and shall betray one another, and hate one another' (Matthew 24:10–11)."

Mike shoves the paper back, seeing other papers beside it.

"But where does all this literature come from, Martha? Some of our critics would jump up and down calling it subversive!"

"It comes from my office only, Mike…doesn't get any better." And she stops, looking at him differently, thinking.

"Is something bothering you, Martha?" Mike asks, waiting.

"Oh yes, something bothers me! Wars and rumors of wars, greed, deceit, political unfaithfulness, all of it, Mike, take your pick. It's out in full view before us, but some can't see it!"

And she stops, getting her breath. "But after a lot of prayer, reading the Bible, I've found the answer!"

Mike is surprised again. He looks back at her, waiting. "Tell me about it, Martha!"

"Add the pros, the cons, only one conclusion, Mike!

"And?"

"We're headed for One World Order: no doubt about it! Remember how Jesus said He would come as a thief in the night, well, it's here, Mike!"

And Mike is looking at her petrified, waiting for more!

"People running our government, they're deceiving us big time. They're good at it, Mike…the best ever! And when they're caught, they look at you mystified, changing the subject quickly. But the sad part comes last, Mike—the part most frightening!"

"The sad part…"

She lowers her head, afraid to speak, and back again confronting him. "People accept it, Mike! They actually accept it! Satan has them—hook, line, and sinker!"

Doug moves beside her, taking over. "I'll make it simple, Mike. They want to change the Constitution our forefathers died for, destroy our heritage, make anything acceptable!"

And he's speechless again, listening forever.

God Help Us

"Today as we speak, hundreds of Christians are being killed throughout the world. In North Korea, Iraq, Africa, all over the Middle East, hundreds wait, starving, just for announcing the Gospel of Jesus. It's here, Mike! Take a look at this, something to make every Christian shout about!" he says, handing him a tract, words written on paper.

> He that findeth his life shall lose it: and he that loseth his life for my sake shall find it. (Matthew 10:39)

And suddenly, Mike is different. His eyes show tears about to move downward.

"What's the matter now, Mike?" Martha asks, innocently.

And he looks up at her, pitiful-like. "I just can't help but think about those twenty-one Christian Egyptian men living in Libya having their throat cut by ISIS just for believing in Jesus!"

Martha and Doug stop suddenly. They're looking again at him, thinking, never, never can this person change so much, a follower of Jesus!

And Doug begins again, "It's all coming to an end, frightening to think about unless—"

Mike reaches out, stopping him. "Unless what?"

"We're moving out! The man with the mark is here on earth, walking among us, Mike!" Doug says excitedly.

"But the Bible, Doug...what does..."

"Read the book of Revelation, Mike! Once he comes in power, once he has their mark, they're his forever throughout eternity!" Doug says, reciting it to him.

> For it is a number of a man; and his number is Six hundred threescore and six. (Revelation 13:18)

"I'll wrap it up for you, Mike," Martha says, moving beside him. "We're in trouble financially, militarily, and morally! And when we lose our morality, we lose it all! People like Billy Graham, his son Franklin, a host of others, they've warned us, Mike! Think back to the flood in Noah's time, think back to Sodom and Gomorra, we've become like them, Mike, it's scary and—"

Mike looks up to her, pitiful-like. "And if we don't change our ways…"

She bows her head, a quick prayer, ready to go again. "We'll be the same, Mike, lost in a cloud of dust, gone forever!"

And Mike listens on and on, marveling!

"But that's only part of it, Mike. There's a cyberspace war going on every minute of the day, a war that can blow this planet to hell and back! It's serious, Mike, serious as it gets. Time we wake up, look around, and see it as it really is!"

"What are you really trying to tell me, Martha?"

"But think, Mike, think! The whole world, they're out in no man's land, searching for a leader!"

"You mean…"

"None yet, but the world is waiting!"

"But the president…why not…"

Again she reaches out, stopping him. "Oh yes…the president: he changes the law as he chooses!"

"But how? I don't get it!"

"A lot of people don't get it, Mike! It's called Executive Authority. That's the way it's done today. He does it quick, sudden, lets them think about it later. A year goes by, nobody cares and it's over," she says, shaking her head disgustedly.

God Help Us

And Mike is thinking hard, remembering something he heard long ago in a little country church. "Now you're in my league, Martha."

"And what league is that, Mike?" she asks, jokingly.

"I'm thinking about something I heard when I was a kid sittin' on an old wooden bench in an old country church."

And she moves closer to him. "Tell me about it, Mike, it's your time to preach!"

"I'll do even better. I'll quote it to you, Martha!"

> For there shall arise false Christs, and false prophets, and shall show great signs and wonders; insomuch that, if it were possible…they shall deceive the very elect. (Matthew 24:24)

And she's caught, staring at Doug, thinking, *Mike of all people…he just could be right!*

Again, she gets her breath, continuing, "But the important part, the part you're about to play, Mike!"

He pauses, beginning to chuckle. "Me…important…you gotta be kiddin', Martha…I'm nobody!"

And her anger erupts again, exploding.

"Stop it, Mike! I'm fed up listening to your whining about something thirty years ago. It's time you step up to the plate and forget the sad stuff," she's shouting, causing him to draw away, looking again at her, waiting.

She points her finger in his face, displaying her anger. "Look straight into my eyes and remember what I tell you once again, Mike Cutler!"

"You mean like this, Martha?" he asks, smiling, taunting her.

And again she's up in his face, shouting, "Whether you like it or not, sweetheart, you're part of us, all the way to the bittersweet end. But it's not only our country, Mike. I'm talking about the world, a world governed by the devil himself…no conscience whatever, full of corruption!"

And she stops, looking at him differently. "This is hard to speak this way, Mike, real hard, but it's the only way I know how to tell you."

Doug moves beside her quickly. "I think maybe it's time we let him know everything, sweetheart," he says, interrupting.

And she turns, confronting Mike again. "But I can do better, Mike. I'll make it the way you like it, blunt, direct to the point!"

And he waits, looking up at her, expecting the worst.

"We're living in a different world, a different time, engaged in a war you're not aware of. There's a war of angels and demonic forces going on everywhere! They're waiting to do battle, Mike! It's a winner-take-all battle, the stakes have never been higher!" she says, her emotions exploding.

"But I am aware of it, Martha! I really am!"

A big lovely smile, glancing back at Doug, she says, "But don't be so sad, Mike, the game isn't over!"

"Isn't over, Martha?"

"Remember Yogi Berra, the baseball catcher, what he once said, Mike?" she asks, grinning.

Mike sits, wracking his brain, wondering. And wham! Right out of the blue, it hits him.

"Sure I do! It ain't over till it's over, right, Martha!"

She moves from her seat, shouting, "You're right, partner! Grab hold of something and hold on tight, it's time we play hard ball—Yogi's game!"

"I'm waiting, Martha!"

"Good! We're a little behind with a couple of innings left. It's time to get our signals straight. We come to bat in the last of the

God Help Us

ninth…time out to make a decision. The stakes are high, souls hang in the balance."

"Yes, Martha, yes!"

"Baseball is life on the field, Mike, but with us, the stakes are higher!"

"Higher! Like what, Martha?"

"It's winner-take-all, Mike! It's either heaven or hell, no in between!" she's shouting full-out.

And Doug reaches out, placing his arms around her, kissing her softly, happy again, enjoying the moment.

11

Assignment Unknown

Bless the Lord, ye his angels, that excel in strength, that do
his commandments, harkening to the voice of his word.

—Psalm 103:20

It's time for a break. Conversation has been fast and furious,
leaving unanswered questions. Mike is reeling from one
question after another. He's the guy ready for anything, but this
is different, growing deeper by the moment.

"We've explained minor things to you, Mike, but now, time
we get down to details. I've been instructed by Nate to move
forward, set our course full out with you in the middle of it,
Mike," Doug says, causing Mike to move closer.

"I've never heard of this guy called Nate."

"You will…depend on it. When Nate speaks, people listen!
We all do!" Martha adds.

"I'll explain Martha's part, Mike. Nate put her in her position
because she's not only good…she's real good, everyone knows it."

Martha moves between them. "This is the way it is, Mike. I'm
tough—maybe hardnose—not because I love the job, I don't. I
do what it takes to get the job done!"

"You're amazing…maybe it's time I tell you something
about Mike."

| 94 |

God Help Us

She moves closer. "I've been waiting for this, Mike! Let it out…let it all out!"

And he wonders where to begin. "It's this certain feeling I have, Martha! It's unexplainable, hard to talk about. It's like I'm lost…searching for something…never finding it. It doesn't go away, it goes on and on, never ending!"

And she's touched, looking again at him. "But you'll know someday, Mike…believe me you will. There are other things to think about: things you alone must find out!"

Mike reaches out. stopping her. "But why are you saying these things to me, Martha?"

And again, she looks up at him, pitiful-like. "I suppose every time I read the Bible, I think about you and what you might be facing! And I'm beginning to wonder if it's about the same as *the Apostle Paul* warned us about," she says, hoping to make him aware of his future.

"Tell me about it, Martha."

"He told us what would come in the latter days, Mike, and with all my heart and soul, I truly believe those days are upon us!"

Again she stops, getting her breath. "Think about it, Mike! Someday soon, maybe sooner than you can imagine, we'll be standing before Jesus, our Savior!"

And again, Mike is stricken, looking at her in amazement. She places a small tract in his hand, and looking up at him, she says, "Take this and read it, Mike, it's something that might help all of us."

And he begins to read.

> Put on the full armour of God that you may be able to stand against the wiles of the devil. (Ephesians 6:11)

Arthur (Mac) Mc Caffry

And his face turns pale, worried. "Tell me something I don't know, Martha. Yes, I believe the Lord is coming. But when I think of my life, I still wonder if I'm worthy!"

She clasps his hand, squeezing it hard. "But you are worthy. Mike!"

"Please don't do this to me, Martha...please don't," he mumbles, bewildered.

Martha holds his hand, guiding him to an open window. "But look beyond, Mike, set your sight upon tomorrow! Your sins are forgiven as far as the east to the west. It's over, Mike, time to think about tomorrow."

And again, he looks up at her worried, muttering, "Tomorrow...explain it to me, Martha!

"You're the recipient of something greater than anything you've ever imagined, maybe something you've always dreamed about! It's waiting for you, Mike, a chance of a lifetime!"

He raises his head, gazing out toward the same old scenery he sees every day; it's different!

A short break, and they're sitting at the dining room table, Martha and Doug looking satisfied, but for Mike, a worried look clouds his troubled face.

"But how do I fit the pattern for any kind of service? My life has changed, but there are other problems."

"Like what, Mike?" Martha asks.

He looks at her, wondering how to explain. "There's something else, Martha, take a look at me as I really am! And when you're finished, I'll tell you what happened to me!"

She reaches out, taking his hand, asking, "What happened to you, Mike?"

He's wanting to cry, but doesn't. "He touched me, Martha, my life has never been the same!" he barely mutters.

God Help Us

She moves beside him, embracing him. "Calm yourself, Mike! We know your history, the good and the bad...everything about you!" she says, causing him to look up embarrassed.

"You know about me...the church?"

"Everyone knows about you and the church, Mike, we're family!"

Mike's head hangs low, surprised again.

"Night after night, I lie awake wondering about myself, my past, my future...whatever! I try hiding my feelings, but there's no place to hide."

Martha moves beside him. "But you fail to understand—"

"Understand what, Martha?"

"You're different, Mike. You have a life ahead, a new life, a life of service to Him. From the moment your name was mentioned, the issue was over...settled!"

He glances at the table before them and back to Doug. "Are you sure about this, Doug?" he asks, doubting.

"I'm sure of it! It's time you forget the past, open your eyes, and look up, Mike. Your future is set, it couldn't be greater!" Doug says, moving beside him.

Mike's eyes strain, staring at him amazed. "But I'm serious, Doug! Believe me I am! But now it's your time to come out with it, tell me the rest of your motive being here!"

Doug moves against him. "We came here for you, Mike, your service to Him! We came here to educate you on other things about you...things you haven't the knowledge of understanding. That's our only motive being here!" he says, looking into his eyes, never blinking.

Mike sits frozen, staring at the blank wall, afraid to speak.

"My service to Him, is that what you said?"

| 97 |

Arthur (Mac) Mc Caffry

"That's what I said, Mike…meant every word of it. Something waits for you that only our Lord knows the outcome. Think about it, Mike! I'm talking about Him…angels throughout the universe…wherever! It sounds unbelievable, but it isn't!"

And again he's shaken, left wondering! "Then let's get it over…tell me the rest of it."

Doug moves even closer. "It's all about you, Mike! You've been given the honor of participating in the second greatest episode ever: history in the making…serving Him forever! It's big, Mike…it has to be!"

And Mike begins to smile, relaxed. "Don't play games with me, Doug. My name is Mike, not Paul, the guy who gave it all for Jesus, not Peter, the fisherman, or Mary, the one who waited for Him at the grave. They were His picks…all different people. They were chosen for a purpose, Doug! Believe me, I haven't forgotten. I knew all about them till…"

And Doug can take it no more. He reaches out, pushing him against the wall without warning.

"Don't say it, Mike! Please don't say it! We're tired of talking about the past. I warn you again, Mike, don't say it!" he says, causing Mike's hands to go limp, frightened by a different kind of nephew, one deadly serious.

And a change comes over Doug, looking down at Mike, grinning.

"Now what's so funny, Doug?"

"It's you, Mike…you! It's all about you!"

"What about me, Doug?"

"You answered your own question. You're one of His chosen, you still haven't recognized it!"

And Mike's face brightens. He remembers Friend, the words he said to him. "You're chosen, Mike…chosen to do His will."

God Help Us

His body goes limp! Slowly, he moves, seating himself across from Doug, puzzled again!

"Your boss in Washington, the one called Nate, he told you this?"

"He did, Mike! When your name began to appear, I wondered if maybe he knew you. I asked him the question, but he didn't answer. He sat in his big chair looking up at me, smoking a big cigar, turning his head away. And then he got up and walked to the window looking out, leaving me sitting!"

Again, Mike runs his hand across his brow, thinking, trying to remember.

"Not too many people give me a recommendation for helping Christians, more of the opposite would be more appropriate," he mutters glumly, never looking up.

"That I don't know, but Nate isn't the kind of person I wish to question. And I'm warning you now, Mike, never question Nate's authority, he's enough authority for the both of us…and then some!"

Doug looks toward Martha, waiting. "It's time we take a break, sweetheart. Let's go some place, clear our minds before we get down to real business!"

And Mike shakes his head, puzzled again, wondering, *Get down to real business? What else can there be waiting?*

Thirty minutes later, they're seated at a fashionable restaurant in downtown Indy. Conversation is open, limited to family. Inquiries of whereabouts, who married who is enjoyable, but the look upon Mike's face displays no interest.

He turns, facing Martha. "Tell me something, Martha."

"Yes, Mike."

"Are you about to tell me what you're really here for, or must I drag it out of you the rest of the evening?"

She looks up, pretending unconcern. "This isn't the place, Mike we're heading home, we'll make you an offer you can't refuse!"

"Can't refuse…and what's…"

And she stops him. "That's the way it is, Mike. Your chance in a lifetime, an offer you can't refuse!"

His mind runs wild, a hundred different thoughts and then some. He wonders if this is another bad dream, one of those crazy heartbreaking dreams.

12

Setting the Stage

Therefore if anyone is in Christ, he is a new creation;
the old has passed away, behold, the new has come.

—2 Corinthians 5:17

Thirty minutes later, they're home with Martha leading the way inside to the living room.

"Sit down, and prepare yourself in today's world, Mike" she says, seating herself across the table before him.

And Mike begins to chuckle. "I'm ready for anything that doesn't kill me, Martha."

"Great, Mike! You just said the magic words!"

"What words, Martha?"

"Kill me! Words that might describe the next chapter of your life! How do you feel now, Mike?"

He can only stare at her coldly, afraid to answer.

"It's time you learn about the real world! A world you've never been told about, Mike! The most dangerous world ever! Can you possibly understand what I'm trying to say to you?"

He shakes his head, looking toward Doug, waiting, hoping, but nothing.

"Evidently you can't, Mike! You're not the first one, nobody can! To understand the world I'm talking about, you have to be one of them! I'm serious as I can get, partner, time you wake up and take it that way!" Martha says, demanding, causing Mike to sit up, focusing his eyes upon her alone.

"But I am serious, Martha, never been more serious."

"And that's the way I like it, Mike, down and dirty, spill it out, lay the cards on the table, that's me all the way, Mike, get used to it!"

And there's nothing but silence, no response! Mike's eyes focus upon her alone, recognizing she's smart, tough as nails, serious for sure!

"In my business, we bring the news before it happens. It's powerful news, describing Christ coming. Kill us, sure, there's always that possibility! They might kill all of us, Mike," Martha says, watching him squirming.

"Anything you'd like to say at this point, Mike?" she asks, expecting.

But only a surly glance, never a response.

"What's the matter, something bothering you, Mike?" she asks, down in his face taunting.

Mike glances toward Doug and back to Martha. "You're talking tough, Martha, real tough to a sixty-two-year-old guy whose only real asset is my undying faith in Jesus Christ! I've changed, Martha! I've really and truly changed! It's about time you get used to it!"

And Martha steps back, glancing toward Doug, wondering. "Good, Mike! We're making progress!"

"Maybe it's time you tell me who we're dealing with, Martha."

She raises her arms high, shouting, "Well, praise the Lord, you're finally getting it! Listen carefully, Mike, this…you don't want to miss…understand?"

"I do understand!"

God Help Us

"But you don't understand, Mike! You don't have the slightest idea what you're about to move into! We're dealing with the supernatural! We're dealing with a different kind of world, a world of evil, filled with darkness!" she says, down in his face, serious.

And he's stunned again! Never anything like this! His eyes stay glued to hers, missing nothing, waiting.

She stops sharply, turning to face him. "It's all about Satan, Mike! He walks the earth this very moment! His time grows short...he's desperate! He will do anything there is to do... knowing—"

And Mike can't wait. "Knowing what, Martha?"

"He knows his time on earth is running out! The war that began in heaven is about to end, end for good, Mike. He's desperate with no way out."

Shock and more shock. "And then, Martha...what then?"

And she's smiling. "He's going to hell forever! It's time for us to celebrate, shout and be happy, Mike!"

Again, he's stunned! Martha tells it like it is...he loves it.

"Think back, Mike, think about something I told you moments ago."

And he's puzzled again, wondering. "Tell me again, Martha."

"We can't lose, Mike! Our God, He's with us always, all the way to the bitter end," she reminds him, moving closer beside him.

"And the rest of it, Martha..."

She stops, looking at him differently. "Sorry, Mike, but I can't! This is different, outta my realm completely!"

Mike studies her every word, tired eyes looking down, feeling desperate. "I don't know how much more of this I can handle, Martha! I'm lost! I'm tired! But why, Martha…why?"

"Who isn't tired, Mike? We all are!"

He drops his head, looking down, worried! "But this guy Nate, what about him? I still don't know if he knows me?"

She reaches out, grabbing his hand. "Who cares about Nate, Mike? It has to be God's will—His alone. That's all that matters!"

"It has to be for sure! But the purpose of the mission, is that too much to ask for, Martha?" he's begging.

Martha turns, pointing upward. "It's all about angels, Mike! They're out there, they're everywhere!" she says, rising from her chair, walking away.

"But, Martha! Martha! Come back! Please come back! You don't understand. I love angels, without angels, I'm lost, nowhere to turn to."

And they stop, staring back at him, wondering.

"Is that part of the change, Mike?"

"It's all of it, Martha! I had help beyond your wildest imagination! Someone called Friend came to me and told me things I never imagined! He knows everything, my thoughts, my weaknesses, the path I'm heading. He's my guardian angel, Martha, without him, I'm nothing!"

A never-ending glance at him proudly, and she asks, "And where are you heading, Mike?"

"Wherever, Martha! Wherever He sends me!"

Again, they're amazed. Mike is different, he's changed!

"We've been waiting to hear you say the words, Mike. We're moving on. We've a lot to do, a lot to explain."

God Help Us

Doug reaches over, calling Martha to the side. "But did you ever think this might be Nate's decision, Martha? Did you ever think about—"

"I did for sure…who else could it be?"

"I'm not sure, but remember who Mike's guardian angel works for," Doug says, grinning.

"You mean…"

"There's no doubt about it, sweetheart! No doubt about it!"

13

Preparing for Battle

For his anger *endureth* but a moment; in his favour is life.

—Psalm 30:5

Martha opens her briefcase, removing a book filled with papers, addressing him. "I'm satisfied the way things are going, Mike! But now the question is are you ready, truly ready for something big, your assignment?"

And a smile crosses his face. "I'm as ready as I'll ever be, Martha."

"Good! I'll give you a schedule for things to come. Pay close attention, keep track of times and dates, they're important, very important! And something else to remember: anything I submit to you today can be changed in a moment's notice. Go look it over, I'll give you dates, times, places, and schedules, still with me?" she asks, moving along, never stopping.

"I am."

She begins again, talking slowly, emphasizing things to worry about, things never to talk about, on and on it goes till it's time to make appointments.

"Exactly forty-five days from today, you will show up in Washington. After you arrive, you'll grab a taxi, proceed downtown to the Mark Twain Hotel, registering immediately. Your room will be paid for, reserved for two days. Ask for your

God Help Us

mail at the desk, you'll find a cashier's check waiting to cover expenses—whatever. You will remain at the hotel the rest of the day, but making no contacts. Still with me?" she asks, catching her breath, waiting.

"I'm with you."

"You'll receive a call at midnight on the first night of your arrival and you'll be told where and when to be on Monday morning. Still with me, Mike?" she asks, persisting.

And Mike hesitates, thinking.

"I'm with you, but the day I arrive is Sunday, two weeks before Halloween."

And she looks up at him, shouting disgustedly, "Just shut up and don't argue with me, Mike, just be there!"

He looks again at her, perplexed! "Sure...I'll be there, but why the secrecy?"

And her anger is showing, reaching out grabbing his hand, pulling him against her. "Just shut up and listen, Mike! I've told you the kind of people we deal with over and over, just sit, be quiet, and listen!"

And his temper runs high, feeling scolded!

"From the moment you embark from the plane, you'll be watched, maybe by us, maybe not by us. Do you understand what I'm telling you?"

"I do! Sure I do, Martha," he shouts as the conversation becomes heated.

"Then don't ask stupid questions: just write it down and do what you're told to do, Mike," she says, lashing out at him wildly.

And turning away, showing a smile on her face, she glances over at Doug, listening to the conversation pleasantly. It's temper-testing time; his short fuse is lit, he's at their mercy.

Arthur (Mac) Mc Caffry

"Once you arrive in Washington, pay close attention to what surrounds you, don't make yourself noticeable! Act normal as those around you, perhaps a business person, someone important. Are you getting it, Mike?"

Mike isn't happy, he's growing tired! And it's showing!

"Yes, Martha, I'm getting it! And I'm waiting, Martha, waiting," he mutters sarcastically.

"And I'm aware you're waiting, Mike. But as I told you before, this is different, a matter of life or death, no in-betweens. The world you're about to enter into is a different world, a spiritual world filled with good and evil, fighting for your very soul. It's a world humans know nothing about, a world where only God, the devil, demons and angels are aware, *an unseen spiritual world.* And very soon, you're gonna be part of it, doing things never before dreamed about, never could have imagined! It's a whole new ball game, Mike...with you in the middle," she says, pointing her finger in his face, frowning.

And he's startled again, staring at the wall blankly.

"You'll be dealing with forces beyond your wildest nightmare...satanic forces, ready to face anything you've got to offer, all of it, guided by the devil! I'm talking about the occult, deadly forces you know nothing about. And we pray for you, Mike, we pray and pray again for you!" she's up in his face, shouting.

Mike looks hard at Martha, shocked! "You haven't the slightest idea what I've faced, you never will, Martha," he says, grabbing her attention.

"You're right for sure, Mike. But get this through that thick brain of yours: this isn't Nam, my friend, this is warfare— beyond warfare...more deadly than anything you've ever dreamed about!"

God Help Us

"Now what are you talking about?"

"Think back to a grade school in Connecticut, Mike. Think about a place where innocent school children were murdered; murdered by a wild beady-eyed young man devil possessed! And he went on a killing spree, over and over, never looking back. He was one of them, Mike, devil possessed!" she shouts up in his face forcefully.

And again, Mike can only listen, on and on, speechless!

"It's still the same old war, Mike! God against Satan... nothing is changing! It's like the days when Jesus walked the earth, Jesus taking you to heaven, the devil sending you to hell!"

And bells begin to ring, things he heard in church thirty long years ago—demons, witches, false prophets, Antichrist, all of them, serving the devil.

She moves against him. "*Do you believe you're up to it, Mike... or is it time we say good-bye?*" *she asks, threatening.*

And he's angered, ready to go to war, confronting her.

"Yes, I'm up to it! I can do it! I know I can do it!"

And Martha is up in his face, smiling pleasantly!

"I know you're up to it, Mike! From the very beginning, I've never doubted. We care about you! We care more than you'll ever know. And it's possible, Doug or I could be with you meeting Nate. If not, you're on your own."

And she turns, glancing at Doug. "But I may have forgotten to mention..."

"Mention what, Martha?"

"You're not going on this trip alone, Mike...you're about to have a partner!"

"That's news...who's the partner, Martha?"

She looks back where Doug sits, grinning. And now she's wondering if she should have mentioned *partner.*

Arthur (Mac) Mc Caffry

"It has to be someone with a record, an established record…someone who knows how to get things done!"

Briefing is coming to a close and Mike sits, thinking about their visit, so short, painful at times, changing his life completely.

"But one more question, a final question, Martha."

"Yes, Mike."

"Is there something special, maybe something specific, I should know before meeting Nate? I don't know why, but I've a feeling this is one time I need to be sharp…really sharp!"

Doug moves beside him. "There just might be something, Mike! Just before I departed, he said something odd, it caused me to take notice!"

"Yes, Doug."

"He looked up at me while puffing on a big old black cigar. And with an old gruff, gravel-coated voice, he said, 'Oh, by the way, Doug—tell Mike to watch a television miniseries, it just might help someone like him!"

"Nate said that?"

"He did, Mike…he sure did. But I had no idea what he was talking about. I asked him, 'What series are you talking about, Nate?' And he answered, '*A Band of Brothers*—you know, the old blood and guts type…the kind he likes.'"

And Mike is puzzled, wondering again, asking, "Something else maybe?"

"Nothing for sure, Mike! But l had a feeling he knew more: maybe your assignment has something to do with WWII. Do yourself a favor…watch it twice."

"Bet on it, Doug! I'll watch it till I can picture it in my dreams and then some!"

Martha starts to move on, but stops suddenly, looking back at Mike. "Oh, but there's something else I might mention, Mike."

God Help Us

"Yes, Martha."

"Doug and I are heading to Hawaii for a week vacation."

"Something special in Hawaii?" he asks, suspiciously.

"Oh yes! There is indeed, Mike, the largest observatory in the world at the foot of Mauna Kea, it's there waiting for us, Mike!"

And suspicion grows. "Wonderful, Martha…wonderful! But maybe another reason, some kind of secret reason?"

"No secret, Mike. It's all about Mauna Kea, a volcano melting pot ready to explode. It's the hot spot for the world's best astronomers, a playhouse for the rich and the famous!"

"And you'll be searching for what?"

She pauses, taking her time.

"Oh! Maybe a trumpet to sound, the heavens to part while Doug and I stand gazing upward, watching Him and His angels coming to greet us."

And Mike is excited, shouting again, "Oh yes! They're out there, Martha, believe me… they're out there!"

"Who, Mike, who is out there?" she's yelling, waving her arms frantically.

"Angels! God's holy angels! They're over the prairies, oceans, mountaintops, they're all over the land, they're everywhere, Martha…everywhere!" he's shouting excitedly, walking away smiling.

14

No Way Out

Cast your burden on the Lord, and He will sustain you; He will never suffer the righteous to be moved.

—Psalm 55:22

Mike hits the sheets near midnight, but sleep doesn't come. He tosses and turns, same as he did before Friend. Things have changed, he's serving a different master, but he's still insecure. He wonders if he's capable of serving his Creator and it bothers him greatly.

He dreads the thought of failure. His bedroom becomes his prison, he considers himself nobody. Worry! Day and night... never going away! He gazes into the mirror, turning away in disgust. And he mumbles the words of Moses time and time again, "Who am I that I should go?"

And there's a soft knock at his bedroom door. He gazes at the clock, showing an hour past midnight, and he wonders if something is wrong with Doug or Martha. Another soft knock—the door opens and before him stands Doug, looking down upon him troubled.

"I don't know why, but I just couldn't sleep. Maybe it's because we're concerned about you, Mike," he says, worried.

Mike is surprised, but grateful. "You're not alone, Doug! I've been lying here for hours doing the same. My mind runs wild, imagining everything there is to worry about."

"Tell me about it, Mike."

And he sits straight up, ready to talk. "I worry if I'm capable of anything, especially what I hear from you and Martha. Can you possibly understand what I'm trying to say?"

Doug looks at him again, thinking, *Maybe it's time to tell him my problems.*

"But you're not the only one who worries. I worry about my own capabilities. This is what they call the human side of us ordinary people. But you, Mike, only you, have something going most people would envy…maybe die for. It's special… something I've never doubted."

Mike points to a nearby table, wanting to explain. They sit quietly thinking, studying till Mike breaks the silence.

"I wrack my brain over and over. I search and search, but never an answer. I plead over and over, 'Why me, Lord…why me?' And I go on pleading, 'Anything, Lord…anything to make me feel better.'"

Doug moves close to him. "I don't have the answer, but there's one thing I know for sure…"

"Then tell me something for sure, Doug…I could use it," he mutters, hopelessly.

"You're not alone, Mike! Everything was set up before we arrived."

"I understand! But the hardest part is…why me of all people?"

Doug grins, shaking his head, wondering, *How will I ever make him understand, this is something greater, something beyond reason.*

"But you don't understand! You haven't the slightest idea what might be ahead of you. But it has to be the chance of a lifetime, Mike! You're going on a trip, a trip that only He knows where. I envy you, I really envy you," he says, placing his hand upon his shoulder, smiling confidently.

Mike moves even closer. "You make me feel proud, but humble, Doug. But never did I believe I would be here sitting beside you talking about a journey to nowhere. It frightens me to even think about it!" Mike says, rising from his chair, going to the window, looking out into a sea of darkness.

"But I can tell you this for sure, Mike…"

"Anything, Doug! Tell me anything to soothe my crazy thoughts, my crazy mind!"

Doug looks up at him, reminding him, "Your selection wasn't done by simply picking a name and number! There has to be something greater, something I'm not privileged to know. But someone…someplace…knows you, Mike, knows you better than you know yourself."

And again, Mike pauses, thinking back to other times, other places. "There has to be, Doug! There just has to be! But who or where, maybe I'll never know."

Doug walks to the window, standing beside him, comforting him.

"But you'll get over it, Mike, believe me you will. I've been in some bad spots, but nothing like this. It baffles me to even think about it! But there's always good news to go along with the uncertain, Mike! Think about something Martha told you, something important."

He looks up at Doug, smiling for a change. "You mean…we win, Doug…is that it?"

And Doug grabs his hand, shaking it. "Sure it is, brother…we always win: we're on His side!"

"But I'm an expert at failure, Doug, believe me I am!"

"You're not alone, Mike, so were others, people you like to talk about! People like Mary Magdalene, the biggest prostitute in Palestine. And Paul, the apostle, the guy who persecuted Christians. And yet another, someone called Peter, the guy with the short fuse, denied the Lord three times before His crucifixion. Remind you of someone, Mike?" he asks grinning, but wanting to laugh in his face, shouting, "They were like you, Mike—*chosen, but only the Lord knows why.*"

"You mean, people like me?"

"You're finally beginning to get it, Mike! They were like you! Just like you! And when your mission is over, you'll never be the same…never again…ever!"

Doug turns away, walking to the other side of the room, looking out toward the highway, where an occasional car whizzes by in both directions.

"But there's more, Mike!"

"More of what?"

"I've analyzed every possibility for your selection down to the last hilt…the last possibility. And when I put all the pieces together, there can be only one conclusion…"

Mike moves beside him, waiting. "And your conclusion, Doug?"

"When there's no other way out, stop, look around, and turn to the Bible!"

Again he's in trouble, thinking back, trying to remember. "But not for me, Doug, I'm nobody, a simple person!"

"We all are, Mike! There's times when logic doesn't make sense, but Him…if it's His will, never question!"

"But still…"

And Doug doesn't wait. He reaches out, placing his hands with his, bringing him alive.

"The Lord has to be looking over you, Mike! Everything's too perfect—falling in place like clockwork. You're in the thick of it…along with His blessing, what better situation could you ask for?"

"Now what are you trying to tell me, Doug?"

He pulls him next to him, confronting him. "Forget about your wants and plans, Mike! If the Lord wants you to serve Him, the issue is settled! With all of your past troubles, you should be the proudest of the proudest, you should be shouting it to the world, knowing He's with you!"

Mike places his hands to his head, wanting to scream, plead for help, but doesn't.

"But, Doug! Can you really believe this is happening to a guy like me? I'm the guy who hated the church as much as the devil."

Again, Doug places his hands upon Mike's shoulder. "But think again, Mike! Your sins are forgiven. He died on a cross for you, others like you!"

Mike moves away, staring at the wall, mumbling words, pleading words.

"But, Doug! Of all the people in the world…"

And Doug turns, looking away. "I don't know! I just don't know! But someday, Mike, someday…with God's help, you'll know! Where or when, only He knows, but you will know, Mike!"

His message is over and Doug is tired. "Let's get some rest, Mike. If the Lord wants you to know, you'll know in His time, not in your time. But in the meantime, pull up your pants, put on your shoes, and get ready to serve.

God Help Us

An hour goes by and Mike still lays awake, thinking back to his youth. He remembers what Friend told him, his dedication to God. He remembers what his mother told him as a child of six, but never understood. And suddenly, it hits him! He remembers something different: it was the first time she called him Mike, not the usual childish name, Mikey Boy.

"You were placed on the altar as a baby. You were anointed with oil by the minister as your father and I submitted your life to God. Your life is dedicated to Him, Mike, and someday, somewhere, you'll understand why."

And Mike begins to relax, feeling at ease, hoping it's about to be over!

15

Farewell, Oh My Captain

For as the heaven is high above the earth, so great
is his mercy toward them who fear him.

—Psalm 103:11

A week has passed and no word from Keith with all his troubles. And just at the break of dawn on Sunday morning, there's a loud rap on the front door. Before Mike can get to it, he hears more loud raps. He looks through the peephole and there's Rosy, Keith's woman, standing outside, crying alone.

He opens the door, inviting her inside, and still, she cries uncontrollably. She's hardly dressed, around thirty-five to forty, about five-foot tall, flaming red hair down to her neckline, dirt and mud all over! She wears only a pair of skimpy red shorts, a shirt covered with mud, and sandals held together with a single strap. Mike has seen her in different attire, but never, nothing as this. He places his hand over her mouth for only a moment, and she stops her whimpering.

"Quiet, Rosy, quiet…get hold of yourself, girl," he says, trying to console her.

She continues sobbing till she begins to choke. And a moment later, she's staring up at Mike, looking like death.

"Keith is dead! Help me, Mike! Help me!" she's pleading, trying to catch her breath. "I'm desperate, Mike, you alone can help me."

God Help Us

Mike studies her again, wants her under control, his control! Police, he doesn't need hanging around asking questions. But there's only one way with Rosy: get tough, real tough, the only way Rosy knows it!

"Shut up, girl! Get your breath and we'll go from there. Now before we go further, take your time and tell me about the police!"

"I will! I will! And don't yell at me! Please don't, Mike. I called them at once from the house, but didn't wait till they arrived—I was mixed up, scared to death, and I'm still frightened, Mike!" Rosy says, panicking.

"You didn't wait! Why didn't you wait?" he asks, exploding. "Are you nuts, stoned, or just plain crazy, Rosy girl? The very first thing they're going to think is you had something to do with it," he's yelling, causing her to draw away, frightened!

And Rosy begins crying again. Mike grabs her, pulling her close. He puts his hand over her mouth, shouting in her face.

"Straighten up! Pull yourself together, Rosy girl! Any more of this crying all over the place, you'll be going on a trip alone… without me, for sure."

More sobbing, and she looks up at him pitifully, ending the crying with her head bowed low, her body quivering all over.

"Sit down and drink this, Rosy girl," he says, handing her a can of Coke.

She walks to the dining room table, sitting, gulping it down without stopping. A couple of minutes later, the sobbing and crying come to an end, and she's looking up at him, speaking weakly.

"I'm okay for now, Mike. I'll make it, but I'm scared… frightened more than I've ever been," she says, motioning him to come close and sit beside her.

But instead of sitting, Mike stands behind her with his arms placed on her shoulders, comforting her. Her body still shakes, quivering with fear.

Mike wants to know things. He tosses his anger aside, getting down to business.

"Tell it all, Rosy! Right now, I'm the only friend you have. Don't lie to me and I'll help you, one lie and I'm history with you forever! And remember this, Rosy girl…"

And again, tears begin to show, looking pitiful.

"What, Mike? What must I remember?" she asks, humbly, sobbing again.

"I'm all you got, Rosy, and don't you forget it! Now, do you understand?"

She turns, staring hard at him, her body still quivers. She can see his look of disgust, knowing he has reason. Her voice is low, tender, pleading.

"I understand, Mike…really I do! Keith always told me I could depend on you above anyone, you alone, Mike! I'm still scared, but I'll begin with this…"

And he looks hard at her again, a voice threatening. "And it better be the truth, Rosy girl…nothing but the truth!"

"Every word I say is true. I swear it, Mike…I swear it!"

"He and I were pretty well stoned, and I still am some. We had a few drinks, smoked some grass, and were getting ready to make love. Suddenly, without saying a word, he jumped up looking crazy like a wild person. And then he ran to the back door, heading down to the boat dock leading to the boardwalk, extending out into the middle of the lake. I ran after him, yelling, asking, 'What's wrong, Keith, what's wrong?' but he just kept going as if he didn't hear me. It was wild, Mike—crazy wild, you know the kind. I was beside myself, frustrated, trying to figure out what he was into, but he kept on acting crazy, going berserk!"

Mike interrupts, "I'm beginning to picture what happened. He must have gone nuts or got hold of some powerful stuff."

"When he got to the end of the boardwalk, I expected him to stop, but he didn't. He never glanced back once before he plunged into the water, and that was it, Mike! That was it!"

Mike reaches out, stopping her. "Get your breath for a moment, Rosy, slow down and begin again!"

"I was screaming for him to stop, but he went under, and that was the last time I saw him. I knew the water at the end of the boardwalk was deep—no way to save him. That's it, Mike, Keith is gone and I'm standing there in the dark…alone, looking down, crying my head off!"

And Mike interrupts. She's talking so fast he can't understand with all the sobbing in between.

"Slow down, Rosy, it's over! This isn't exactly the time for all the sobbing. It's only gonna be a while till the cops come looking for you, and when that happens, you better have your story straight for sure, Rosy girl! And in the meantime, you better start praying your heart out like you've never done before!"

And she looks up at him, pitifully asking, "Praying! Praying for what, Mike?"

"Just pray they don't take you in for further questioning! But if they do, you're in trouble…trouble like you've never seen before, Rosy girl."

"I know! I know!"

"Listen to me! Now listen to me, Rosy!" he's shouting.

And she peers up at him, sobbing again. "I am listening, Mike…I really and truly am!"

His eyes turn away, showing some pity; a moment later, he's facing her, beginning again. "There's no use letting the police think you had anything to do with any part of this. Now stand up straight, pull yourself together, think back, and answer my questions. Do you fully understand, Rosy girl?" he asks, calmly for a change.

Mike sits across from her, waiting for an answer. Long lingering moments, and finally, she looks up at him, stopping her sobbing.

"I do understand, Mike…I'm just upset! Please don't be angry with me—guess I just wasn't thinking good…maybe I just panicked!"

"But you're doing okay now, kid! I can understand why you might have panicked! Now, tell me about the dirt covering your body, top to bottom."

"Yes! Yes! I'll try to explain. I was running around like mad trying to get rid of the drugs, it was everywhere. It was in the kitchen, hallway, and bedroom. We always were sloppy, sometime crazy I guess. I gathered it all up and put it in a big old sack, and then, I hauled it across the road to an empty lot. I was looking around trying to find a way to get rid of the stuff. I was beginning to panic till I finally found a spade lying nearby. And I dug a hole—buried it about two or three feet down," she says, stopping to get her breath.

"And then what?"

She takes her time, studying again, thinking back. "Oh yeah, now I remember! I ran back to the house and called the cops before coming here. And that's the truth, Mike…every word of it is the truth," Rosy says, calming.

Mike walks around the kitchen, slow and calm, occasionally glancing over at Rosy before saying anything. He's thinking of every possible angle to cover, knowing the police will be asking questions fast and furious. And finally, he glances at the clock, looking satisfied; it's time to give her the word. He moves beside her, staring down at her, speaking sympathetically.

"Now, here's what I want you to do, Rosy!"

And again, she looks up at him pitiful-like. "Yes, Mike, yes."

"Go into the bedroom and find some clothes of mine to wear. Leave nothing lying around and take a shower, making yourself presentable, but not too presentable. I hope you understand! Afterward, go back to the house, walk boldly inside where police and emergency people will be waiting and tell them the same story you're telling me, except using the drugs and hiding the grass, of course."

She heads for the bedroom to prepare herself. A quick shower and an assessment of her other parts, she comes back into the living room. She's dressed in a pair of loose-fitting jeans, a shirt looking halfway presentable, and stands before him posing.

"How does this look, Mike?" she asks, turning herself completely around before him.

Mike grabs hold of her hand, turns her around a couple of more times, and smiles. "Better, much better, Rosy girl," he says, giving his final approval. And for the first time, Rosy begins to smile, looking up at him. He guides her to the door, she hugs and kisses him, and off she goes to the lake house filled with confidence, a grin on her face, smiling.

A couple of days later, there's a short story in the newspaper obituary column about Keith's death, explaining he was of ill health—without cure. And the funeral service will be at Raccoon State Park on Wednesday morning at eight, a short distance from Indy.

16

Someone for Rosy

The Lord is nigh unto them that are of a broken heart.

—Psalm 34:18

Days waiting for Keith's daughter to arrive from England are miserable for Mike. Friends call and ask if he's attending the funeral; if some of his pals might be needed for pallbearers. But he doesn't want to be reminded, shutting them off quickly.

Sleep doesn't come easy the night before Keith's burial. Again, his mind runs wild, thinking of the good times, but hiding the bad times. He wishes somehow he could have reached him spiritually, but didn't…over and gone forever.

Morning comes and Mike drives to Raccoon Lake alone, feeling miserable. Arriving, he glances around, and at the entrance gate, a small sign shows Keith's name and area of the ceremony taking place. He heads into the camping area, noticing a gathering around a small pond, where about twenty or thirty people sit upon the ground with legs crossed near the water. He parks his car, walks over near the pond, becoming one of the participants, all waiting to honor Keith.

Morning sun has arrived and a warm breeze blows briskly, causing a couple of trees with overhanging branches to bend slightly. In the middle of the gathering, Mike can see Rosy

God Help Us

sitting in the midst of a small crowd waiting for the ceremony to begin. She's dressed in a flowered white silk dress reaching down past her knees and a blue silk bandana is wrapped neatly around her neck. Rosy doesn't look like the same Rosy he met the last time. She waves at him, displaying a lovely smile, a far different-looking Rosy from just a couple of days ago.

Most participants wear garb of the sixties and seventies, displaying red and white bandanas tied around the forehead. Women wear skin-tight shorts, barely hiding their butts, low-cut blouses, hiding little or nothing above. Mike doesn't like the style, but this is for Keith, Keith only! Looking further, he notices a couple of men off toward the back, dressed in business suits, different from most.

But he doesn't notice someone moving up from behind: Keith's daughter, Brittany Ann, the love of his life from England. She moves next to him, blurting out loudly with an ever so pretty Brit accent, "I'm Brittany, Mike…Brittany Lincoln, from London!"

He's speechless! He's caught off-guard at her sudden appearance, but soon recovers. He puts his arms around her, hugging her as a long-lost daughter. Another quick glance and he begins to realize she's as Keith described her: beautiful…a supermodel, top to bottom. Heads turn, looking to where Mike and Brittany stand dressed differently, not their usual. And Mike is different, peaceful for a change, forgetting his anger from the past, seeing flower children from the sixties and seventies, seated on the ground at the other side of the pond.

Someone begins humming a song of the sixties and seventies while Mike and Brittany stand, holding hands, watching from across the pond, wondering, *What's next for these friends of Daddy?*

Brittany squeezes Mike's hand, whispering, "I suppose they all knew Daddy, right, Mike?" she asks while singing continues loudly from across the pond.

"They did, Brittany. They all knew Daddy, but none knew Daddy...like I knew Daddy," he says, grinning.

A couple more songs of the sixties and seventies ring out, and there's a sudden halt, time for Keith's eulogy.

An elderly hippy-looking guy rises up from the grass, takes off his cap, raises his arms high in the air, beginning, "I knew Keith well, knew him thirty years, and never a better guy have I yet to meet. We had a friendship, a deep respect for one another...Keith was like a brother. He trusted me and I trusted him, sometimes we argued, sometimes we laughed. And when it was over, we never looked back! And that's the way it was, folks: *everything was beautiful.*"

Mike sits at Brittany's side when a slightly graying lady, about Keith's age, rises to offer her eulogy. She tells of Keith's love of nature and all the hidden beauty from the soil they once enjoyed. A recording begins to play and she waves her outstretched arms, looking upward toward heaven. *Peter, Paul, and Mary sing an oldie,* "Where Have All the Flowers Gone," finishing with "The Age of Aquarius." Music from the sixties and seventies fills the morning air, and the distinct smell of marijuana comes blowing in from across the pond, making them happy.

Brittany pulls hard on Mike's arm. "Is that what I think it is, Mike?" she asks, grinning.

Mike shudders to think of it. He looks at her disgustedly before replying, "It is for sure, darling, I'm sorry to say."

From across the pond, a gentleman about Keith's age dressed in full hippie attire rises slowly to his feet. He wears a bandana wrapped around his forehead, no shirt, bare to the waist. He walks slowly toward the water with a large silver metal urn filled with Keith's ashes. And he stops suddenly at the water's edge, holding it high above his head, gazing upward.

Brittany tugs at Mike's arm, pulling him closer. "What are they doing, Mike? The urn he's holding, is that supposed to be Daddy?"

And Mike is thinking hard, searching for an answer. "Maybe, honey, but not the way I knew Daddy," he says, grinning.

Again, they begin singing "The Age of Aquarius". And with all eyes fixed upon the big silver-looking urn held high above his head, he hurls Keith's ashes high into the cool morning air above the pond. And instantly, there's a resounding shouting of joy ringing out over the pond, praising Keith and his life of happiness. Keith's ashes reach the highest point, slowly begin drifting downward, falling lightly upon the still water. And from out of nowhere, a beautiful robin redbreast appears, landing on an overhanging branch of an elm tree. A breeze begins to blow and the branches bend downward, touching the still water.

And the audience below rise, standing as petrified, looking upward, staring in awe. Shouts ring out, "A miracle! A miracle! And suddenly, imaginations run wild, sending the crowd into a wild shouting frenzy. An older lady wearing a long white skirt, a red thin blouse, and a blue bandana raises her arms, pointing upward. And the crowd goes even, more wild, yelling hysterically, "*Look! Look everyone! It's Keith! His spirit parts the branches before us.*"

Standing far off at the other side, Mike laughs without end while Brittany hangs on to his arm, shaking her head, wondering, "What's next with these old friends of Daddy's?"

Proceedings are over and people begin to leave. Keith's ashes become part of the mud and water. Mike and Brittany hold

Arthur (Mac) Mc Caffry

hands heading for the car when suddenly from afar, Rosy comes running with arms outstretched. She's winded, but able to speak.

"Brittany! Brittany darling!" she shouts, out of control, rushing toward her.

Mike watches surprised as she greets Brittany like an old friend with hugs and kisses. And it's love...love at first sight, making Mike feel proud, happy for the ones Keith loved most.

A couple days later Brittany calls Mike, expressing gratitude for his friendship with her father. Mike helps her in a couple of financial matters, and life goes on after Brittany departs to her home in London.

And a couple of weeks later, Mike receives a beautiful letter from Brittany. She informs him she has a new friend, a loyal, most charming friend, Rosy girl, her personal maid from America.

17

Person of Interest

Rejoice with me, for I have found the coin which I had lost.

—Luke 15:9

Nine a.m. on a beautiful Sunday morning and Mike heads off to church once again. He remembers only a month ago, he gave his life back to the Lord after thirty years of hatred. Life is great, though lonely for companionship. Financial problems plague the church, but there's no worry about the future.

He's about to enter when suddenly, a sound from above causes him to stop, looking up. And at the top of an old wooden belfry is an iron cross where a beautiful mourning dove sits chirping away, looking down. He shrugs his shoulders, moving inside, gazing around the audience.

Ethel and Marie sit waiting at the front as usual. He passes the center pew, noticing someone sitting alone, not just someone, but a very attractive lady looking up, smiling at him.

"Good morning! My name is Mike Cutler, we're pleased to have your presence."

"And I'm Ailene Brooks, reporter from the Indianapolis Star Newspaper, Mike Cutler."

"You're a reporter! Wow! This is something new for Morris Avenue Baptist Church. Make yourself comfortable, Ms.

Brooks. And if I can be of help, call and I'll answer," he says, turning away.

She reaches out, stopping him. "But hold it a moment, Mike, don't walk away, maybe you can help."

Another casual look back and, "Then, just tell me how I can help, Ms. Brooks."

"I'm looking for a story, Mike, something like a human interest story!"

"A human interest story, Ms. Brooks?" he asks, quickly interested.

"Oh...you know...one of those kind of stories...that makes you wonder what life is all about, tearing your heart out... making you want to sit up and think!"

Mike looks at her again, surprised!

"But why here? Nothing unusual happens at Morris Avenue Baptist Church."

She motions him to sit. And pausing briefly, she says, "Well, here's the way it is, Mike, plain and simple..."

"Wonderful!"

"I'll make it short and sweet, Mike. I'm here to find out what's happening in America...what's happening to our churches all over the nation. You know what I'm talking about, whatever happened to the old Billy Graham, George Beverly Shea type of meetings; the ones that made you stand up and shout, ready to pray your heart out?"

Wow! He's surprised again! Here sitting beside him is a reporter from the Indianapolis Star Newspaper, asking him a question he's afraid to answer.

"But why is it important? Everyone knows churches are having a hard time watching their speech, preachers or priests afraid to say things they truly believe, all because of something

God Help Us

called political correctness. It's a brand-new world, Ailene, a brand-new culture, one you and I will never get used to!"

She likes him! He's different, a like-or-not kind of person.

And she looks again at him, looks him over good.

"Well! That was quite a speech, Mike. But I'll give some credit for—"

And he reaches out, stopping her, asking, "Credit for what, Ailene?"

"You're not afraid to speak the truth about how you feel, partner! In my book, you hit it right on the head! But let me explain something, Mike."

"Please do, Ailene, I'm always interested in learning from someone."

"I'm a reporter first, it's my job. But there are other things, important things that matter! I've made some notes, things of interest. And surprisingly, Morris Avenue Baptist is exactly what I'm searching for," she says, moving beside him.

Again, he looks her over, hesitant to say something he's thinking!

And she moves even closer, whispering, "I believe I know what you're thinking, Mike, but I don't mince words. I'm what people call a straight-out person, others call me a little more than aggressive person. I'm the kind of person that isn't afraid to call a spade a spade, even if it breaks their heart listening!"

And he looks at her again. "That's good to know, Ms. Brooks, you're different for sure, not like most of them," Mike barely mutters.

"But there's something else, Mike!"

He looks at her interested. "Tell me something else, Ailene!"

And she looks up at him ever so pleasantly. "I'm crowding sixty, Mike! And I'm still waiting!"

Arthur (Mac) Mc Caffry

"Waiting…for what, Ms. Brooks?" he asks, suspiciously.

"Oh, you know, Mike…every reporter's dream! A big story! I'm talking about one that never goes away…making you wonder…whatever!"

And his eyes roam, her dress, her eyes, her hair, he loves it. She wears a navy-blue business suit trimmed in white, about five foot five in height, a figure fit for a model And she tops it of with coal-black hair with a touch of silver neatly combed, dropping slightly below the ear, a dream woman, something special for a guy like Mike.

"But you look so young, so vibrant, never sixty, Ms. Brooks," he says while she reaches up brushing back her hair, smiling.

And she likes the way he says things, someone she might like to know better, a friend for sure.

"I'm aware I don't look sixty, Mike! And if you tell me you're not interested in what you see, I'll stand up before you and call you a dirty good-for-nothing liar… right here in church!" she says, shrugging her shoulders, brushing back her dark long hair flirtatiously.

And he likes it! He likes the way she talks, a fast-talking, right-to-the-point kind of person.

She leans hard against him. "But the best part is…"

"Yes, Ailene?"

"I still have dreams, Mike! Dreams yet to come! Maybe something wild, something different, who knows where or when…"

And he can't wait. "Tell me some more, Ailene…the rest of your dreams…"

She turns her head, looking up at him smiling. "But the best part is life isn't over, it's just beginning! I've a long way to go, dreams and more dreams, all about tomorrow!"

"You mean…dreams yet to be filled, Ms. Brooks?"

A long pause. "Oh! I suppose! There's always something you hope for, you know, the kind of story every reporter dream about…till the day they die!"

Again, he's speechless. It's the way she says things, things that make you think of, maybe, some of your own dreams.

And she moves ever closer, grinning mischievously. "But you, Mike, tell me your hidden dreams, your desires, everything," she whispers, touching his side playfully.

And his face turns pale! He's caught…caught in her trap with no way out. Maybe this is it! Tell his long-hidden secret, one that never goes away.

"We all have dreams, Ailene! Dreams of things to come, fantasies of faraway places, places like somewhere I once read about or maybe dreamed about," he says, leaving her hanging, waiting for more.

"I like it, Mike, tell me the rest of it, sounds interesting!"

And he pauses, thinking about it, his dream that never goes away.

"I call it Shangri-La! My make-believe place, far away, somewhere over the mountaintops."

And suddenly he stops, thinking hard, continuing, "But somehow, I never find an ending. My dream always ends as suddenly as it began, leaving me wondering…"

"Wondering about what, Mike?"

He gazes up at her, starry-eyed! "I always end up wondering what else might be waiting for me, somewhere on the other side of the mountaintop," he says, shaking his head sadly.

And she likes it. "But that's good, Mike! It's called human interest at its best, keeps you wondering. But there's one thing for sure, Mike."

Arthur (Mac) Mc Caffry

And he looks full straight at her, asking, "And what's that, Ailene?"

"You're definitely not the kind of person I ever expected to meet in church," she says, leaving him guessing.

And he doesn't know whether to frown or smile, but he's pleased, waiting, ready to hear more.

"But what are you truly looking for, Ailene?"

She's surprised! She takes her time, gazing elsewhere, undecided to answer.

And finally, she says, "You got me, pal! I really don't know! But maybe I'm looking for something simple, a person with a story worth telling."

And he's surprised again.

"It's not me for sure, Ailene. But maybe—"

"Maybe what, Mike? Now come on, Mike, open up…tell me all about it," she says, her dark blue eyes looking into his, waiting.

And he's caught, wondering, "It's my seemingly, wonderful, impossible friend, Ailene…he saved me!"

And she comes against him hard, nudging him forward, waiting, "Don't stop, Mike! Tell me the rest of it…you know… like how, when, and where," she says, pursuing him forward.

Mike stammers, wondering how to say it! *How do you tell someone about an angel?*

"But he's different, Ailene! He's really…truly different! Maybe…"

She waits, but it doesn't come. "Then tell me about other things, Mike, tell me what's happening at Morris Avenue Baptist Church. I need a story bad…something different! And if I find the right words: it's Sunday morning's front-page story!"

God Help Us

And he's caught! "Oh! Nothing special, but there is one thing…"

"Keep going, Mike…all of it," she says, urging him on.

"As I was about to enter the church, I noticed a beautiful mourning dove sitting at the top of the belfry perched upon a cross."

"A mourning dove?"

"Yes, but this mourning dove was different!"

"But…why different?"

And he studies hard, hoping to remember, "The poor little thing just wouldn't quit chirping, on and on and on, staring down at me, causing me to wonder…"

"Wonder about what, Mike?"

"Oh! I don't know for sure, but he never turned his head, he kept gazing down upon me only!"

And she listens, looking again at him, interested!

"But let's talk about something different, Mike."

"Like what?"

"Like what has happened to all the young people, are they so perfect they've all gone to heaven, Mike?"

He turns his head, searching. "A thousand times I've asked myself the same, Ailene," he says, turning away, afraid to answer.

She reaches over, grasping his hand, stopping him. "But let's talk about you, Mike, what's happening in your life, maybe a love affair, hiding in the closet?" she asks, teasingly.

He wants to chuckle, but doesn't. "Take a look at the one sitting in the front row waiting for me, Ms. Brooks. Her name is Ethel, and boy, oh boy, can she tell some stories," he says, wanting to laugh, but doesn't.

"Your lady friend…perhaps…"

And this time, he can't hold back chuckling. "Look again, Ailene! She's twenty years my elder. But she's my dearest, most pleasant friend ever!"

"Tell me about it, Mike. This could get interesting."

Again Mike pauses. "She alone knew my loneliness, my sorrow! She alone invited me back to church after thirty long miserable years going nowhere," he tries to explain, remembering how it all began, how it all happened.

"Wanna talk about it, Mike?"

"Sometime maybe, but not today, Ms. Brooks. It's a long story, hard to talk about."

She grasps his hand, squeezing it tightly. "But I'm a reporter, Mike, that's what I do! I listen to stories. If they're good, I write about them."

Mike turns, looking away. "But I was bad, Ailene...real bad, lost without hope," he says, fighting back emotions.

And she likes him more; the guy is honest, though it hurts.

"You're interesting, Mike! Perhaps when the service is finished, we'll talk outside...agreed?"

Mike begins to grin. "Agreed...I was thinking the same, Ailene."

And her thoughts and mind move quickly; no time to say hello, no time to say good-bye, only time to write the story; a human interest story...a story for everyone!

She opens her briefcase, grabs her laptop, taking off running toward the entrance. She's breathless, continuing on, before reaching a small wooden table near the doorway. And she's at her best, her very best, pecking away on something she calls the story of all stories: "The Dove That Never Stopped Chirping."

A week goes by, still nothing from Ailene. Mike can't help thinking of her—she's interesting, exciting, something long missing from his dismal, tiring life. And finally, it's Sunday! He rushes to the newspaper box and there it is, spread out in bold letters across the front page. Mike reads it over and over, missing nothing.

Headlining the top of the newspaper, it reads, "Story of All Stories: 'A Miracle from Above!'...*The Dove That Wouldn't Stop Chirping!*" Ailene's picture is displayed with a picture of the dove sitting atop the cross. The phone rings and Mike's heart begins to pound.

"Hello, Mike. I've been wondering if you're pleased. I wanted to write something about you, write something touching that would please you. And now I can't sleep from wondering if you liked it?" Ailene says, ever so pleasantly.

And her words, so warm and tender, causing Mike to picture her standing before him, her arms around his shoulders.

"It was great...beyond my wildest expectations!"

"I'm glad you liked it, Mike...really I am. I've been thinking about you...I truly I have," she says warmly, making his heart flutter.

"And what's on your schedule next, Ailene—maybe some more of this human interest material again?" he asks, jokingly.

And he can hear her sighing, saying words he's dreamed of hearing, "Only the Lord knows, Mike. Maybe something different, some place crazy—like your dreams of Shangri-La or perhaps some place high on a windy hill, sound exciting, partner?" she asks before hanging up, looking in the mirror, watching herself, grinning mischievously, leaving him guessing.

18

Someone to Think About

The Lord is my light and my salvation; whom shall I fear?

—Psalm 27:1

Days pass and still no word from anyone concerning the mission. Time has run out, Mike's anxiety runs high, it's the night before D-Day. He sits at home thinking of tomorrow, a day he has waited for so long. It reminds him of Nam, heading out on a mission. But this is a different kind of enemy, warned about thousands of years ago. He tries to sleep, but can't. He thinks of David, what he might do. He opens his Bible, reading the *Twenty-Third Psalm;* his mind is soothed, his worries are over.

Sunday church services are short for a change, and Mike bids farewell to Ethel, Marie, Brad, and Mary. He discusses nothing, talks about taking care of some overdue business in Washington. They ask no questions, and he drives to the airport alone, wondering, *What lies ahead for someone like me...Mike Cutler...nobody.*

He sits alone inside the concourse at the Indianapolis International Airport thinking, unable to comprehend the reason for his selection. To him, it sounds like Mission Impossible, something unattainable! He thinks about Friend, his guardian angel, and Nate, the mystery guy he's yet to meet.

| 138 |

God Help Us

There's no rest during the trip. He watches a young couple holding hands across the aisle, sneaking a kiss or two when none are watching. It reminds him of his own young love, his great expectations. But now, his life is suddenly turned around without known reason. He only knows he's been selected to do God's work. *Keep the faith…keep the faith*, he tells himself over and over.

Time passes quickly, and soon, he arrives at Dulles International Airport a few miles out of Washington, the city where laws are made governing the nation he loves so well. He thinks of George Washington, Abraham Lincoln, Franklin Roosevelt, and his hero, Ronald Reagan, all presidents, residing here in the White House. He feels proud to be a part of a nation so great in history, but now he's beginning to worry, wondering if the nation he adores is the same—a nation proud, blessed… under God.

He stands outside the airport entrance waiting for a cab to deliver him to the Mark Twain Hotel. Cab after cab go whizzing past till one stops in front of him. The driver gets out, grabs his baggage, and off they go.

"Where to, buddy?" the driver asks, nonchalantly.

"The Mark Twain Hotel, please."

"Washington new to you?"

Mike pauses before answering. "It's been a while," he says, remembering Martha's words: *friendly with the unknown.*

Mike watches the scenery as they speed away without conversation. Twenty minutes later, they pull up in front of the Mark Twain where a bellhop stands waiting. His baggage is placed on the curb and another bellhop grabs it, taking off before Mike is able to say "hello." This is Washington, one

Arthur (Mac) Mc Caffry

of the busiest cities in the world, and Mike begins to realize, *Washington isn't Indy.*

He walks inside the hotel, heading to register. An older grey-haired gentleman greets him at the counter with a smile, politely asking, "And your name please, sir?"

"Mike Cutler, I've reservations. Will you please check to see if I have mail waiting?"

The clerk hands him the card to room 217 while checking his mail.

"Only this, Mr. Cutler," he says, handing him an envelope with his name only.

And turning to move on, he stops suddenly. "Oh, by the way, Mr. Cutler, I do remember several phone calls asking for you. They left no messages, but another couple called back again and again. Enjoy your stay at the Mark Twain, sir."

Mike heads for the elevator while the bellhop places his luggage in another elevator nearby. He tears open the envelope and inside finds a cashier's check bearing his name as the payee for five thousand dollars. This is a surprise, a welcome one.

Soon, he's unlocking the door, hearing the phone ringing. But before he reaches it, the ringing stops. The message light is lit and Mike hears what sounds like a man's voice say, "Glad you made it, Mike," and suddenly, it goes dead, without leaving a name.

The room is comfortable, elaborate for Mike. It's a well-maintained room with a Jacuzzi big enough for four, a bar with booze, a bathroom with shower, and an excellent view of the outside from the second floor. Everything a guy like Mike could want, except the booze he no longer needs. He watches television the rest of the evening, heading to bed about eight. So

God Help Us

far, everything is going smooth and he begins to anticipate what lies ahead tomorrow.

The phone rings at midnight, as Martha said it would.

"This is Mike Cutler," he says, sleepily. "And to whom am I speaking?"

A female voice responds quickly, "I'm Grace, your contact. Be at the *Sampson Building on Massachusetts Avenue* at ten a.m. Any cabbie knows the place, and you will recognize it by four large marble pillars at the front. Go to the tenth floor, room 7, and ring the buzzer. Someone will answer and ask for identity. After your identity has been cleared, you will meet your representative inside and receive your indoctrination. Clear enough?" she asks.

"Clear enough, Grace, look for me."

And the line goes dead.

The phone rings at six. "This is the front desk, Mr. Cutler. It is six a.m. as you requested," a sleepy voice announces.

"Thank you so much!" Mike says, wondering who made the request, assured it wasn't him.

A quick breakfast and he heads to the Sampson Building, ready for action. And minutes later he stands outside, looking up, admiring four huge stone pillars of stone. *What a work of art*, he's thinking, but what lies inside waiting for him he worries about. And he begins to think about another Sampson, the one in the Bible, the one who lost his long dark hair, succumbing to his earthly desires and pleasures with a raging beauty called Delilah.

He carries only his briefcase loaded with papers. And soon, he's standing inside the magnificent work of art gazing throughout, but seeing not a single soul waiting to greet him. He looks upward where small cameras point downward, viewing the large entrance near the elevator. His eyes roam—encasing everything

| 141 |

Arthur (Mac) Mc Caffry

without a smile. Up, up travels the elevator till it reaches the tenth floor. He steps outside, glancing around, seeing cameras posted everywhere, but still not a soul. Finally, down the long marble hallway, he sees room 7, his place of destiny. He touches the outside buzzer and a voice from inside says in a rough but clear voice, "Come inside, Mr. Cutler, it's indoctrination time!"

And he pauses, gazing around before entering. Slowly, he opens the door, and from atop the ceiling, a light shines bright, displaying a drawing of Moses covering the eastern wall. And hanging further down, an ancient-looking scroll displays the *Ten Commandments.*

Row after row of metal filing cabinets are lined against the wall. And at the far end of the eastern wall is another entrance leading into an office area without human presence. He continues, following bold marked arrows along the path.

Far off to the western end of the large room is an enclosed area, where what looks like an extra-large office designed to withstand an earthquake. And looking ahead, a large poster outside displays the words, "Enter, Friend." He pauses, wondering what the word Friend means to a guy like him.

Is it possible it could be someone like his guardian angel or maybe someone like him, a lonely guy in Washington searching for the unknown. He makes his move, pressing the buzzer... waiting.

"Enter and take a seat," a rough graveled voice bellows loudly from inside. Slowly, Mike opens the door, confronting something unexpected. The room is large, decorated with picture after picture of famous scenes of history. On the far side of the room is a large mahogany desk, where someone sits in a huge swivel chair turned backward. Smoke rises from the chair, indicating someone

God Help Us

is smoking more than normal, with an aroma he will never forget. And the swivel chair turns—facing him directly.

Wow! Right in the face, staring at him sits former Colonel Nathaniel P. Roberts, 101st Airborne, Vietnam.

Mike's heart begins to flutter, staring at him, noticing a change, a massive figure that could tear you apart. But the once-blond hair turned silver. That's Nate, a man destined for a place in military history.

A big Cuban cigar protrudes from the corner of his mouth and his face, a grin he'll never forget. He wears a dark suit, open white shirt, a golden necklace with two large diamonds fitted tightly around his huge bull-like neck.

"Semper fi, marine…it's been a while!" he bellows, clearing the air. "I've heard some scuttle-butt about you, lad, but the biggest shock of all was when I learned you've finally decided to get your act together. Am I right?" he asks, puffing away, looking up to him, chuckling.

But the shock is so great Mike can only stare, unable to speak. Never did he dream he would be facing the guy who helped load him into a chopper forty years ago in Nam, a place of memories, all of them bad!

And he stiffens, standing at attention, saluting without thinking.

"Colonel, sir!" he says, loud and clear, gazing into his former colonel's eyes.

Nate rises from his seat, placing his hand upon Mike's shoulder. "None of that, Mike, it's time to forget. Nam is over and from this moment forward…I'm Nate…and no saluting!"

And Mike breathes easy. "But you'll always be Roberts to me, sir. Is it okay if we just keep it that way?"

"Sure it is, Mike, between you and me only."

And Mike turns, looking up to him. "But there's something bothering me, sir…"

Nate looks at him suspiciously, asking, "Now what's bothering you, Mike?"

And Mike takes his time, finally saying, "When I first heard the name Nate mentioned, I became suspicious. And later I began to wonder…wonder about you, sir. I was wondering if Nathaniel was Nate."

And Roberts is roaring, chuckling without stopping. "I never dreamed you would be the one to say something about it, lad, but you did. You found my secret."

"Your… secret…"

"Sure it is. When I was at the Point as a young cadet… Nathaniel wasn't a name to be proud of…more like a lady's name in those days."

"And…"

"Well, lad, I did what you would have done. I had my buddies call me Nate, it worked perfectly!"

And Mike looks up, grinning. "It's still Roberts to me, sir."

Roberts glances up toward the clock, pointing to a chair across from him.

"It's time we get started, Mike, the best part comes later."

"And what's the best part?"

A grin covers his face. "The part you could never understand, jarhead…taking orders!"

Mike lowers his head, not replying.

"We're moving fast, Mike! We have a job to do and you're in the middle of it! I'm not sure what you know, but believe me, you are!"

And Mike looks again at him, hard. "Some people been telling me same, but it's not the kind of news I like to hear!"

God Help Us

A big grin crosses Roberts's face immediately. "Time you change your attitude, lad, you're gonna hear a lot of it. But I do have some good news for you."

Mike looks away and back. "Now, what are you talking about, Roberts?"

And he can't hold back chuckling!

"Only this, lad, you're part of it…like it or not! Now do we understand each other, marine?" he says, growling.

Mike stiffens, staring at him. "We understand each other, Roberts, always have and always will! But in case you're interested, this isn't news. I've heard the same before a thousand times… most of it by you," he says, heatedly.

Roberts sits, glaring at him, enjoying the moment, wanting to laugh, but doesn't.

"What words?"

"You know what I mean, 'like it or not'! I was tired of hearing it in Nam…and I'm still tired of it, sir."

Again, Roberts tries holding back, but can't! He watches him stiffen, standing before him as he once did in Nam, wanting to spout back something, something to hurt him, but can't.

Roberts looks up at him, grinning. "You know, jarhead, you're lucky I wasn't permanently assigned to your outfit at Phu Bai."

"And just what does that mean, sir?"

And Roberts begins to roar, chuckling. "I would have straightened your butt out for sure lad. I can't believe it! I just can't believe it! You're the same old Mike I left in Nam. You're never going to change…never!" he's shouting, moving from his chair, chuckling even louder.

Mike's head lowers! He wants to be angry, but can't. It's time to apologize.

"I'm sorry to show my anger, sir. I'm truly sorry," he says humbly, barely mumbling.

Roberts watches him squirm, enjoying the moment. It's time to add some more, the same kind of flavor.

"But there's something about you I'll never forget, Mike, never changes…always the same…"

And he's confused. "And what's always the same, Roberts?" he asks, pleasant-like.

"It's your short fuse, lad. You were born with it! It's gonna haunt you till the day you die," he says, enjoying the moment.

Mike lowers his head, looking down. "But I'm trying to stop, Roberts, really, truly I am," he barely mumbles.

And suddenly, outta the blue things change, the mood is different!

Roberts walks from around his desk, placing his hand upon Mike's shoulder, smiling, "But never worry, Mike, everything works for the best on this team," he says, surprisingly.

And what a shock it is! Mike moves closer beside him, looking again. He was expecting a few curse words, a few insults, maybe a quick good-bye with a final pat on the back. All from a guy he once feared more than the enemy.

Roberts stands rigid, gazing down at the floor, searching for something different. He looks up at him, placing his hand upon his shoulder.

"Let's start over, Mike! Time is more precious than gold, and you're about to find out just how precious! There's information coming to me by the hour, and you're in the middle of it. I'll put it to you plain, Mike, the way you like it."

"I'm waiting, sir."

God Help Us

"Our mission is the same. We work as a team for the same leader: we're brothers in Christ...waiting for His coming! You know who *Him* is, I hope."

Mike's grin turns to a smile. Roberts is human after all; not the same guy he last saw in Nam threatening to have him court-martialed, but always defending him in trouble. His thoughts ramble on and on, searching for words he might understand. Finally, a frown turns to a smile, covering his face.

"Yes, Roberts, I know Him! Oh yes...how I know Him! I know Him, personally, Roberts," he says, looking into his eyes proudly.

And his words ring loud and clear, causing Roberts take notice thinking, maybe he is a different Mike...not the Mike he remembers crawling into a chopper, cursing him and the world, shouting the vilest language ever.

He looks him over again. "We don't have time for the past, Mike...it's time we talk about tomorrow!"

"I'm ready, sir!"

"I'm with you today only, Mike. There's trouble in the neighborhood and you and I are out to stop it. But we're aware of the trouble ahead, it's not ordinary trouble, it's the kind of enemy we've never seen before: only God himself knows how powerful. We live in one crazy world, my friend...not a happy world like it once was! But Nam, it's time we get over it."

Mike watches and listens to him stunned. "But not forgotten, Roberts, never!"

"Agreed, from this day forward till the day we die, okay, marine?"

"It's okay with me, sir, we'll do it your way till the day we die...agreed!"

"You'll be here only a couple of days...plan your time well. You're about to get an education you'll remember the rest of your life. And when your mission is completed, there's one thing for sure, Mike."

"Sure, about what, sir?"

He rises from his chair, moving around his desk, confronting him. "Never again will you be the same person standing here before me today, Mike. You'll be changed...forever!" Roberts says, leaving him guessing.

Again Mike is confused. "But there's something else, sir. Something important..."

He looks up at him surprised! "I'm listening, Mike, it's a pleasure I've never enjoyed before."

"This may sound difficult for you to believe, but I've no ambition to be the same person you remember from Nam. I was the worst of the worst...but I've changed! Truly, I've changed, Roberts!"

He holds his breath, waiting for him to laugh, but he doesn't. He can only stare at him, beholding something different. He's not the same foul-mouthed marine wanting to kill 'em all and then some; he's sounding like a down-to-earth born-again Christian! And he can see something else about Mike: he's proud, announcing his faith in Jesus!"

"I'm proud of you, Mike. No matter where our paths may turn, I'll remember Phu Bai, your unrelenting will to win. I loathed you, despised you as a dangerous animal! But yet, when it was over, I was always wishing I had a dozen more like you!" he says, causing Mike to back away, looking again.

And they sit gazing at one another till Roberts breaks the silence, pointing to the chair next to him.

"But now, it's time for business, serious business!"

"I'm ready, sir," Mike says, causing Roberts to look again.

God Help Us

"Everything you're told within the concept of this building is critical! There are things you must be able to recite in a second... life-threatening things...matters of life and death in a moment!"

"I can do it, sir...no doubt about it."

And Roberts moves closer, reading something from a paper. A moment later, he looks at him surprised, grinning. "But there's something else, Mike...something I just became aware of..."

Mike looks up at him smiling confidently. "Whatever it is, just name it, sir."

And again, he can't help from grinning. "Neither you or your partner will contact anyone disclosing your mission till the mission is over. Questions, Mike?"

"Well, there is this one question..."

"Then out with it. Better now than never!"

"Who assigned me to this mission? I've gotta know... please..."

Roberts wants to laugh, but doesn't. He's choking on the big Cuban cigar held tightly between his teeth while his mind is gloating as never before, enjoying the moment.

"Well, it wasn't me for sure, Mike!" he says, turning away, gazing out the window, grinning.

And he turns, looking back again. "I notice you quote phrases from the Bible, something like, Paul the Apostle once said," he offers, nonchalantly.

Mike is surprised! Never before has Roberts referred to the Bible in his presence.

"I'm reading your mind, sir! I know what you're thinking, 'I'm *the least of the least,' that was me and then some*, Roberts!"

"And how's that, Mike?"

Arthur (Mac) Mc Caffry

"Paul was nobody before he met Jesus. And I was nobody till I met the same. But this talk about a journey to nowhere, it's driving me nuts thinking about it!"

And Roberts hesitates. "But don't forget the prize when it's over, Mike."

"Now what are you trying to tell me, sir?"

And he turns, facing him; he isn't the same grinning Roberts he's used to seeing; he's serious. "It means a life in heaven forever, Mike, what better deal could anyone have?"

Again, Mike looks at him stunned, waiting.

"But tell me, Mike."

"Tell you what, sir?"

"Your secret…you gotta have a secret!"

Again, Mike looks at him puzzled. "But I don't have a secret, Roberts…honest, I don't!" he barely mutters.

"Sure you do, Mike. Tell me what happened in your miserable life. The last time I saw you, you hated everyone, carried a chip on your shoulder against the world and then some!"

And he's speechless! He can only lower his head, thinking back. "You're right again, sir. I hated the world and everything within it! But I met an angel…my guardian angel. His name is Friend. He helped me, sir! Oh, how he helped me!" he says, fighting back a flood of tears as his voice drifts away ending.

And Roberts looks again at Mike, staring at him in disbelief. "I believe you, Mike…I truly believe you! It had to be a miracle, a real down-to-earth–shaking miracle to change a guy like you," Roberts says before again nearly choking on the big cigar held tightly between his teeth.

Mike's head lowers even further, searching. "I know what Friend told me…and I believed. He looked me in the eye and told me I was one of His Chosen, and it frightened me,

God Help Us

frightened me as I've never been frightened before. Just imagine, sir, someone like me...one of His Chosen."

Roberts moves slowly to the other side of the office, picking up his briefcase, turning to face Mike. "But I remind you again, Mike, it took an absolute miracle to change an animal like you!" he says, looking down upon him, enjoying the moment.

And Mike rises, standing. "You're right again, sir...nothing but a miracle to save a guy like me, but He did, sir," he says, humbled.

Again, Roberts looks at him, shocked, barely able to say the words, "Take a break, Mike, it's time for you to travel."

"Travel where, sir?"

"Wherever, Mike! But I'd bet my last cigar...it's bound be interesting."

"But you, Roberts...what about you?" he shouts, as he heads for the door leaving.

And he stops, turning to face him. "God only knows, Mike! But it's time for me to say good-bye and God bless you, my friend till we meet again...tomorrow!"

19

Thirty-Nine Steps to the Upper Room

For their stood beside me this night the angel
of God, whose I am, and whom I serve.

—Acts 27:23

Thirty minutes pass and back to work, but not with Nate. Another person, about six foot three or four sits in the big swivel chair dressed in a long white shining robe ready to take his place. And from first glance, he's different! His long dark hair hangs down to his shoulder, teeth shine as pearls, and his eyes burn as fire. And Mike is taken, looking up at him, wondering.

He slowly rises from his big swivel chair with his fiery eyes blazing! "My name is Rueben, Mike. I have good news for you, words to make you feel happy!" he says, ever so pleasantly.

And he's shocked again! Angels, everywhere...angels! His mind is reeling, wondering about the good news, but afraid to ask. "What can it be, maybe another episode like first meeting Friend?" he keeps asking himself over and over.

He moves closer. "You have something to please me, Reuben...some good news?"

Mike waits and waits. "I do, Mike! It's time you meet your partner, someone you'll be pleased to see, someone familiar!"

God Help Us

Quickly he turns pushing a buzzer announcing loudly, "Mike is here, bring forth his partner!"

"Yes, Reuben!" a sweet voice from the other side says, making Mike wonder where and when.

Mike rises from his chair and the door burst open wide, causing him to get his breath, swallowing hard. He's gazing into the dark blue eyes of Ailene Brooks, reporter for the Indianapolis Star Newspaper.

A couple of moments standing in shock and it's over, with Mike holding his hand out, greeting her warmly.

"This is an unexpected pleasure, Ms. Brooks, a pleasant one," he says, regaining composure.

"It's a pleasure for me too, Mike. We'll talk about it later," she barely mutters, forcing a smile.

A quick glance toward Reuben, and they're settled at his desk, looking up at him, ready for business.

Reuben glances across his desk, seeing them waiting. "I'll inform you of things ahead, details and places, you'll learn later," he says bluntly, causing them to look again at him, wondering.

And he hesitates, moving closer, wiping his brow. "The mission you're about to participate in comes from Him: I'm His messenger!"

Again, he's glancing down upon papers before him, turning, looking back at them.

Ailene moves closer, worried. "Don't hold back, Reuben. You're the one we came to hear...just tell us!"

And his eyes turn fiery red, staring hard into hers. "But there's something that must be said."

"Yes, Reuben," Ailene barely whispers, waiting.

Rueben moves from his chair, guiding them to the window, staring upward, mumbling words only he knows. Moments go by quickly, and suddenly he turns, gazing back at them, announcing, "Jesus, the Son of God, will never leave you or forsake you. He will watch over you, protect you!"

And they're startled, afraid to speak further. Ailene moves even closer, touching his robe. "But you sound as if you're about to leave us for good, Rueben."

But still, he only sits in his big swivel chair transfixed, motionless. Minutes go by and quietly, he rises, reaching down picking up his briefcase, saying so elegantly, "And you're correct, my dear! I am leaving. It's time we say good-bye and farewell till we meet again…tomorrow!"

And they're puzzled again, wondering.

"But, Rueben! What about us? And tomorrow! When is tomorrow?" Ailene is shouting.

Rueben turns, glancing back, and with a wave of his hand, he says, "Oh yes! Yes, my darling! To mortals, it's always tomorrow! Above, it's always forever! But now, the candlelight is blinking. When the candle blinks, it's good-bye and farewell till we meet again tomorrow!"

Mike runs to him before leaving. "But Ailene and I…where do we go from here, Rueben?" he's shouting.

Again, he turns looking surprised! "But I thought you knew! When you're finished here, step outside to the Upper Room."

"But the Upper Room is where, Rueben?" Ailene asks quickly.

"I thought you knew, dear! Follow the cross, follow it thirty-nine steps to the Upper Room," Rueben says leaving, never looking back.

He's gone, and they move together without talking. A quick backward glance and they head for the door, ready to find the cross leading upward, thirty-nine steps to the Upper Room.

God Help Us

Outside, looking around it's empty, except where far over to the side a light blinks, sending a streak of light displaying a golden cross pointing the way upward.

They move near the cross nervously, expecting anything... whatever. Numbers begin to flash upon the long narrow wall. They stop, looking around nervously, joining hands, counting steps, 1-2-3 all the way, ascending upward to the very top. And there it is, an arrow showing 39. And out from nowhere, another majestic structure of stone appears just ahead waiting. They stop, reading a sign at the door in bold letters: Remove your shoes. Enter. I'm waiting.

A few moments pass and they're sitting on the floor, removing their shoes, ready to enter. Their heart pounds faster and faster as they move forward, searching. And suddenly, they stop abruptly, staring before an altar without blemish, made from mahogany, the finest wood ever. At the center of the altar sits a huge golden candelabrum with seven candles, and the middle candle looks to be gold, shaped as a cross spreading light over and above throughout the area.

Hanging down from the large marble ceiling, a silver chain dangles up and over the altar, where a beautiful silver dish holds sweet-smelling burning incense. And they stop suddenly, glancing at one another, hesitant to move beyond, wondering who or what they're about to encounter. And again, their thoughts run wild! They're wondering if this is some kind of a holy place or maybe a place like the Holy of Holies, or maybe the Inner Sanctuary! And they bend, kneeling in the fullest of reverence.

And from out of nowhere, a loud resounding *bang*! And quickly, a thumping sound from the other end of the long mahogany table draws their attention. They stand gazing everywhere, and at the very end, Friend sits in a huge golden chair, dressed in a long bright white linen robe, waiting.

He reaches out beckoning them to come closer, sit at the table before him. His eyes burn as fire, his smile is noticeable. And without notice, he reaches out, grabbing Mike's hand, causing him to shudder, feeling faint, lifeless!

"Mike Cutler, *the eye of the Lord dwells upon you,*" he shouts, *causing Mike's body to shiver, vibrating all over.*

He's speechless! Patiently waiting for the other part of his message, but there's none to come.

Friend turns to Ailene spreading his arms open, and with a booming voice, announces the same, "Ailene Brooks, t*he eye of the Lord dwells upon you.*"

And she's faint, feeling lifeless! Both gaze upward, staring in awe, waiting, expecting, till Ailene breaks the unrelenting silence. "Is this all we're to know, Friend?" she can barely ask reverently.

His eyes close, he's hardly breathing. "Quiet! His presence is with us!" he barely whispers.

Mike glances toward Ailene, afraid to ask, afraid to speak!

And again, Friend speaks solemnly, "Stand, both of you! Bow your head in holy reverence! Make the sign of the cross!"

And he stops, barely breathing, looking down upon them announcing, "You're standing on holy ground! You're about to receive His protection for the remainder of your days upon earth."

Wow! Magnificent words, strong and powerful! And still they listen and listen, all within God's most holy of sanctums.

Bowing his head reverently, Friend moves slowly toward the front of the altar, speaking solemnly, "Bow down upon your

God Help Us

knees, Chosen Ones, you're standing on holy ground in the presence of Him...God Almighty!"

His words dig deep into their heart and soul, words never dreamed about, coming from an angel. Nervously, they glance at one another, their bodies shake uncontrollably. They look upward, seeing Friend standing over them, his fiery eyes blazing.

"I carry a message from Him!" he announces with a voice rocking the Sampson Building.

Again, Ailene's body turns lifeless. Mike holds her hand, afraid to look where Friend stands over them. His eyes glance toward where the candelabrum's seven candles burn brightly while the smell of sweet-smelling burning incense grows stronger and stronger.

Without waiting they perform the sign of the cross working as one, while Friend stands over them, removing a beautiful mahogany box from a golden case. And slowly, he opens the box, removing two golden necklaces adorned with diamonds.

And it's silence, deadly silence, except for the ticking of an ancient-looking clock hanging upon the wall formed in the shape of a cross. They wait and wait, watching in awe, while Friend still stands before the cross, his face showing nothing but reverence.

"Bow your head and remain kneeling, most honored ones!" Friend says in a low tender voice. "I'm about to fit each of you with this golden necklace touched by the Lord, our most gracious!"

But still, they wonder! They wonder if they're in another world, a world they've often dreamed about, maybe another *heaven*! They remember the words Friend said praising Him. They think and think again, ending facing reality! This is the time, this is the place, there's no way out!

They're spellbound, motionless, kneeling in awe in the presence of God. And they're praying within their very heart and soul; He's beside them or maybe looking down upon them from above. They want to contain themselves, but it's useless! It's their moments of all moments as tears drip downward exposing their heart, their soul, everything for the love they have for the one above: the great and wonderful I Am, their God, Him only!

Friend slowly removes one of the golden necklaces, placing it gently around Ailene's neck, pulling it closed. He repeats the same with Mike. And moving closer, he kisses the cross. His hands rest softly upon their head, and in a very solemn voice, he's speaking loudly, clearly.

"You, Mike Cutler, and you, Ailene Brooks, are His Chosen Ones, kneeling before the altar of the Most High on Holy Ground. You're in the presence of the Lord, our God. Therefore, *in the name of the Father, Son, and Holy Spirit, I commend you to His will to perform His work from this moment forward. Wear the cross as your sword against evil and never remove it till your mission is over and forgotten."*

Complete silence.

"Arise and place your hand upon the altar of God, Ailene!"

His words are strong, spoken magnificently, again causing them to shudder. Never in their wildest dreams could they behold a ceremony so great, filled with sacredness, beyond human comprehension!

Frightened, still kneeling beside Ailene, Mike waits to hear his name called. His head remains bowing, listening. A brief pause and Friend places his hand upon his head, bowing downward and back up again before the altar of God.

"Rise, Mike Cutler, look into my eyes," Friend says, soft and reverently.

God Help Us

Shaking and fearing, Mike complies, waiting.

"Fear not, Mike! The Lord is with you. And with the will of God, I release you from your burden!"

And again, Mike is confused, left wondering! He doesn't know the meaning. He peers upward, looking at Friend, muttering with a shaky, quivering voice, "A burden! I carry a burden!"

And Friend looks down upon him, smiling. "Yes, Mike. The burden you placed upon yourself the day you left the church! It's over, Mike...forgiven! Forgotten! From this moment forward, you will never refer to yourself as Nobody. You're chosen, Mike, chosen by the Lord Our God...Him only!"

Again, long moments of silence. Moments to think, erase the shock! Tears fall from tired-looking eyes.

Mike opens his arms, gazing upward, pleading, "I understand, Friend, I do! Thank God...thank God...I do understand!"

He moves close to Ailene, grasping her hand. Legs and arms once weak and trembling, now firm and strong, waiting. And they begin to smile, gazing upon something sacred: power, wonder-working power filled with love and grace beyond human comparison!

20

Finals

And at the ninth hour I prayed in my house, and,
behold, a man stood before me in bright clothing.

—Acts 10:3

A thirty-minute break and back to work in what used to be
Reuben's office. But now, someone new sits behind the
desk, a manly figure dressed in a shining solid-white linen suit
prepared for business. He's a massive figure with long silver hair
dropping down to his shoulder, eyes sparkling, burning as fire.

He looks across the table introducing himself as Raymond,
a messenger of the most high. And again, they're speechless,
afraid to ask.

He removes folders from a briefcase, spreading them out
before them. "Mike, tell me what you're seeing."

A hurried look. "It's the Village of Berchtesgaden...I'll never
forget it," Mike says quickly.

They open folder after folder, viewing atrocities never
imagined: gas chambers, naked dead bodies thrown one upon
one into holes of dirt during the time of Hitler and his reign
of terror upon Jews. An hour goes by, still they sit looking at
pictures showing inside the Eagle's Nest.

Another hour goes by and the showing is over. Again,
Raymond begins lecturing.

God Help Us

"Moving further into your mission, you will learn the history, the torment, the people, a time of war...hell on earth, never forgotten!"

"But the Eagle's Nest?" Ailene asks, interrupting.

And he's different, rising from his big swivel chair, fiery eyes blazing. "It's a symbol of horror unimaginable, Ailene...the occult, demons...all that goes with it!"

"But I don't understand!"

Raymond moves close to her, his fiery eyes blazing. "But you will understand, my dear! When your mission is completed, you will leave Kalkstein Mountain. The Eagle's Nest will be only a hole in the ground that never was...never existed!"

And she's staring at Raymond mystified, feeling scolded! "But I was thinking as a mortal, not someone special, Raymond," she says humbly, causing his eyes to drop, focusing upon her only.

"Your move-out time from Dulles International Airport is scheduled for tomorrow night. From Berlin, you will be moved to the village, Berchtesgaden, near the foot of Kalkstein Mountain. You will stay the night at a local inn while forces of evil begin gathering around you. You will grow restless waiting, but He within you will guide you!"

A moment of silence, Mike and Ailene lost in a sea of questions, meditating together, and Raymond begins again.

"Prepare for the worse! Pray without ceasing! And when your mission is over: the Lord and His angels will look down upon you...rejoicing in heaven."

Again, they exchange glances, marveling the way Raymond says things, heavenly things, God, angels rejoicing.

"But Halloween! Berchtesgaden! Why?" Ailene asks, nervously.

Again, his eyes turn dark, fiery red!

"It's Satan's holiday, celebrating the killing of millions of Jews…God's Chosen people! It's a holiday filled with blood, murder, debauchery, a place remembered for devil worship, along with Hitler and the occult!"

And again, she's worried, asking, "But my job, Raymond… my obligation to the Star…"

He holds his arms out, stopping her. "You will never write the story, Ailene! Your memory will wilt…disappear as blades of grass that never was to be!"

And she's shocked again, sitting quietly, wondering! She wonders how something so great, so historical, will be lost, never again heard from. She glances away to the side, searching.

"But why, Raymond?" she asks, begging.

"It's the history, my dear, a dreadful most evil history!" And he stops, knowing her thoughts.

"Understand? No, Ailene! You don't understand, you or the world around you will ever understand!"

Ailene has struck a point with Raymond, a painful point she wishes she could take back. She joins her hands with his, wondering if she has offended him.

"I'm sorry, Raymond, truly I am," she says, again wishing she could take it back.

"But the mystery! The reverence! Why, Raymond?" Mike asks.

"Step outside please," he says, beckoning them to follow. And outside in an open area, he joins their hands with his, raising their arms upward. Deadly silence as Raymond speaks words only he can understand, words with no meaning to mortals, holy words, mountains of reverence! And moments later, he lowers his arms, turning to face them.

"The time has come! Your mission is in the making. Soon the heavens will shake showing His glory, your mission…over!"

Mike follows behind, his mind reeling. Wanting to know more, afraid to ask, "You mean…it was Him…He told you this?" He moves back to the window, staring up toward the heavens, a moment of silence, and he's back at his desk, looking up to them, announcing, "You will be at your post on the night of Halloween ready to destroy the satanic Bible! You will lead the way showing His power, His glory, all of it to a bunch of infidels, idolaters, liars, blasphemers, and traitors. And when your mission is over, a thousand legions of angels will sing, 'Glory to God in the highest, praising His name forever!'"

Again, they're frightened! Something far beyond their wildest dreams is about to take place! They're about to be part of the other world—the unknown world, a world of demons and principalities, foretold by Paul the Apostle two thousand years ago.

They move inside, and again, Ailene floods Raymond with question after question.

"But, Raymond, a satanic Bible! Our Holy Bible says nothing about a devil's Bible. This sounds like something Satan himself might come up with."

"Stop, Ailene…stop!" Raymond shouts, frightening her.

"But I don't understand, Raymond…" she barely can mutter.

And his fiery eyes sparkle. "But, Ailene, you've found the secret, the answer to your very own question!"

"Impossible!"

Arthur (Mac) Mc Caffry

Raymond reaches out, getting her to attention. "But possible when the devil authors his own Bible, Ailene," he says, causing her to back away, trembling.

And the room becomes deadly silent, meditating the consequences of something so evil, the devil himself, writing the future!

"We've come a long way…the easy part over. And now, an adventure into the unknown, a view into darkness only messengers of God are privy to view!"

And again, he's gazing upward toward heaven praying, using words only he and his God can determine the meaning.

Slowly, they begin moving away, beginning to realize Raymond's world is a different world, a world filled with angels, demons, fighting a war that began in heaven thousands of years ago.

Ailene moves close to Raymond, bowing low. She holds out her hand, pleading, "I'm sorry, Raymond, truly I'm sorry! We're not as you, we're mortals sent by Him to serve you," she says sadly, looking up again at him, waiting to be scolded.

And his eyes sparkle as diamonds. "All is well, Ailene, we serve the same master! This very moment, the satanic Bible lies deeply hidden within a vault at the National Library in Stockholm, Sweden—"

And Mike reaches out, hands trembling, stopping him. "Stockholm, Sweden?" he barely can mumble.

"Yes, Mike…Stockholm, Sweden! But it's about to be moved to the Eagle's Nest…atop Kalkstein Mountain, near the village Berchtesgaden."

"But, Raymond, it can't be, it doesn't make sense! Why expose the Bible now?"

God Help Us

And his eyes brighten! "Open your mind, Mike! Think of history…Bible history! There's a place called heaven, a place called earth…"

"But here on earth why, that's what I wanna know…just why?"

Raymond moves beside him, gripping his hand tightly. "But it's only part of it, Mike! The war in heaven is over, on earth…it's never ending!" And again, he stops, gazing upward toward heaven.

"But now you're smiling, Raymond…why?"

"It's coming to an end, Mike…about to be over!"

"But when, Raymond?"

Again, he moves to the window, looking upward. "Only He knows, Mike…Him only, Mike!" Raymond says, leaving him guessing.

On and on it continues, information flowing from an angel, talking about another time, another place, a place they hardly know about, only what's written in the Holy Bible, what angels tell him!

Mike looks up, confused again. "And the rest of it…?"

"Your mission is here, Mike! No longer must you wait for an enemy to appear! They're here, Mike. They wait for his call to perform a ceremony as Jesus once did, pledging his life to his father!"

And again, Mike is staggered, wiping his brow, bewildered.

Raymond lays his hand upon his standing beside him, calming him, "But you will understand, Mike! You're one of His chosen! You're a player on a mission that only He knows the reason!"

And he's startled to even think about it, pleading, "Tell me more, Raymond…please, Raymond, tell me more."

Arthur (Mac) Mc Caffry

"Everything is falling in place as planned, Mike! It's like clockwork from a master, Mike…it's perfect! Absolutely perfect, Mike!" he shouts joyfully, raising his arms upward unexpectedly.

But a worried look clouds Ailene's dark blue eyes as she moves closer beside him. "But tell us more, Raymond…please…"

Again, he moves to the window, looking upward trance-like: his eyes close and he's praying words, nothing Ailene has heard before. And he stops, looking pleased, smiling.

"You're about to view the destruction of the once famous Eagle's Nest in the village of Berchtesgaden! A celebration is planned for the most hideous Halloween ever. It will be the Halloween of all Halloweens, planned by the devil himself!"

Long frightening moments and Mike regains his poise. "But why important, Raymond?"

"Maybe not important to you, Mike, but to Satan, it's everything! It's the timing, Mike!" he whispers, close to his ear.

"But the timing…what's timing got to do with now, Raymond?" he asks, confused.

And his eyes sparkle, showing his pleasure. "The time has come, Mike! It's time to look up! Soon…very soon…the earth will shake! Mountains will tumble! And His mighty power will be known to all forever and ever!"

Ailene pulls closer to Raymond, staring up at him, begging, "And then what, Raymond…then what?"

He reaches out, placing his hand upon her shoulder. "Ailene darling! It's time to get ready! Open your eyes…hold the necklace against your heart, it's power, Ailene! Power unthinkable! It's your lifeline to heaven and nothing between heaven and hell can harm you!" he says boldly, heading for the door at breaktime.

21

And Then, There's Grace

If I have told you of earthly things, and ye believe not,
how shall ye believe, if I tell ye of heavenly things?

—John 3:12

A ten-minute break and they're back seated with Raymond,
ready to move on.

"False prophets will come, displaying love and affection,
learn to discern them, avoid them bitterly!"

"But how do we recognize them?" Ailene asks, looking up
at Raymond.

"Think! Remember your teaching, your Bible teaching,
Ailene. Think, girl, think!"

"You mean, within they're nothing but ravenous wolves ready
to devour you?"

"Yes, dear! Along with government traitors betraying their
very own."

Mike moves beside her. "But what part do we play in the
mission, Raymond?" he asks.

"Oh yes…your part! You'll be among them…ready to greet
them, armed like nobody ever!"

Ailene looks over to Mike and back to Raymond. "Ready to
greet them with what, Raymond?"

He reaches out, pulling them closer. "You'll greet them with the necklace dangling down from around your neck, it's power unthinkable…indestructible!"

Again! Mike wipes sweat from his brow, hands cold as ice, shaking nervously. And slowly, he runs his hand over the necklace, feeling its power, magnifying its beauty; and solemnly, his eyes open widely, gazing upward toward heaven, marveling!

Raymond watches him, waiting. "Use the necklace only when necessary, Mike. You're living at the end of the age, about to witness history in the making!"

"End of the age…"

"Yes, Mike! The fulfillment of the book of Revelation, the coming of the devil's most fearsome: false prophets, the Antichrist!"

And they're mesmerized, worried again!

"And then what, Raymond?" Mike asks, holding his breath, waiting.

Raymond hesitates, head bowed low, contemplating.

"It's debauchery at its worst…beyond human imagination! It's Satan's last hurrah…his final party!"

Ailene moves closer. "But Mike and I…our part, Raymond?"

His arms and hands lay spread out wide before them. "Smile and be proud, Chosen Ones! You're chosen to deliver the first blow that will destroy him!" he says, as his voice grows louder.

And silence! Nothing, but silence! Mike listens as his heart pounds hard and fast, waiting.

"But when will all this end?" Ailene asks, growing weary.

He hesitates, thinking, *The day you meet the Lord, my dear, the day you're home forever!*

God Help Us

And on and on it goes, Raymond showing the way, explaining, "Devil worshipers by the hundreds…all at the Eagle's Nest waiting…ready to proclaim allegiance to Satan!"

And he stops, moving to the window, peering upward. Long tense moments and he returns, standing before them smiling. "But all praise to God, they'll never leave the mountaintop!" he announces powerfully, causing them to back away, frightened.

Mike pulls Ailene close to him. "Does this mean what I think it does, pretty lady?" he whispers.

"It does, Mike…undoubtedly it does!"

They remember Martha's words, "We win," and the thought of it rings home: knowing the outcome before it begins.

Ailene holds her hand outward, joining Raymond. And a beautiful smile appears upon her tired-looking face.

"But, Raymond! Oh, how I love Him! I feel His love, the beauty He brings. And when I gaze upon the necklace, it soothes my heart…my soul…everything within me!"

And she stops short, puzzled again. "But why, Raymond, why do I fear tomorrow?" she asks, begging.

He looks up at her smiling, moving close to her. "But you're mortal, my dear! And you're blessed by the one who has conquered hell and beyond! But tell me your weapon, Ailene… the most powerful weapon ever!"

And he waits, but never an answer.

"The cross, Ailene! Power unthinkable…filled with love and glory!" he shouts, causing her to move away, frightened again.

Again, she's stunned, searching for composure, thinking, *This is too much! I can't take it no more!*

And on and on it goes, explaining, shouting, never letting up.

Arthur (Mac) Mc Caffry

"Tomorrow, we enter into the critical part. You'll be shown film making you acquainted with the "Village Berchtesgaden," Raymond announces loudly!

Time passes without notice, both tired, never resting! They wonder if they're in another world, maybe a dream world, one they read about, but never want to see. And the very thought of something so evil, a satanic Bible written by the devil himself, unbelievable but true!

"But the others...the ones we're yet to meet?" Mike asks, more and more weary.

A sudden turn of his head, looking back. "Yes! Yes! The others, they too are Chosen."

"Chosen... when?" he asks, pursuing further.

And his face glows brighter. "Chosen as you, from the very beginning!"

And Mike rises, moving closer. "But one final question, Raymond, a question I dream about, hoping it's true. I want to believe, believe it will happen, but if I could only be sure..."

"Yes, Mike?"

"You tell me you were with me from the beginning...and I believe! You tell me you're an angel sent by God, and I believe you! But the one everyone desires to know..."

"Yes, Mike?"

"I read about angels, how they serve God here on earth..."

"Yes, Mike..."

"But Ailene and I...it's different! It's just gotta be different!" he says, moving even closer, waiting.

And Raymond is smiling. "Brilliant, Mike, brilliant! You see things others wonder about. It pleases me greatly!"

"But the answer, please, Raymond," he's begging.

God Help Us

And again, he gazes upward, searching. His eyes close. He wipes his brow, again meditating. And he stops, turning to face them.

"But soon, very soon, things will move! And then, only then, Mike, you'll find what you've been searching for!"

Mike waits, lingering, another mystery to worry about. "But when is soon?" he keeps asking himself over and over, never an answer.

Raymond rises from his chair, walks to the window, staring back, facing Ailene. "Return to the hotel and be here tomorrow for finals, Ailene! After finals, you leave for Berlin: problems, contact Grace!" he says, his eyes never blinking.

And again, she's glaring at him, dumbfounded! Raymond reads her mind before she can tell him her problem.

"But, Raymond! I've yet to meet Grace!" she shouts frantically.

Raymond stands at the door ready to leave. "But Grace is with you always, Ailene…even to the end!" he says, departing.

And from over at the window, a slight noise from out of nowhere, the candle is out.

22

Ready to Roll

The Lord knows those who are his.

—2 Timothy 2:19

It is six a.m. on a cool clear autumn morning and the phone rings in room 217 at Hotel Mark Twain; it's Grace.

"Be at the Sampson Building at eight a.m., the both of you. Today's the final day before departing, understand?"

"I understand."

A quick shower, a shave, and he phones Ailene, asking, "Ready for finals?"

"Meet you in the dining room in ten minutes."

Thirty minutes later, they're seated in a large dining room just off the front entrance of the Mark Twain. A briefcase lies beside each, prepared for business. No shaking hands, no pleasantries, nothing but business.

Ailene breaks the silence, never smiling. "Are you worried about something, Mike, maybe something we need to talk about?" she asks pleasantly.

He looks at her puzzled, thinking what a question to ask being this far along.

"I'll put it to you this way, Ailene. I'm as happy as I'll ever be. I was made for something like this!" he says, jokingly.

| 172 |

God Help Us

Moments of silence, no looking around. "But I've a question for you, Ailene!"

"A question for me?"

"Oh, yes…a very important question!"

"Then spill it out, dearie!" she says, never looking back at him.

"Many nights, I've laid awake wondering about something, but never an answer."

She looks at him, grinning. "Quit your hedging around, Mike…fire away. Tell me what keeps you awake."

"But I've gotta know the truth for sure, Ailene…it's important…understand?"

"Then don't take all day…out with it, time's wasting!" she whispers, agitated.

"Did you come to Morris Avenue Baptist by the wishes of the Star…or was it Friend?"

She looks at him, grinning. "Does it bother you, Mikey boy?" she asks, taunting.

"Sure it does, bothers me a lot. Last night, I lay in bed thinking about you, how we first met."

"Now, I'm interested, tell me about it."

"Well…it just might be, that's why we're here together!" he says nervously, looking away.

And she turns, facing him, grinning. "Guess, Mike! Guess!" she says teasingly.

And Mike's temper begins to flare. He isn't about to guess. He picks up the newspaper, pretends to read, wait another day.

Breakfast is over and they head back to the Sampson Building. Raymond sits inside the office, waiting at his desk.

No greeting, nothing, just business with Raymond taking over, beginning.

| 173 |

"Later today, you'll leave for Berlin. You will have a last-minute briefing en route. Make notes of nothing, but be faithful in everything explained to you perfectly. And again, I must warn you, the enemies you're about to face are soldiers of Satan! They're sent to destroy you and all who serve Him!"

And he stops! Beginning again, staring downward. "But most important is…"

"The most important is what…Raymond?" Ailene asks anxiously, never waiting.

And his fiery eyes flash as lightning. "The power of the devil! It's frightening, beyond your imagination! Thousands upon thousands of unseen demonic forces wait for the day he proclaims himself God, God of heaven… earth…all over and beyond!"

And they sit stunned again! Raymond waits, staring at them in silence. "Questions?" he barely asks.

Mike glances over at Ailene, seeing her eyes looking down. "No questions, Raymond…none!"

"Before you leave, get rid of everything written, every note, every notation. Store it in your mind, let it rest till needed! Check your room again and again, but don't check out!"

"But why, why not check out?" Ailene asks quickly.

Raymond moves closer between the two, whispering, "Let them do the worrying where you've moved in case they're after you! I'm talking about unseen forces, the kind of forces the Apostle Paul warned us about! I'm talking about unknown *principalities, demonic, evil forces…watching, waiting for you!*"

And slowly, he moves away, moving on.

"Sometime in the next twenty-four hours, you'll be notified by Grace to leave the hotel, don't wait…move out quickly!

God Help Us

Take nothing except the clothes on your back, everything else is useless!"

He pauses, gazing again at them, moving on. "Outside the hotel, you'll meet Rainbow."

"Rainbow! And who is Rainbow?" Mike asks.

"She's your pilot, Mike! She will deliver you to the airport where you'll meet Golden, her fellow pilot."

"And from the airport?"

"Leaving Dulles, you'll move to Berlin. Later, you'll continue by helicopter directly to Berchtesgaden, a small village in the Bavarian Alps."

"And Berchtesgaden?" Ailene asks.

"A place in history not often mentioned, the home of the greatest devil worshiper ever, Adolf Hitler: killer of Jews, leader of the occult!"

A short pause. "Watch your surroundings, take nothing for granted."

Over and over, it goes! Grilling without let up.

"Arriving at Berchtesgaden, things will pick up!"

Again, Mike wipes sweat from his brow, asking, "But our part begins when?"

Raymond rises standing before him, staring down at him, announcing loudly, "Your part! It begins the night of Halloween, move over to the window and look out, see who will be with you."

They move to the window, gazing out. And before them stand a hundred strange figures dressed in white: protectors! And Mike turns quickly, looking back...no Raymond!

23

Berchtesgaden:
A Place in History

The chariots of God are twenty thousand,
even thousands of angels: the Lord is among
them, as in Sinai, in the holy place.

—Psalm 68:17

Ailene and Mike sit waiting for someone taking Raymond's place, and from out of nowhere, an unknown voice, "I'm Golden, your pilot, Rainbow isn't coming!"

They glance toward the door and back to the swivel chair. A beautiful young lady with long blond hair sits alone, wearing a white linen pilot's uniform, strikingly adorned! It's fitted with gold buttons, red stripes running down to her black leather shoes. And covering her head, she wears a matching cap displaying a small but noticeable golden cross.

Anxiously, they wait for her to speak, but she only stares back at them smiling, settling back in the big swivel chair. And again, they begin to realize they're in a completely different kind of world, the kind of world Golden knows, a world of angels, messengers of God!

She opens hers arms, beckoning them closer. "Prepare for excitement, Chosen Ones! Things are happening fast and

| 176 |

God Help Us

furious! I'll brief you. deliver you later. Once we land at the village of Berchtesgaden, you'll be briefed again! Questions?" she asks, catching her breath, waiting.

And again, they're shocked, left wondering.

"But the remainder of our schedule, Golden...where... when?" Mike asks.

"Within twenty-four hours you'll move on, prepare for it, Mike. Three nights from now will be Halloween. And when the clock strikes midnight in the village of Berchtesgaden on Halloween night, your mission will be over, completed... forgotten!"

Wow! It's news from the highest, but Mike isn't satisfied, wanting more.

"And when the mission is over, Golden?" Mike asks, moving closer.

"You'll be going home! The Eagle's Nest...a hole in the ground...soon forgotten."

Ailene moves beside her, worried! "But Berchtesgaden! The children, the people...the homes..."

Golden places her hand upon her mouth, hushing her. "The Eagle's Nest only, Ailene...nothing more, but I must warn you..."

"Warn me about what?" she asks, suspiciously.

And she rises, standing, looking down upon Ailene alone, shouting, "It's all about prayer, Ailene! Prayer and more prayer, only He has the answers!"

Again, Ailene sits shocked! Muttering a silent prayer, she knows so well, "Lord, help me, please, Lord, help me."

Golden opens a briefcase, spreading maps across her desk, motioning them come closer.

"Placed before you is something to read before departing for Washington. Read every detail, memorize every hallway, stairwell, elevator—whatever strikes your eye important. Once you leave the motel in Berchtesgaden, things will begin to happen, frightening things! Things only He knows. And in minutes, you'll be on your way to an elevator at the base of Kalkstein Mountain. From the base of the elevator, you'll zoom upward, reaching the top of Kalkstein Mountain!"

She stops, waiting briefly, continuing on.

"When you arrive at the top of the mountain, stop, look up, look around: you're inside the notoriously famous Eagle's Nest, when things get busy, when time becomes precious!"

And their eyes stay focused upon her hypnotized, missing nothing.

"You'll be given three hours to complete your mission. Evil, unseen satanic forces will surround you. But there's nothing to fear…nothing to harm you…"

Ailene can't wait, breaking the silence. "Yes! Yes, Golden," she shouts, waiting.

Golden reaches out, clasping her hands, surrounding her. "The Lord is with you always, Ailene. He will never leave you! Never forsake you!" she says, consoling her.

Time is moving fast and again, Golden reaches out, spreading maps, diagrams before them. And again, she's explaining every nook and cranny within the Eagle's Nest, occasionally stopping to mention Hitler's reign of terror, living in an atmosphere of luxury. And the Great Room! A place of pleasure for Hitler's Gestapo, the most feared killers ever!

She mentions *Joseph Goebbels*, the Nazi madman; *Hermann Goering, the* political leader who hung himself in prison; *Eva Braun,* Hitler's long-time mistress; the occult, devil worshipers forever.

God Help Us

She mentions Jews, millions put to death in concentration camps. On and on, she continues while Ailene sits next to Mike, fighting back an urge to vomit.

A twenty-minute break and she's back, continuing. She tells of the American occupation by the 101st Airborne at the end of WWII. She tells of priceless relics falling into hands of the victors. On and on, hours upon hours describing history till finally she comes to Halloween night, the night all nights, the night all hell breaks loose at the Eagle's Nest in Bavaria.

Halting, regaining her breath, Golden reaches out joining hands, beginning again.

"You will be dressed as waiters in black trousers, white shirts, black bowties. And from the Inn, Hans will escort you and others to an elevator at the base of the mountain. And from the mountain base, you will proceed farther to the highest point on Kalkstein Mountain, gazing upon the one and only Eagle's Nest. Questions?"

Two quick nods, and Ailene asks, "And the Eagle's Nest, describe it please."

"There's nothing like it, made of solid marble stone, carved into a playhouse at the top of the mountain. It's a magnificent work of art, a history, indescribably horrible!"

And she stops, staring at them sadly. "But the most spacious of all is the large ballroom leading out onto a large overhead balcony. Evil plans were set in place, witchcraft, never ending! Long nights of debauchery, sexual depravity, a playpen for Hitler and his cult of devil worshipers conceived by the devil himself," she says teary eyed, staring down, away.

"Questions?" she asks.

But looking again, she's seeing only stares of pity, heads bowing low, never questioning.

"Nearing the ballroom, you'll be met by Jonathon, one of our own! He's knowledgeable of the territory, a take-charge person, directing a procession of twenty or thirty waiters and waitresses throughout the parade, ending up before the altar!"

And Mike interrupts, "The altar?"

Golden looks at him differently! Afraid to say the words, but she does. "The altar of Satan, Mike, none other!"

He's shocked, but carries on, asking, "But how do we recognize Jonathon from others?"

And her face brightens, showing her pleasure. "Look for the biggest, the sweetest, the most handsome waiter ever: that will be Jonathon. He will place you behind a cart at the end of a line of waiters and waitresses dressed the same. Ailene, you will be at the head of the cart. Mike, you will follow, trailing at the rear. And the two of you will remain this way till you reach your destination!"

"And my destination is where?" Mike asks.

"It's wherever the satanic Bible is placed, Mike. It will be spread open, lying upon an altar, honoring Satan as God. Every eye will be fixed upon it from the moment it's placed. The top of your cart will be neatly displayed with wine, liquors, drinks of every brand. And under the cart's cover will be hidden the Holy Bible, the same Bible used for the swearing in of President Ronald Reagan in Washington. Now the both of you look at me! Look me in the eye, tell me you're with me!" she says, staring hard into their eyes boldly.

Again, they're shocked, wondering why. Ailene grabs her hand, moving up in her face. "But, Golden! We are with you! We love Him too!" she's shouting, excited, wondering the question.

And her eyes brighten, looking at Ailene, satisfied.

God Help Us

"Sometime before midnight, you will deliver the cart with the Holy Bible hidden on the second shelf below. Surrounding you, celebrants will gather in the main ballroom. Look them over, but never worry. And when you see figures dressed in black standing one against one at the wall, disregard them, they're Satan's own, his best ever. But more important is—"

And Mike can't wait, interrupting, "More important!"

"It is, Mike…far more important! Never shudder, never doubt…look up, keep your eyes upon the cross!" she says, standing upright, spreading her arms, gazing upward.

Excited, Ailene asks, "But the cross, Golden, what happens if they see the cross?"

And she begins to smile, showing her delight! "But they will not see the cross, Ailene, they're blinded by those standing before them."

"You mean—"

"Yes, my dear! Light before darkness…"

"But then what, Golden?"

And her lovely smile turns cold. "Look up and pray, my darling! Pray…pray and keep on praying you're up to the task!"

"But, Golden! Tell me what…tell me what then?"

She gathers her folders, clasping Ailene's hand. And pointing upward, she smiles so beautifully, "He will never leave you or forsake you, Ailene—even unto the end."

24

Halloween

*Therefore being justified by faith, we have peace
with God through our Lord, Jesus Christ.*

—*Romans 5:1*

It's here! The night of all nights—Halloween! Plans are laid, time grows short. Ailene and Mike stand outside the Inn gazing up to the mystery place, Kalkstein mountaintop.

They struggle to visualize the past, what the Eagle's Nest had been during Hitler's reign of terror against Jews. Nervousness, filled with apprehension, runs rampant in their minds. It's six hours till take-off and Mike can't bear the thought of failure. Victory is the way, the only way, and with Mike as always, failure isn't an option.

His eyes close, trying to visualize the 101st Airborne making this same journey at the end of WWII, a winding road upward to the Eagle's Nest. He remembers Nate's message and will never forget: Watch a television miniseries, *A Band of Brothers.* And now he's part of it, in a different way, a holy but deadly way! A battle more deadly than anything Hitler could offer, a place in hell filled with devil's advocates.

Heavy blowing rain falls outside the Inn, flooding ditches and gullies, as the two stand beneath an overhead shelter. Off

God Help Us

in the distance, they see a large wooded forest at the base of the huge stone mountain. And from far off in the forest, they hear the unmistakable howling of bloodthirsty banshees, signaling the coming of death. It's something Mike swears he heard as a child, just before someone in the neighborhood was about to die.

And farther off in the distance, they hear the sound of helicopters landing, taking off one after another, bringing dignitaries from faraway places. And the atmosphere surrounding the Inn has suddenly changed, it's an eerie, dreary evening, chilling to the bone.

Ailene looks upward, seeing nothing but darkness. And suddenly, she grabs Mike's hand heading him back inside the Inn. Inside, they stand in the lobby, gazing upon a never-ending line of chauffeur-driven limos, winding their way upward—headed for the Eagle's Nest. Ahead of them, they can imagine a prize of all prizes—a glance at the first and only appearance of the one and only satanic Bible. And down the road, families gather outside, watching an endless line of traffic with no idea why this Halloween is the greatest, greater than all before.

Ailene holds Mike's hand tightly, and for the first time, she's different, looking worried.

"I'll be happy when this night is over, Mike, seems as if the weather is against us," she barely mutters.

Mike looks at her surprised. "This isn't going to be easy, reporter lady," he offers, agreeing. "It could get a little rough before this episode is over."

She squeezes his hand hard. "You're right, Mike, but don't forget who guides us."

"You mean—"

She places her hand over his lips.

Yes, Mike—Him! The one who calms the sea, parts the waters, He will be with us, Mike," she reminds him, holding the cross, squeezing it tightly.

And Mike turns, looking again at her surprised!

"You're amazing, Ailene! Absolutely amazing! I've met some tough ones, but never one like you, afraid of nothing, willing to die trying."

And she looks up at him, smiling. "But God is with us, Mike, that's all I ask," she says, surprising him again.

Minutes later they return to their rooms, hoping for rest-time, but resting is impossible! A lot of tossing, turning, thinking, regretting, wishing, and repenting...all of it, engulfing their next couple of hours till the phone rings, it's Grace!

"Be in the lobby prepared to leave with the rest of the waiters and waitresses in ten minutes. Say nothing to anyone except Jonathon, the handsome one."

Bang! The phone goes dead and Mike is ready, anxious to move out.

Outside in the hallway, they hear people moving toward the lobby where a large bus sits in front of the doorway ready to deliver them to the scene of action, the Eagle's Nest. Boarding is accomplished in minutes, and soon they're sitting in the middle of a crowded bus with people unknown. Mike gazes across the aisle seeing a gentleman nodding back at him, grinning; Hans is here!

And it's party time! The party of all parties, Halloween of all Halloweens, and they know it.

Ailene nudges his side. "You seem pleased, Mike...why?"

He holds her hand, gazing back at her. "I'm very pleased, Ailene. I'm thinking of a song I heard just before I left home... it doesn't go away."

God Help Us

She squeezes his hand. "Tell me about it, Mike," she barely whispers.

And with his eyes gazing out into darkness, he says, "It's one of the old never to be forgotten kind of songs, one of those you don't hear about anymore."

"Just tell me about it, Mike, I'm waiting!"

"It was called *'What a Friend We Have in Jesus.'* There's *something about it that comforts me when I need it.*"

She snuggles close to him, squeezing his hand, looking up into tired bloodshot eyes.

"This might shock you, Mike, but I'm beginning to change my opinion of you…maybe a little and then some."

"But why, darling?" he whispers, looking around, seeing who might be listening.

"Well, I've discovered something new about you—finally!"

"Good! Tell me about it, sweetheart…"

"Oh, maybe you're not really such a bad guy after all. I don't know why, but you're getting to me good…real good!"

And Mike begins to grin, moving his head upon her shoulder, getting closer.

Rain pounds hard upon the bus top as it makes its way among a heavy flow of traffic heading toward the mountaintop. Up, up, and up they move over the curvy road till finally the elevator is reached. A quick hasty move and they're zooming skyward toward the Eagle's Nest. They're met at the entrance and quickly ushered down to the waiter's quarters near the main dining room. Ten or twelve persons greet them eagerly, but one stands above all. He's the big handsome one, Jonathon, a perfect example of manhood at best. He's a Scandinavian-born offspring about six feet two or three, blue eyes, long blond

Arthur (Mac) Mc Caffry

hair and instantly noticeable. He greets them with a strong handshake, causing Mike to glance twice, noting the size of his large brawny hands.

"Follow me, we need to talk," he barely whispers. And in moments, they're standing in a secluded area outlining his plan with Jonathon in charge.

"You've been drilled on this before, but we'll go over it again. Slip-ups we can't afford, there's no second chance," Jonathon says, watching their reaction, waiting.

He begins again, "We have two and a half hours left before the real action begins. And once we're there, Mike, you will be placed at the very end of a long line of carts loaded with food and drinks headed for the dining room. And you, Ailene, you will be at the head, guiding the way forward. Take nothing for granted! Listen carefully, be suspicious, understand every move *you make, your lives depend upon it.*"

Ailene moves closer against him. "We understand, Jonathon, we're with you all the way, ready to move forward," she says, standing beside him.

"I'll be in charge of the operation. During the move down where the satanic Bible is to be located, my eyes will never leave you. The Holy Bible you placed your hands upon at the Sampson Building is placed at the bottom of your cart. Disregard the revelry, it doesn't matter! It will disturb you, make you sick! But the only thing that really matters is doing His will, sending the satanic Bible up in flames…never to be mentioned again!"

And he stops, thinking, "But there's something else important—"

"Something else?"

God Help Us

"There is, Mike. Every move must be synchronized to perfection. We're dealing with the best there is, headed by the devil himself. Every move we make, it must be flawless!"

Mike moves close to him. "Stop your worrying, Jonathon. I've waited for this moment forever and then some!"

Jonathon places his huge hand upon his shoulder.

"You'll do great, Mike, I know you will. This could be the last time I talk to you till the mission is over. But I warn you again—"

Mike interrupts, "Warn me about what?"

"This is the devil's show! He's powerful beyond your imagination…the greatest deceiver ever!"

They move forward cautiously, following instructions perfectly. Minutes later, they arrive outside the kitchen area. Mike pulls one of the maps from his pocket provided by Raymond; it's perfect, down to every nook, every cranny.

Crowds of people have gathered in the main dining area. Music, never-ending speeches, all of it giving praise to Satan; booming out over loudspeakers, followed with wild hysterical moments, cursing the name of Jesus and the cross.

Evil runs amuck, reminding them of stories about Hitler and the occult. They need something to console them, something to depend upon. They hold the cross praying silently, fear disappears, worry no more.

A huge German-made clock hangs high against the stone wall showing two hours before midnight. A signal from Jonathon and the march begins. On and on, proceeding toward the center of the dining room where people crowd together, waiting for the moment of all moments; a view of the one and only satanic Bible.

A glance back and Ailene sees Mike trailing at the end of the procession guiding a large metal cart. His face is filled with

Arthur (Mac) Mc Caffry

confidence, looking at ease. On and on, they move till finally it's here, their destination. And they stop sharply, staring ahead.

And suddenly, it happens! This has to be it: his never-ending search for peace. It's over! It's over forever! He wants to shout. His mind works overtime thinking back, this is the place, the time, his destiny; it has to be the answer to his never-ending prayer. It's his lifelong desire, the one he has waited for, prayed for never ending.

And he stops short thinking, remembering how it all started: his visit from Friend, his forgiveness, his meeting Ailene. His mission is clear: destroy the one and only satanic Bible. And suddenly he's different, the old Mike back in Nam, feeling unstoppable!

A large mural upon the wall depicts Jesus on his knees pleading forgiveness to Lucifer; forgiveness for proclaiming himself the Son of God. Figures dressed in SS uniforms from WWII stroll throughout the crowd, dragging human-looking Jewish mannequins, while the place goes wild with onlookers shouting obscenities, laughing hysterically. And an unmistakable female, the image of Hitler's whore lady friend, Eva Braun, dances nude at the center of the crowd, shouting praise to Satan and his Bible of all Bibles.

And Mike is furious! He fights back his temper, controlling his rage. He remembers what Jonathon warned him about, looking away. And from the other side of the room, he can see a man figure dressed in a Gestapo uniform holding a crucifix high over his head. He's shouting vulgarities against Jehovah over and over. And suddenly, he plunges the crucifix downward into a large picture of a Jewish child wearing the Star of David. And it's too much! He can stand it no longer.

He walks to the nearest door leading out to an iron railing, overlooking the forest below. And off in the distance, he hears the sound of animals howling, running wild in all directions. From far overhead, birds of prey screech their eerie wails, searching for food down below. And off in the distance, he can hear the sound of wolves sending their eerie sounds without end, signaling the coming of death. Once again, he grabs the necklace, kisses the cross, gathering his thoughts, reviving.

And boom! A jolt from out of nowhere shakes the mountaintop. Revelry stops as worshipers stand, gazing in all directions. High above the bar, a barometer runs wild, showing disturbance below, a shaking and it falls to the floor, breaking into a hundred pieces.

And memories of WWII strike fear into hearts of the white-haired ones, nights of horror, bombs falling from high above, searching for Hitler, the madman, killer of Jews! Minutes go by and the shaking ends. Mike makes his way back inside, staring in shock; celebration runs full, resuming in all its glory and splendor!

High above, the clock shows an hour and fifteen minutes till midnight when hell will be let loose in all its fury. And forty or fifty feet away sit the sacred twelve, *Satan's disciples waiting.*

Mike stands hypnotized, his eyes glued, staring hard. This can't be real! It just isn't possible! He keeps muttering to himself over and over! He recognizes some of his own, American dignitaries, long-time public servants in life.

And suddenly, the unthinkable! The older gentleman sitting near the head of the table with arms folded showing reverence to Satan, a past vice president of the United States, holder of the Nobel Peace Prize and all that it stands for. Next to him sits another white-haired elderly looking gentleman, not-long-ago secretary of state. Next to him sits the world's richest atheistic billionaire. And finally, a breathtaking glimpse of the one and only Club of Rome, atheists all, disciples of Satan!

The clock shows ten minutes till eleven, and Mike moves the cart in a slow rhythmic walk. Slowly, he's trailing at the rear until he's standing before the magnificent piece of art, the *altar of the most high*. Upon the altar lies the satanic Bible, spread open at the center. And it's large, a showpiece for a thousand drunken, sadistic revelers, shouting obscenities against Jesus. Mike's eyes strain to look, viewing letters in red, written in blood.

And far out against the wall, human-looking figures dressed in black stand motionless, guarding their masters seated below.

At the head of the table a figure stands ready to proclaim Satan's Bible to the world. A bugle sounds far off to the rear. Eyes turn, and from out of nowhere stand four Nazi storm troopers dressed in uniforms from WWII. And suddenly, it grows quiet—deadly quiet! A huge black masked figure appears before the altar of stone.

Outside becomes alive. Guard dogs strain at their leashes, running, barking, howling in circles. While inside naked females run shouting and screaming, in and out around the altar of Satan. And from far off in the distance again, there's an unmistakable sound of bloodthirsty banshee wailing the night away. It's Halloween at its highest, reigning in the full power of Satan.

Moments of all moments, it's finally here! Ailene signals Mike it's time to begin. She raises her arm high, and with a quick stabbing motion, her thumb points downward, time to begin!

Worshipers watch, standing motionless petrified! Mike stands high over their most precious of all possessions, the one and only satanic Bible. And quickly from the bottom of the cart, he removes the Bible of God Almighty, pulling it close to him, kissing the cover. He raises it high above his head, and

God Help Us

before a stunned audience of devil worshippers, he shouts ever so loud defiantly, *"Jehovah! Our one and only God—He lives! He lives today, tomorrow, forever...throughout eternity!"*

And with a mighty thrust of his arms, he delivers a swift move downward, sending his Bible of I Am into the heart of the satanic Bible.

A loud resounding woof! A huge puff of smoke and it's history! Where only moments ago the Bible of Satan reigned high upon the altar, Mike stands looking proud, holding the Bible of Almighty God tightly against his heart, watching ashes from the satanic Bible drifting into the wind...gone forever.

25

Why, Oh, Why, Lord?

For I can do all things through Christ
which strengtheneth me.

—Philippians 4:13

His moment of glory is over as quickly as it began. From across the room there's a change of guard. The once-dark figures lined against the wall have disappeared, replaced by angels of the Lord, standing boldly in their place, dressed in long white shining garments.

All hell should be breaking loose, but it isn't. There's a gathering of the faithful, a loud resounding cheer, and the unexpected—Halloween continues, moving ahead in all its glory.

Both move quickly away from the rowdy, cursing celebrants. They move fast, picking up speed, and now they're running full out.

"Are you okay? Is everything okay, Ailene?" Mike shouts at the top of his voice, breathlessly.

"Keep running, Mike! We need to get away from this hellhole before it gets rough," Ailene says, pushing the cart in front of her like a locomotive out of control.

And with a quick move of her arms, she shoves the cart hard and away, bounding out into the crowd of worshipers. One more glance and Mike stops suddenly, seeing the twelve disciples!

God Help Us

They're sitting near the altar looking helpless, till chauffeurs and bodyguards move quickly leading them back safely. It's party time, the Halloween of all Halloweens at the top of Kirstein Mountain!

They walk fast, sometime running toward the entrance. And without warning, Mike reaches out, grabbing her hand, turning her around, shouting, "Stop, Ailene! Stop! This place is out of control, growing more serious by the moment!"

And quickly, he reaches into his jacket, pulling out the Sacred Bible of God, handing it to her. "Keep this with you, it's precious! But don't worry, darling, I can handle this! Just hang with me and pray as you've never prayed before!"

Wow! Things change quickly! She's a different Ailene! She's angry, more than angry—she's furious! She moves up in his face, shouting, "You can handle this, Mikey boy!"

And he moves back, surprised! "Sure I can, honey. We're getting out of this place. We're heading for the departure point…understand?"

And her face fills with anger, shouting, "Now hold on a minute, sonny boy, it's time for Momma to take over!"

And Mike moves, backing away, shocked again!

"Here's the way it is, sonny boy. We have fifty minutes to make it down the hill, find the chopper, and get away from this godforsaken place from hell."

"I know! I know!" he's shouting back at her, but to no avail.

And instantly, she's back in his face, exploding again. "Now you listen to Momma, sonny boy! It's time you get something straight!"

"Yes, darling…"

"I'm not your honey, your darling—whatever! I need no advice from you. I've been around…done it all…seen it all! I

| 193 |

know the score better than you ever will!" she barks, loud in his face, threatening.

And he's shaking his head, speechless again. He wants to speak, but can't.

"Are you finished, sweetheart?" he asks meekly.

And her anger explodes again. "You'll know when I'm finished, sonny boy! Don't just stand here looking at me with your mouth open, we're moving on…gettin' outta this hellhole before something else goes wrong, up to this point, I'd call it a pushover!"

And he's shocked again! "A pushover!" he mumbles to himself, wondering why the sudden change.

Again, they begin running, slipping, falling on frozen ground, stopping briefly, checking locations.

And abruptly Mike stops, reaching out, grabbing her arm, pulling her to him. "Where's the Bible, where is it?" he's shouting hysterically.

Ailene's anger erupts again. "It's where it belongs, you idiot. here in my satchel!"

"Good! Hold on to it, protect it!" he says, breathlessly.

And her anger explodes in all her fury. "Now, slow down a moment, big boy! I've had enough of your giving orders. It's time you wake up and get your act together, or I'll leave your sorry butt out here alone, praying for some angels to come get you! And there's something else you better learn, cowboy."

He moves close to her, looking into her eyes. "About what, sweetheart?"

And she's out of control, overflowing again.

"It's just this, cowboy! I'm not your sweetheart…never will be! And never in your miserable lifetime do you need worry about me!"

God Help Us

And suddenly, it grows quiet, a long uninterrupted silence. "Sorry, Ailene, guess I had you wrong. But I've other things on my mind."

And her anger subsides; she's different.

"Maybe I'll never know your problems, Mike, but let's move on before we miss the chopper."

Mike doesn't respond, and she's beginning to worry. "Now what's wrong with you, Mike? You're beginning to act hesitant— almost like you're not ready to leave this godforsaken place."

He pauses, thinking without speaking. He takes her hand, and again, they move slowly ahead, feeling their way down the winding slippery slope.

And from far off in the distance, a familiar voice yells from out of nowhere, "Over here, over here, Mike, Ailene, over here!"

It's Jonathon, and they recognize his voice immediately. A few yards away, Jonathon moves swiftly standing before them. He's breathless, trying to speak. He grabs both, bringing them between him, his big brawny arms wrapped around them.

And Mike is surprised, wondering why Jonathon is here, unexpectedly. Was it planned or mentioned before or has something gone wrong? But before he can ask the question, Ailene does.

"Why are you here, Jonathon? You weren't supposed to see us again, correct?"

"Plans have changed, Ailene. I'm going with you all the way to Berlin," he says, regaining his breath, breathing hard in the cold night air.

But they're still puzzled, wondering why the sudden change of plans? Jonathon was supposed to be finished.

"But why the switch, Jonathon, something wrong?" Ailene asks.

He looks at Mike, hesitant to answer, but does.

"Someone called Nate called the base. He was like an old grizzly bear, kinda rough, mean-like, you know the type."

And Mike grabs his hand, worried. "Nate! Did you say Nate?"

"That's right, Nate. And from the tone of his voice, I didn't wait, this guy was serious. Before I could say a word, he was giving orders, giving orders to me like a general. And the worst part was, I've never met the guy!" he says, excited.

"Giving orders about what, Jonathon?" Mike asks calm and innocent like, searching.

Again, Jonathon looks over to Ailene, hesitating.

"Nate said, 'Stay with Mike. Stay with him till it's over. I know him from way back, and when he gets mad, nobody between here and hell can stop him, nobody! And I do mean… nobody!'"

"Is that all?" Mike asks meekly.

"That was it, Mike! I like you a lot, but I didn't wanna argue with this guy called Nate!"

Mike turns away, glancing back toward the Eagle's Nest, worried again, wondering.

And Jonathon begins to explain. "I'll be leading you down the mountainside. It's dangerous for sure, but you'll get used to the turf once we begin moving. Follow my light, do as I say, and we'll be back at base in no time."

And from out of nowhere, *boom*! *Boom*! Another aftershock rocks the mountainside. Rock and debris rumble down the mountainside like lava spilling from a volcano. Screaming and shouting fills the cold night air, till finally, the mountaintop begins to settle again.

Ailene lies flat on her stomach, spread out on cold barren rock searching for Mike. But Mike's plans have suddenly changed.

God Help Us

He's on his back, flat on the ground, looking out into a different direction. And he's different again, looking up, meditating!

Without notice, he stands upon his feet, running back toward the Eagle's Nest. Minutes later, he's standing, gazing upon the entrance door blown loose from its foundation left hanging. And he's horrified...gazing over the mountaintop, wondering what's left of the Eagle's Nest.

Jonathon and Ailene continue, moving slowly over frozen rock and stone headed downward without speaking. But their thoughts are of Mike, wondering, *What's happening?* And they're asking themselves over and over, *But why! Why, Mike! Back to the Eagle's Nest, a place filled with nothing but evil?*

And they stop, standing without speaking. Ailene can hold it no longer. Again, she's furious, staring out into the cold dark night where Mike has disappeared into a sea of utter darkness. She wants to cry, but can't.

She looks up into the cold dark night with tears streaming down from her tired lovely face. And she's shouting at the top of her voice, angry again.

"I knew it! I absolutely knew it! Nate pegged you right, Mike, clear up to the finish line. Now, when you're finally finished playing your games, just come back to Momma! But when you do, Momma's gonna grab hold of you, pick you up, and drag your sorry butt all the way down this mountainside, Mikey boy!" she's shouting all out, rebounding over the mountaintop.

Jonathon hears her shouting, but can only remember Nate's final words: stay with Mike, till it's over.

Off in the distance, Mike is about to enter the Eagle's Nest once again. He stops, looking up into darkness, shouting at the top of his voice.

"Sorry, darling! Sorry, Jonathon! But I've unfinished business with my Lord and Savior. It's between the two of us, personal business…only He and I can understand! I love you, darling, always will…forever!" his voice rings out, vibrating over the mountaintop.

Jonathon and Ailene stand huddled together fifty yards away, unable to respond.

Cautiously, Mike moves forward inside the Eagle's Nest, and again, he stops, falling upon his knees, looking up toward heaven, shouting, "Oh, Lord! Oh, Lord! Hear my prayer! The mystery of my life, the search for peace I've still to find. It isn't over…it can't be! But show me, Lord, the other half, the half I've yet to know. Please, Lord…help me, Lord."

Farther away, Jonathon moves close to Ailene, hoping to move on, but again, another wave of anger overruns her senses.

"Have you completely lost your mind, Mike? It's time to go home, leave this godforsaken place now and forever," she's shouting loud and clear, sending echoes bouncing off the mountainside.

And Mike searches for words; peaceful words to soothe her anger.

"Please don't be angry, darling. But this is why I'm here in this godforsaken place. It is! It has to be! I was hell-bent with no way out, but now…I'm free! Free at last! Please, darling, try to understand me," he pleads, on and on, stopping only to get his breath, beginning again.

And her heart begins to melt! Anger turns to forgiveness.

"But if you must continue on, darling…do it well, do it for His sake! For your sake, but do it, darling! I'll be waiting and praying for you, sweetheart," she yells as her voice drifts away out into the cold night air.

"But it's not over, darling! I need another look, a look into where I might have been, except for the *grace of God!" Mike shouts, stepping farther out into the unknown.*

He tugs at the door; finally, it opens. And surprisingly, there's someone waiting. Friend stands before him, smiling. His heart skips a beat, reaching out to hug him, but quickly, he turns, moving away.

"This isn't the time or the place, Mike, don't touch me," Friend says without explaining.

Mike stares at him, wondering, "But why, Friend?" he asks, worried.

"I have a message for you, Mike, a wonderful, exciting message."

"For me?"

"For you only, Mike."

He waits and waits. "The message, Friend…"

And his eyes sparkle as diamonds! "Jesus, Our Lord and Savior, He will never leave you or forsake you, Mike!"

Mike stands, looking again at him, comforted! He moves toward the front where devil worshiping ran wild only minutes ago. And he turns back, searching, but no Friend.

He's alone, running wildly toward the dining room where music fills the air, festivities run their highest. He stops at the edge of the balcony overlooking the ballroom, looking down. And again, it's sickening! It's nothing but human degradation at its highest! Damage is everywhere, but the show goes on, revelry at the highest. But how! How can this be? He asks himself over and over, again and again, but never an answer.

At the center of the large room stands a well-known Hollywood starlet…naked. Music plays softly as she slowly moves her naked body before the twelve disciples. And it becomes louder and louder as the rhythm moves the audience into a wild sadistic frenzy, lust without shame! And suddenly, she increases her movements, working her body into wild gyrations of passion.

Disciples reach out, motioning her to come closer, and she does, motioning the same. Glaring eyes, filled with lust, follow her every movement. And selecting the moment she has been waiting for, she moves quickly atop the large marble table, shouting obscenities. And quickly, the former American secretary of state pokes at her breast, showing his pleasure. Never waiting, she responds to his wishes, straddling his lap. Music stops with a bang; quiet reigns throughout—deathly quiet! Slowly, she walks to the center of the room where a painted figure depicted as the Son of Man lies prone on the floor, nailed upon a wooden cross.

And again, Mike becomes sick, holding back vomit. Cheers ring out unrestrained, blasphemy against God, reigning in the night of Satan! She moves slowly, straddling the image of Jesus. And it's an orgy of wild indescribable decadence only Satan himself could enjoy. Her legs spread wide over the image of Jesus hanging from the cross while she urinates over what's supposed to be his body.

And Mike can take no more. No! No! He's shouting from atop the balcony, but his voice goes unnoticed drowned by yells of passion. And it's time to move on, get out of this place of hell and debauchery forever!

He struggles to contain himself, but fails. His first thought is, *Kill or be killed, kill them all*. He's wishing he could spill their blood, feed their guts to animals below. He takes another look, nothing but sin at its fullest, beyond human imagination!

God Help Us

He has to get away from this place of horror and debauchery. He takes off, running wildly toward the entrance. Outside, he stops to vomit and off again, running over broken rock with mud up to his ankles. And suddenly, he comes to a halt, breathless, thinking. He gazes up toward heaven, spreading his arms, yelling all out, *"But why, oh, why, Lord? Why?"*

26

To Hell and Back

For if ye forgive men their trespasses, your
Heavenly Father will also forgive you.

—Matthew 6:14

And the nightmare comes to an end. He stops, looking out and around, regaining his breath. Again, he takes off, running wildly headlong into the cold night air. Faster! Faster he runs screaming, shouting hatred toward the celebrants, never looking back. And again, the unthinkable happens!

Ba-boom! *Ba-boom*! Another huge underground blast explodes like a thousand bombs. Kalkstein Mountain shakes, rocking the mountainside greater than before. Mike lies flattened out on the ground, lost, groping for something to put his hands around, something to cling to, for only a moment.

Minutes pass like hours, and finally, he's able to stand, looking out into nothing but a sea of darkness. He turns looking back to where just minutes ago, satanic revelry reigned in all its glory, praising the devil.

But it's different! The mountaintop is changed completely! He looks back to where he stood moments ago, seeing smoke billowing upward, spewing gases from a bottomless pit. His legs are numb—no place to rest. And he's thinking of Jonathon and Ailene out somewhere, searching for him in darkness. He's in trouble, and he knows it! He gazes upward toward heaven, holding the cross and kissing it softly: his heart is slowing, beating normal.

His thoughts change again! He's wondering what the once great celebration at the Eagle's Nest must be like now. And the very thought of it hits hard, an unquenchable desire to go back to the place, a horrible place, a place he calls h*ell...hell on earth.*

Gazing far out into the night, his eyes search the mountainside, getting his bearing. One more glimpse of the Eagle's Nest becomes his only thought. Enough is enough! He can stand it no more! It's an obsession without end, something only he and God might understand. One more chance to look into hell, all of it; it's waiting for him here on this barren, stinking, frozen, mountaintop. And he feels it! He knows it!

And he remembers what he was told before leaving: pray, pray and keep on praying. He falls to the ground, pounds his fist upon the cold barren earth, and looking upward, he's shouting at the top of his voice, *"Please, Lord, please, Lord: one more look— please, Lord...please!"*

Far out to the left, Ailene and Jonathon yell his name without stopping. He musters his strength, crawling on frozen ground toward the sound of voices. "Mike darling, where are you, where are you, darling? Answer me, please, darling...please," over and over, never stopping.

Slowly he rises from the ground, shouting, "Over here! Over here! Walk this way. I'll be looking you in the face."

Ailene and Jonathon walk hand in hand, groping through cold bitter darkness, searching, only a flashlight showing the way. And suddenly, not far away, an outline of a figure shows; it's Mike, standing with his arms held out, waiting.

Ailene stands rigid, staring at him breathless. She breaks away from Jonathon, running recklessly toward Mike, smothering him with kisses.

A yell from afar, and in moments Jonathon arrives, looking ragged and dirty. He reaches out engulfing them, hugging them forever.

But again, it happens. Ailene's anger explodes full out, shouting, "You're a blasted idiot, Mike. What were you thinking, running back to the Eagle's Nest? It's over, Mike! It's finished! Have you lost your senses?" She's raving recklessly, on and on, never stopping.

Jonathon moves to interfere, but quickly, she reaches out, pushing him away, angered.

"Nate had you pegged, Mike! He pegged you right the second time I met you. You're never gonna quit, Mikey boy…same old Mike forever!" she's yelling close to his face, turning away angry.

And without waiting, Mike moves against her, pulling her closer. "Are you finished, my darling? And if you are, I'd like to reply," he says, ever so humbly.

Before she can answer, Jonathon moves between the two without speaking. And they're one, huddled together, feeling the cold, looking upon someone different!

But Jonathon's mood is worrisome, his defiance is noticeable! Time runs short, his face shows the strain, he's desperate! And they know it!

Jonathon faces Mike full out, speaking sharply, "Listen to me, Mike, time you pay attention! You've been there, did your job, it's over! It's time we leave this godforsaken place. Time has run out, no more options!"

They're speechless, standing before him, waiting.

God Help Us

"The situation is serious, Mike! And looking from here, we have no idea what's left of the Eagle's Nest. Below, it has to be the same, but only a guess!"

And Jonathon stops, taking their hand, pulling them closer. "But this I know for sure, the last blast was no ordinary earthquake. It was a completely different power within power!"

Mike moves against him, surprised. "But what else could it be, Jonathon—what?" he asks instantly.

"There's only one thing it could be, Mike, it had to be an ammo dump left from WWII," he says, leaving both speechless, thinking.

"Now, do you understand the seriousness of our situation, my friend?" Jonathon barks, causing Mike to look at him again serious.

Mike holds Ailene's hand, barely able to distinguish her face. And in a very humbling way, he tries to explain.

"Yes…, I do understand the seriousness, Jonathon. But sometimes, things—impossible things—occur like maybe the one and only chance of a lifetime kind of things. And again, maybe it's a time when you can't think of your own life, but maybe something personal…even sacred…between a person like me and Him. He and I alone, Jonathon, that's how it is…today, tomorrow, forever!"

Jonathon reaches out, stopping him. "Maybe it could be that way, Mike, but why here? Why now, Mike? You've been there, it's over…time to forget," he says, calming.

Mike looks downward, hand upon his brow, thinking. And the urge to return, it's unstoppable! It's never going away…it's never ending.

He reaches out, grabbing Jonathon's hand without waiting. "But please, Jonathon, listen! Please listen to me! It's all about

what life means! What it means to a crazy guy like me...
something sacred, between God and I alone. You know what I'm
talking about, Jonathon...what really counts in life...when our
days on earth are over!"

An eerie feeling engulfs the three standing high upon the
cold barren mountaintop. Silence reigns throughout, filling the
night air with an unexplainable feeling. Ailene and Jonathon
hold hands, gazing upon each other, trying to comprehend his
meaning, words that Mike alone can explain. He talks about
something past with only God and him a part. And it makes
them wonder, where, why, and when! But there's something
else: why so everlasting important? Why something to worry
about? Why something to search for?"

And Mike is at his end, watching them, hoping they might
understand. But within his heart and soul, he knows he's alone,
only he knows the story of Friend, himself, his mission! And
he remembers words from Friend, words sounding immortal!
*"You were Chosen, Mike...chosen and anointed on an altar of God.
Placing the golden chain around your neck means something most
sacred, it's touched by God. And nothing! Nothing is more important!"*

Far off in the distance, they hear choppers leaving the airstrip,
flying away, one after one, never ending. And in the distance,
animals wail while people cry...never ending! Some curse the
day they were born, others shouting in pain, pleading.

It's decision time! Time to leave or stay! And Jonathon
breaks the silence, moving up in his face, unexpected, grim,
ready for war.

27

A Place of Torment

And he cried out and said, "Father Abraham,
have mercy upon me. And send Lazarus that he
may dip the tip of his finger in water, and cool my
tongue, for I am in torment in this flame."

—Luke 16:24

Jonathon moves against him, confronting him. "This is the moment, Mike! Time we decide, one way or the other."

Mike reaches out, stopping him.

"And my choices, Jonathon?"

"We've only two choices Mike. We either move from this mountaintop now or stay and die later! If we move down to the chopper now, we might stand a chance of going home. But it's up to you, Mike, time for you to make the decision!"

Mike looks at him, puzzled again, "A chance…and what does that mean?"

"It means, I have a place for us on the backside where we can climb down without getting killed, Mike! Golden waits for us in the chopper, and once we're with her, we're on our way home…outta this place forever. Think hard, my friend, it's now or never!"

Mike gazes at the two, studying hard; his words are true and he knows it. But once again, something becomes more important. He needs something else, something that needs to be explained between him and his creator. But all that runs across his mind is one last glimpse of the Eagle's Nest, his last chance to solve the mystery, God selecting him, the worst of the worst, for the greatest operation ever: Un-Holy Ground.

He reaches out, placing his hand upon their shoulder. And his voice becomes different, peaceful, filled with humility.

"Please, please, both of you…quiet! I beg you to listen, try to understand…"

And Jonathon's eyes focus hard upon him, worried.

"We do understand, Mike. My only question to you is why the big change of plans here on a mountaintop at the very last moment? Have you lost your faith? Is that it, Mike?" Jonathon asks, waiting.

He wipes tears from his eyes as many times before. He pauses looking out into the cold dark night smelling fire and brimstone; the kind of place the Holy Bible describes as hell for the unbelievers! And his thoughts drift back, before the Lord spoke to him through Friend.

"No, Jonathon, it's the opposite," he says, ever so humbly. "My faith alone tells me there's something out there in this sea of darkness waiting for me. But always remember, my most dearest of friends, no matter how disgusting or bad I might be, I'll always love you…the both of you forever."

Ailene moves close against him. "And we know that, Mike… the feeling is mutual. But tell me again your reason to find the answer. It's important, most important to me, someone who loves you!"

"It is important, sweetheart. But God alone knows how I've suffered from hatred within. And now, I'm here, here on a

God Help Us

mountaintop, thousands of miles from home searching for the answer. I can feel it! There has to be someone somewhere out there in this sea of darkness waiting for me," Mike says, gasping to get his breath.

"Is this you're final decision, Mike?" Jonathon asks, standing next to him, waiting.

"It has to be! I'm going back, Jonathon! It's something that has to be answered, no matter how I fight it. And please, Jonathon, please don't try stopping me!" he mutters defiantly.

Ailene is shocked! He's not the same Mike; he's determined and she knows it. She wants to be angry, but can't. She holds his hand, moving against him, looking up at him. "I'll be waiting, darling," she barely mutters, as tears begin to fall from her pretty blue eyes once again.

He reaches out, grasping her hand, kissing it softly. And tearfully, he says, "I'll return, darling, but if not, leave me, leave me here on this mountaintop, the place I've always searched for... maybe it's my Shangri-La, the place I once told you about. But I'll be in the hands of the Lord and there's no place safer. And it's time you know my love for you, sweetheart...no matter where, no matter when...I'll always love you...today, tomorrow...forever!"

Silence reigns over and throughout the mountaintop. Peace! Wonderful peace! Their hearts become one, engulfing their worry. Mike joins his hand with theirs, bringing them together for one last moment. He looks up toward heaven, and without a further good-bye, he pulls away, bounding out into a sea of darkness, heading toward the *Eagle's Nest, his unknown destiny.*

But Ailene's thoughts are different. She can only stand looking out into the cold night air, wondering about the time they first met and his dream of-Shangri-La, somewhere high over the mountaintop, far, far away. And she wonders if he's right, maybe this is his

Arthur (Mac) Mc Caffry

long-sought-after place called Shangri-La, just over the mountaintop, waiting.

Jonathon moves beside Ailene, hoping to change his mind.

"But you're a fool, Mike…it's not worth it! Listen to me, come back, please…please come back. Ailene and I need you. God needs you. Please, Mike, please come back," Jonathon is shouting, sending vibrations over the mountaintop.

Mike stops abruptly. It's pitch-dark…hard to breathe. He looks back where they last stood, close to him.

"Someday, yes, maybe someday, they'll understand," he mutters, to himself, satisfied.

And he moves inside where only minutes ago, revelry and celebration ran rampant, hundreds shouting blasphemy toward God. Slowly, he moves, picking his way forward, searching for what's left of the once-large glamorous mountain of stone. And suddenly, the scene is visible.

Onward, he moves, heading to where he watched celebrants chanting their insults toward his Savior as one of the lowest of the lowest! Closer and closer, and finally he's looking down upon the scene where revelry ran highest, but now it's different! It's unbelievably different! He hears people groaning and moaning far down below! And he moves even closer, stopping at the edge of the massive structure. And he's peering down into a dark bottomless pit filled with nothing but human anguish, nothing but horror. Unbelievable but true!

Eyes…human eyes! Thousands of eyes gaze upward through a sea of darkness, moving in circles gazing toward heaven. He hears their moaning, their groaning, begging forgiveness, but useless. He wants to move away, but can't. And it's horrible even

God Help Us

to think of, but true! It's a picture of what the Bible said it would be, hell in all its darkness!

And looking down into the bottomless pit, he begins asking himself the question that bothers him most, "But why, Lord, why did this all happen? But why me, oh Lord, why me of all people? Please, please, Lord, why am I here on this barren mountaintop looking down into this bottomless pit with thousands of eyes staring up at me as if I'm guilty of something? Please, Lord, please answer my never-ending question: might this be me without Friend?" he pleads, again and again, over and over.

And someone taps his shoulder, sending him reeling. Friend, his guardian angel, stands beside him smiling, looking pleased.

A slight twist of his head and sparkling eyes are fixed upon his. And Mike can sense his time has come, someone with authority stands over him, someone with an answer.

But he's afraid to speak. He can only look upon him breathlessly waiting, praying for the thing he's been searching for forever!

Friend reaches out grasping his hand, bringing him alive again. And he doesn't wait, he squeezes his hand, bringing him to attention!

"And the answer to your question is yes, Mike! You would be among the unforgiven without His forgiveness!" he's shouting loud and clear, his words bounding over the mountaintop, causing animals down below to scatter, running frightened, wailing.

Mike is speechless! Friend reads his mind as always.

"But, Friend…Friend…I don't—"

"Mike! Stop! Stop and listen," he says, moving against him.

Again Mike is lost, afraid as never before, listening.

"Listen to what, Friend?"

"Your prayer, Mike...it's answered! Your prayer is answered!"

"You mean..."

"Yes, Mike, the one He taught you: the Lord's Prayer. Say the words, Mike...say the words!" Friend shouts, over and over, excited.

And standing close to him, high upon the mountaintop, Mike begins reciting His words loudly, "Our Father who art in heaven, hallowed be thy name. Thy kingdom come, thy will be done, in earth, as it is in heaven. Give us this day our daily bread. And—"

Quickly, Friend reaches out, stopping him!

"Wait, Mike! Wait!" he shouts again, causing Mike's knees to buckle, trembling.

"But...why?" he asks, frightened.

And a broad smile crosses his face, a heavenly beautiful face, Mike has never seen before.

"It's time for you to think, Mike, read the next part, the part you've been searching for. And when you're finished reading, read it again. Read it till you know the meaning, something only you and Him will understand, Mike!"

And slowly, he begins reading again. "And forgive us our debts, as we forgive our debtors," he finally is able to mutter.

Friend reaches out, grabbing his hand, pulling him next to him. "Now tell me the words again! Words for you alone, Mike. Think back to thirty years ago, Mike..."

And again, tears begin to show, his face fills with remorse.

"Please, Lord...please forgive me! Yes! Yes! I forgive them! My heart bleeds for them, it never goes away."

"And the rest of it, Mike."

Again, he looks up at him, pitiful-like.

"Oh yes, I'm hoping that somehow, some way, He forgives me, the one who hated them, the one who wouldn't forgive them," he says, pitifully pleading.

Suddenly, the necklace around his neck moves in circles. And it's the most wonderful feeling ever, a feeling of blessed assurance, soothing his worried mind. He falls to his knees, lying upon the cold ground, looking up to heaven.

And for the first time in thirty long years, he feels something different, loved again, a sense of holiness. And he thinks of words Friend once told him: "The Lord's mercy and love look over His Chosen."

Slowly, he rises to stand, but can't, hurting from the cold night air. Another attempt and he rises from the ground, looking down into the bottomless pit. He hears the pleading, the crying, never-ending begging forgiveness. And he begins to wonder if maybe they view heaven—where saints and loved ones dwell with Christ sitting next to his Father. And the very thought sends chills vibrating throughout his body.

And he's humbled, opening his arms looking up toward heaven, shouting with a mighty voice, *"I thank you, Jesus. Oh, how I thank you, my great and wonderful Savior, how I thank you! This could have been me, but you sent Friend, your messenger, to save someone like me, a sinner, the worst of the worst. Thank you, Jesus! Thank you,"* he repeats over and over till satisfied.

He rises from the cold ground, looking out where once a mountaintop filled with evil reigned throughout the cold dark night. And he turns, gazing out into empty space gathering his thoughts. It's frightening to even think about, and he begins running all out, back toward friends waiting. And again, he stops, pondering his past and his future. He has looked into the bowels of hell, found the answer to his long-sought question. And only through the grace of God, he has survived a place in hell, reserved a place in heaven!

28

Decision Time

Therefore being justified by faith, we have peace
with God through our Lord Jesus Christ.

—Romans 5:1

Jonathon and Ailene stand shivering in the cold night air atop of what's left of the once-great mountaintop. It's decision time, and they're trying to hold on desperately. Wait for Mike or depart immediately becomes the question, a matter of life or death between the two of them! Jonathon is worried, and it's showing.

Jonathon stands looking down toward the cold barren ground, imagining, thinking.

"I can't leave him, Ailene. I just can't! I couldn't live with myself leaving him here alone. Let's stay a while longer. He's worth it no matter how bad the situation is or becomes. I just can't do it!"

Standing beside him cold and tired, she barely mutters, "You're a wonderful guy, Jonathon…a lifesaver for all of us. I was hoping, praying, you would come to your decision. I agree with you, he's worth it. No matter how his crazy mind seems to work overtime! I know…oh yes, how I know! Mike gets a little out of control sometimes without known reason, but maybe… just maybe, there's things we know nothing about."

Jonathon senses her feelings immediately. He reaches out, grabbing her hand, pulling her close. "And you know something, Ailene..."

"Know what?"

"I believe you're actually falling for the guy," he says, chuckling.

She wants to shout back at him, no, no, a thousand times no, but she can't.

"Sure, I'm in love with him, tell him I said this...I'll be kicking your butt all the way back to Berlin."

Jonathon flashes his light down to his wristwatch, ten minutes past midnight, time to depart has come and gone. But he doesn't want to think of leaving Mike behind. And again, it's decision time, time to live or die on this barren mountaintop.

From far in the distance, someone is yelling at the top of his voice, the one and only...it has to be!

And suddenly, from out from the darkness, a form appears. Mike Cutler, the crazy one...he's back with them.

Ailene can't wait! She's running all out toward him, shouting without stopping, "Mike darling! Mike darling! Thank God you're safe...it's a miracle!" And a moment later, she's hugging and kissing him, over and over till Jonathon appears, standing beside them.

But again, things begin to change; her warm, loving attitude is no more, it changes dramatically! She's like the old Ailene, tough as nails, back at the Star Newspaper, spouting orders. She remembers him running away, and it sends her into a wild shouting savage rage as usual.

"You insane good-for-nothing stupid Irish idiot, what has happened to you? Have you lost your mind again?" she's yelling up in his face, uncontrollable.

But as quickly as she began berating him, she suddenly stops, gazing up into his tired weary-looking eyes.

He pulls her tightly against him. She shivers, shaking from the cold. His lips touch hers, she's warm, she's pleased...all resistance ceases. Anger turns to desire, love turns to passion, and in a single moment of time on a cold, godforsaken mountaintop, they're together again, in love, happy. He holds her close, whispering words of tenderness, while a tear moves slowly down her beautiful loving face.

"I believe you love me, don't you, darling?" Mike whispers.

And like the old Ailene, she pulls herself away, pretending to be angry.

"That'll be the day, sonny boy. Never in my wildest dreams could I fall for a crazy Irish imbecile like you, never in a million years," she mutters, hoping Jonathon doesn't hear.

Jonathon stands to the side, listening and waiting, though the mountaintop temperature heads downward fast. Again, he glances at his watch, time to make decisions...it's action time.

"Bundle up and get ready to move out. With luck, the weather could change, allowing us to move faster. Right now, we'll move down the backside, hoping and praying that Golden doesn't take off without us."

But Mike isn't worried whatever; he places his hand upon Jonathon's shoulder, and with the other hand, he touches the cross. And smiling ever so happy, he says, "But, Jonathon, we're going home, my friend, the Lord our Savior...He's in charge; forget your worry!"

Jonathon turns, looking out into the darkness, wondering, *But why so sure, why so pleased?* Asking himself, *Is this the same guy Nate worries about?*

Arthur (Mac) Mc Caffry

The journey is rough from the start. A heavy splattering rain falls without end, causing treacherous footing. Every curve, every stone and tree has been moved, but Jonathon knows his business. Struggling, winding moves and the sky begins to clear, bringing hope.

And it happens! The unbelievable wonderful thing of things happens!

An amazingly beautiful moon shines over the mountainside, displaying everything below. They're thrilled, moving full steam ahead till they're standing on solid ground where earth becomes level.

Far off in the distance, they hear the undeniable sound of chopper blades warming for take-off. And Jonathon doesn't hesitate; he's heading for the chopper running full out. His arms spread full out, stumbling again and again, getting up and beginning again. And before him, he can see Golden sitting inside the chopper, waiting, observing his every step closer.

Chopper blades cease their swirling and Jonathon stops, looking around, finding his bearing. His eyes strain, viewing hundreds, dead and injured bodies, scattered over and throughout the base of the mountain. He looks upward, viewing birds of prey circling, sensing the scent of blood far down below. And from the forest, animals run wildly devouring human remains, reminding him of something he read in scripture: a place yet to be, but not far away, Armageddon, on the plains of Megiddo.

> Thou shalt fall upon the mountains of Israel, thou, and all thy bands, and the people that is with thee: I will give thee to the ravenous birds of every sort, and to the beasts of the field to be devoured. (Ezekiel 39:4)

God Help Us

And through the misty haze two figures emerge out from nowhere, ragged and dirty.

Jonathon is shouting, his arms flailing upward. "Over here! Over here, hurry," he shouts over and over, watching them clasping hands, running in a full fit of joy headed toward him.

Golden can stand the excitement no longer. She moves down from the chopper, running toward them, gathering them beside her. Her voice is broken, her words unmistakable.

She's excited as never, standing before them gasping, barely breathing. She pulls them close, explaining breathlessly, "I was about to leave, time had run out. But something happened!"

And they gaze at her stone face, wondering. "And what happened, Golden?" Ailene is finally able to mutter.

"Someone spoke to me, telling me, 'Wait! Wait!' He was saying! And I knew without doubt from where it came from!"

"You mean…"

And she reaches out, placing her hand upon her lips, stopping her.

"It was Him, Ailene! It had to be, Him!"

It's time to move away from this nightmare of hell. Golden turns, glancing back from her pilot's seat, seeing Mike's arms engulfing Ailene. And she's smiling, beginning to realize the mission is over!

Chopper blades roar; they're off into the wind. They're tired, exhausted, but looking ahead.

Mike sits silent, gazing up toward heaven, remembering how this all began. He thinks of Nam, the church that turned him away, the hatred he bore for them. It's over, finally, it's over! Peace, wonderful peace, love as never before, for their God only! *He thinks of himself before and after, risen up from the pits of hell to celebrate the Lord in all his glory.*

His thoughts ramble again and again, thinking of a song his grandmother would sing just before bedtime. And silently, he begins to hum the words Grandmaw taught him early in childhood.

"Jesus loves me yes I know, for the Bible tells me so, yes, Jesus loves me…yes, Jesus loves me…"

He drops his head, thinking back, wanting to cry. But it's over, he's happy again. And looking upward, he holds the chain, kissing the cross. His head bows low, commencing a prayer.

"Thank you, Lord. Thank you, Friend, it's over, finally it's over! Never again! Oh, Lord, never again! I look up into your heavens, gaze upon your mighty wonders, and I'm free! Saved forever! But only by the grace of God: my Lord and Savior."

29

Looking Ahead

Therefore be ye also ready; for the in such an hour
as ye think not the Son of Man cometh.

—Matthew 24:44

Election Day in America has come and gone. Weeks have passed and Mike hasn't heard from Doug or Martha. He's enjoying the company of Ailene; love is in the air.

He lays sprawled out on the couch at home, drifting off to a well-needed sleep. The phone rings in the middle of the night, causing some quick apprehension. Mike listens to a familiar voice; it's Doug, speaking excitedly at the very beginning.

"It's great to talk to you, Mike. I've some things to inform you about and little time to do it. Just pull up a chair and prepare to listen."

"I've been worried about you Doug, been wondering what's going on with you."

"There's a lot going on, Mike! Things are moving fast all over the world. People who never worried before are coming awake, beginning to realize life is changing for the worst…it's frightening, Mike! Are you with me?" he asks, excitedly.

"Maybe I'm ahead of you, Doug!" a sleepy voice mumbles.

"Good! I have some information you might be interested knowing about, only between the two of us…you understand!"

"I understand, but are you going to Africa?"

"I'm not sure. But I'm heading for the Middle East definitely. The place is on fire, burning from one end to the other. First it was Egypt, Libya, and Somalia. Now it's all over Syria, Iraq, Lebanon, Jordan, Yemen, and the United Arab Emirates! It's spreading like wild fire, Mike, there's nobody to stop it!"

"It makes you think about the Bible, doesn't it, Doug."

"You mean wars and rumors of wars?'

"I do! I'll quote it to you. 'For nation shall rise against nation, and kingdom against kingdom: and there shall be earthquakes in diverse places, and there shall be famines and troubles; these are the beginning of sorrows' (Mark 13:8)."

"I've seen it coming, Doug. And the sad part is, Christians are in the middle of it, hunted like animals. Seems like everyone's holding their breath waiting for something big to happen, praying it doesn't."

"I don't know the answer, Mike, nobody does. Countries we never worried about are suddenly important! But the scary part is…"

"Scary part is what, Doug?"

"It's all part of biblical prophecy, Mike, something everyone should worry about!"

"It is, Doug…it definitely is. But what else is going on?"

"I've been assigned as an aide to retired General Nathaniel P. Roberts, a former member of the 101st Airborne, US Army. He's in charge of our five-person think tank commission along with others from different cultures, different countries. And from what I've heard about Roberts, it could end up becoming a little messy…maybe before we get started."

And Mike is fully awakened, shaking his head, wondering if it will ever stop. Roberts, Doug's new boss, is none other than Nate, his worst nemesis ever!

"What do you know about Roberts, Doug?" he asks, innocently.

"I haven't met him yet, but I understand he's one of those guys who tells it like it is—no matter who it is. My part is complicated, a little more than complicated!"

Mike sits straight up. "Tell me about it."

"Some people describe our mission as the mission of all missions. We want to set the stage for peace talks, Jews and Arabs living side by side…in and around Jerusalem."

"But where at around Jerusalem?"

"Historical places like the Dome of the Rock, the Temple Mount, the Wailing Wall. It's big time, Mike, places with religious history going way back."

"How far back would you guess, Mike?" he asks, waiting for a long-drawn-out answer.

But Mike is ready, giving him his favorite quotation, "Only He knows, Doug, could have been about the time He created us."

And Doug takes his time answering. "That's one for you, Mike. I was thinking I gotcha," he says, chuckling.

"But the time element…when are you leaving?"

"I'm not sure…but soon."

"And Martha?"

"She's staying in Washington."

"But she's qualified, why not her?"

Arthur (Mac) Mc Caffry

"She's qualified for sure, Mike! But we need her, she's more valuable for our own use. She knows what's going on here at home. But there could be another reason she wasn't included."

"Another reason?"

"Think again, Mike you know she's outspoken, always ready to give her opinion freely. But again, it could be due to the fact she's an aide to Roberts: they deplore the guy! The word is out he's too harsh dealing with Muslims, makes them feel uncomfortable. There's gonna be about six or seven of the same heading out with us."

Mike pauses, wanting to chuckle but afraid to. "I'm surprised Roberts made it, Doug!"

"Everyone is surprised! He wouldn't be in charge of our group unless Military Intelligence insisted upon it. But there's one thing for sure: the administration isn't happy about it!"

"And what else, Doug?"

"There's suspicion about everyone! I'm talking about people running the government: it's like a game of who's for who and who isn't! It's getting crazy, Mike, and nobody knows what to do about it. And there's something else, Mike—"

"Yes?"

"Suddenly, the State Department has adopted a kinder attitude toward Muslims."

"That's different for sure! We've been friends of Israel forever."

"It's really hard to explain, Mike, but the only straight-out way to say it is the way a Jewish friend of mine told me…"

"And what was that?"

"He looked up at me with tears in his eyes and said, 'America is no longer America!' And when he said those words…it almost made me cry!"

"Just what does it mean, Doug?" Mike asks quickly.

God Help Us

"He shocked me again, Mike. He didn't bother to hesitate. He said, 'Americans are changing partners in the middle of the dance, leaving their best partner ever!' And this time, Mike, I couldn't hold back. I cried without stopping!"

Mike takes his time, pondering his words over and over. "Maybe that's a good way to put it, Doug. He's probably right! Now tell me some more."

A long pause. "Maybe it's time we talk about something we're sure of, Mike…something we don't have to think twice about!"

Mike pauses, troubled! "You're talking Bible…right, Doug."

"All the way. I'll quote it to you. 'And I will bless them that bless thee, and curse him that curseth thee' (Genesis 12:3)," Doug says waiting, letting him think about it.

"Makes you feel sorry for America if we desert them, doesn't it, Doug!"

"It sure does, Mike, it makes you wonder if that's the reason our country isn't mentioned nowhere in the Bible, concerning end-time prophesy."

"They're His chosen and it's never gonna change, Doug. It's time the rest of the world begins to think about it. But what's in your mind for a solution to this never-ending problem?"

And again, he hesitates. "I'm not sure if there is a solution! The biggest hurdle is trying to find a way to keep Jews and Arabs from killing each other!"

"It's biblical history, Doug! It's been that way since Abraham, the father of Ishmael and Isaac: one son went one way, the other son went another!"

"It has to be the reason, Mike. I've studied the subject night and day forever, but I'm still hoping something can be worked out to end it. Maybe an agreement, something like the one presented to the world by President Bush, Prime Minister Rabin, and PLO Chairman Arafat back in 1993."

"The Oslo Accord, I presume?"

"Yes, Mike. You remember how they gathered outside the White House shaking hands, celebrating forever!"

"I'll never forget it. I thought it was a bad idea then, and I still do! It was a lot of work for nothing!"

Doug pauses, thinking. "But some are thinking maybe something more enticing could be offered, something special, like the Oslo 11 Accord in 1995 with a different leader, a different director!"

"Enforced by—"

"Maybe the UN or the European Union, someone powerful. I'm thinking someone with clout, a political leader, a religious leader, coming onto the scene from out of nowhere."

"You mean maybe someone charming, playing dumb, deceiving everyone?"

"Perhaps...but God only knows!"

Mike is suspicious, probing. "But partitioning Jerusalem, Jews would never go for it!"

"The world is aware of it, Mike! But this is a new world. Not the kind of world we know. Something has happened to our world, Mike, hard to put your finger on it!"

Another long pause. "No doubt about it, Doug. Wish I was wrong, but I'm not."

"But there's something different this time, Mike, scary to even think about. The previous American president tried it, the one before him tried it; but for some unknown reason, I've a feeling this just might end up being a treaty both Jews and Palestinians might go for."

God Help Us

And Mike hesitates, suspicious. "Maybe something like a seven-year treaty between Arabs and Jews sharing Jerusalem?"

"As we said before, Mike, God only knows!"

"Tell me some more, Doug. My bell is ringing. I don't wanna stop it!"

"I'll do my best. The Oslo Accord fell apart when the participants began throwing rocks at each other. Today, with some persuasion from the right people, who knows what might happen. It just might end up changing the course of history!"

"But tell me the rest of the story...you know what I'm talking about."

"And I'm beginning to understand your meaning, Mike. If someone could come up with a treaty between Jews and Arabs, side by side in Jerusalem, the greatest treaty ever...no doubt about it!"

"But maybe there's something else, Doug, something else to think about..."

"About what?"

"Think about the orchestrator of the treaty, Doug, he would be the greatest negotiator ever! He would be someone people would follow to hell and back, maybe someone like a god!"

"Especially if they go back to *existing boundaries before the Six-Day War back* in 1967, Mike!"

Mike's head is swirling, trying to keep up. "But hang with me, Doug! You're talking some serious stuff! You're talking about Israel putting their worst enemies in their own backyard with tanks and rockets?"

"I am, Mike! But I can't forget what the book of Revelation tells us about a seven-year treaty being agreed upon just before the Lord's return. And I'm beginning to wonder, wonder about some biblical quotes! You know what I'm talking about!"

| 227 |

"Sure I do! A lot of people are doing the same, Doug!"

"But calm yourself, Mike. Only a magician could sell the Israelis something as dangerous this," Doug says, trying to sooth him.

Mike gets his breath, rubbing his forehead. "But there are other things for Jews to worry about, Doug."

"Tell me what you're thinking."

"Israel is a very small nation, eight million citizens at best. They're surrounded by enemies on every side. They're alone, pleading, but peace isn't coming. Now think about it, Doug, imagine what we would be doing if we were Israelis…"

Doug doesn't hesitate. "Drop dead, brother—forget it! That would be us, Mike!"

Mike gazes up at the clock showing past midnight. He's tired, growing impatient!

"Tell me some good news for a change, Doug…there has to be something we can cheer about."

Again he pauses. "Maybe there is, Mike, I'll tell you something about the Israeli leader."

"Tell me about him."

"He's tough to deal with. He's smart as they come, he knows what he's doing! He represents the Likud Party. But most important, he has a lot of respect from some of our own."

"Our own! And just what does that mean?"

"It means people like you and me, Mike, evangelicals, God-fearing people, hard to convince people!"

And Mike comes alive. "Don't say the word, Doug. It has to be Jacob Behrman."

"He's the man, Mike."

"And Roberts! What's his feeling about all this, Doug?"

Again, he pauses. "We haven't talked privately, but he takes orders like everyone. President Forestall gives orders, we carry them out! It's just that simple, Mike, the way it was meant to be."

Mike pauses. "And where do you begin this journey for peace...or is it a secret?"

"It's no secret, Mike. The first part of the journey is scheduled to leave New York heading for Rome, home of the Vatican! We need the blessing of the new pope, Peter II."

Words are flying, his mind running with it. "Rome's moving up, a hot spot since Peter took over. But after Rome then?" Mike asks.

"Who knows where?"

"Makes you wonder, doesn't it, Doug?"

"It does, Mike. But we're heading for the Middle East for sure! We had our sight on Dubai being the next place after Rome, but things are changing all over, causing some to think differently. But Bali, you can be sure of, why I don't know!"

But Mike isn't satisfied. "Why all Muslim countries, Doug?"

"It's where the trouble is, Mike. It's a dog-eat-dog situation: to hell with the rest of the world to put it plainly!"

"I'll be praying for you, that you can be sure of..."

"I'll need it, Mike. We're in serious trouble! Gloom and doom everywhere...you know what I'm talking about."

"Sure I do! I'll read it to you, Doug."

> So likewise ye, when you see these things come to pass, know ye that the kingdom of God is nigh at hand. (Luke 21:31)

"You're right, Mike. Jesus gave us signs of His coming over 2,000 years ago and still people can't see it."

Arthur (Mac) Mc Caffry

"What are you trying to tell me, Doug?"

"We're coming down to the final countdown, Mike, it's here! The things we talk about are coming true, scary to even think about it! Everyone is choosing sides, the clock is ticking. We're entering into a stage the Bible refers to as the "Time of Sorrows," a time to pray, a time to get ready!"

"I've been thinking the same, but afraid to say it. And what do you hear about Europe?"

"It's the same all over. People are frightened, grabbing their money, searching for a place to hide it!"

"They have good reason to run scared, Doug. There's no place to hide, their money's becoming useless, their confidence shattered!"

Again, Doug hesitates. "But there are other problems, Mike, problems within!"

"Now, what are you talking about?"

"Think back to a guy named Judas, you know the guy who kissed our Lord while sitting at his table, eating, drinking wine."

"I know what you're thinking, believe me I do!"

"Some of our own…they remind me of Judas, they worry me, and I don't know how to stop it! I can't talk about the subject at present, but I wanted you to know the facts before I leave. It's getting crazy, Mike. I'm talking real down and dirty crazy, the kind you never see coming till it hits you!"

"But there has to be a solution, Doug! There has to be!"

Again, he takes his time, searching for an answer. "There's only one solution when you think about it, Mike! It seems impossible to attain, but it's out there, it's always out their waiting!"

"Like what?"

And he stops, getting his breath. "When I was a kid going to church, people got down on their knees at an altar of God *praying* forgiveness! *They called it repentance! And when they finished, they would stand straight up, gaze around, staring at their friends, feeling better!" Doug says, leaving Mike thinking.*

And a smile crosses his face instantly. "But a friend of mine told me another way, Doug."

"Now, it's your turn to straighten this old world out, Mike, tell me about it!"

"I'll be glad to, Doug. This guy I knew…he never took things light, he said things blunt, right to the point! He was my uncle… my Uncle Joe I would call him."

"And?"

"He said, 'You have a choice in life, lad!' And it made me think! I'll never forget his answer."

"Yes, Mike."

"It was plain and simple. He would look up at me with his big old Irish grin and say, 'There's only one way to put it, Mikey boy, it's repent or perish! The king is coming, time to get ready!'"

Doug glances at his watch, remembering his timing. "Thanks for the warning, Mike, you told me the same when I was seven! Call Martha if you wish—at home of course."

30

Help Us, Lord—Help US

Eye hath not seen, nor ear heard, neither have
entered into the heart of man, the things which
God has prepared for them that love him.

—1 Corinthians 2:9

Doug and Roberts stand waiting to board the plane inside Kennedy International Airport. It has been interview after interview, ending with a question: can peace become reality in Jerusalem, dating back to Abraham?

Thousands hold signs, wishing hope in what has been described as the Impossible Dream. Boarding begins, and they're ushered inside with other staff members seated behind them.

Another twenty minutes and the huge A380 Airbus rumbles off the air strip amid roaring applause: destination, Rome! The eternal city of Rome, home of the Vatican!

Inside the giant plane is a crew of twelve and a twenty-member think-tank commission selected by newly elected American president, James R. Forrestal, a political leader, a negotiator!

Think-tank members are proven persons with impeccable records. They've dealt in diplomatic work throughout the world, but never important as this: peace between Jews and Arabs in the holy city of Jerusalem. American delegates are headed by

| 232 |

God Help Us

Nathanial P. Roberts, a disclosed past member of US Military Intelligence, now serving as a retired statesman with impeccable credentials. He's assisted by aide, Doug Cutler, another with ties to the Intelligence Department. Doug is known to be a person with a future, bright as they come.

Everything moves like clockwork, and soon, they're seated ready to move on. Doug sits next to Roberts as the plane settles down to a speed of 623 mph. Across the aisle sit three other members of the delegation: Ann Rabin, a prominent lawyer; Susan Brantley, a well-known medical advisor to members of Congress; and Howard De Plume, a bright young man well-known for handling world financial problems. Roberts' selection of Doug for the journey remains to be known, but already, critics are hearing the name "*Friend,*" praising Doug's ability to lead when things look hopeless.

It's time to relax and Roberts gazes down below, looking into a sea of white clouds. He feels like someone lost in a dream world, a place where war and hatred no longer exist. His mind reflects back to a different time, a different life. He wonders why he finds himself about to enter an era never before known. Most of his career has been spent in the Far East, serving in the army he loves so well. And now he's headed to something on the other side of the world as an *American statesman,* ready to tackle the biggest problem ever: Jews and Arabs living alongside in the holy city of Jerusalem.

Roberts wants to relax: think of tomorrow, draw from the past, knowing this might be the end of his adventurous career. He reaches over, punching Doug at his side, signaling him to look toward the rear, across the aisle behind them.

"Take a look at the older guy reading the book, Doug. Remember the face and don't forget it," he whispers.

Doug glances toward him, turning back, whispering, "Someone important?"

"He's very important! He's Israeli, Joshua Steinberg. I last saw him at the Israeli Embassy in Washington. He never draws attention, but knows what's going on everywhere. Some call him a genius!"

Doug glances at Joshua again, turning back to Roberts. "Can we trust him, sir?"

"We can, a hundred times more than others. In case he makes contact with you or anyone aboard, let me know immediately. He's a member of the Likud Party a friend of Prime Minister Behrman."

"I'll do it, sir."

"Inform the others, Doug, we're a team, it pays to have back-up. But now, time you take a break, get some shut-eye. I'll do the same later," Roberts whispers, turning away satisfied.

It's not long till Doug drifts away in deep sleep, but for Roberts, his thoughts run different. He's busy reminiscing his past, maybe his future. He's wondering what life will be like settling down at his ranch in Montana…if this could be the last trip of his journey.

He gazes down below, his thoughts shifting back to childhood. He remembers how his mother came to him at school during WWII at the ripe old age of seven. And he remembers how she gave him the news with tears streaming down her face, emitting words of sorrow, frightening words he didn't want to hear. "*It's up to you and me, son…your daddy isn't coming home, he was killed at a place called Normandy!*"

He sighs long and hard, continuing in a dream world. He's remembering how she accepted the news as part of life, military life, God and country first, now and forever.

God Help Us

And now he sits with Doug flying high above an ocean of water, asking himself the age-old question: *was it all worth my father's life? That dreadful, horrible day at a place Mom called Normandy?*

From across the aisle, newspeople move closer, gathering information.

His mind wanders again, remembering how he stood by as a young boy holding his mother's hand on a cold winter day at Arlington National Cemetery. Soldiers, sailors, and marines stood at attention near his father's casket, giving him a feeling of family, one of them, the proud, the faithful! He remembers the sound of taps being played as they lowered his father's casket into a grave at the ripe old age of twenty-nine. He remembers tears flowing down his mother's face in a never-ending stream. He remembers the American flag being handed to his mother and how she protected something most precious, holding it tightly against her, listening to her heart pounding. He remembers going to the White House, where his mother accepted the Medal of Honor for his father's action displayed on the field of battle. He remembers his mother's words like only yesterday: "It's called patriotism, Nathaniel, and nothing except serving God is greater." Again, he wonders if his father's life was worth the price he paid, fifty years later in a world of turmoil and trouble.

Several delegates have traveled this road seeking peace before; here today, back again still dreaming! And soon, there's a mingling of personalities and cultures, all hoping and dreaming the same, something Doug calls the Impossible Dream: love the world over, peace never ending!

Time passes quickly, details, subjects to be discussed, people moving back and forth, never ending.

Arthur (Mac) Mc Caffry

A short stop in London and wheels hit the ground landing in Rome. And from the cabin door a flight attendant stands, ready to give an announcement.

"Give your attention please! I wish to express the crew's sincere wishes for you to have a safe and successful mission. Our hopes and prayers go with you."

He stops, getting his breath, continuing, "And I'm pleased to announce a crowd of thousands are here to greet you, wish you well on your journey for peace. Limos stand waiting just outside the concourse, ready to deliver you to Vatican City."

A few standing applauses greeting his announcement and he's ready again.

"But there's more awaiting you at the Vatican! After your blessing by Pope Peter II, you will be ushered to the Library... the most prestigious library ever. There, you will be given the privilege of viewing manuscripts written thousands of years ago, some written by prophets in the Bible. This is a privilege granted by His Holiness, Peter II."

It's noontime at Vatican City! Thousands stand waiting in St. Peter's Square waiting for the appearance of their new heroes, ones headed to the Middle East searching for peace in Jerusalem. Pope Peter and an entourage of bishops and priests sit high upon a platform in St. Peter's Square, waiting to greet them.

The sun shines brightly upon a crowd of the faithful, moving quickly before the pope, waiting. And suddenly, it happens! Peter II raises his hands high up and over their heads, blessing them! And it's deafening, shouts of praise and glory while the crowd stands in the midday sun, clasping their rosaries, sweltering.

They move to the library walking behind an army of well-wishers, police by the hundreds, cameramen and reporters

God Help Us

trailing. And inside the library, things become different, it's silence…deadly silence all over!

Roberts and Doug stand off to the side searching for manuscripts from the Bible. And suddenly, Roberts reaches out, pulling Doug away, looking pale…speechless!

"What's wrong, sir, you look like you've just seen a ghost, speak to me, what's the matter?" he keeps asking.

Roberts moves closer. "You're right, my friend. I have seen a ghost! The guy I just saw walking by heading for the door is someone I know as Anthony De Marco. A couple of years ago, some friends and I were chasing this guy all over the planet."

"Chasing him for what, sir?"

"He was laundering money for the Iranians here at the Vatican Bank during sanctions imposed upon them by our country and the rest of the world in 2007 and 2008. Iran sold the oil on the black market, handing the currency over to De Marco. He would move the money to different currencies, handing it back to the Iranians keeping them going. He's a genius, Doug. He was running the place, making millions, we couldn't touch him!"

And Doug grabs his hand, stopping him. "You couldn't touch him! I don't get it!"

And Roberts can't hold back, chuckling. "He was inside Vatican City, Doug, he was on holy ground. No one travels on holy ground unless they're invited!"

"But the Iranians…"

"Oh yes…the Iranians, they loved him like a brother! He saved them from going under! They're brothers, but only they know it!"

"This is crazy! What's the guy doing here parading around like he owns the place?"

| 237 |

"But why not? He doesn't need to worry, he's been exonerated from everything...given a pass to go anywhere. The best way to say it is—"

Doug interrupts, "Go ahead...tell me!"

Roberts is angry and it's showing. "It's hard for me to say this, Doug, but we can't touch him...no matter what he does. The guy has connections all over the world, and the hell of it is, nobody knows where he came from!" Roberts says, barely whispering, becoming angrier by the moment.

"But, Mr. Roberts..."

Roberts reaches over stopping him, "Let's say no more about this here, Doug, it's far too dangerous! De Marco is a guy to be reckoned with, but you better be sure you know how to do it! This guy could be dangerous...believe me, he could."

"I'm glad you warned me, Mr. Roberts."

Roberts moves closer, barely whispering, "Move back over to the manuscripts...act normal as if we're enjoying the moment. We can't just stand her gawking at him, lad."

"I understand, believe me, I do!"

Moments later, librarians stand beside them, explaining. And two hours later, they've only looked upon a couple of the priceless manuscripts, still wondering about De Marco, his business.

Dining at a nearby restaurant two hours later is pleasant, but not what Roberts planned for. He motions Doug to follow outside, take a walk, see the sights around St. Peter's Square.

They walk slowly, over and around the square, till Roberts pulls him to the side, ready for business.

"I haven't the slightest idea what we're about to get into, Doug! We've only began and I can feel something different... not natural. When I see someone like De Marco hanging around, my blood runs cold!"

God Help Us

"What are you talking about, tell me the story!"

"It frightens me to think about it, Doug, but there has to be a leader among this group somewhere, a takeover guy or gal, there has to be!"

"Maybe, it's better that way till you take over!" he says, grinning.

"That'll be the day! I can already tell I'm not loved by the ones sitting behind me. They only look at me when they have to."

"But you do have all the newspeople watching you. They're about to go crazy, waiting for something to happen with you in the middle of it."

"Let's get serious, Doug! When I see someone like De Marco appearing from out of nowhere, it's scary...believe me, Doug... it's scary!"

Doug gazes far out, seeing Joshua sitting upon a bench reading his Bible.

"This may sound like treason, sir, but my honest belief is..."

Roberts waits patiently. "Is what, lad? Spill it out before I grab you by the neck, choking it out of you!"

He gets his breath, exhaling deeply. "I believe we're being betrayed within our own government, sir."

Roberts hesitates, looking him over again. "Now you can tell me the rest of it. Let it all hang out!"

Doug's head drops even lower, looking miserable. He's thinking, never ever before...something like this...with a guy like Roberts!

"I don't know what has happened to America. It's like we're a different nation without a goal, lost, wandering in the wilderness! I'm convinced the American people have been deceived by our very own! Believe me, Mr. Roberts, never in my lifetime would I say such words, but facts don't lie, sir, they just don't lie!"

Roberts watches him, struggling. "Something else you would like to say, Doug?"

"Only this, sir...Martha agrees with me! She's in the middle of this mess every day. She hears conversations from the highest, the lowest—it's frightening!"

Roberts lowers his head, turning away and back again. "You've got a lot of nerve to tell me this, Doug, but the sad part is..."

"Is what, Mr. Roberts?'

He looks up at Doug, staring hard into his eyes. "Believe it or not, Doug, I believe you!" he says, surprisingly.

"I'm glad you believe me, I thought I might have to convince you."

Roberts places his hand upon his shoulder, surprising him. "I believe you because there is a problem we need to deal with, lad. Facts are facts, never dismiss them!"

"And the problem is what?"

Again, he pauses. "I've suspected a lot of people for some time, some close to me...very close to me! I too, have learned some things, things that make me miserable to even think about!" Roberts says, barely able to say the words.

"Like what?"

Roberts doesn't hesitate. "Our every move has been monitored since we began this trip to nowhere, the bad part is it's being done by some of our own people!"

Doug looks up at him, barely muttering, "I've never thought differently, sir."

Roberts watches him, seeming to be helpless, seeing the strain he's in, feeling his pain.

"Need some help, Doug?" Roberts asks nonchalantly.

He sighs, pausing briefly. "Nothing I can't handle. But I could use some assurance, in case everything fails."

And Roberts's face brightens immediately. "But there's always something we can depend upon, Doug. Walk with me where nobody can listen. When I give you my nod, we'll repeat the *Twenty-Third Psalm*."

"You mean about right now?"

"Why not? This is as good a place as any. It makes me feel like David with a slingshot facing Goliath!"

They head toward an open area in the concourse, reciting the words, taking every word seriously.

> *The Lord is my shepherd; I shall not want. He maketh me to lie down in green pastures; he leadeth me beside the still waters. He restoreth my soul: he leadeth me in the path of righteousness for his name's sake. Yea, though I walk through the valley of the shadow of death, I will fear no evil: for thou art with me; thy rod and thy staff they comfort me. Thou preparest a table before me in the presence of mine enemies: thou anointest my head with oil; my cup runneth over. Surely goodness and mercy shall follow me all the days of my life: and I will dwell in the house of the Lord forever.*

It's finished, and again, Roberts places his hand upon Doug's shoulder. "Did it help, Doug?"

"It did, sir…it really did! David was always at his best, talking to the Lord."

31

A Stranger from Nowhere

He shall magnify himself in his heart,
and by peace shall destroy many.

—Daniel 8:25

Daylight comes and everyone is loaded aboard the giant airbus, ready to visit the golden city of Dubai, a city part of the United Arab Emirates. A loud sound of motors revving up and they're on their way across an ocean of water toward a land of sand; a land where once Nomadic tribesmen traveled on camels, searching for food, water, and shelter.

A film displays the wonders of this great and wonderful city while the audience sits, marveling in awe, its beauty, its wealth unbelievable. The film shows a city with condos rising high up in the heavens, built upon sand, while Doug and Roberts sit among them, remembering a song they once heard in church, "On Shifting Sand," beginning to wonder.

At the front of the plane, a tall dark-haired gentleman emerges from the cabin, dressed in a dark blue suit standing before them. His long dark hair and piercing eyes causes Roberts to freeze; it's Anthony De Marco, the man he searched the world over... forever!

Doug doesn't wait! He reaches out, pulling Roberts closer. "That's him, sir. He's the guy you told me about, it's Anthony De Marco! It has to be him!"

His lips barely move, never facing him. "Quiet, lad...I'm thinking. Give me some time...we'll talk about it later!"

Instantly, all attention moves upon De Marco only, waiting.

He moves closer, spreading his arms before them. "My name is Anthony De Marco! I've been designated as the one to serve as your leader under the authority of the United Nations, the European Union, and the president of the United States of America!"

And quickly, a stirring of onlookers, looking again, wondering, who is he?

He doesn't wait, beginning again, his voice growing stronger by the moment.

"Presently, there is no leader among you. History has proven over and over: without a leader, your mission is helpless. Therefore, I've volunteered my services to become a part of you, someone to lead you, someone to guide you. My knowledge of world affairs has never been greater."

And he stops, looking out, beginning again. "World peace is something near to my heart, my greatest ambition is to see peace and love the world over. We will act as one! We will be joined together with something in common, our love of humanity, no matter who we are!"

And from the Arab delegates, cheers ring out while Joshua sits at the back of the plane, listening, reading his Bible.

And he continues, looking out over them peacefully. "Peace in Jerusalem isn't impossible! But with the right leadership, there's nothing impossible! I've been placed in this position as your leader. I will lead you today, tomorrow...forever!"

And again, cheers ring out from the rear.

"With your help and service joining me, the world is ours, there's nothing impossible!" he's shouting, his voice blooming.

Still, Roberts remains sitting speechless, his head bowing low, waiting.

Doug punches his side, gaining his attention. "What's wrong, sir…tell me what's wrong with you."

"Wait, lad! Wait! This isn't the time, this isn't the place. I told you before…this isn't going to be easy!" he barely whispers, still watching De Marco, waiting.

And without expecting, Susan Brantley from the American delegation raises her hand ready to speak, nodding to De Marco. "Mr. De Marco, please…"

"Yes, Ms. Brantley."

And the audience comes alive, staring at Susan!

"Sir, I'm sure we all agree in our effort for peace, but tell us your background, your knowledge of world affairs, the people we'll be dealing with!"

Again, there's a stirring all over…waiting.

An amazingly beautiful smile. "Your question is well taken, Ms. Brantley. I have served the world over for a lifetime. But I still search for a way to make people happy. Previously, I spent years of faithful service in Vatican City, serving as president of the Vatican Bank. My record is spotless! People I've befriended are thousands, millions, they think of me as one of their own!"

Again, Roberts lowers his head, biting his tongue, holding back his temper waiting, while Doug still waits, expecting an explosion.

Thirty minutes into the trip and the same, question after question to De Marco, always pleasing. His words come easy, his desire to lead them relentless, his drive is perfection!

God Help Us

And suddenly, a slight wave of his hand, he's heading toward the cabin, promising to join them later.

Roberts moves quickly. He motions his delegation to come together. He's worried and they can see it.

"I have no idea what's going on, fellow delegates! I've been this route before, this procedure isn't normal! I knew about this guy back in 2007 and 2008 during the sanctions imposed upon Iran for going ahead with their project developing a nuclear bomb. Myself and two other guys attached to the CIA searched the world over for this guy, never finding him. But I'm warning you now, this guy is dangerous, he isn't normal. He frightens me!" Roberts explains, his voice uncontrolled for the first time ever.

And heads lower, gazing around at other delegates seated, wondering!

Tenseness is showing! And from the back, one of the Arab delegates moves to the front, addressing Roberts.

"Mr. Roberts, I believe we need a break. Some of my friends are worried, we need to talk among us freely."

Roberts reaches out grasping his hand, shaking it. "I believe you're right, sir, let's take a thirty-minute break…get our minds together and begin again."

Without waiting, Roberts brings his delegation together, discussing the situation, while at the middle of the plane, other members gather doing the same, except for Joshua, he still sits at the rear, reading his Bible.

Thirty minutes later, breaktime is over, everyone is seated, waiting for the leader. And bang! The cabin door opens with the Captain and De Marco rushing to the front to address them.

De Marco looks worried, showing stress for the first time. He motions the captain come forward, handing him the microphone. "I believe you need to perform this, Captain, it's hard for me to give the news," he says, sadly.

The captain stands tall, looking out over his delegates gaining their attention, beginning, "My name is Captain Roger Craig. I bring sad news, my American friends! I have just been notified a terrible earthquake has just occurred all along the California coastline extending up into Oregon and southward as far as the Mexican border. Deaths and injuries are unknown at the present time, but there has never been anything like it in America before!"

And he stops, thinking. "And there's something else my friends, I've been instructed to collect all cell phones, computers, cameras…whatever, due to high intensity over the Internet."

Shock sets in immediately, causing Americans to stand gazing upon Captain Craig afraid to ask further.

His head is still lowered. And finally, he opens his teary eyes, beginning again, "I can only tell you what I was informed about minutes ago. I'll leave the rest to your imagination!"

Still none asks, waiting.

"At about seven a.m., an earthquake approximately 8.5 in magnitude struck all along the Pacific coastline, causing terrible loss of life and damage. The center of the earthquake was in the San Francisco area along what is known as the Hayward Fault Line. There is another fault line in the same area called the San Andreas Fault Line, just as dangerous."

And he pauses, wiping his eyes, looking them over again. "This area has long been known for this possibility! The Hayward Fault Line is the same fault line that nearly destroyed the city of San Francisco a couple of hundred years ago."

And from the center of the delegates, someone asks, "And what about tsunamis, sir?"

God Help Us

"There is a possibility tsunamis could be created rolling across the Pacific Ocean, causing damage in Japan or Hawaii. All traffic is shut down except what the government deems necessary. The only good part of all this is the San Francisco Bay Bridge is left standing!"

And heads are lowered, some crying.

American delegate Ann Rabin rises from her seat, standing bravely before the captain, waiting.

"Yes, Ms. Rabin."

"My husband is in the area you described to me. He's there on business. What am I to do, Captain? I love him! I can't leave him alone helpless!"

And it's silence all over, while heads are bowed, waiting.

"I give you my sympathy for sure, Ms. Rabin. But I have already been informed this flight to Dubai is cancelled! We turned this aircraft around minutes ago, heading back to Rome, waiting for someone to decide the future."

And the American delegation sits, waiting to hear something from Roberts, but he only listens, sitting passively beside Doug waiting.

Again, Captain Craig is ready to address the audience further.

"The death toll and injured isn't known. The National Guard is on duty throughout western states expecting trouble: looting, shortages of gasoline, food, clothing...whatever. Things are happening all over America, terrible things...making you wonder..."

Still there's no shouting or screaming, only miserable looking faces throughout, staring downward, some praying.

247

32

Welcome Aboard, Marla

He tends his flock like a shepherd; He gathers the
lambs in his arms and carries them close to his heart.

—Isaiah 40:11

A night of rest in Rome, and early the next morning, they're on their way to Bali, Indonesia, the journey to Dubai cancelled. No comments about the cancellation, most expressing feelings for the journey to be over. There's trouble at home, worry is everywhere.

Roberts doesn't wait, moving next to Doug, whispering, "It's time I brief you on something!"

"I've been waiting for this, Mr. Roberts."

"We're heading for the finals, Doug, settle back and take it easy, time I brief you on a couple of things to look out for in Bali."

"Tell me whatever you know, Mr. Roberts…I'll need it."

"Once we arrive in Bali, things will pick up for sure. De Marco knows this place and everyone in it; he was born here!"

And Doug sits back, wondering why he didn't tell him before. A couple seconds later, he whispers, "Why didn't you tell me earlier? I could have been thinking about it."

Roberts moves against him, "With someone like De Marco sitting close to you, anything can happen. He isn't ordinary, Doug... get ready for it."

"And what else?"

"I wouldn't fool around with the populated areas, stay close to our quarters and be ready for anything. With a guy like De Marco hanging around, pray, lad, pray!"

"I always pray, especially since I met you!"

And Doug hears him barely chuckling, continuing to mutter, "Bali is a highly populated city with about three million people...99 percent Muslim. And for you, a Christian, it wouldn't be healthy."

A bulletin moves across a screen, announcing Ms. Marla De Marco, a twenty-three-year-old young lady has been added to De Marco's staff. Quickly, they glance up where De Marco sits, viewing a nothing but a perfect-looking blond-headed beauty seated beside him.

And moments later, Chairman De Marco moves to the front of the plane, joined by Club of Rome members. A few pats on the back making them welcome, and De Marco pounds his fist hard upon the table, gaining attention.

"I'm sure you're aware this is our one and only destination before heading back to New York because of the earthquake. Once we arrive in New York, I will submit my recommendation for a peace treaty affecting both Jews and Arabs in Palestine and Jerusalem. It is my intention to bring it before the UN General Assembly as soon as possible in order to stop the killing and mayhem throughout the area."

Nothing but silence! A quick look out over his audience, beginning again, "My assistant will pass among you, placing documents before you explaining my recommendation for peace in Jerusalem. For the past couple of years, I've worked endless hours drafting a peace proposal that would be fair and just for both Arabs and Jews living side by side in Jerusalem."

And quickly, American delegate Susan Brantley rises to asks, "Is this something new, Mr. De Marco? I've never heard of a peace treaty drawn up by you!"

De Marco's face turns fiery red, glaring at her ruthlessly.

"No, it isn't new, Ms. Brantley! Your president, the pope, and some members of the UN are aware of it!" he says, causing her to look again at him, wondering!

Roberts punches Doug in the side, grinning. "Thank God for one of ours, she didn't let it pass unnoticed!"

"But, Ms. Brantley, my only desire is to bring peace to a place the world has given up on. It's been tried many times, and I'm aware of it!" he says, frowning, showing displeasure.

And he stops, looking out over his audience seeing them waiting, continuing, "But after days and nights of sleeplessness, I've come up with the answer, something the world has dreamed about—"

And again, Ms. Brantley stands before him, interrupting, "Tell us your secret, Mr. De Marco, the whole world is waiting for something like this, tell us how you're going to save the world and all the people in it!" she says defiantly.

And his mood changes! Suddenly, he's looking down upon her differently; he's pleased, showing his pleasure, continuing. "I've drawn up a treaty to satisfy everyone! It will be a treaty for seven years, moving further into an era of peace and prosperity, Ms. Brantley."

"And then what, Mr. Chairman?" she asks boldly, her eyes never blinking.

A very pleasant smile and he stands, spreading his arms, shouting, "It will be peace forever! The whole world will be as brothers and sisters, Ms. Brantley!"

And his audience sits spellbound, their eyes still glued upon him, loving him.

He stops, motioning his friends from the Club of Rome forward beside him.

"And now, I wish to thank my most trusted and able friends from the Club of Rome. When I began this project a couple of years ago, you alone gave me faith when I most needed it! And for your loyalty, you'll be sitting beside me, guiding the world into a new eternity!"

And quickly, he reaches out pulling them closer beside him, hugging them.

Roberts moves against Doug, whispering, "This will be good, lad, fireworks will begin early…get ready!"

Marla moves from delegate to delegate, placing documents before them. She reaches Roberts, places a document before him, glancing over at Doug without notice. And a single paper falls to the floor unnoticed. She bends low, reaching down to pick it up, waiting for Roberts's signature.

He glances over it without reading; it's huge—126 pages written in English, Arabic, and Hebrew, while Doug sits smiling, waiting calmly.

Roberts doesn't wait! He faces De Marco, shouting, "Mr. Chairman! I have an objection!"

"State your objection, Mr. Roberts. We've a busy schedule ahead, make your objection brief, to the point, Mr. Roberts!" De Marco says contemptuously.

Roberts is at his best, letting his words out, exploding, "I'm about to do just that, Mr. De Marco! As representative of the

United States, I'll state my position plain and clear for the world to see regarding your plan for Jerusalem. You and I both know it's nothing but a charade! Your true purpose is to destroy the nation of Israel! I sincerely hope you understand my position clear, Mr. De Marco!"

De Marco stops, fighting to contain himself. "Proceed as you wish, Mr. Roberts."

Roberts turns, gazing out over his audience, continuing, "Do not consider the United States one of your protégés, Mr. De Marco. Even though, you've made it plain you're a friend of our president, it doesn't make you a friend of the American people!"

De Marco's fist close quickly, clenching his gavel! His eyes show rage, his breathing noticeable.

"We began this trip with the understanding our purpose was to solve problems between Jews and Palestinians. But you, Mr. De Marco, have turned it into a political issue to benefit your ambitions. Many times, I've had to bottle my emotions, listening while you heap praise upon yourself and your Club of Rome brothers! But it's not working, Mr. De Marco, never on Christian Americans!"

And De Marco interrupts, pounding his gavel. His eyes stare down at him delighted, enjoying the moment. And suddenly, he lets it all out, beginning to chuckle.

"I assume you're not happy, is that your problem, Mr. Roberts?" De Marco asks politely.

Roberts' temper erupts again. "Your assumption is correct, Mr. De Marco. I'm mad as hell! And now with your permission, I'll continue."

"Permission granted, Mr. Roberts, again, the floor belongs to you!"

God Help Us

"Now, as far as the United States of America is concerned, your days being chairman of this trip, it's over! America will not give in to your wishes, now or ever, Mr. De Marco!"

And across his audience, a lot of staring, murmuring; while at the center of the crowd, Roberts remains gazing upon De Marco, waiting.

De Marco explodes in all his fury! "Sit, Mr. Roberts, sit! I command you to sit, take your place with other delegates. Further demonstration from you, I'll summon your president to silence you—understand, Mr. Roberts?"

Roberts calmly seats himself while Doug and other American delegates sit collecting their thoughts, wondering.

And moving forward, pretending it never happened, De Marco looks out over his audience differently. He's suddenly the old De Marco, smooth-talking, peaceful-looking person, telling them his favorite words ever; there's a better life to come…hang with me!

"You've made yourself very clear, sir…very clear indeed! You've given us a full display of American diplomacy. And as I've stated to the world before, I'm a man of peace, willing to negotiate with anyone—even Israelis. You simply don't understand the way we negotiate our problems today. You're own president has made this very clear. I will never force myself upon this delegation."

"May I have one minute to reply, sir?" Roberts asks peacefully.

"You have one minute, Mr. Roberts…proceed."

Again, Roberts turns, gazing back and around, seeing only Joshua returning his smile.

"Who has given you power to assume the chairman's seat?"

253

Arthur (Mac) Mc Caffry

"Your president has, Mr. Roberts! Surely, you must be aware of it! There is no opposition to my plan other than Evangelicals and Catholics like you, Mr. Roberts, you're laughable!"

Roberts turns, looking at Doug shaking his head in disbelief. And finally, he sits, contemplating.

De Marco moves forward, showing a different part of him—no longer the loving, caring, forgiving person. Hatred overwhelms his display of piousness.

"My American friend, little do you know whom you have offended this day. Once this Jewish situation is over, things will change as never before. A new millennium of peace and prosperity shall prevail…my power unthinkable!" he shouts, slamming his gavel hard upon the table.

Doug whispers, "Now we see the other side of him…the side we've been waiting to see. Does it cause you to fear him, Mr. Roberts?"

And Roberts begins to laugh up close to his face. "I was born without fear, Doug. You should have been in Nam with your Uncle Mike and I back in the sixties and seventies. Ask him the same question. Give me the pleasure of his answer."

"I doubt it, sir. The word Nam irritates him."

"I understand."

"One more question, sir."

"And?"

"Why does De Marco put you down? He enjoys making you sound ridiculous?"

"It's obvious, lad! He knows I've got something important, something he can't touch. It causes him sleepless nights, frightens him more than all put together!"

"You're losing me again."

God Help Us

"Think again, Doug. We've never doubted Jesus. He alone is the Son of God! It's something he can't live with. It's the one thing he fears most, something he can't destroy."

"But I'm lost again—why only us?"

Roberts looks up at him, expressionless. "It's simple, Doug. *De Marco 'wants to be God'* and we stand in his way! He wants to destroy us, doesn't care how he does it!"

33

Strangers in Paradise

And they four had one likeness: and their appearance and their work were as if a wheel within the middle of a wheel.

—Ezekiel 1:16

Marla moves slowly down the aisle collecting objects. And coming to Doug, she bends low, picking up his phone while Roberts watches a couple teardrops fall unnoticed.

"Find out why the tears, Doug, could be important," Roberts whispers as she remains bending low, hurriedly placing away articles.

"But why do you cry, Marla?" Doug whispers.

Her head is yet bowed, barely mumbling, "Take this…we'll talk later."

She slips him a note moving on, while De Marco's eyes remain glued to Roberts, expecting.

Twenty minutes pass and De Marco again stands at the front about to address his audience.

"My dear friends, there's good news for everyone, especially Americans! I've been in contact with President Forestall and members of the European Union. All the aid necessary needed to heal the wounds in America will be rushed from France immediately. My heart bleeds watching them suffer."

And Roberts whispers to Doug, "When I look at the expression on these people's faces, it's unbelievable, they absolutely love the guy!"

Doug heads for the restroom, pulling the note from Marla from his pocket.

Dear American friends.

My message is short, but urgent. I was born in Los Gatos, California. At the age of two, I was kidnapped near my home and taken to England. Today, I'm twenty-three years of age, and life has been a living hell. While in England, I was with Arabic-speaking people till the age of six. Later, I was sent to Dubai as a servant to a very wealthy Saudi sheik, Omar Khatami. He's a friend of De Marco with unimaginable wealth. He has many women from different parts of the world serving his needs— whatever. And he truly believes it's his given right by Allah to use them as slaves. Many come from Russia, Indonesia, France, England, and Italy. Most live without hope, doing anything to please him. I ask Russian girls if they want to go home, and they answer the same, "Why would anyone wish going back to Russia to live in poverty?" But I'm different! I'm still an American and want to return home to California and see my mother. I've prayed to God without end, but still no answer. But if you are the answer to my prayers, help me, I beg of you... please help me.

Your fellow American,
Marla

Doug reads the note twice in the restroom before tearing it to bits, flushing it down the toilet, returning to join Roberts.

"How's everything going, Doug?" Roberts asks, nonchalantly.

And without warning, the plane rolls from side to side! Panic takes over! Shouting and screaming throughout while passengers scramble, searching for oxygen masks. And from overhead storage bins, luggage comes plummeting downward.

Moments later the plane levels again, under control. And from the cockpit, the door slams open wide; the pilot is standing alone, gazing in shock. He's covering his eyes, crying as a baby till De Marco's aides rush to his side, grabbing him violently, shouting and cursing.

And in seconds, De Marco is standing before him furious, shouting obscenities.

"Explain, you idiot! What happened?"

A pitiful look upward facing De Marco and the pilot's fear begins to subside.

"It's them, sir—the ones we talked about," he mutters, with a slow, shaking voice.

"Who are you talking about, imbecile? Have you lost your mind entirely?" he's shouting angrily.

And the pilot stiffens, staring back at him normally. "The ones you told me about, sir, the same ones I can never see because of their brightness!"

"Shush! Careful what you say, you coward! You mean—"

"Yes, sir! The ones you call cherubims, it's them, sir, I'm positive!"

And De Marco's face turns pale, his body shivers, he's shouting obscenities.

"Get back to your senses, man, explain yourself; tell me what happened!" he says, shoving his fist in his face, causing the pilot to back away frightened!

Doug looks toward the front where other delegates sit motionless, never speaking.

God Help Us

Roberts moves quickly against Doug, whispering, "Look over to the Arabs, did you see the fear upon their faces when they heard the word *cherubim*?"

"They should be afraid, they serve a different master!" Doug says, grinning.

De Marco's arms remain wrapped around the frightened pilot! And again, an outburst of fury.

"Get yourself together, you idiot! Now think, man…think! Tell me what happened. And I'm warning you, never ever again mention the word *cherubim*!"

Sweat shows upon De Marco's forehead as he holds the pilot's arms, pulling him to the side without warning.

"Did you notice the Jew and the Americans? Were they smiling when this happened?"

"I did, sir. They were enjoying the moment, smiling. Others sat watching, afraid to move, speechless!"

And again, his anger runs out of control. He reaches out, pushing the pilot hard against the cabin door.

"I saw you looking at the Americans smiling, do it again… your head will be hanging from the nearest tree when we arrive in Bali. Now, do you understand, pilot?"

And he can barely get his breath, staring, looking up at De Marco, his face frozen, afraid to speak!

But De Marco isn't finished. "What they believe doesn't matter! Continue on with your story, continue till I tell you to stop! I want it all, everything…the whole story," he says, holding the pilot pinned against the cabin door, barely breathing.

And the pilot breathes hard, wanting to speak, shaking with fright.

"I was flying at 621 mph at 60,000 feet when out from nowhere, objects appeared; streaks of light so bright they blinded

Arthur (Mac) Mc Caffry

me. They came without warning, passing me as lightning bolts. They had four eyes, six wings, and color of beryl, it was like nothing ever before, sir, it was unbelievable!"

"Speak lower, you idiot. Can't you see people watching, wanting to hear our conversation?"

"Sorry, sir, I guess I'm still excited," he can barely mutter as De Marco again presses his body hard against the cabin wall.

"Everyone was frightened, sir. I've never seen such unearthly creatures. Their lights were as bright as the sun pulling up next to me, flying a straight path, passing by, again and again. And their speed, sir, faster than the blinking of my eyes!"

"Tell me the rest of it, you idiot! Hurry, man, hurry!"

"Vibrations took over, the plane was shaking, unbelievable but true, sir," he's barely able to mutter

And again De Marco shakes him, banging his head against the wall.

"How many?"

"I don't know. There could have been ten, twenty, or a hundred, all looking the same. I was frightened! My crew was frightened! And I swear to you, sir, it wasn't our imagination!"

Again De Marco shoves him hard against the wall, enraged!

"But a description, any kind of description. Tell me, man! Tell me!"

He's shaken, but takes his time thinking. "But I did notice one thing…something I'll never forget…" he barely can mumble.

And De Marco's temper begins to ease, waiting, excited.

"What was it, man? Let it out! Tell me all of it," he's screaming, while around him, an audience of delegates sit frozen, all but the Americans and Joshua smiling.

God Help Us

"Well, sir, I saw what looked like a bright shining cross, the kind the Christians wear around their neck, displaying it proudly. I swear to you…it looked like blood, real red flowing blood!"

And De Marco's face turns ghostly white! His hands shake, his body trembles. He remembers something from the past, a place called Calvary.

Silence rules the air. "Is that all, is that all you have to offer, pilot?"

And his eyes look upward, pleading, beginning again.

"Inside the cross, sir! Something was different! A wheel…a large wheel! A wheel like I've never seen before. And inside the large wheel, I saw a smaller wheel. And it, too, was beryl, red as fire. It was like blood…red blood…pouring downward from a cross. And I couldn't look at it any longer. I had a feeling, a guilty feeling like never before! I found myself turning away, feeling different! And when I looked again, the cross, it was gone, sir!"

De Marco stands rigid, afraid to move.

"Shut up, you idiot! Say the words to anyone, you're dead!" he barks, shaking his fist at him, threatening.

"But, sir, what does it mean?" he asks, his shaky voice quivering.

"It means the cross, the blood, you idiot! It's all about Him, the Jew, called Jesus; the holy one sent by his father sent to die on a cross at a place called Calvary!"

And he turns, explaining again, "It's the prophecy told by Ezekiel, another worthless Jew! And the thing you call a cross, it's a myth worshiped by fanatical Christians, troublemakers. Now back to your post, you idiot. Call my friends at Mauna Kea Observatory, they'll know what's going on for sure. Hurry, man, hurry," he's shouting.

Arthur (Mac) Mc Caffry

Roberts looks over at Doug, nudging his shoulder. "A penny for your thoughts."

"You know my thoughts better than I do, sir."

"De Marco knows Ezekiel's dream: wheels within wheels better than anyone, except his master!"

"You're right, Doug, but this time, a cross has been added. I've been waiting for something like this all my life, couldn't be happier! It makes me want to stand up and sing to the world."

"What would you be singing?"

And a smile appears. "There's only one way to say it, Doug. 'How Great Thou Art!' It soothes my mind, it soothes my conscience!"

Minutes go by and the pilot appears, facing De Marco puzzled. "This is crazy! Absolutely crazy, sir! Mauna Kea saw absolutely nothing, except a large number of shooting stars heading toward earth. But they did mention increased activity from the volcano above the observatory."

And De Marco is furious again.

"Enough of this foolish nonsense, pilot! There will be no more bad news. Forget about it…understand?"

"I do, sir. No bad news, even if it kills me."

De Marco's eyes stare hard at him. "And for once, you're right, pilot…your head is at stake! Now get back where you belong and never again will you utter the word *cross*."

He turns, looking pale! "Never again, I swear to you, sir."

It's not long till wheels strike the surface in Bali, causing a screeching sound. Doug moves to the window viewing a never-ending sea of people, ready to welcome home their greatest hero ever.

An attendant leads the way to the exit with De Marco beside him. And standing high above his cheering followers, he opens

God Help Us

his arms wide, shouting all out, "What a beautiful wonderful day this is! Home again, among old friends, childhood friends from yesterday!"

And the feeling is mutual, the crowd goes wild shouting his name forever.

Doug whispers to Roberts, "Evidently, these people love the guy, Mr. Roberts. It makes me wonder..."

"Wonder about what, Doug?"

"Why they love the guy so much, Bali, Indonesia...of all places!"

"But evidently, they do love him, Doug. Maybe this is where he got his charm...his magic!"

"Whatever you're thinking, sir...count me in!" Doug whispers.

But Roberts simply smiles, gazing upon De Marco, thinking again.

Marla stands close, returning confiscated computers, cell phones, whatever. She hands Doug his computer with a note attached to the backside. It reads, "Talk to you later—Marla."

He slips the note in his pocket, moving away, unnoticed. And he's thinking, *Maybe it's time we find something more about this lovely person serving De Marco, who wants to go home to America.*

34

Celebration

The Lord knows who are his.

—2 Timothy 2:19

Back home in America, Mike and Brad leave Indianapolis International Airport headed for New York a week ahead of the church delegation. There's places to see, people to talk with, praying together.

Passengers have settled down to rest and Mike is feeling happy again. He sits next to Brad gazing out the window while his thoughts creep back to the past—three years ago, before his new life began. He remembers his attitude, filled with anger, and now he's a free man with love for the church and what it means to him. Peace, wonderful peace he has finally found. And it's time to discuss some things with Brad.

"I've been doing some reminiscing, Brad. And for the first time in many years, I feel good about myself. I guess you could say I made a change, right, partner?"

Brad lays his book down, beginning to laugh. "For a guy like you, it's more like a miracle, Mike."

"And I agree, pal, nothing but a miracle. A couple of years ago when we were about to go under, never did I dream this day might come true."

Brad is surprised. He has been waiting to talk with him about the subject.

"Neither did I, Mike. Today, now that we're back home again, things are looking up. I can speak freely about our financial condition without frightening everyone."

"Really that bad, huh, Brad? Tell me about it."

"There's only one way to describe it, Mike. We were going down for the count, and a miracle happened!"

"What are you talking about, Brad?"

He reaches over, grabs his hand, confronting him. "It was you, Mike. You're our miracle. God intervened in your life, He sent you to us!"

Mike shifts in his seat, a bit uncomfortable. He looks over to Brad, searching for some words, but impossible. A tear drifts downward, giving him courage.

"It could be, Brad. I was at my lowest, but He wasn't finished with me. Sometimes, even today, it's hard for me to believe I was sent to Berchtesgaden."

"I understand, Mike. It's a mystery to everyone—except Him. Even today, people don't know the story, they only know there's a hole in the ground where once Hitler and his friends ruled everything, along with the devil!"

"I'll never forget a remark Ethel said to me when I first came to Morris Avenue Baptist."

"I'd like to hear those words, Mike. Give me the pleasure…"

"She looked up at me with that certain little twinkle in her eyes, and said, 'Quit your worrying, Mike, just trust in the Lord, and He'll provide.' She always wanted to let me know He was there for me and not to worry."

"You mean trust, prayer, and faith?" Brad asks, grinning. "You're a very lucky guy to have met her, Mike, it took a fixer... to fix someone like you!"

And there's no way to stop their laughter.

"I'm aware of it, Brad. She doesn't hedge, right to the point, she's a fixer, if there ever was one. But God alone planned it that way! It had to be! And for some time now, I've wanted to talk to you, you know, some confidential matters."

Brad reaches out, placing his hand upon his shoulder. "And you know I'm here for you, Mike. Our relationship has been wonderful. We've understood each other from the very beginning, but if you're going to tell me about your past, forget it, my friend, it's over."

And suddenly, he sits, looking downward silently. He's searching for words. He doesn't know where to begin. He wants to explain something troubling him, never ending. He wants Brad to listen and understand.

He reaches out, grabbing his hand, getting his attention immediately. "But you don't understand, Brad, believe me you don't. It's not only the thirty wasted years, there's more, honest, there is, Brad. My debt is paid in full, my heart, my soul are finally at peace. But still, I've a yearning, a yearning for something greater, something special. It's something I can't get away from, Brad, never have and never will!"

"Slow down, Mike, take your time. I'm trying to understand what you're telling me!"

Mike begins again slowly. "It's something different, Brad. It's something greater than me, something far beyond my imagination!"

"Why different?"

"I've no idea, but I can't get rid of it. It never leaves me."

God Help Us

Brad is surprised the way Mike talks. He's never before heard him so sincere. This is something between God and him alone; it has to be something only they can decide.

"I hear you, Mike, believe me, I hear you! But this is strictly between you and Him. The only advice I can give you is—"

And Mike can't wait. "Yes, Brad, yes…"

Brad takes his hand, looks deep into his eyes. "God bless you, my friend, do or go wherever He leads you! There's no other way, Mike…remember the story of Jonah and the fish!"

And his face brightens, a smile returns, relieved immediately.

"I knew you would come up with some pleasant words to soothe me. But whatever comes or whatever goes, I'll be waiting, I'll be ready!"

Brad pauses, studying his words, never commenting. He wonders if it has hidden meaning, maybe something like what happened upon Kalkstein Mountain!

"You're losing me, Mike. Are you saying you're not satisfied after your trip to Berchtesgaden?"

Mike hesitates to answer. "It may sound irrational of me, Brad, but there are other things I must know."

"Like what, Mike? You did it all…and then some!"

"Not all, Brad. After my trip to the Eagle's Nest, I felt sure that was the end of it. But there's more, there has to be more. I want to go back, back to the time I loved Him with all my heart and soul. I want to go back before my problem with the church and the hatred I had for them, it's hard to explain without getting down on my knees and asking forgiveness again."

"But it's over, Mike. I've told you this repeatedly, it's time to move on, forget it!"

"I wish I could, but I can't get rid of it. There's something left for me to do—something important. Never forget my dedication, Brad, it was sacred! Friend hasn't forgotten, I'm sure he hasn't," Mike tries to explain.

"But I've got news for you, Mike!"

"Good or bad, Brad?"

"I really don't know. But this I can assure you…"

"Yes…"

"Just rest assured, partner, no matter when, no matter where, Friend will be with you, Mike; he's your guardian angel…with you till the end!"

"You might be right! It's something to look forward to be with Friend again," Mike says, joining his laughter.

"But we're talking seriously, Mike. Whatever He might have in store for you will happen, no matter where, no matter when, it will happen, there's nothing you can do about it. Remember how it was before your mission to Berchtesgaden. You surprised us all, but the world still doesn't know the story. And when it's all finished and over; it's only what He knows that really counts."

Mike is surprised his words are welcoming. Especially words like "That's what really counts."

"Thanks, Brad. Now…time for the rest of the story."

And again, Brad is surprised, left waiting. He's ready for a break, but Mike isn't ready.

"This is hard to explain—truly it is. But for some unknown reason, I feel my time on earth is short. But it really doesn't bother me. I remember how I lay wounded in a rice paddy in Nam…still wanting to kick butts. But I'm different today, my wounds are healed, my hatred gone forever!"

And again, Brad tries to understand, thinking, *Maybe, just maybe, the Lord isn't finished with Mike.*

God Help Us

And now, they sit quietly concentrating till Mike breaks the silence. "'I remember Ethel telling me how life is so short, like a vapor disappearing high up in the sky. She was right, Brad, it's that way for us all of us."

"You mean, here today, gone tomorrow?"

"Maybe. But for the first time in my life, I've no fear of tomorrow! He will be waiting. I've no doubt of it! I look forward to it."

Brad is amazed, but happy. "But you're different, Mike, completely different! Most of us want to hang on forever... whatever. Wish I could feel as you, partner!"

"I've a lot to be thankful for, Brad. I've met you, Ethel, Ailene, Doug, and Martha. I'm the luckiest guy in the world. Who could ask for anything better?"

And again, Brad is upset, hearing his remarks.

"But why do you talk this way, Mike?" he asks. "This isn't you at all. Let's change the subject...forget it!"

And Mike shows his biggest smile ever. "But I can't forget it, Brad...everything is beautiful! And for the first time in thirty-three years, I've no regrets...strange, isn't it?"

And Brad is shocked again. "I wish you wouldn't talk that way, Mike. But I'm envious of you in a loving sort of way."

"You're envious of me! That's a new one! I'll remember that remark till the day I die!" Mike says, chuckling.

And a couple hours later, they stand registering at the hotel in New York. Ahead of them, nothing but a week of pleasure before Doug's arrival.

35

A New Player

And God shall wipe away all tears from their eyes;
and there shall be no more death; neither sorrow.

—Revelation 21:4

It's Sunday morning in Bali, and Doug sits alone in his hotel room, watching news from America concerning the great earthquake. San Francisco lies in ruins, looting runs wild, while citizens live in fear without food and water. Mountainous tidal waves over the Pacific destroy everything in its path.

National Guard units are called in from other parts of the United States; military bases around the world are closed temporarily. Martial law is put into action throughout while churches remain filled to the brim and food and gasoline rationed.

A news bulletin flashes across the television screen, announcing the United Nations Assembly has temporarily cancelled the proposed meeting in New York. A later meeting is planned in Rome at the Vatican.

Doug sits on his bedside, ready to call Martha when there's a slight knock on the door arousing him. Peering through the peephole, he can see Marla's face looking downward, nervously.

He opens the door stepping out into the hallway. She's standing alone, suspiciously glancing back from where she came

God Help Us

from. And quickly, he changes his mind inviting her inside where she cries without stopping.

He seats her at the nearest table where she begins wiping away teardrops. And she comes to her senses, staring up at him pitifully.

She looks up at him, pointing toward the phone, whispering, "The phone, Doug...it's bugged!"

He looks back at her, grinning, "Forget about it, Marla...I took care of it when I arrived here. Now tell me what your problem is and get out of here before someone comes looking for you!"

She looks up at him pleadingly, holding back tears about to roll downward. "I need your help, Doug. I need it more than you can ever imagine!" she's frantically trying to explain.

"Tell me about it. Tell me what's going on and maybe I'll help you. Tell me a lie and you're outta here immediately, my lovely lady."

And she doesn't wait! "I'm desperate with nowhere to turn. Friends, I have none, except maybe you and Roberts, the ones I'm hoping for. You and Roberts alone, you're part of me, you're the good part of me and my problems!" she says boldly, looking into his eyes, never moving.

Doug places his hand over her mouth again. He's worried, wondering crazily.

"What do mean we're part of you?"

And she's surprised. He's not the same person she assumed him to be; he's tough, knows his business well, and isn't afraid to use it.

"I sent you my note, you know the story. I know what's going on between you and Roberts. I'm totally aware you're opposed

Arthur (Mac) Mc Caffry

to De Marco. We're friends…like it or not, Doug. I deplore him, need to get away from him…once and forever!"

And he's thinking hard, afraid to answer! He only stares hard at her, his mind rambling.

"It's nice to know some good news for a change, most everyone else adores him."

"I despise him, Doug, but there's nothing I can do. You're my only hope. I really and truly mean it."

Doug looks her over again. "Tell me some more, Marla, you're getting interesting!"

"Your friendship means everything. It brings me hope when I thought there was no hope. You're my last and only chance to get away, Doug, there's no place to hide," she whispers softly.

Doug stands close to her, thinking about the many times Roberts warned him to never be involved with a woman, no matter how innocent it may seem. He remembers the time he warned him of dirty tricks, set-ups looking innocent, always ending in tragedy!

Again, he looks her over wondering. He watches tears falling like raindrops while she's trying desperately to stop them.

Doug knows this is a situation he shouldn't be a part of, but Marla could become a player, someone they can depend upon. Her pleading for help looks genuine, and he's beginning to think of her as an American. A minute standing next to her seems like a lifetime, his brain runs like a computer.

She whispers, "Please, Doug, I'm American as much the both of you. I can't disguise my feelings to De Marco any longer. He's a beast without a heart! And if I'm not able to get away from him, I'll kill myself and get it over with!"

He brushes a tear from her eye, hoping to console her. She stops crying, but he's not finished with her.

God Help Us

"What's wrong with you, Marla? Think again, girl, think! Do you realize what you're saying, do you know the position we're in? Think about it, girl, you and me, alone in my room at this time of the evening?"

She moves her head trying to answer, but he cuts her off quickly. "This is crazy, unbelievable. How do I know you're not one of De Marco's plants, sent to find out what we're thinking?"

And the crying stops. Her eyes show fear as nothing Doug has seen before. She moves, backing away, speaking in a whisper, "What I tell you is true, hard to believe, but true, Doug. I swear it from the bottom of my heart as a Christian! I'm aware my being here is danger unthinkable, but I've no choice! My entire life has been lived with this kind of existence, a life of shame and misery from the beginning, never a way out for Marla!"

A long moment of thought, another moment of pity. "But explain to me again, why now?"

She lowers her head, finally able to speak, "This is my last chance to get away from De Marco, Doug. He treats me as his slave, I'm afraid to cross him! I can only plead with you from the bottom of my heart, return me to the country and family I love," she whispers, desperation showing.

Doug listens, head lowered thinking, wishing Roberts was present, but he isn't.

"But can you possibly understand the situation Roberts and I will be in if it all goes wrong?"

And she looks up in disbelief. "I'm aware of everything, Doug, believe me I am. I've been with these people my entire life! But when there's no other way out, I'll do most anything to get away from him. It's either help from you or I'm dead…no doubt about it!"

And he's speechless, looking at her pitifully. He believes her, but he's an aide, an aide only. He wants her to understand: Roberts alone makes decisions!

"But understand something, Marla…"

"Yes, Doug…'

"Roberts is the man! He alone makes the decisions. He's rough, he's tough, there's none better! I'm his aide, I do what he tells me. If he believes your story, we're in all the way. But if you're setting us up for something different, you're dead as hell, and so are we! Do you fully understand my message, girl?" he asks, frightening her.

Her body quivers, her voice is broken. "But I do understand, Doug. I've played this game all my life, but never with friends. I read something long ago…today, it's all I can think about."

"Fill me in, Marla."

She hesitates, thinking back. "It was a book I found stuffed way back in a library, a history book, Doug. A person named Patrick Henry…one of our own during the American Revolution. He said some words, meaningful words…words I'll never forget!"

Doug waits, thinking how to respond, but useless.

Again, she looks up at him, pitiful-like. "Patrick said, 'Give me liberty or give me death!' That's me Doug, all the way or nothing to the bittersweet end."

And again, he's surprised, but pleased. He wishes he could say it so well.

"But I must ask you a question, Marla!"

And her head lowers. "Help yourself, Doug. I've nothing left…nothing to lose."

"What does De Marco say about Roberts and me in private? Hold something back, anything between us is over," he says, demanding.

God Help Us

Her body goes limp, tears disappear. "I've heard him tell others you're CIA. He knows your every move, and you're right about the rooms, they're bugged. They listen, recording every word you say. He doesn't like you, Mike, but he hates Roberts more. He tells everyone he despises Roberts so bad, he wishes he could strangle him, shut his mouth forever. There's more, a lot more, I could go on forever!"

Doug sighs, displaying a smile for a change. "That's what I've wanted to hear, Marla. Now we can do business, serious business with Mr. Roberts."

And she begins to relax, relieved! "But understand this, Doug! I don't care if you're KGB or CIA. I just need to get home…I need to live again!"

And again, he looks her over, smiling.

"I know you do, Marla! And you will get home! Just pray that everything you told me is correct. But you'll be checked and double-checked before Roberts makes a move. That's the way he does business, all the way or nothing!"

"And I understand. I know the risks he's taking, but I'll be doing the same. It's all true, Doug, I swear it. But never forget this…"

"And now what, Marla?"

"It's far worse than you could ever imagine. Everything about De Marco is rotten!"

"Nothing about De Marco surprises me."

"But it's true. Just wait till you hear the tapes in their entirety. This is all I ask of you."

Doug pauses briefly, thinking of Roberts and his reaction. "But I warn you again, Marla."

"Warn me about what, Doug?"

| 275 |

"You better be telling the truth. If not, your days on earth are numbered. I'm serious, Marla!"

She only smiles, doesn't move or flinch while he watches her.

"Now one more time, Marla, spill it all out before I talk to Roberts. He's not as nice as I am," Doug says, causing her to shake her head, frowning.

She looks up at him, facing him squarely. "I am telling the truth, Doug, this is all I can tell you."

Quietly, he moves from the room, heading for Roberts's quarters two doors down the hallway. He knocks repeatedly, but no answer. Finally, he gives up, returning to Marla for more questioning. And she's waiting anxiously, something to tell him.

"Roberts isn't available at the present, Marla. Will you be able to continue, or would you prefer waiting for Roberts?" he asks, trying to be pleasant.

She smiles, concentrating.

"Let's get it over with, Doug. Some of the things you need to know are too important for me to be the only one with the information. I'll be okay, now that you know why I'm here."

And calmly, she's talking easy, letting it out.

"Last evening, I was sitting in the lounge next to De Marco's meeting room and the door wasn't fully closed. People were going in and out like a bunch of tourists, and for some reason, nobody paid attention to me. The only reason I could imagine, was because what was going on inside the room, De Marco, was all they wanted to hear!"

"Keep going, Marla."

"Later, I noticed the situation changed!"

And Doug stops her.

"Changed…and how?"

God Help Us

"Numerous persons entered his office, but none were coming out. And naturally, I was curious."

"How many? A rough guess, Marla?"

She pauses, thinking back. "Oh, I'm not so sure, maybe up to a hundred. I wasn't counting. They were laughing, talking loudly, everything seemed pleasant. I could hear every word they spoke and they never dreamed it. I speak five different languages and know most of them by face. Many I met serving the Sheik before he sent me to De Marco."

Doug stops her. "Are you telling me you heard their entire conversation and you're willing to tell the same to my boss?"

"Sure I am, that's why I'm here pleading you help me. I took pictures, recorded conversations, all of it on my recorder. I've got it all, Doug, right here with me. But now, I'm worried!"

"Worried...about what?"

And she stops, looking at him differently!"

"If they have the slightest thought of what I'm into, I don't even wanna think about it! Some of these people are ISIS! The most vicious ever, they're animals, killing who or whatever!"

Doug moves closer, can't wait, never satisfied, wanting more. "Are you saying you've seen De Marco or his people killing people?"

And her emotions are over. She pauses, burying her head, looking downward without answering. "Sure I have! I've seen him kill people many times! I'll never forget the last one, a young British soldier serving in Iraq. De Marco stabbed him with what looked like a writing pen. And in minutes, the young soldier lay on the floor dead, never knew what hit him. That's the way it is, Doug, that's how he plays the game...all or nothing!"

Arthur (Mac) Mc Caffry

Doug bristles with anger, holding back till he can stand it no more. "But why an ordinary soldier? It doesn't make sense, Marla."

And her head lowers again, trying to find the words, hating to explain.

"He refused doing what De Marco wanted him to do, Doug!"

Doug slows his questions, seeing her pain. "What was he asking from the soldier, Marla?"

"Same as usual. He wanted him to sign a statement—a false statement, saying he killed women and children for his pleasure! But that's only part of it…"

An angry moment thinking about it. "Keep going, Marla, tell me the rest of it!"

"I was forced to watch as they cut his tongue out, feeding it to the dogs," she says, intermittingly, her voice broken.

And Doug can only stare at her, shaking his head disgustedly, again looking at her pitiful-like.

"Sorry I had to ask, Marla, it's part of the game we play, things I must be sure of," he says, apologizing.

She looks across the table, fighting back tears. "Don't ever ask me to say this again, Doug. I won't do it, I can't do it!"

And he begins to wonder about Roberts. "But have you thought about the other side…what they might do, Marla, if everything doesn't work out?"

A deep breath, a long sigh. "There's nothing left for me to do, Doug, nothing! But I'll never go with De Marco again, whatever!"

He waits, pausing again. "And the other people, Marla, the visitors…do we know them?"

God Help Us

Doug watches as her body begins to stiffen again. "Sure, you do! Some were from the beginning, delegates, sitting close to you during the trip here. But now it's becoming crowded, all them waiting for his word to move forward. But the ones who really led the crowd were the think-tank commission members from the Club of Rome, De Marco's best, his most ardent followers!"

"Give me names of some of the people present, Marla."

"I know a lot of them but wish I didn't. They're the most dangerous people on the face of the earth. They come from Russia, Iran, China, the Muslim Brotherhood…all over! And there are four or five new ones from Myanmar, but those I didn't know. They flew into Bali this week while others were here getting acquainted."

"And ISIS?"

"Oh yes! ISIS, the most vicious of them, right in the middle of it, enjoying every moment!"

And again, silence, getting her breath.

"I'm frightened, Doug! I'm afraid they'll find out what I'm holding."

Another long pause. "I understand…believe me I do!"

"You and Roberts are my last resort, my only ticket out, Doug. I'll do anything but let them kill me! If worse comes to worse, that's the job I'll hafta do."

Doug keeps digging on and on. "But don't forget this, Marla…"

And again, she looks up at him. pitiful like. asking, "Forget what, Doug?"

"Roberts is one of the nicest guys ever, but if he even suspects you're lying, you'll wish you were never born!"

And she stares hard at him, challenging. "Don't try to frighten me, Doug, it doesn't work! I've wished I was never born a thousand times. Many times I was used by some fat miserable-looking pig from a place l like to call hell. I even tried the suicide route, but thanks only to God, it didn't work!" she says, looking up at him disgustedly.

And Doug looks at her strange, wondering. "Suicide!" he barely mumbles.

She turns her head, displaying marks around her neck. "A rope, how else?" she barely mutters.

And Doug looks at her again, convinced it's the truth, but never an apology.

But Marla isn't finished. "I told you I'm desperate. I've told you how De Marco killed the young soldier. But there are other things, things I'll never forget!"

"Like what?"

"I was in Saudi Arabia with De Marco. He and some of his friends were reading American newspaper articles explaining how terrorists in the United States were read their rights under the American Constitution. They were laughing so hard it made me laugh along with them. It's the truth, Doug," Marla explains in the only way she knows how, sobbing, crying.

"And you! What were you thinking, Marla?"

Suddenly, tears disappear and she's holding her hand over her mouth to keep from laughing.

"What the whole world thinks, Doug? Americans are fools when it comes to justice! In America, they read them their rights and let the lawyers take over. In the Arab world, they stone them to death and let the dogs take over! It's a different kind of justice, Doug, it's the Muslim way of justice!"

He looks at her differently, pausing. "Maybe they're on to something, Marla, it's cheaper for sure! But the cell phone, the pictures, the recorder, all of it, do you have them with you?"

God Help Us

She looks up at him, smiling. "I do have them with me, glad to get rid of them, Doug." Marla says, reaching into her purse, handing them to him.

His mind begins rambling on and on, thinking.

"You've been through a lot, Marla, a lot more than the average person could stand. But understand the seriousness of the situation."

She smiles for the first time. "I understand it all, everything. Doug, tell me what's next?"

Doug sits across from her, thinking, while she sits across from him, wondering.

"This could end up being something far more important than you ever dreamed, Marla. I'm talking international affairs, the whole bag of tricks in one…whatever! Are you ready for it?"

She brushes back her hair, staring at him.

"I've had enough, Doug! I can't stand it no more! You have the evidence before you, and now, it's my time to speak earnestly!"

"Yes, Marla."

"I want you to promise me one thing for sure."

Doug hesitates. "If your story is true, consider it done, Marla!"

"Something else?"

"Yes, there is something else! We need a plan to move what you gave us! Right now, Roberts isn't aware of what we've been planning, he either goes with it or he doesn't. I'll be talking to Roberts about our discussion and I'll get back with you later!"

And she looks up at him for the first time, smiling, asking, "Later…but when, Doug?"

"Before we arrive in New York for sure! Roberts is shrewd as they come and he'll have a plan worked out to protect the material you gave me. And knowing Mr. Roberts as I do, you'll be part of whatever he decides, I'm certain."

And her face begins to glow.

"But there's something else, Doug, something for you to know…"

Again he's surprised. "And?"

"Always remember no matter whatever happens, there's one thing for sure…"

Doug stops her. "But nothing is gonna happen—forget it!"

"But I mean just in case!" You know what I mean…"

"Yes, Marla."

"Always remember, if worse comes to worse and our plan doesn't work…"

"Yes, Marla…"

"No matter the outcome of our venture, win or lose, I'll die happy, knowing we tried!"

And he looks her over again, thinking, *She's good, real good.*

"I hope I haven't missed something, but that's up to Roberts. Do I make myself clear, Marla?"

"Very clear! But there's something else for you to know, Doug."

"Yes."

"Something has happened to me since I met you. I'm beginning to feel like I'm being born again, a life beginning over!"

And he smiles. "Could be, Marla…we Christians do it all the time!" he says, grinning.

She hugs him warmly, kissing him on the cheek. "But I believe it, Doug, I really do. Someone called a missionary stopped to help me a couple of years ago when I was at my lowest. She told me about Jesus, and from that day forward, I believed! I truly believed…and still do!" she says, looking up to him, smiling so pleasantly.

God Help Us

He leads her toward the door, stopping her abruptly. "But there's something else, Marla. Roberts could make a change even at the last moment. Be ready for anything and don't be surprised whatever might happen. And once again, Marla…"

"Yes, Doug…"

"Never panic! It never works out and it isn't worth it."

A soft kiss on his cheek, and quietly, she leaves the room, satisfied.

36

Changing Plans

There is therefore now no condemnation
to them which are in Christ Jesus.

—Romans 8:1

Doug sits alone, pondering how to present the information to his boss. He hopes he approves his action with Marla without his presence, but worries about his decision.

He quits his pondering, heading for Roberts's room once again. He knocks lightly on the door and Roberts appears dressed in a long black robe, inviting him inside.

A couple of moments to get his breath and, "I've something of importance to show you, it's dynamite, Mr. Roberts!"

"Be careful how you speak, Doug. Dynamite can blow up and kill you," he says, chuckling.

"Marla came to my room unexpected, and she began showing me some things that shocked me! I discussed some matters with her, and I'll tell you about it later. I couldn't believe what I was seeing, some of the things she showed me were frightening! We made some plans for the future...all depending upon you making the decisions."

"That's the way I want it, Doug, you made the right move. And as I told you before...we're a team and I'm the leader."

God Help Us

And in moments, they're seated, ready to do business. Doug doesn't wait. He reaches into his briefcase pulling out the recorder and cell phone handing them to Roberts. "Keep these, Roberts, you're gonna need them."

"I'm gonna need them…"

"That's what I said, sir, you keep them 'til we're ready to use them. When we're finished here, you'll understand why, believe me you will!"

Soon, they're at the table across from each other viewing something unthinkable, photos showing Europeans, Arabs, Chinese, and Russian diplomats huddled together with a couple from the Muslim Brotherhood. They're showing American military being blown to pieces by roadside bombs in Afghanistan. And halfway into the showing, Roberts reaches out stopping him.

"Stop where you are, Doug! I can't believe what I'm seeing, look who stands next to De Marco."

"You're referring to whom, sir?"

"None other than the past president of Iran. He's the same guy who stood in the United Nations Assembly in New York blasting our country before the world. The same liar that told the world the Holocaust never took place in Europe during WWII. He's the same devil who wants to wipe Israel off the map. But the most amazing thing is—"

And Doug can't stand the suspense, reaching out, interrupting, "The most amazing thing is what, sir?"

"I'm beginning to believe he doesn't really care for us Americans," he says, covering his mouth to keep from laughing.

"You're right on, sir, it is him! I don't know why, but I never recognized him. Look who stands next to the Chinese delegate.

| 285 |

It's the delegate from Russia, Brutus Zorkov, one of the old communist pals of Brasov. Standing next to him is their Foreign Minister, Victor Mein Hoff!"

"This is hard to believe, Doug. But take a look at the guy standing next to the door near the Chinese delegate."

"Wow! It's Randy Branson, a former member of Congress. I'd recognize him anywhere! He was supposed to be one of the think-tank members selected by De Marco and our president, but for some reason, he was replaced at the last moment."

Roberts begins to grin. "And now we know why, lad, he was more valuable here."

Doug ponders on and on, never speaking till he looks up, moving across from Roberts.

"I don't know why, but suddenly I've got a bad feeling about this situation! Something is telling me they're gathered here to unite forces with De Marco. It's scary, makes you believe something big is in the air or these guys wouldn't be here. All of them, heavy hitters from way back, good at their business."

"Are you referring to—?"

"I am, sir."

"I believe you're right! They're preparing something big! Are you ready for it, lad?'

"Ready as I'll ever be. But do you think we'll get a chance to show this stuff to the right people before someone tries to stop us?"

And he looks up at him, surprised! "There's no limit to what they'll do to stop us, Doug! From this moment forward, remember everything I'm telling you, and you just might be able to live a while longer!"

"You truly believe it, don't you?"

God Help Us

"Sure, I believe it, so should you, lad! Everything in this game is serious, life means nothing to these guys!"

And Doug looks up at him surprised again, apologizing, "I wanted to be sure, sir. What's our next move?"

"I might sound a little blunt at times, Doug, but when you described the things we hold as dynamite, you described it lightly! Right now, most book-makers would probably say, odds are about ten to one against us making it back home safely! This is gonna be a tough job to pull off, lad, but we'll do it, we have to do it!"

"Tell me how, sir?"

"We live with it, lad! This is our job! We play the game the way we like it, not the way they like it! This is our game and our rules! The kind of rules that gets us home safely, now do you understand?" he asks, heatedly.

Doug begins to smile. "As you would say, sir, 'Sure I do—clear as hell!' And for the last time, quit worrying about me! I'm a big boy, Mr. Roberts!"

Roberts stops, looking up at him again, wanting to chuckle, reminds him of himself thirty years ago and then some.

"I'm glad you told me you're a big boy, Doug! The only reason I asked was to make you realize what we're into, who stands with us, who stands against us!"

And he stops, thinking.

"Something wrong, sir?"

And Roberts looks at him differently, worried! "There's a lot wrong, Doug. I'm searching my brain, trying to find out the ones against me! I've a different feeling, a mountain of doubt! Tell me something, Doug…"

"Tell you what, Mr. Roberts?"

| 287 |

Arthur (Mac) Mc Caffry

"Tell me what Marla thinks about all this happening in her backyard!"

And he pauses, thinking again.

"She thinks the same as I do, sir. She's ready to do anything to protect the information, she's positive about everything, and she isn't afraid to do it. She has a lot of guts, afraid of nothing!"

"And her plans are what? Tell me what she's looking for."

"She's waiting for you to make the decision as I am. We're waiting for you to decide."

Roberts stares at him pleased; it's showing.

"I want you to remember something, Doug, something important to think about before this mission is over."

"Like what, sir?"

"Right now, my mind is running like a locomotive without an engineer, heading nowhere. But before we reach Kennedy, I'll have a plan ready for you to go over with Marla. In the meantime, don't ask!"

And he looks up at Roberts, grinning. "I'll be waiting, and I'll be wondering. The rest is up to you, sir."

"Good! Whatever I decide to do between here and Kennedy, we'll do it my way! I'll make the plan, I'll study the strategy. And whatever happens in the meantime before we reach New York, I'll still do the deciding! Understand?"

And Doug grins, getting his message. "I expected no less, sir. I've already told Marla what your decision would be."

Roberts pauses, wondering. "That's good, Doug, that's the way we play the game, the way it has to be!"

"But sometime before we reach New York, I want you to get with Marla and go over everything I decide upon. Whatever you want to tell her beside the plan is your game, make her feel like one of us. She deserves it!"

"She does for sure. She told me things about the scum she had to serve under, made me want to vomit! She's a good person, an American, probably a Christian!"

"What makes you believe she's a Christian, Doug?"

And again, he grins. "I know Christians, Roberts. They have a heart, willing to help somebody! She's that kind of person!"

"I'm beginning to feel the same, Doug. But now's the time we get ready for some more of this crap, we're going big time with this one for sure!"

Doug looks at him, wondering whether to ask, and he does. "Big time! That's a new one! Tell me about it, Mr. Roberts."

Roberts looks up at him, grinning, "It means all the way, lad…all the way! And by the way, I've warned you before about hanging out with guys like me."

"Warned me about what?"

Again, Roberts chuckles. "Well, it just could end up sending your butt to heaven sooner than you might have expected, lad!"

Doug begins to grin. "That doesn't bother me either, sir."

"Now what are you trying to tell me, Doug?" he asks, jokingly.

"I'm covered, Mr. Roberts. The blood of Jesus took care of that about twenty years ago!"

Roberts's face grows serious, looking worried. And Doug senses it immediately.

"Something's wrong, isn't it, sir? I see it in your eyes."

"Sure as hell is, Doug. I just realized we've been had big time! It's time we play the game the way they do, down dirty and nasty! Understand?"

Doug looks at him, puzzled again. "No! I don't understand! We have the proof here with us. It shows to the entire world

De Marco can't be trusted. Surely, you don't worry about its authenticity."

"Not in the least. It's dynamite, Doug!"

"Then why the worried, disgusted look? It's easy for me to recognize your thoughts, good or bad as they might be.

"It's all about this trip to nowhere! This trip is nothing but a sham, but a real good one…I've got to admit!"

"Now what are you talking about? A sham! What are you trying to tell me?"

"De Marco is using this trip to nowhere as a front for his real purpose. He's here to gather his armies together for the big one coming later! This is the time! This is the place! It's exactly why all these people from all over the world are here. They're the big boys coming later, the leadership, the greatest army of all time! If the Seven Year Plan meets approval of both Arabs and Jews, De Marco becomes the best of the best, the greatest hero ever!"

Doug looks at him, shaking his head, interrupting, "Now you're getting to me! Are you thinking the same as I am?"

"Of course I am! This has gotta be him. He has appeared, coming from out of nowhere, using the world as his footstool. We've been had, Doug, in the biggest scam ever! It's time we take a break and get used to it."

Doug is lonely. He wants to call Martha from some place safe. He heads out toward the ocean with only the sound of waves splashing up against the sand. Twenty minutes later, he calls Martha, hearing the voice of someone close to his heart for a change.

God Help Us

"Hello, darling! I miss you more than you'll ever know. I'm lonely, want to be with you, hold you in my arms, never leave you again," he exclaims before she can say a word.

His voice and feeling is mutual. She worries about him constantly, knowing it's impossible to be with him.

And she's overwhelmed! Her heart pounds, filled with anxiety. "When will you be coming home darling?" she's shouting.

"Pretty soon, honey, maybe only a couple more days. Hang with me a few more days and don't worry. But I just wanted to remind you, I miss you terribly...I want to be with you forever!"

"You're on my mind always, sweetheart, night and day... you only!"

And Doug's heart beats faster while she listens forever.

"I've been doing some thinking, all about the two of us. It's bothering me a lot."

"Thinking about what?"

"I've been thinking about how time is so precious, sweetheart, how important it is!"

She interrupts, "And I'm doing the same, Doug. Have you found a solution to the problem? I haven't!"

"Well, I was thinking when this is over, we might take another vacation, maybe a vacation with no end. I'm beginning to think this isn't the kind of life we planned. It's a long story, honey, something to talk about. We'll discuss everything once I'm home with you in my arms forever, doing what's natural!"

And Doug can hear her gasping, him wanting to be with her.

"We will, darling. And I will be in your arms doing what's natural. It's hard being without the one you love, needing him always. I've dreamed of you every night, think about you constantly! And now of all things, some of my friends are beginning to tell me I'm gettin' a little hard to get along with."

Arthur (Mac) Mc Caffry

"It's the same here in Bali, sweetheart! I'm not the most pleasant person around and Roberts is even worse. I'm afraid to talk on my cell phone…they watch everything I say or do. I don't wish to frighten you, but this is one dangerous place, a place to stay away from!"

"When will you be coming home, sweetheart?"

"I'll be in New York Tuesday for sure. Meet me inside the airport near the concourse and be careful who's standing around you. There'll be a huge crowd, so be there early. Do you understand?"

"I do, and I'm glad you let me know. I'll be there before anyone. I've talked to Mike, he and Brad are already in New York. I'll leave tomorrow with the rest of the group from church. Okay with you, darling?"

"Sure it is. I'm anxious to see all of them, a lot to tell Mike. I was thinking of him the other day. From out from nowhere, a song he and a friend used to sing came to my mind, causing me to feel better."

"Tell me the name, darling? I'll sing it for you sometime."

"I'll never forget! 'Everything is Beautiful.' And when I heard the words, I felt it had to be named after you!"

"You say the nicest things, darling. I suppose you know how bad the earthquake has affected us all over America, how people gather outside churches, hoping to get in."

"It's always that way, honey!"

"It's worse than 9/11. People appear on television crying, begging for help and there's no help to give them. It's pitiful, honey, plain pitiful!"

And Doug pauses, thinking about her statement.

God Help Us

"Get used to it, sweetheart. It has been that way since the beginning of time. When people have it all, they follow the flow. In trouble, they head for the churches begging forgiveness, been that way since Adam and Eve in the garden. Gotta move on, sweetheart—see you soon."

"And I'll be waiting, honey, get ready for lots of huggin', lots of kissin'...lots of lovin'...and then some..."

37

A Time to Heal

I have made a covenant with my chosen; I
have sworn unto David my servant.

—Psalm 89:3

Roberts is beginning to feel the strain he's under. He's tired, weary, walking toward small palm trees a short distance from his quarters. He sits glancing out across the scenery, and he stops looking again; his friend, Joshua Bernstein, a member of the Israeli delegation sits close by meditating. He watches him pick up his briefcase, approaching him, looking worried.

"I've been taking a stroll to nowhere, Mr. Roberts, mind if I join you?" he asks, casually.

"Please do, Joshua. I've been hoping to meet with you. There's some unfinished business between us, issues we should talk about."

"There has to be, Mr. Roberts."

"It's important we talk low without drawing attention, Joshua, there's cameras, listening devices everywhere."

"I'm sure there is. You begin and I'll listen, Mr. Roberts."

Roberts looks at him, grinning. "But for the moment, just refer to me as Roberts—okay, Joshua?"

And he looks up at him, smiling. "I was just going to say the same, Roberts...just call me Josh."

God Help Us

"It's a pleasure, Josh, but everything we say or do could mean life or death for a lot of us. I'll speak the truth, expecting the same from you."

"And you'll hear the truth, Roberts. I give you my word in the name of Jehovah," he says, while his bloodshot eyes remain barely open.

"Jehovah is good enough! Consider the same from me. We're off on the same track at this point. Now, let's get started, tell me what's bothering you!"

A deep worried look, desperation showing at its highest, all of it displayed upon a tired rugged face before he speaks.

"I don't know if I'm doing the right thing or not disclosing this information to you, Roberts, but I've no other choice. Night after night, I lie awake imagining the worst, sleep becomes a nightmare. My heart grows weary…no place to turn…no place to rest!"

Roberts listens, seeing him suffering.

"I know your feelings, Josh, hasn't been easy for Doug and me either."

Josh drops his head, looking down to the ground, barely muttering, "But in all the trouble I've ever known, never have I felt so desperate, Roberts. I try to understand what's going on in this crazy world of ours and I wake up finding it useless!"

And he stops.

"Let it out, Josh…all of it!"

"I'm desperate! I've searched the world over, climbed every mountain! I've come to a conclusion."

Roberts grows impatient and it's showing.

"I'm waiting, Josh."

"My conclusion is this, Roberts, you and your group are the only friends Israel has left in the world, but…"

| 295 |

Arthur (Mac) Mc Caffry

"But what?"

And Josh breathes hard and long. "There are times I worry about your president, his ambitions, his actions! It causes me to wonder about things, unbelievable things, like what if America doesn't stand with us?"

"It would be disastrous, Josh! There would be nowhere to turn. I don't want to think about it."

Josh moves closer. "But there are other problems, Roberts!"

"Like what?"

"I've just learned persons in our government want to go along with De Marco and sign the peace treaty immediately."

"And what's your opinion, Josh?" Roberts asks, turning his head, looking away.

"There's only way to put it Roberts: it would be like signing our death warrant, treason, beyond treason!"

Again, Roberts gazes out, looking around, watchful. "Are you saying there's no trust within?"

Josh looks up at him, pitiful-like. "I am saying it, Roberts! There's definitely a problem of trust! If this could keep us from going to war…that's good! But then I ask myself, for how long will peace last, I can't find the answer, causing me to worry."

Roberts doesn't let up. "But there has to be more, Josh, there has to be!"

Again, his head bows low, barely muttering, "It's him, De Marco! He has only been on the scene a short time, but he's got the magic, millions can't get enough of him, standing in line waiting!"

Roberts turns, looking back at him different! He's impressed, urging him on.

"Keep going, Josh."

God Help Us

And he stops, looking at Roberts differently. "I can't, Roberts. I shut it out of mind completely!"

Roberts moves closer. "Tell me some more, Josh!"

"The whole world is in trouble—big trouble! I'm not sure how it's going to end..."

"Go ahead...tell me some more, Josh!" Roberts keeps urging.

And he begins again, barely whispering, "Perhaps I shouldn't say this, but sometimes, I worry where your president fits in the picture, whether he's trustful!"

Roberts turns his head, looking away, barely mumbling, "I can't blame you for your feeling, Josh. I've done the same a hundred times over. But I remind you again—this conversation between the two of us, never was...never happened!"

Josh holds out his hand, joining his. "This was never discussed...never happened, my friend!" he says, squeezing his hand forever.

"But rest assured of something important, my friend..."

"Assured of what?"

"Doug and I are only two, but we stand with you, today... tomorrow..."

And he looks up at Roberts, puzzled.

"But why? Tell me your reason, Roberts?"

He reaches out, placing his hand upon his shoulder, barely muttering,

"Jesus, the Son of God, was a Jew, but he died for millions of others, Gentiles like Doug and I, Josh!"

And his eyes light up. He takes Roberts's hand, looking up, smiling, "I'll sleep well tonight, Roberts! I needed to hear those words from someone like you, a Christian!"

Josh turns away, looking over the scene around him. "But I need your confidence, something important…something you must hear!"

Roberts takes his time answering, "But maybe if it's that important, you shouldn't tell me, Josh."

A worried look shows. "But I've got to trust someone: you and Doug are the only two I can trust!"

Roberts stops! Looking at him, pitiful-like! "But think it over again, Josh, perhaps I shouldn't know!"

And sweat shows upon his forehead instantly.

"I'm talking as serious as it gets, Roberts. I'm talking about peace for the whole world!"

Roberts stands, looking over the scenery surrounding them. "You have my trust, Josh, get with it!"

"I've been informed this very day, if the treaty isn't approved, our forces will take all the necessary action needed to stop Iran from completing their nuclear bomb. Our agents are positive the bomb will be deliverable in two months."

And Roberts's face turns pale, staring at him, asking, "Are you sure about this, Josh?"

"There's no hope left, Roberts! The UN will do nothing to stop it! They're nothing but a joke and everyone knows it!"

Roberts's head drops looking down, feeling hopeless! "With all my heart and soul, Josh…I hope you're wrong this time!"

"I hope the same, but it comes from the top, Roberts. We have no choice but fight back."

Roberts lowers his head, concentrating, feeling his lowest.

"You're right, my friend. But De Marco…where does he fit in? Has he promised his protection?"

God Help Us

And he begins to grin. "Of course, he has, Roberts. But we trust him only so far, after that, we check him again. He tells us his Seven Year Treaty has a covenant as good as the one God gave Abraham."

"And then?"

Josh looks up to him, surprised. "God, we trust! De Marco is someone we worry about!" he says, turning his head away.

Roberts grows tired, but can't stop. "You have reason to worry. But the outcome...the most important part, what's it going to be?" he mumbles, barely heard.

Again, Josh hesitates. "I don't know, my friend. I truly don't know! This is why I'm here with you. I need your input."

Roberts hesitates, afraid to answer. "This is beyond me, far beyond me! But there's a way out of this mess for sure, Josh."

Josh looks at him, hesitating. "Out with it, Roberts! I'm desperate as I'll ever be, tell me man, tell me!"

And a big smile crosses his face while he's shouting, "Pray, man! Pray with all your heart, your soul, your mind...everything!"

And Josh is stunned, wondering why he didn't think of it. Quickly, he turns his head away, laughing.

"Now what's so funny, Josh?"

"Only this, Roberts, you—a *gentile*, telling a Jew like me to pray. Our people were born to pray! But somewhere along the way, we've forgotten how to pray. Thanks, Roberts. Maybe someday, we'll understand one another."

And Roberts looks up at him, grinning. "Happens to the best of us, my friend, but it works!"

"I've wracked my brain till it hurts, ending up with nothing. I'm beginning to think we have no other choice, Roberts."

"Sure you do. Everyone gets a second chance sometime in their life. Stand up and we'll take a little stroll around the palm trees. It's time to think about things, time to clear our minds from all our worries," Roberts says, standing beside him.

Josh looks at him suspiciously. He turns looking at the palm trees, walking side by side with Roberts. And all the time Josh is thinking, *What's next with these gentile friends of mine?*

Ten minutes go by, and they return smiling. "I believe the walk did us some good, Roberts. It made me think about something different!"

"Different...what does *different* mean, my friend?" Roberts asks.

Josh sits next to him, wondering how to tell him, it's hard to explain.

"I've come to the conclusion, De Marco holds all the aces. He's the shrewdest I've ever met. He has promised to restore King Solomon's temple at the Temple Mount. This means everything to our people, every Jew on earth knows it."

Again, Roberts is shocked. He's thinking hard, his brain is rambling. The very mention of a Jewish temple built near the sight of the Temple Mount—impossible! A Jewish ambition for centuries: King Solomon's temple in Jerusalem!

But Roberts finds it hard to believe. "Hold it a moment, Josh! Did I hear you say he has promised you King Solomon's temple would be restored in Jerusalem?"

"He has! Jubilation is going on among my people like never before. Hundreds of years, we've dreamed of this moment and it's finally here! Even the thought of such an event causes our people to rejoice, wanting to get started."

"Unbelievable!" Roberts mutters to himself, shaking his head, doubting.

And Josh looks up at him surprised, seeing a different Roberts, a worried-looking Roberts.

"I know what you must be thinking, Roberts. But my people are willing to agree to almost anything to see the temple restored, it's their dream of a lifetime…becoming reality."

But Roberts is still in shock. He wonders how Jews have fell for his promise so easy. He can't hold back; it's time to tell him.

Roberts takes his time, searching. "His promise means nothing, Josh! Haven't you learned anything from the past?"

"And now what are you talking about, Roberts? His plan is supported by the world."

Roberts wants to laugh, but doesn't. "The UN is a joke, you said it…you know it! It's plain and simple, man, plain and simple! Offering your people to rebuild the temple of Solomon has to be the best bait ever! It's the one thing he knew you would fall for! It's time you wake up, man—get real for once! Quit smelling nothing but roses, and take a look around seeing the real world, man!" Roberts shouts, up in his face.

And Josh is speechless! He didn't expect this from Roberts. He wrings his arms up and around without thinking.

"But, Roberts! Roberts! I don't understand," he says, meekly.

Again, Roberts places his hands upon his shoulder. "It's all about him, Josh, not your people. Jerusalem is where he wants to end up as God. Read the Bible, read the book of Revelation. According to the prophet John's writing, he ends up in Jerusalem, inside the temple pretending to be God! This is going to happen during the last three and a half years of the tribulation! It's all in the Bible, my friend, it's time you read it!" he says, becoming louder and louder, angrier and angrier!

Josh lowers his head and back again, staring at him. "You're sure of this, Roberts?"

"No doubt about it, Josh, you and your people have been taken like the rest of the world has! The Bible tells us God has blinded your people because of your unfaithfulness. It's serious, time you open your eyes, look up, and pray your heart out before it's over!"

Josh is speechless again, barely able to ask. "And then. Roberts...what then?"

Roberts looks down upon him, barely mumbling, "Only one thing to do, my friend, asks His forgiveness. Sometime in life, we all must do it. I have for sure!"

Bam! Roberts' words are tough, right to the core...hurting!

"But are you sure about this, Roberts?" he asks, still not convinced.

"I'm sure! Time you wake up. Read the New Testament! Read Matthew, Luke, and John. It's all about the Antichrist, unfaithfulness, deceit...all of it before the return of Jesus!"

Josh reaches up, holding his head between his hands, afraid to look Roberts in the eye. Tears drip down before he can speak.

"But, Roberts, if I try telling those same words to my brothers, they'll laugh for sure. They don't understand...they'll never understand," he tries to explain.

"I'm glad you mentioned your brothers, Josh. It brings up another question."

"Lead on, my friend, today is your day...your day of glory! Out with it."

He pauses briefly, wanting to make it easy.

"But this isn't my day of glory, Josh, it's my day to make you aware of the danger you're facing! It's hard to say this, but it's time we understand each other before we continue."

Josh's head drops even further; again his face turns pale, pitiful-like. "You can't hurt my feelings, Roberts. I've been

God Help Us

accustomed to live in doubt my entire life, go ahead—out with it!"

"I've always wondered why Jews in America criticize Christians for everything, everything they should be doing! Throughout the Middle East, they call your people the Little Satan, Christians, the Big Satan! You've heard it a thousand times undoubtedly," Roberts says not too happy, hoping he gets his message.

"But you're wrong, Roberts…you're wrong!"

"And why am I wrong?"

"I've heard it ten thousand times, Roberts, and then some!"

And Roberts stops, feeling his pain, wanting to make his point without hurting.

"Christians always have and always will support your people: I'm talking about real Christians, the ones that study your history, knowing you're His Chosen. It's what binds us, Josh, time you find out about it!" Roberts is preaching to Josh, never stopping.

And he stops suddenly, asking, "Are you following me, Josh?"

Surprisingly, he's smiling, different. "I'm ahead of you, Roberts. I thank my Christian brothers wherever!"

Roberts is surprised to hear *Christian brothers*! And he wonders.

"I'm glad you call us brothers, Josh. But there's something else, something that never goes away!"

"Like what?"

"Your fellow Jews in America, their disregard for their mother country, Israel!"

Again, Josh sits with his head bent downward, wondering how to respond. He can't understand why one so friendly can turn so suddenly angry.

He looks up to Roberts, showing his emotions. "You get right to the point, don't care who it hurts, right, Roberts!"

"I was born that way, Josh. I'm not one to beat around the bush just to make you happy! I get to the point...no matter who it hurts! I watch wealthy Jewish millionaires strolling down Wall Street with no regard for the poor, the needy! I see them politically support the ones who hate them most, the ones the Bible calls Pharisees."

Josh can only hang his head, thinking back to a time he knows about, he's read about.

"You're right about many of us, Roberts. But I'm at the end of my rope with no place to turn. I try to explain this to my brothers, but they never listen. I'm tired of preaching to them, no way to change things!" he says, becoming emotional again, lowering his head downward.

And Roberts looks at him, seeing his pain, his unselfishness. His eyes light up, looking pleased.

"But there is a way to change things, Josh! I've a message for you, a wonderful message...something different!"

And Josh looks up at him again, waiting.

"A message, something different, you say," he barely mumbles.

Roberts reaches out, placing his hand upon his shoulder. "Jesus, the Son of God, He loves you, Josh! He paid the price for your sins and mine at a place called Calvary! We're brothers, my Jewish friend, brothers to the bitter end...no matter..."

And again, tears drip downward on a tired, worried face. "But what must I do, Roberts? I'm ashamed, don't know how or where to begin. Help me, show me, please—tell me what I must do," he's pleading.

| 304 |

God Help Us

Roberts reaches out, grasping his hand. "Josh! Josh! Look up, my friend! Do what we all must do! If you truly believe within your heart and soul Jesus is the Son of God, then repeat after me."

And suddenly, he's smiling as never before, looking up, shouting, "With all my heart and soul, I believe Jesus is the Son of God."

And he stops, wiping away tears, looking up to Roberts, asking humbly, "Is that it, my friend…now are you satisfied?"

Roberts shakes his head, stunned again! He has a brother, a Jewish brother in Christ. He turns confronting him.

"That's all it takes, my brother, your faith, your belief in Him, Jesus is *the* Son of God! Questions?"

And Josh doesn't hesitate. "But our Savior, Jesus! When is He coming back, Roberts…when?"

And Roberts can't hold back. "The day or the hour I don't know, Josh, but He's coming! He's just around the corner waiting for your Jewish brothers to come home, my friend!" he says full out, placing his arms around him, hugging him as a long-lost brother!

38

A Time to Pray

For through him we both {Jew and Gentile}
have access by one Spirit unto the Father.

—Ephesians 2:18

A short break and they're gazing around the area once again, observing it all. Suspicion grows, seeing strangers huddling together, causing them to wonder who and why.

"What else do you know about De Marco?" Roberts asks.

"I know one thing for sure…it frightens me to even think about it."

"Tell me about it."

"I know the world supports him while we stand with our back to the wall, our used-to-be friends running like a bunch of scared rabbits."

But Roberts only sits, thinking, while Josh looks out and around, still speaking.

"I ask myself repeatedly, 'What can seven or eight million people do against millions upon millions?' And even the thought of it causes my sweat to turn red, looking like blood!"

And quickly, Roberts shakes his head, disagreeing.

"But you're wrong, Josh! There's always a way out!"

God Help Us

And he looks back at him, puzzled again. "Explain it to me, Roberts. I've wracked my brain forever, searching for an answer."

Roberts moves closer. "But your searching in the wrong place, my friend, the answer you seek isn't here, it's up there waiting!" he says, pointing his finger upward.

And he looks up at him, wondering.

"Explain... Roberts," he barely mumbles.

"Have you forgotten your past? Open your eyes and think back to the Six Day War! Can't your people ever learn that God is watching your every move, standing beside you, waiting? Maybe now you might understand why I'm disgusted!"

And again, a pitiful voice says, "But I don't understand, Roberts, I never understand."

Roberts takes his time, thinking. And finally he pulls him against him, whispering, "It's because it's the way your people think, Josh, you're always leaving Him out, the one who will never forsake you!"

Still, Josh sits, looking blank, contemplating!

"I look at you and I'm pleased. But when I see how your people shun what God has given you, it's hard to understand for someone like me a Christian! You've gotta be the most hard-headed people in the universe without saying," Roberts says disgustedly, turning his head, wanting to say more, but doesn't.

Josh still sits with his head turned, looking away dumbfounded, while Roberts fights his inward thoughts, continuing.

"Think about His covenant with your people! It's unbreakable, Josh! Are you blinded, my friend?" he's shouting. "I'm a Gentile, but I know your history better than you know it!" he says, wringing his hands before him, still hoping.

Josh only looks at him worried, thinking of his past, wanting to explain.

Arthur (Mac) Mc Caffry

"But world political pressure—"

And Roberts can't wait, stopping him quickly.

"I know the position your people are in, but agreeing with De Marco isn't the answer," he's says, tired, wanting to shout it at him, but can't, frustrated.

Josh speaks even lower, sadly looking up to Roberts, pitifully. "But I doubt if you do. Roberts, you'll never know how I feel... you're not a Jew! Some want to strike first and worry about it later. I'm not part of it at present, but may be forced to do so later!"

"Then why the big hurry, Josh?"

He moves even closer, next to him, barely whispering, "De Marco has set back his appearance at the United Nations due to problems in America. But it only adds to his preparedness time, making it even more dangerous!"

"And then what?"

He doesn't hesitate. "In the event his plan is approved at the UN, he'll come looking for us with blood in his eyes, prepared to destroy us! He has the world behind him, what can we do about it?" he mutters, his head still bending.

And Roberts can't wait. "But it's already approved! Haven't you learned this by now? Look around when he's present, see how people adore him! It's time your people get down on your knees and beg forgiveness. Either that...or you're history!"

Again, Josh hangs his head, showing desperation.

"I've no other words to express, Roberts, time is running out, nowhere to turn. We're at the end of the rope...going nowhere!"

Roberts looks at him again, wondering if he will ever understand his message.

"I hear what you're saying, Josh. But still, you're not getting my message. In our Holy Bible, we were warned of him

God Help Us

thousands of years ago by one of your own, a prophet called John. He referred to him as the Antichrist, a world political leader...a man of peace. And another he referred to as the false prophet, a religious leader, both of them appearing at the end-time. I've wanted to tell you this before, but knew you wouldn't accept it. I've studied long and hard, come to a conclusion..."

And Josh reacts quickly, placing his hand against his without notice. "And your conclusion is what, my friend?"

Roberts can't wait, blurting out, "Now that you're a Christian, it's time you understand the Bible our way, the Christian way!"

"The Christian way..."

Roberts takes his time, reaching out, grabbing his hand, squeezing it hard, gaining his attention.

"The Messiah has been here before, Josh! He was crucified upon a cross, and in three days He rose again, ascending into heaven."

Joshua reaches out, stopping him. "But now, Roberts, now!"

Roberts doesn't wait, pleased to hear his question.

"Today, Jesus our Savior, He sits next to his father in heaven waiting to come back again!"

"What's that, Roberts?" Josh can barely mumble.

"You, my friend, and all like you, you're in serious trouble if..."

And Josh's face only shows sadness, asking, "If what, Mr. Roberts?"

Again, Roberts looks at him, pitiful-like.

"If you don't recognize the one you've been waiting for, Jesus, the Son of God, the one who died on the cross for you; you're in serious trouble, my friend, trouble like you and the rest of the world has never seen before!"

Joshua smiles for the first time, looking up to him. "But I believe! I do believe! But it was hard for me, a Jew to recognize him without seeing!"

Roberts looks again at him, still wondering.

"But you can rest assured of one thing certain, Josh!"

"One thing certain, Roberts?"

"Oh yes! Very certain, my friend! Your people will understand someday! But only He knows the hour, the day!"

"But when, Roberts?" he asks, never satisfied, still pleading.

Roberts grows more and more impatient, still trying.

"Now listen closely, I'll tell you again."

"Yes, Roberts…yes…"

"Before the end of the tribulation period, Josh, your people, then they will know! They're eyes will be opened, their sins forgiven, and they will accept Jesus as there Lord and Savior!"

And again, he's lost.

"But when is the tribulation you talk about, Roberts?"

Roberts shakes his head disgustedly, growing weary. "One more time—one final time, Josh…listen carefully! The tribulation period begins after signing a seven-year treaty between Arabs and your people. And then at the middle of the treaty when the Antichrist and the False Prophet take over, heads will begin to roll, all hell will break loose and people will suffer! And finally, it's here, the answer you're searching for…"

"Yes! Yes! Tell me, Roberts!"

And Roberts pulls him against him, "Your people will know Jesus is the one you've been waiting for, your-long sought-after Messiah! And something else, Josh!"

God Help Us

And again a pitiful voice asks, "And then what, Roberts… then what?"

"It will be over, Josh! Your people will understand: the Antichrist, the false prophet, the one who came to you as a lamb, they're nothing but the devil incarnate, waiting to send you to hell with them."

His head drops even lower, asking, "But how, Roberts, how can I warn them before it's too late?" he's pleading without stopping.

Roberts shakes his head, hoping he's wrong, but knowing he isn't. He has read the scriptures, knows their suffering.

"I haven't the answer. Jesus told your people over two thousand years ago and they didn't listen. How can I—a Gentile, tell them the same today? If they wouldn't listen to Him, when He walked with them, talked with them, all the way to the Cross?" he asks, looking into his bleary eyes, dripping tears unashamedly.

Josh shakes his head, wringing his arms, lost again!

And once again, Roberts places his hand upon his shoulder, comforting him. "I understand the pressure you're under. All I ask is keep me informed of your whereabouts."

"I'll do it, Roberts. I will."

"But there's something else we need to understand before you leave, Josh."

And he looks at Roberts, expecting the worst. "Hope it's not something you're irked about, Roberts," he says, grinning.

"Nothing irks me now, Josh. I've warned you. You'll know what to do, I'm sure of it."

Josh begins walking slowly away, never looking back. And suddenly, he stops, looking back toward Roberts, smiling. "But there's always one sure way out of this mess, Roberts," he's shouting.

"What are you talking about, Christian?"

"Remember the Six Day War you asked me about?"

"Remember it as yesterday, Josh!"

"He was there for us then, he hasn't changed…He will never leave us or forsake us. He gave us a covenant we hold dearly!"

Roberts wants to send him away feeling good. "You're right, my friend! You'll win again…no matter what's waiting!" he yells at the top of his voice, no longer worried.

Josh keeps walking slowly away. And now he turns again, looking back.

"But, my friend! Now I'm a Christian, depending upon something different!"

"And what's that, Josh?"

"Faith, Roberts! Faith! Something the Apostle Paul wrote about."

"It is, Josh—it is! But I'd like to hear the words from you. Just one time, my friend…just one more time before you leave me… please, Josh, please…"

And Josh stops, removing a Bible from his briefcase. He begins reading, shouting back to Roberts words from the book of Romans."

> For I am persuaded, that neither death, nor life, or angels, nor principalities, nor powers, nor things present, nor things to come, nor height, nor depth, nor any other creature, shall be able to separate us from the love of God, which is in Christ Jesus our Lord. (Romans 8:38)

Josh gives a farewell wave to Roberts, walking slowly away humming a song Roberts taught him. His voice rings loud and clear: "What a Friend We Have in Jesus."

God Help Us

And Roberts listens proudly, enjoying the words, deciding to let him know something important before leaving.

"He is our friend, Josh! And it's nice to have a Jew remind me," he's shouting loud and clear, hoping the world hears him.

Josh is gone while Roberts remains sitting upon the bench, reminiscing their meeting. He's finished and begins walking back toward the hotel, shaking his head, muttering a prayer.

"Oh Lord...my God...I hope he's right. Israel's very existence hangs in the balance, leaving them wanting! Help them, Lord! Help them please. I pray you will be with them throughout eternity!"

Back at their quarters Doug sits alone, gathering his thoughts. He's lonely, wishing Martha was here beside him. Never before has he missed someone so greatly, haunting him day after day, night after night!

He begins walking slowly toward the water's edge not far away. A beautiful bright red sunset far off against the horizon hovers down to meet everlasting blue water below. And it reminds him of God's great power, the great everlasting beauty, all His creation.

He wonders why he ever became involved so young in life with people so unsure. Again, his mind runs rampant, beginning to wonder if everything will go as planned before reaching Kennedy. He continues walking, at times stopping to kick the sand, watching it scatter in the breeze, falling all over. And he stops at intervals, gazing back toward the hotel, being sure he isn't followed. The sun is about to settle over the beautiful clear blue ocean water, bringing him a sense of calmness. And it's welcoming!

Arthur (Mac) Mc Caffry

And appearing from out of nowhere, a beautiful lady with long dark hair flowing halfway down to her waist appears. She walks beside him toward a never-ending sunset.

Doug stops, gazing upon her beauty; she's perfect, beyond imagination. And he's wondering why she's out here on a sandy beach with him alone in the middle of nowhere.

They reach the water's edge where huge waves rush in from deep blue water, splashing up against sand, flowing back with the tide. Doug peeks at her shining blue eyes, riveted to the evening sun about to disappear.

And her white nylon pants, her red silk blouse expose a golden cross over her heart. She's petite, perfect bronze skin, teeth white as snow. And her sandals glide across sand like petals from flowers falling upon still water.

And he pauses, gathering his thoughts.

"I didn't see you coming, beautiful one. Have you come to warn me about dangerous waters?" he asks playfully.

She smiles beautifully, but doesn't answer. Her eyes remain as if glued to the blazing red evening sunset.

Finally, she turns, facing him with eyes shining bright as the sun above.

"I've came to warn you of something only He knows, Doug," she says softly, tenderly.

Doug looks at her differently; she knows his name, but they've never before met.

"You know me from where?"

"I know you, Doug—know you well. You prayed asking for help," she reminds him as a longtime friend from somewhere.

Doug needs time to gather his thoughts. He begins slowly, walking closer toward the water's edge with her moving beside

God Help Us

him. Once again, he stops suddenly. He stares at her, wondering where or when.

"I've a feeling we've met before, beautiful one, but can't remember where or when."

And still gazing out toward the evening sunset, never turning, she says so sweetly and tenderly, "I've heard the same many times, Doug. Some call me Deborah, others, *sunset at eventide.* It was given to me by the one I serve."

Doug likes the name and wonders about her friends.

"And the one you serve is?"

She looks at him amazed. "I serve the great I Am, our Father in heaven," Deborah says proudly.

He moves from her side, looking upon her in awe. And suddenly, she stops her walking, not wanting to frighten him further. Her eyes glow like fire, reaching out for his hand, pulling him beside her. And without asking further, he's standing, gazing upon her, helpless, wondering.

"How can this be, how do you treat an angel—a beautiful wonderful creature of God. But why—here looking out toward the ocean with someone like me?" he asks himself, over and over, but never an answer.

She bends low, writing letters in the sand, while Doug watches her every move in admiration.

"You write letters well, Deborah," he says, feeling helpless, trying to be pleasant.

And she's happy. She begins humming a song, bringing her pleasure. She gazes up into Doug's eyes, and the brightness of her face causes him to look away with deepest regret. Another beautiful smile and Deborah moves beside him.

"Look into my eyes and don't be frightened, Doug! The Lord is with you!"

| 315 |

Arthur (Mac) Mc Caffry

He feels paralyzed, unable to move, helpless to reply.

"Listen to my words, Doug, take them seriously! I watched His son—as you watch me. He wrote words in the sand in the holy city of Jerusalem. An angry group of Pharisees stood gazing down as he wrote. And when He was finished, they looked upon it unaware that He, the Son of God, was the long-awaited Messiah!"

Doug's knees bend, his mind reels on and on, lost without thought, unbelievable! This beautiful one has been with Jesus. He wants to fall down upon his knees and worship her, but worship is for Him. And long moments of silence till he's able to speak without crying.

"You mean—"

"Yes, Doug, Jesus, the son of the great I Am!" she says, gazing toward the setting sun.

Doug bends his knees, touching the sand. And moving closer, he reads big bold letters written in the deep white sand.

"Danger ahead, arrival: Kennedy Airport"

And he rises slowly, staring at Deborah, wondering further. But still, she remains, looking into the sunset, seeming unaware of his presence.

He feels as if he's in another world, and this is only a dream. But it isn't, and he knows it! He gathers his senses, looks up above, seeing only heaven, and slowly, he's walking to her side, still wondering.

"I thank you for bringing the warning, but a question, please."

Deborah turns, smiling. "And your question, Doug?"

"The song…the one I heard you humming. I've heard it before, but can't remember where or when."

God Help Us

"But I heard it only yesterday, Doug. It touched me, made me happy. And now, I can't keep from humming the words, so beautiful!"

"Heard it where?" Doug asks, anxiously.

"Oh, yes, Doug. Words from someone you love dearly, beautiful words."

"But the words…tell me!"

And she smiles, ever so beautifully. "On Eagle's Wings," she says, turning back and away looking into the sunset.

And he's thinking, "*On Eagle's Wings*"…*no. No, it can't be, that's Uncle Mike's song.* He turns, searching for her, but Deborah's no more!

He rushes to the waters' edge, gazing out toward an ocean of blue. And a glimmering brightness shows Deborah far out, dancing on ocean waves, heading into the evening sunset. And gazing far out as his eyes will take him, he sees a beautiful rainbow hanging low, just above the clear blue water.

His heart pounds as he watches her skipping over waves of never-ending water. Faster! Faster! Her figure begins to diminish, smaller and smaller, heading toward the beautiful sunset at the end of the rainbow. And finally, she's only a dot, fading beyond the sunset.

He rises from the sand, walking slowly back toward the hotel. And he's thinking of her beauty, her mission, and where she might be headed. He wonders if she's headed for Paradise, the Garden of Eden, or maybe over the rainbow, a place his Uncle Mike calls Shangri-La.

39

A Stranger in Paradise

The angel of the Lord encampeth round about
them that fear him, and delivereth them.

—Psalm 34:7

"This can't be true," he keeps telling himself, wondering what Roberts is going say. It's hard to believe, but too important to let it pass. He heads back toward the hotel, hoping and praying Roberts accepts his story.

Roberts stands outside the hotel, motioning him to come and join. Doug wonders where to begin, feeling uneasy.

"You look like you've seen a ghost, lad, something wrong?" he asks, jokingly.

Doug breathes hard, trying to catch his breath. He thinks of words to answer his question. Deborah is an angel, never a ghost. Surely, he will believe and understand, he prays.

"Not a ghost, sir, something better, a real live breathing beautiful angel. I didn't know how to tell you this, but it's true!"

Roberts wants to calm him.

"Get your breath and tell me about your angel."

Doug, for the first time, looks at him, worried. He doesn't know where to start, but finally, he begins explaining his encounter with Deborah.

| 318 |

God Help Us

"I was walking on the beach heading down to the waters' edge when I was approached by the most beautiful person I've ever met. Her name was Deborah, meaning *sunset at eventide*."

Roberts reaches out, placing his hand over Doug's lips.

"Slow down, Doug, we have the time, this could be important!"

Doug pauses to regain his breath.

"Deborah told me she had a message from the Lord, and it frightened me. She told me God sent her, and I was the one to receive her message."

Roberts pretends to be uninterested, turning his head away, but listening.

"Sure it was an angel, Doug, not one on the other side?" he asks, seriously.

Doug looks pale. He thinks back to the time and scene. "Definitely an angel sent by God, sir, definitely an angel," he repeats over and over till Roberts stops him again.

Roberts doesn't look excited and Doug wonders why. Angels he knows!

"Calm yourself, Doug. It's about time your eyes are opened."

And he wonders what he's talking about. But the thought of heavenly bodies speaking to him, he's sure about. He moves close to Roberts.

"I guess I just couldn't believe it could happen to me, sir."

Roberts wants him to know things, unseen things, good and bad things, from below and above.

"Prepare for it. Do you not remember how we discussed the subject before? Angels, God's holy angels, they're among us! It's time to shout with joy, Doug."

Arthur (Mac) Mc Caffry

"I do remember, but I never once thought it would happen to me. It's like a dream come true, sir. But I had a bigger problem after she left me."

Now Roberts doesn't understand.

"Tell me about it."

Doug looks around, searching for words. Finally, he says, "Well, Mr. Roberts, I felt maybe you would think I was losing it, you know, imagining things I wished would happen. I don't know why, but I can't seem to get her out of my mind. Her voice, so sweet and tender, eyes blue as sparkling diamonds."

Roberts tries to vision her beauty, but determined to move on.

"But let's talk about the message, Doug. She wouldn't have been there if it wasn't important."

"You're right, sir. It was shocking how she took over."

"Shocking?"

"Yes, it was unbelievable the way she took over! She did everything so easy. I'll never forget how she took her finger and wrote in the sand, the same as Christ did using His finger before the Pharisees 2,000 years ago."

Roberts becomes as excited as Doug.

"And the message, out with it!"

Doug gets his breath again, breathing deeply. "She wrote, 'Danger ahead at Kennedy airport when you arrive.' And that was it, sir. I was overwhelmed, couldn't believe what she was writing, trying to figure out the meaning!" he shouts, excited.

Roberts looks at him, somber-like. "Then why did you believe her, lad?"

"I knew she was on my side, sir. She told me about Jesus and the Pharisees and I never doubted her. But it's still hard to believe I've been visited by an angel, but I have... I really, really have," he says, excitedly.

God Help Us

"Calm yourself, Doug. Get your breath and tell me the kind of trouble she spoke about. Was it something we can handle before leaving this place?"

"That's up for you to decide. But I do believe there's something planned to stop us from making our delivery. There's nothing else it can be, sir."

Roberts pauses long, looking troubled.

Finally, Doug asks, "Are you going to make a change, sir?"

"No other way out, it has to be done! We'll call it the big switch, one made at the last moment."

Doug waits for more, but Roberts is still waiting.

"Mind explaining it, sir?"

"Yes, I'll explain it! It's about a dream I had last night."

Doug holds his breath, waiting. "Good or bad, sir," he finally asks.

"It was bad, real bad. A horror story I couldn't run away from. But now, I'm beginning to believe it's coming true."

"Are you telling me you can't make a change in your plans at Kennedy?"

Roberts looks embarrassed. "No way in hell, Doug. But you're not gonna like this one either. I've been doing some research about what's been going on within the department, it doesn't go away!"

Doug interrupts. "You're losing me, sir."

"Hang with me! This dream I had is about to come true—and that's no crap for sure! I dreamed we were being double-crossed by our own arriving at Kennedy. And now, it's beginning to fit perfect. It's all about Deborah's warning."

Doug looks at him again. "But I still don't understand. I thought you knew these guys meeting us at Kennedy."

| 321 |

Roberts looks disgustedly at Doug. "I've told you before, things change at any moment. There are times it becomes necessary to make a switch, maybe now…maybe later!" Roberts says heatedly.

And Doug can't wait, moving closer. "Give me the details and I'll get started immediately!"

Roberts glances at him, grinning. "Now hold on…just hang with me, Doug! We've did a lot of talking during this journey, now I'm putting you to the test."

"What kind of test?" he asks, surprised.

"You and Marla will make a switch."

"A switch!"

"That's correct. It's time I find out who our friends are: ones within the department, wherever. It's time we get serious…no time for slip-ups! We're about to end this journey to nowhere… it's no time to get sloppy!"

"You're referring to our fellow agents, I assume."

"I'm talking about you…I…and Marla…none other!" he says, heatedly.

"But…explain to me why, sir?"

I've been worrying about some of our own, this is the place, the time to find out. But before going further, there's one thing I'm sure of…"

Doug interrupts quickly, asking, "Sure of?"

Roberts begins to chuckle.

"You and I will be at the scene of the action, but not delivering the tapes."

"Then who will be delivering the tapes?" he asks, suspiciously, waiting.

"Nobody other than our lovely Marla, she's the deliverer… nobody but Marla," he says, grinning.

God Help Us

Doug looks hard at him shocked, still wondering. "This is a surprise, sir. Do you feel she's competent enough?"

"Marla's the one! I make the decisions—understand?"

"I do understand, sir. I talked to her briefly, she understands our relationship, she's waiting! But I begin to wonder..."

Roberts begins to chuckle. "There are times, Doug, you just don't get it. Try to think of a better one for this job, my friend, you can't!"

"But I don't intend to try for a better one, I think she's perfect! I only wanted be sure there's no slip-ups."

"Then it's settled! I'll explain it to you and you'll get with Marla and inform her of our discussion. If there are problems, get back with me immediately, understand, lad?"

"I'll get with her for sure, now tell me the switch."

"I'll explain how it's going to work. You will arrange to be in a position able to pass the tapes to Marla as we make the walk to the concourse, a question maybe?"

And Doug looks at him, perplexed.

"Only this, sir: why Marla? I still wonder if she can be trusted when the chips are down, it makes me worry!"

"But think about this for a change, find someone better for this situation and I'll kiss your butt on Main Street. She's perfect, my boy, absolutely perfect!"

Doug has never seen Roberts like this before, and he's wondering why.

And Roberts begins again.

"Sometimes, Doug, you just don't get it! If there's a better one for this job than Marla, I'd sure as hell like to meet her. She's been to hell and back at the ripe old age of twenty-three."

Doug looks at Roberts, feeling differently for the first time ever.

| 323 |

"Think back how Deborah delivered her message to you about trouble at the airport, Doug. Trouble calls for action, quick action…not waiting till you're sorry it happened. Time is running down and the only thing that really matters is delivering what we have to the proper authority!"

"I understand, Mr. Roberts. All you need do is give me the word and I'll get with Marla before take-off. But your friends with CIA, how are they to know the change?"

And Roberts looks again at him, wondering why the question.

"They won't know, Doug! I don't want them to know! Let 'em guess the way I do! Telling them without being sure who is with who, it would be like playing with a stick of dynamite about to go off! And that's why I'm switching messengers!"

Doug looks surprised again, asking, "But why? They still look at you…talking as friends?"

"But no longer, Doug. Politics has a way of changing people, friends come and go. I've got to be sure of this one, this is a tough one…no margin for error!"

Doug studies his every word, listening without end.

"I understand, Mr. Roberts, keep talking. I don't wanna see any slip-ups as much as you, sir. I don't wanna miss anything, for sure!"

"By now, word has gotten around at the Pentagon what we're coming with. And someone in the crowd with opposite views than ours will know were coming with material they'll die for," Roberts explains.

"And how do we pull it off? Marla expects us to take the tapes all the way. All she's thinking about is to get away from these people as fast as possible."

"Write a note to her plain and simple, Doug. And tell her to tear it up in pieces when she's through with it. Tell her to put a satchel or travel bag on her left shoulder before leaving her station departing, leaving the top part open. And when we pass her moving forward, toward the concourse, you will plant our material back inside, giving it to her. Now do you get it, lad?" he asks, once again grinning.

Doug takes his time, thinking hard, going over every word... thinking again.

"Now I get it! I definitely do. Sounds smart...tricky... something you're good at. Carry on, sir."

"Now here's your part, Doug! The part we can't have any slip-up..."

And he looks hard at him, waiting anxiously.

"Yes, Mr. Roberts?"

And Roberts can't help from grinning again.

"Put yourself at ease and store this in your mind, you'll need it later. Picture the scene in your mind as you would be part of it now."

And Doug can't wait! "Yes...yes...then what?"

"It's going to be body against body as we walk through the concourse. When we pull up beside her, you place the tapes inside the bag without stopping, plain and simple, lad, that's the way the pros do it, once, quick, precisely, and it's over!"

"I can do it. What about the men we're to meet? Have you got a message or something to give them?" Doug asks innocently.

"Oh yes! I sure have, Doug. I've got something planned they'll never forget. In fact, I'm probably going to send them off with a bang, maybe a big bang. Nothing is too good for some of my old buddies," Roberts says, with a chuckle that only he can do.

"I'll get with Marla for a couple seconds yet today and let her know what to expect. Now that you've solved Deborah's

Arthur (Mac) Mc Caffry

message, I'll feel a lot better on the plane heading home, sir. It's beginning to sound like something like Uncle Mike would say."

And Roberts looks at him surprised. "And what would that be?" he asks, waiting.

"Everything is beautiful in its own way!" Doug says, with a huge grin, waiting for him to chuckle.

And he looks up at him, smiling all over. "Couldn't be better, Doug, we're heading home, and nothing is sweeter."

"And where's home?"

Roberts begins to smile. "Oh, I suppose it's wherever you find happiness, maybe some place… just over the rainbow," he says, walking away.

40

A Plan for All

For this God is our God forever and ever:
he will be our God even unto death.

—Psalms 48:14

Early the next morning, the Airbus glides off the runway headed for New York. De Marco enters the assembly room, and it's silence throughout. He stands behind a small podium, brushing back his long dark hair, smiling.

"My faithful colleagues, you have shown your faith in me during this journey, and again, I come to you humbling myself, asking your support!"

And instantly, Roberts nudges Doug, looking at him grinning. "This is gonna be good, Doug…get ready," he mumbles.

"Again, I thank you for your cooperation during this crisis caused by the earthquake in the United States. It has created a situation where it's no longer feasible to hold the upcoming UN meeting in New York. Travel, both air and auto, isn't back to normal and isn't expected to be for months, maybe years from now. Therefore, I will contact other members along with you, asking permission to address the United Nations Assembly concerning my Seven Year Plan to be held in the ancient city of Rome, one hundred and two days beyond the present date."

| 327 |

And there's a stirring among his delegation quickly. Some show no interest; others show ecstasy!

"This moment in history will never be forgotten. It will live for eternity! This is an agreement the world has dreamed about: peace in Jerusalem between Arabs and Jews forever! The significance of this precious agreement must be someplace of great world importance, a place that has stood since the beginning of time. And I ask you, my most honored delegates, can there be a better place than Vatican City?"

And the applause is deafening!

"It has stood silent since the immortal days of the Roman Empire. And now it is my promise to you, we will rebuild not only Rome, we will rebuild the entire world under one government for the benefit of not just the few and the privileged, I will build you a new empire for all the people! I, Anthony De Marco, will lead you into a new eternity!"

And again, the applause is deafening, except where the American delegates sit motionless, listening silently. And at the rear of the plane, Joshua sits alone, his eyes focused upon his Bible.

"I'm therefore going to meet with all concerned leaders throughout the Middle East, Jews especially. They have seen the reaction of the rest of the world to my Seven Year Plan. They should therefore welcome this occasion as the rest of world: shout, stand up, and be happy. Israel, above all nations, stands to benefit from my personal guarantee for their security forever and ever."

Cheers ring out again, waiting.

"Enthusiasm for my plan has never been greater! The entire world searches for peace and security, and I'm the one to see they get peace and security!"

God Help Us

Doug reaches over, touching Roberts. "They're gonna get anything but peace if they go along with his agreement," he mumbles to Roberts, watching him grinning while Ms. Brantley sits listening stone-faced, wringing her hands, angry.

"Soon, I'll be meeting with my entire staff along with members of the UN and others just before the signing in Rome. After the signing in Rome, I'll travel extensively throughout the world. But eventually, my headquarters will be moved to Jerusalem. And from Jerusalem, I will govern the world: the home of the New World Order!"

And again, the applause is deafening!

De Marco is at his highest; it's showing! His eyes burn like fire, his face shows his glory, strain appears every moment, but he's loving it!

And he continues without ending.

"My signing must go forward—with or without American support! The world is waiting, the time is right. I can't delay something so precious forever!"

He stops suddenly, beginning again. "And with your support, I'll move forward with you behind me, there's none to stop us!" he's shouting, stepping back, heading for the cockpit, leaving them in wonder, applauding.

And Roberts is furious! "He's done it again! Now he's rubbing our noses in it. He's undoubtedly the shrewdest character I've ever witnessed in my entire life. I simply can't believe what he's just pulled right under everyone's eyes," Roberts says, looking back and around the American delegations, seeing Joshua sitting, holding his Bible, listening.

But Doug is puzzled, resting his head between his hands, wondering.

"I don't believe I understand your remark, sir. Fill me in."

Arthur (Mac) Mc Caffry

"It's obvious he's deceived us again. He deceives the whole world with every utterance from his mouth, and here aboard this plane to nowhere, he's performing his best ever! He's got the magic son, but nobody can see it."

"Explain it, Mr. Roberts…

And instantly, he's staring hard at him, up in his face, "Listen good, Doug, I'm about to teach you something!"

"I'm listening!"

"De Marco has arranged for the signing on the day Christ was crucified, Good Friday. Wake up, lad! It's time you see De Marco who he really is! Not only has he the guts to insult us further, he will be sitting in Rome the same day Christ arose from the grave on Easter Sunday. We're not in the same league with this guy, Doug. De Marco thinks and plans while we're lying in bed sleeping. But we do have one consolation!"

And Ms. Brantley moves beside Doug, joining the conversation. "Tell me our consolation, Roberts," she says, without waiting.

He moves close to her, whispering, "God is still in charge, Ms. Brantley! The signs of His coming appear every day, it's time for us to get ready!"

And Doug moves closer. "You're ahead of me, sir. We need to protect the cell phone and recorder more than ever."

"You're right, Doug! It's about time for you to visit Marla!"

He looks up at him, nodding. "They'll never leave my body till I'm handing them to her, you can count on it!"

Roberts holds his hand out, joining Doug's hand, shaking it. "Let's get some sleep before we reach Kennedy, Doug, I'm beginning to feel we might need it."

"But before we do, there's something I need to say, sir!"

"Then please do."

"Amazing things are happening. The cherubims, the sudden appearance of De Marco. It seems like every day, De Marco is changing the world scene to benefit him only."

"He is, Doug! Things are beginning to happen just as our Lord told us they would happen! Remember these two phrases He used warning us: 'I will come as a thief in the night.'"

Doug is mystified, listening, as Roberts keeps looking out blankly, continuing, "He told us we will be caught up in the twinkling of an eye to meet Him in the air. I've been thinking about the words, kind of looking forward to it."

Doug stops him. "But I don't understand your message, sir."

Roberts's face turns different. It's a face Doug has never viewed before. It's almost like something holy, a peaceful face waiting.

"I don't understand your meaning!"

"As a thief in the night, Doug, that's the secret of His return. All throughout the Bible, people questioned Him about signs of His coming. The signs are here, but people can't recognize them!" Roberts says smiling, while Doug watches, wondering.

Doug has never seen Roberts like this. He wonders why, but there's no way of knowing.

"I believe the same! It worries me too, sir."

"I know only God himself knows the day and the hour of the Second Coming. But I've read the Bible a lot in my lonely hours away from home. I'm positive about some things."

"Like what?"

"His coming will be according to the book of Revelation, seven years after the treaty is signed, ending with the battle of Armageddon."

Arthur (Mac) Mc Caffry

"I've never thought of it that way before."

"Remember this, Doug. Two prophets will appear in the Holy City of Jerusalem with great power. And they'll remain in the street three and one half years till they're killed by the Antichrist. And when he takes over for the next forty-two months, you don't wanna think about it! It's prophesy, Doug… nobody can change it!" he says, enjoying it.

"Will that be the end, sir?"

"Think, lad, think! Think about the treaty De Marco has been talking about! It's scary, makes you wonder! There's forty-two months to go after the two prophets are taken up! And during the last forty-two months, the Antichrist takes over, and that, my friend, is when all hell breaks loose! Satan will give unbelievable power to the Antichrist and the False Prophet. The Antichrist will be killed, rise again after three and one half days, people all over the world will view it, worshiping him as God! It's coming, Doug, it's coming fast and furious! But I know one thing for sure…"

"What do you know for sure?"

"I don't expect to be here during the seven year treaty. Now let's talk about something a little more pleasant, if possible. Read this, Doug, something again from the Bible," he says, handing him a tract of paper. And his face turns pale, finally able to face him.

"It's frightening, sir. It truly frightens me."

> And I will give power unto my two witnesses, and they shall prophesy a thousand two hundred and three score days.
>
> And when they shall have finished their testimony, the beast that hath ascendeth out of the bottomless pit

God Help Us

shall make war against them, and shall overcome them, and kill them. (Revelation 11:3, 7)

Doug reads the tract, looking up to him. "It's frightening, sir…I don't wanna be here."

"But don't worry, my friend. You're safe as I am. We're covered by His blood and that's all it takes. But there's something else…"

"Like what?"

"The last discussion I had with Joshua, he said something I keep thinking about."

"And what is it, sir?"

"He used the words, 'We won.' And now, I'm beginning to realize how important the words are. When every battle is over, those two words decide the outcome and the future."

"It's always the end result that counts, isn't it?"

"It is, Doug. And I want to tell you about a dream I had last night. It was the most realistic dream I've ever had! And when I awoke, it was hard to convince myself it really hadn't happened!"

"Sounds interesting…tell me about it!"

"I dreamed I was about to die. I seemed to be in a meeting and there was a large screen, like a movie screen. And when I read the words on the screen, I recognized them as Paul's words when he was about to be killed."

"And?"

"I dreamed I was standing before Jesus! He was about to judge me. My rewards would be according to my works here on earth. I was baffled, but then it came to me."

Doug waits for the finish, but it doesn't come.

"And what happened?"

"Well, there was only one thing to do: use Paul's words…I couldn't think of any other!"

Arthur (Mac) Mc Caffry

I have fought a good fight, I have finished the fight, I have finished my course, I have kept the faith. Henceforth there is laid up for me a crown of righteousness, which the Lord, the righteous judge, shall give me at that day: and not to me only, but to all of them also that love His appearing. (2 Timothy 4:7–8)

41

Looking Ahead

My help cometh from the Lord, which
made heaven and earth.

—Psalm 121:20

The trip is long, tiring, without the usual conversation going on throughout. Delegates stare out to nowhere, displaying a worried look. Everyone seems to sense something big is about to happen, something so big the entire world will end up being affected. Who do you trust becomes the greatest worry ever, while Jews and Arabs alike wonder relentlessly.

Roberts has been reading his Bible. And finally, he's finished, placing it inside his briefcase, ready to talk.

"I've made a decision, Doug. As soon as we take care of business here, I'm throwing in the towel and retire."

And Doug places his book down, looking at him, surprised. He's wondering if he's in one of his joking moods again.

"You, retire! That'll be the day."

"But I'm serious, Doug! I've been there and done that all over the world. And now, I'm tired. I wanna go home!"

"I'm beginning to believe you, but why?" Doug asks, trying to understand his sudden statement.

"I'm worn out, Doug! I've had it! After this trip to nowhere, I'm heading home without regret. I've spent my last thirty years working in Intelligence, one way or another. My wife is gone, and there are times, I get lonely, never satisfied. I should have called it quits when she was killed twenty years ago, but didn't. And now I look at you and Martha...and I'm envious...wanting the same."

Doug still can't believe what he's hearing. To him, there's never an end to someone like the colonel.

He looks at him seriously for a change, asking, "And what's on your mind for a year from now, sir...maybe a woman or a place somewhere to settle down?"

And Roberts looks at him surprised, wondering if he's reading his mind.

"Who knows what might happen to a guy like me? I might still find someone to enjoy life with me for a couple of more years."

"What will you do with your leisure time, sir?"

Roberts looks at him confused. He's prepared for this a long time, but now it's time to think again. And finally, he does.

"Years ago, I bought a ranch in Montana, but never had time to enjoy its pleasures. I love good music, you know the kind that gets to you when you're feeling lonely, the kind that makes you think, enjoy the pleasures of life."

But Doug is having a hard time understanding his words.

"When I look at you, sir, I can't help but think of an old warhorse, the kind that enjoys action every moment of the day. It may take some time to get in the swing of just sittin' and rockin' all day in the sun."

Roberts takes his time explaining. "But not for me, Doug. I've seen it all—the good, the bad, and I've nothing to regret. My time is well planned from the very first day."

God Help Us

"Tell me about it. Who knows—I might wanna come calling on you sometime."

"I'll sit in an easy chair and listen to some of the old ones, like Perry Como singing, 'Let the World Go Away' and then, I'll listen to Julie Andrews sing, 'The Sound of Music.' I'll have a glass of wine and smoke a cigar. And when I'm finished, I'll quit smoking again for the ten thousandth time."

And it's Doug's time to laugh, and he does.

"Well, I've solved the mystery of all mysteries, Mr. Roberts, you just let it slip!"

Roberts turns his head away again, grinning. "Just what are you talking about, Doug?" he asks, sheepishly.

And Doug can't hold back. "Oh, yes you do know! Montana is your Shangri-La…or maybe someplace just over the rainbow, the place you've always searched for, but never been able to find," Doug says, as his boss turns his head away, chuckling.

"You got me, Doug! You've finally got me! I'll sit in my rocking chair, watching the sun go down over that big red Montana sky. And I'll be dreaming of snuggling up close to Maria."

Doug is taken again, filled with emotion! His mentor talks about things his Uncle Mike talks about, enjoyable things, things that make him want to be there with them.

"What was your wife doing at the time of her death, sir?" he asks, wishing he hadn't.

And instantly, he can tell Roberts doesn't like the question. He doesn't answer quickly as usual; he's looking out the window at a sky full of clouds down below. He moves his head downward without looking at Doug, barely able to let it out.

"She was killed in an automobile accident. Her name was Maria, maybe that's why I have a feeling for Marla. She was beautiful, Doug. Every cadet at West Point had their eyes on

Arthur (Mac) Mc Caffry

her from the time they saw her. Her dad was military all the way, had it in his blood. But the thing I didn't know was her blood was different than his or mine. She had her own ideas concerning success. And today, I'm beginning to believe she was the smart one," he says, turning his head, wanting to cry, but doesn't.

Doug is talking personally and Roberts is ready to respond.

"But what led you to Christ, sir… or am I out of line asking the question?"

"It's okay to ask, Doug. It was a cold winter night in Chicago and I was about to hit the hay after a bad day at the airport. Billy Graham was on television preaching, and he was explaining how life is short, like a vapor, as he put it. I thought about it over and over, and I began to realize it was true. I listened to George Beverly Shay sing 'How Great Thou Art' and my heart began to melt. And the next thing I knew, I was on my knees beside the bed, spilling my heart out to Jesus. He touched me, Doug—He touched me! And I was never the same thereafter."

Roberts begins to chuckle.

"But what's so funny, why the sudden look of pleasure upon your face?"

"I'm thinking of De Marco. He's the man of the hour, the bright and shining star to most everyone aboard."

Again, Doug looks at him, puzzled. "I don't understand, sir. I'm out in left field once again."

"It's only this, Doug: it's been tough for me to listen to his lies during this venture for peace, but maybe it's worth it."

And Doug is puzzled again, wondering. "What are you trying to tell me, sir?" he asks, moving closer.

God Help Us

A big enjoyable grin suddenly appears upon his face, showing his pleasure. "Maybe we've just defeated the greatest deceiver of all time, the Antichrist! We've been with him almost one month and still have our souls within us. Look around you, Doug, see how he has won every single person's soul during this trip, except members of the delegation. We have defeated the devil's very own, and he hates our guts without ending!"

Doug shrugs his shoulders, looking over the rest, relieved.

"I believe you might be right, but I've never thought of it that way, sir."

"But that's what it's all about, Doug. It's all about souls and more souls! Good against evil. That's it exactly! His destiny is set by our Lord above and it never changes, Doug. He learned a long time ago, he's going to hell for sure and there's nothing he can do about it."

And suddenly, he stops, pausing to say, "And yet his biggest desire still remains—"

Anxiety takes over and Doug can't wait, asking, "And his biggest desire is what, sir?"

Roberts begins to smile, elated. "He wants to take you and me with him, Doug," he says, waiting for his reaction.

Doug is overcome, thinking hard. "You're right. But I never looked at it that way before, sir."

"I've explained it to you before maybe in a different way, Doug, now I'll tell it to you again. Without the Holy Spirit, we would be like putty in his hands. He can't touch us, lad, and he knows it. The very minute we first acknowledge Christ as the Son of God and ask forgiveness, our sins are forgiven; we're new people...born again! And during this trip, I've never felt more sure, more secure...never ever."

Doug is puzzled and it shows. "But why, sir—tell me why?"

And Roberts begins to grin full out, reaching for his hand, looking pleased. "My name is in His book, Doug—the greatest book ever written. The same book Jesus will open on Judgment Day. It's all in the book, lad, it's everything! All in one," he says, getting loud and emotional for the first time ever.

Doug looks at him speechless, contemplating the meaning before replying.

"I've learned a lot from you, Roberts, but I honestly believe this is the most important issue I've come to understand. Never before did I ever understand the power...the fullness of the Holy Spirit."

"Maybe someday, Doug, we'll understand things better. But more than everything, I pray for the ones who haven't accepted Christ as the Son of God as their one and only Savior. Someday very soon, they will look up and see heaven's glory, and it will be their saddest day ever!"

And he stops, pausing again, saying, "But never forget Ethel's quote, Doug!"

Doug can't hold back, interrupting, *"You mean, 'He's just around the corner.'"*

And Roberts begins grinning again. "I do for sure, lad...I do for sure," he says, enjoying the moment.

Marla walks among the passengers serving their needs, but never glancing toward Doug or Roberts. De Marco comes from the cockpit making an announcement, but nothing important. The journey is about to end, some look sad, but the Americans seem happy. The expectation of meeting friends is growing. Concern for those injured or dying in the quake grows deeper and showing.

God Help Us

Marla moves forward, announcing touchdown at Kennedy will be in approximately twenty minutes. She returns after briefly talking to De Marco. She moves to the departure door and begins to speak.

"Please listen, fellow passengers! Everyone aboard will leave in an orderly fashion beginning from the front of the cabin. A huge crowd awaits us and it's important to be aware of everyone and everything around you. Thank you for your patience and consideration."

Roberts is worried and it showing. He looks at Doug, uttering a deep sigh of relief.

"I'm glad this journey is over, Doug. I'll not feel safe till we hand everything we have over to headquarters, even then, I'll be worrying."

Doug looks at him again, wondering why, but never asking.

"Stop your worrying, Mr. Roberts, we're home free," Doug says confidently.

"Wrong again! This is where it just might get interesting: lots of people, lots of noise, it's the perfect setting. Keep your eyes peeled, Doug. This could be what some people might call *party time at the Big Apple!*"

"Tell me again…I don't get it!"

"For the first time in my life, I'm not sure who our friends are. I wonder who to trust no matter who they are. I suppose that's the way it is when trust runs down with no way out."

"Everything is gonna be fine, sir. I'll be at your side, count on it."

"I know! I know you will, Doug; couldn't want anyone better. When we walk down the steps leaving the plane, hang with me, stay tight, nobody gets between us—understand?"

"I'll be beside you, Mr. Roberts. Don't worry!"

"But still, for some reason, I've got one bad feeling. If they've found out about the cell phone and recorder, all hell could break loose. Pray, Doug, pray your heart out for this one, it just might get interesting…one for the books!"

42

The Reception

Greater love hath no man than this, That
a man lay down his life for friends.

—John 15:13

Wheels screech loudly as of the plane strikes the runway at
Kennedy International Airport. The huge plane taxies to
a passenger unloading zone, and in a short time people are ready
to move out. Marla moves near the door, holding a loudspeaker,
ready to begin unloading.

"Please listen, everyone!" she shouts loudly over the speaker.
"We want everyone to comply with our instructions during the
unloading. And as you can see, there's a huge crowd of people
here to greet Mr. De Marco. In order to make this quickly and
safely as possible, I want all delegates, other than Mr. De Marco,
to leave the plane at the head of the line."

Unloading begins with Doug and Roberts at the head of
the procession. As they move past Marla, she leaves her station,
walking between the two toward the inside of the concourse.
Her travel bag fits snug against her side open at the top, and
Doug moves against her, slipping the cell phone and recorder
inside without notice.

Standing among the large crowd of people is the delegation
from Morris Avenue Baptist Church searching for Doug, their

hero, while De Marco moves from the plane with thousands shouting his name in wild jubilation.

And from throughout the concourse, the praising begins, "All hail De Marco! All hail De Marco!" On and on, never ending!

Still moving quickly ahead, Doug feels a tug at his shoulder from behind. And suddenly, beside him stands Joshua, the Jew, the one he's been searching for.

"Tell Nate we're on hold till we see what happens once the seven year peace treaty is in place. He will understand, I'm sure," he says without waiting.

"I understand, Joshua. I'll tell him as soon as we meet some friends," he says, turning to see the crowd following behind.

And turning to look back again, Joshua is gone, disappearing out into nowhere.

They never stop to look elsewhere. They continue walking swiftly onward toward the airport entrance. And from out of nowhere, two large well-built men approach dressed in black suits with white shirts and blue ties.

Roberts begins to smile, recognizing friends from past. A meaningful handshake, a grateful hug. "Hi, boys, take good care of this beautiful lady from nowhere, she's special…one of our own," he says, proudly.

"She will be in safe hands, Roberts, the worry is over, my friend!" one replies, glancing around, searching.

Without waiting, they grab hold of Marla's hand, heading to a waiting limo with two occupants Roberts also knows from past. Doug and Roberts are fixed, standing, watching their every move from well inside the concourse. And when she reaches the front entrance, she turns smiling, waving a farewell kiss with her arms held high. And she's yelling something hard to hear, but sounding like "I love you! I love you! I thank you!"

God Help Us

They return her wave as the driver gets out of the limo, seating her in the rear seat while waving a farewell and a thumbs-up to the both of them.

Doug and Roberts continue onward, walking slowly toward the front entrance expecting contact from Intelligence to appear at any moment.

On and on till seemingly from nowhere, appear two friendly faces walking directly toward them. And instantly, Roberts's face brightens, recognizing old friends from the past. They shake hands smiling, hugging as brothers, while Doug's eyes remain fixed, searching the crowd, looking for Martha.

Roberts reaches out grabbing his arm pulling him closer. "Meet a couple of my old friends, Doug. This is Glenn Orwell and Ernie Duncan. I didn't want to upset you at the end of journey, but I've been concerned about our safety carrying the kind of cargo we have with us. But now, I'm finally relieved! I feel safe for the first time in several days. I've known these two guys for what seems like a lifetime. We served ten years in the Far East protecting each other, and it wasn't a picnic, was it, boys?" he asks jokingly.

Orwell begins to chuckle, exploding loudly, "You can say it again, my friend, it was never a picnic!"

"You boys got your credentials?" Roberts asks jokingly.

Orwell puts his arm around Roberts and begins laughing.

"You're a fine one to ask for credentials, after what we've been through, you old dog-faced sky-jumper," Orwell says, hugging him.

And surprisingly, Roberts hesitates to go further, looking them over good, changed from a moment ago.

"Do these look good enough for you, sir?" he says, handing him his papers.

Doug takes his time looking them over, and finally he looks up at Orwell, smiling, "Good as gold, sir."

"You got the cell phone and recorder?" Orwell asks, looking at Roberts, smiling.

"Sure we have it! And I'm ready to turn it over to the two of you, but just as a matter of formality, tell me the code word for this operation," Roberts says, staring at Orwell, waiting.

And Orwell is different! He's pale looking, serious for a change, never joking, never speaking. And Roberts, stares again at him, noticing.

"We'll step inside the restroom across the way to make the transaction, boys, there just might be someone watching us," Roberts says, watching the sudden news, changing their expressions.

Mike and Martha stand a short distance away with the church group, looking for Doug when suddenly, Martha recognizes Doug talking to Roberts. Her heart begins to pound, taking off, running, shouting his name, never stopping. "Doug darling! Doug darling! Here I am! Here I am!" she's shouting, running all out toward him.

Mike stands frozen, watching her running toward something she knows nothing about. He isn't waiting any longer, handing his clothing bag to Brad, taking off beside her.

Dodging in and out between people, she reaches Doug, throwing her arms around him, smothering him with kisses.

Things are changing fast! Doug, Roberts, Orwell, and Duncan, all huddled close, searching for a code word that only Roberts knows; it doesn't exist! And the once peaceful atmosphere of meeting friends with honor and trust is changing quickly into a cursing, swearing of words at its highest. All hell is breaking loose just outside the restroom where people listen, scattering in fear without waiting.

But only Martha is the one unaware! She's holding on to Doug in another world, thinking of him and her only, together forever!

And Orwell and Duncan become transformed, two different people completely! They're no longer old friends of the past. Attitudes change without notice. And suddenly, their fists begin pounding Doug and Roberts without provocation.

They're cursing, pounding on Roberts and Doug like persons with a vengeance, hatred at its highest, out of control completely! It's betrayal within the Intelligence Department, America's most trusted!

Again, Mike's brain works overtime, realizing it's time to take action! He doesn't wait, heading for the center of the action, grabbing Orwell around the neck, breaking his grip upon Doug.

Across the room, Roberts struggles hard with Duncan, having trouble holding on to his briefcase. All hell is breaking loose while police stand afar, afraid to move forward after some are yelling, "Guns!"

Mike raises his hand, motioning to Martha, shouting loud and fiercely as never before. "Get the hell out of here immediately… both of you! Don't stand there looking at me like a couple of zombies. I'm serious. Go! Do as I say," he's shouting, causing them to take it seriously.

And he stops staring at them, maybe for one last time, pleading. "Please, Martha…please, Doug…get out of here and do as I tell you," he pleads, as they look at him wondering how suddenly he's in the middle of the fray knowing nothing about nothing.

Arthur (Mac) Mc Caffry

Doug is struggling with himself, wanting to move back to assist Roberts, but Martha holds tight to him, shouting, screaming for him to stay. She has no idea what's taking place, but Doug knows Mike well and knows when he's serious!

Mike, Roberts, Duncan, and Orwell suddenly stop, standing, staring at each other in the middle of the concourse outside the restroom entrance. Without warning, Orwell pulls a pistol from his side, shoving it hard into Robert's stomach, causing him to grunt with pain. Duncan stands beside him, glaring toward the two, ready to join in the action.

Bystanders have cleared most of the area, waiting, but seeing the pistol drawn, panic sets in, shouting, "Guns! Guns!" And from the far side of the concourse, another shouts, "Bombs! Bombs!" And from far down the concourse, all hell is again breaking loose as police come running from out of nowhere.

Orwell and Duncan stand looking at each other, panicked. It's time for action, no way out but to fight, kill them all, die for the cause!

Duncan grabs Roberts by his arm, opening the restroom door, seeing occupants left inside, crying hysterically. And instantly, he's yelling all out, "Get out of here, you cowards…unless you're prepared to meet your god this moment!"

Orwell places his pistol to Mike's head, threatening to do the same, shoving him inside ruthlessly. And from the far corner of the restroom, there's a sudden stampede of half-dressed men running for the door, looking for safety.

Time is running out, and Orwell knows it. He pushes Mike against the wall, striking him hard with his pistol, till he staggers, falling to the concrete floor, losing his senses.

God Help Us

Outside the restroom sirens wail, people are screaming, but none are about to enter. Duncan stands over Mike, poised like a giant, a man gone wild, blood in his eyes, wanting to kill all.

Roberts remains calm, never speaking. Slowly, he begins moving closer to Mike, seeing eyes blinking, looking upward. And he smiles, looking down at him pleasantly.

But Duncan isn't finished. He shoves Roberts hard against the wall again, pounding him with his pistol. Blow after blow falls hard upon Roberts's head and shoulder 'till finally, he drops, looking up, joining Mike beside him.

Fear filled with anger shows deep upon Duncan's face as he announces, "You two boys can make the switch real easy for yourselves by handing over the tapes here and now!"

And he stops, beginning to grin, saying, "Or you can take the other route by making it your final day on earth! The decision is up to you alone! Time is running out! And we're not about to leave this place without the tapes, it's now or never…so hand them over!"

Roberts stares toward Mike's bloody wound still bleeding. And quickly, his sense of pride overwhelms everything surrounding. Mike can only smile back toward him with the same look he saw over thirty years ago at a place called Phu Bai. It makes him grin, being part of this, enjoying the moment, maybe his last moment…whatever! But he's enjoying it, staring at Roberts while his thumb points upward smiling. And blood begins flowing from Robert's nostrils like a fountain. He looks toward Mike again, displaying his usual big grin, satisfied, muttering lowly.

"Maybe I don't know how to say this, but it looks like we're right back at the Phu Bai airport with our back to the wall, doesn't it, Mike?" Roberts asks, beginning to enjoy the moment.

Mike grins, trying to move closer, but the pain is bad. "Well, I'd say it's this way, sir. We sure as hell didn't quit then, and it's too late to even think about quitting now, Colonel," he says with a forced smile, but yet a pleasure.

Duncan's anger explodes. He pulls Roberts up from the floor, ramming his pistol hard into his ribs, so hard, it makes him yell with pain.

Orwell can stand it no more, letting an outburst of cursing and yelling. "Shut up, you old bastard, you haven't yet learned what it's all about, have you?" he's shouting. "Well, my old and faithful friend...you're about to learn the facts of life the hard way."

Duncan joins the act, making the situation worse. He picks Mike up bodily, dropping him to the floor, kicking him, over and over, again and again.

"I'm telling you, Roberts, for the last time, give us the tapes here and now, or I'll shove this pistol down your throat and blow your brains all over this place," Orwell shouts strongly.

Roberts looks at Mike lying beside him in pain. "You're right with the Lord, aren't you, Mike?" he asks, grinning.

"Never better, sir! My score is settled: my name is in the book. And for some unknown reason, I'm beginning to feel like the Apostle Paul, thinking of some famous words he once uttered when things looked the worst."

"What words. Mike?"

'I'm the least of the least, Colonel! "Maybe, just around the corner, he and I will meet, and I'll be somebody...someday!"

Roberts looks upward to where his captors stand looking down at him, showing no mercy. And he returns their smiles, showing some unexpected delight.

God Help Us

"I guess you boys have us in a hard spot for sure, not that I haven't been there before. But I'm old enough to know when I'm licked and there's no use to go further!"

And Orwell can't resist, asking, "And your choice is what, Roberts…what?"

He motions for Orwell to bend down, move closer beside him. "You really surprise me, Orwell, you're smarter than I gave you credit," he says, grinning as if pleased.

Orwell moves even closer, waiting for more.

"I'm done for, Orwell, no use to fight further! I'm going to give you what you came for, the prize of all prizes belongs to the victor always! But I do have some pride left within me, something you alone can do for me," Roberts says, head bowed in shame before him.

"Yes! Yes! Tell me, Roberts…" he's begging.

And Roberts looks up at him, pitiful-like. "My only hope is that you two let bygones be bygones," he says, pleading.

Orwell moves even closer, ready to take the case from Roberts.

And Roberts doesn't hesitate, pulling his key from inside his suit vest, unlocking the chain, holding the case bound to his wrist.

Orwell rises from the floor, moving across the room where Duncan stands waiting. And surprisingly, he hands the case to him before opening.

"You're the one who settled our score with these guys, Duncan. Only you should have the honor of removing the tapes and recorder, my friend," Orwell says, handing it to him, grinning.

And a huge smile of triumph appears on Duncan's face, displaying his pleasure. Slowly, precisely, he places the key in

| 351 |

the lock turning it quickly, and *boom*! An explosion so loud it can be heard far and away.

The large restroom is gutted in a second! Walls fall, like dominoes, one upon one from all four sides, blocking the door from without. Smoke begins to show while broken pipes send water spewing high into the air above. Mike still lies on his back bleeding from within while his arm hangs limp, shattered in three parts, dangling. Roberts lies close to him no better, both legs shattered, bleeding from his side, feeling pain as never before while both Duncan and Orwell lay in pieces, beyond recognition.

"Can you hear me, Mike?" Roberts can barely ask.

"Hear you well, Colonel."

"I've got something to tell you—something important!"

"What's important at a time like this, Colonel?" a weak voice barely mumbles.

"I just want you to know something, Mike…"

And a still weaker voice asks, "Something about what, sir?"

A moment of hesitation, and finally an old gruff-sounding voice from the past says, "You were one helluva marine, Mike! I never liked the way you wouldn't listen to me, but I was always proud of you!"

Mike tries to laugh, but it's useless, he can barely speak.

"You mean Phu Bai, where blood flowed like water in a storm? But now, I've a question for you, Colonel."

"Let it fly, Mike…time's wasting."

"Do you believe in predestination, like what the Bible teaches us, sir?"

He grits his teeth, trying to speak.

God Help Us

"Never really thought about the subject, Mike, but it sure is beginning to look like we're about to leave this place pretty soon together!"

"I wouldn't be so sure, Colonel," Mike barely can mutter.

"But it's different this time, Mike…it's different for sure!"

"How different, sir?"

"I see someone coming…coming closer and closer. And she's beautiful, Mike…so beautiful! And now she's dancing upon water! And the sun, so bright, so heavenly…"

And his voice stops…silence all over!

Roberts's shattered body remains lying on the busted concrete floor covered in blood. And from a short distance away, a white shadowy figure moves closer and closer, while Mike struggles to see who's coming, barely breathing.

And suddenly, his face begins to lighten, recognizing him. It's Friend, his guardian angel, reaching out to him smiling. And the pain, the suffering, all gone in a moment!

Friend reaches down to him pulling him closer, while his fiery eyes dance, sparkling as diamonds. And softly, he whispers the words he's been waiting to hear, "It's time to go home, Mike. He's waiting for you, today, tomorrow…forever and ever… throughout eternity!"

Outside the concourse, the welcoming delegation stand gazing within toward the massive amount of destruction feeling sadly. And suddenly, their faces brighten! They're gazing upward toward heaven, beginning to realize life isn't over! It's just beginning! Mike is gone from this world, but his spirit lives with His Lord, and Savior, forever and ever, in a place called heaven!

43

Predestination

For whom he did foreknow, he also did predestinate
to be conformed to the image of his Son, that he
might be the firstborn of among many brethren.

—Romans 8:29

Cries ring out throughout! Calling people's names go unanswered. Hundreds stand in shock observing death and destruction before their very eyes. Firemen, policemen, all are running, shouting orders, hoping to restore order in an uncontrolled situation. And in the middle of the crowd, a policeman stands upon a platform addressing a crowd of hundreds of stunned onlookers, shouting over a bullhorn.

"Attention! Attention! Do as we instruct! It's necessary you comply with my instructions for your own safety. I've taken measures to keep this situation from spreading further, and with your cooperation, we'll get this matter under control."

And from out in the crowd, someone yells, "But what 'bout the ones inside, the dead, the injured?"

"My men are about to reach those trapped inside, sir, but give us time—please. As soon as possible they will be brought forward, and with your cooperation, things will soon be under control. Injured bodies are everywhere, and all I ask is that you stay back and away, so we can handle this situation without interference. But I must remind you, officers will not tolerate civil disturbance in any form or any way!" he tries to explain over the screaming and yelling from all directions.

The mounting crowd of persons grows even larger and the captain decides to act immediately. Time is wasting, time to clear the area from hysterical screaming onlookers.

"I want every person to move out quickly unless you're absolutely sure your loved ones are inside the damaged area hurting. Now move out slow and orderly where security personnel can take your names and talk to you as you pass forward."

He steps down from the platform, handing his horn to another, heading toward the restroom.

Doug moves toward Intelligence people he recognizes, offering his credentials. They walk quickly to a nearby undamaged office where a tall thin-looking agent about sixty or sixty-five with a weathered-looking face sits looking up to him, announcing, "Step inside and take a seat, Doug. I'm William Reynolds, agent in charge of this operation."

Doug looks at him, surprised. "And I'm Doug Cutler, sir, associated with Mr. Roberts as his aide, glad you're here."

"Sit, Doug, I'll brief you on some matters, along with the services of a dozen of our own. I'm aware you're not up on everything, so I'll bring you up-to-date on our part in this matter."

"Great, Mr. Reynolds, it's time I know."

Reynolds douses a cigar he's smoking, throwing it into a nearby empty trash dispenser.

"Bad habit, I know, Doug, trying to quit. Suppose we get down to business and go over some things, things both of us need to know before moving further," he says, friendly.

Arthur (Mac) Mc Caffry

"You begin the conversation by telling me what you know, starting at the beginning with Marla. I'll see if it jibes with my information, and when you're finished, I'll brief you on what we know up to now and the part we're about to play. But in the meantime, gather all your thoughts and mind together. This just might take a while, my friend," he says, removing his coat, ready for business.

Slowly and deliberately, Doug gathers his thoughts."

Perspiration shows quickly upon his forehead as he thinks back to Marla, De Marco, the secret meeting of De Marco and other leaders gathering in Bali. He continues on and on, describing contents of the cell phone, the recorder, information valuable to the department. When he comes to the part of meeting Orwell and Duncan, he wipes his eyes and takes a break, trying to visualize traitors, ones to speak about in the same tone as persons he loved so well.

Finally, he's able to bring his words together without paying the price of crying. He finishes it up with their words of betrayal.

"It was Orwell and Duncan, sir, from Military Intelligence. Roberts knew them from way back…knew them well," he mutters, holding back tears.

Quickly, a fellow agent next to him reaches out, placing his hand upon his shoulder, offering condolence.

"He knew them back when, Doug?" he asks.

"Years ago, sir, while serving in the Far East…all over the world. He once told me he never trusted a lot of people, but when we watched them coming to us, he seemed pleased, as if they were old friends, some of our own," Doug tries to explain.

Reynolds looks him over again, shaking his head, finding it hard to believe, but knowing it's true.

God Help Us

"It's a sorry state of affairs, Doug, no fault of yours or Roberts," he says, rising from his desk, showing his anger.

Without warning, he begins slamming books around lying on his desk in a sudden display of anger. Doug watches in silence as Reynolds walks in circles, cursing his once friends, now traitors, without stopping.

And Doug can take it no longer sitting, watching Reynolds display a sense of futility, madness without end.

He rises from his chair, confronting him. "But to me, Mr. Reynolds, the whole affair is very simple!" he says, causing Reynolds to stop, look up at him, taking notice.

He confronts Doug instantly, still angry.

"And now what are talking about, Doug? This is serious as it gets, no time for foolishness."

Doug moves against him, letting the same attitude he speaks with back at him, strong and meaningful.

"There's no other way to put it, Mr. Reynolds—we've been had, not something too pleasant a subject to talk about! For some unknown reason, all the facts point to two of our own!"

"Keep going, Doug…I'm listening!"

"Roberts and I were in charge of delivering some secret information back to headquarters here in Washington. And at the end of the journey, we were taken…taken by two of our very own, the ones we trusted most! We did our job and we did it well, but when it was over, it carried a price…a heavy price, sir."

"Carry on, Doug…tell me the rest of it."

"Simple, sir. We made the switch with Marla and delivered the tapes as expected without a hitch. The switch at the last moment arranged by Roberts was the only thing preventing them from getting away with it."

Reynolds's anger subsides, becoming calm. He shakes his head, stunned again, staring at Doug as in disbelief. Finally, the shock is over, moving next to him, offering his hand, apologizing.

"You're right, Doug, your plan was brilliant. Roberts was one of the old warhorse type of guy, a step ahead of everyone."

"But what bothers me more than anything, sir, is the fact Duncan and Orwell had credentials as good as mine. Roberts knew their history after serving with them for years. But if he hadn't asked for the code word, they could have pulled it off for sure."

Reynolds stops suddenly! Looking again at him, shocked!

"Code word! What codeword?" he asks, surprised. "Hell, there was no code word, Doug. This gets crazier by the moment: nothing was ever mentioned about a code word."

They rise, staring at one another, wondering. And Reynolds begins to chuckle.

"But now, what's so funny, Reynolds, let me in on it for God's sake."

And he stops chuckling, gets his breath, facing Doug.

"Think about this for a change, Doug. The sly old fox just put it to the ones that killed him, they didn't have the slightest idea what he was doing. It was Robert's way of giving them his final check. Smart move from a smart guy, one we'll always remember...that's for sure!"

And Doug is speechless! It's his time to stare at Reynolds in wonder.

"Oh no, it can't be! That dirty wonderful old fox! That double-dealing old fox!" Doug is shouting as he circles the desk with his arms flailing upward. "The guy I thought I really knew actually pulled one on me, his aide!"

God Help Us

Standing close, other agents join the laughter, heading to the door, leaving the office.

Only a couple agents remain as Doug and Reynolds continue on and on without stopping.

"Roberts explained to me the possibility of traitors. He worried about others, but never these two, Mr. Reynolds."

And he stops, confronting Reynolds. "But something bothers me, sir...something I must know before going further—"

"Let it out, Doug."

And he doesn't hesitate asking, "But why did this happen from the most trusted, our very own?"

Reynolds becomes speechless again, looking away, searching for an answer.

"This isn't easy, Doug, but there's only way of saying it—we slipped up! We slipped up bad! Orwell and Duncan were let go two years ago, and for some unknown reason, you weren't notified," he says, with a shaking voice filled with humility.

Doug is stunned again, gazing at Reynolds in disbelief.

"You failed to notify us! No! No! This can't be!" Doug is shouting, facing the other two agents.

Reynolds can only barely mutter, "But it happened, Doug... it happened!"

"But these two guys had credentials, sir. I checked them over and over, time and time again, just before Mike grabbed me from behind. I swear they had credentials, credentials as good as my own, sir. They were our friends, Roberts's best friends!" Doug is shouting for everyone to hear him.

And pity begins to show upon Reynolds's face unexpectedly. He wants desperately to make Doug understand, but can't find words fitting the occasion.

With his head bowed low, Reynolds moves next to him, placing his hand upon his shoulder ready to explain.

"They were no longer ours, Doug! I can't put it to you any other way! The love they once felt for our country was turned to De Marco, turned against us, traitors to their country."

Doug looks at him hard again, dropping his head, feeling his sadness.

"And what's next on the menu, sir?"

"You'll be briefed on what's taking place in this country you and I love and adore. It's getting scary, Doug…real scary! And when I try explaining the situation to others, everything goes silent…they don't want to hear it."

"Trouble's ahead of us for sure, Mr. Reynolds. Roberts and I been preaching it."

Reynolds takes his time, studying Doug, waiting. "I made a mistake, Doug, a terrible mistake! I believe everyone has."

Doug glares at him, waiting, hoping.

"Out with it, Mr. Reynolds…I'm a big boy now, I've learned a lot!" he says, staring him down, waiting.

A long pause, staring back at him a couple of times and Reynolds confronts him, "You have indeed, Doug. I see it in your eyes. Time we talk about some private matters, our thoughts, our beliefs…our faith!"

"It is, sir. Someone has to."

"I've underestimated our enemies, my friend! We're playing with fire and people can't recognize it. We're in trouble as never before, searching, hoping for a way out!"

Doug hangs his head, thinking back, reminiscing, as Reynolds continues.

"I wish I knew the answer to this problem, Doug. We lost one of our best, and you lost an uncle willing to give his life for you.

God Help Us

By all reports coming to us from Bali, we knew the relationship you shared with Roberts was far greater than just boss and aide, more like father and son."

"We were close, sir, very close. And Uncle Mike…one of the best! He knew what he was doing. I remember how he shoved me away, giving his life for me. And, Mr. Roberts, how can I better describe him? A man of his own, a man of honor if ever…how else, how else can I better describe him?" Doug says, hanging his head as his voice begins to break once again.

And Reynolds has heard enough; he can't take it anymore. He extends his hand in friendship, looking puzzled indeed!

"Shut the door and lock it, Doug. There's something I need to tell you…something important…why I went to pieces."

Doug sits across from him at the desk. Reynolds hesitates slightly, looking casually around the room seeing none other.

"I'll begin with this, Doug. Roberts was close to me, much closer than anyone knew. We served in Nam together back in the late sixties and early seventies. I was a young second lieutenant, just out of West Point assigned to the 101st Airborne under the command of then Colonel Nathaniel P. Roberts. Things were happening fast and furious all around us, hardly anyone knew where we were at most of the time. And our unit helped evacuate most everyone left alive at an airport, a place in hell, I'll never forget."

And Doug reaches across the desk, stopping him.

"Stop—please, Mr. Reynolds, don't go further till I ask you a question," he says, holding back reluctantly.

"You sound as if you know something, Doug. Go ahead, ask."

A wide grin appears upon Doug's face.

"The airport you speak of, could it possibly be near the village Phu Bai?" he asks.

Arthur (Mac) Mc Caffry

And quickly, Reynolds pulls back staring at him.

"It was Phu Bai!" he shouts. "But how in the hell do you know about Phu Bai? You're not half the age it takes to know about things with memories of hell on earth."

He doesn't let Doug respond.

"I left Phu Bai ahead of the colonel on a chopper back to De Nang. Roberts always insisted on being the last chopper out, but this time for some reason, it was a little different.

"But what does different mean, Mr. Reynolds?"

"Before he could get away, something bad happened, bringing him under fire."

Doug knows the ending, but says nothing.

"When Roberts finally arrived at De Nang, he had a couple of wounded marines with him. One was shot all to hell, and the pilot told us how the colonel was about to shoot the other one he called one crazy-ass marine."

Doug waits, listening only.

"Later, there was a board of inquiry set up at De Nang with a couple of naval officers present wanting to press charges for Mike's action of disobeying orders, something marines don't like," he tries to explain.

"And what was the end of it," Doug asks, innocent like.

Reynolds begins to laugh.

"This will kill you, Doug, it's unbelievable! I was there with Roberts and got the shock of my life. They questioned Roberts about Mike's refusal to leave—wanting to kill everyone in sight, and the colonel just sat there laughing without end. It was hilarious, and nobody knew why. But I'll never forget his answer when they asked him if Mike deserved to be court-martialed."

"And what was his answer?" Doug asks, anxiously.

Reynolds can't hold back; he chuckles loud before answering.

God Help Us

"How can I ever forget? He looked toward the jury and said, 'Court martial, hell! This crazy-ass marine is a hero. I saw him kill a dozen of the enemy and loved every second of it. Hell, General, if I had a hundred like him, I could have won that stupid-ass war. I hereby recommend him for the Silver Star, and that's my final!'"

Doug can't wait. "And then what?"

"He got up from his seat, looked over at the General, and left, along with everyone. Investigation—over! And I still remember the day, the time, and the look on every marine's face hearing Robert's statement. And oh brother! How they loved him."

And Doug explodes, thinking, *That's my Uncle Mike for sure... nothing like him!*

"I can't help but laugh, Mr. Reynolds. This has to be one for the books."

Reynolds looks at him perplexed, wondering. "And now... what are you talking about, Doug?" he asks, surprised at his statement.

"It's simple, sir. The crazy-ass Marine you so easily describe was my uncle, Mike Cutler," he says proudly.

Reynolds rises from his chair, looking petrified. Finally, he mutters, "You're joking, of course—"

"It's true, Mr. Reynolds. They met three times for only a few hours total, but there was something greater directing their movements. Something I believe strongly, something I call predestination!"

And interest begins to build within Reynolds.

"I've always wondered about predestination. Come and see me at headquarters tomorrow. After you make your report, someone will brief you on what's going on within. You're welcome anytime, Doug. Anything else I can do... I will."

Arthur (Mac) Mc Caffry

"Thank you, sir. Maybe I'll be seeing you sooner than you think."

And Reynolds begins to think again.

"I believe you need some time off, Doug! Time to get your thoughts together…realize what you're about to get into. You've earned it, Doug."

They shake hands and Doug moves out satisfied. He begins thinking back to a time he sat across from Mike, wondering if he was going make the grade for something called, Mission Impossible. He remembers Mike telling him about a friend who told him he was chosen, and how often he wondered what it meant. But now he understands; it's predestined, something you can't get away from—no matter how hard you try…ever.

44

A Man to Remember

He will swallow up death in victory; and the Lord
God will wipe away tears from all faces.

—Isaiah 25:8

There's no celebration in order for Doug's return. Ailene writes a stirring memoir of Mike's life appearing in the Star. It tells of his love, hatred, and forgiveness. She tells of his life on the battlefield with Roberts, their death together at Kennedy, and his long-sought search for a place he called Shangri-La. And she tells how he sacrificed his life for another, believing His will.

Her newspaper days are ended, their plan for marriage over, all in an act of betrayal by some of his own. And when you read between the lines, her story isn't just a story of heroism, but a hidden note of love and devotion.

Body parts gathered from the floor of the restroom arrive home unnoticed, and on burial day, hundreds gather. Ailene sits with family members along with Ethel. And it's silent throughout as Brad stands tall beginning his eulogy.

"I'm heartbroken as many of you. But this I know for sure, Mike, our friend, ended up where he always wanted to be. He came to this church a couple of years ago and made a difference. We became friends, more like brothers. Recently, he made a personal request to me. He asked me to have someone sing a

| 365 |

couple of his favorite songs if he should depart this world soon after. But Mike was different! He was always talking about being some place different, places like the New Jerusalem or meeting people like Peter, Paul, and Mary Magdalene, or like someone he met when things looked bad—a guy called Friend.

"Mike had no fear of death: as a matter of fact, he kind of looked forward to it, causing me to wonder! But today, thinking again, I believe maybe it was because of his best friend, Ethel. She told him about a place called the New Jerusalem, and he fell in love with it like nobody ever!"

Complete silence, and suddenly it's hard for some restraining their laughter.

"We talked aboard the plane to Kennedy and he expressed hidden desires, his desire to serve the Lord. But it was Mike's time to go—as it will be for all of us, and I can assure you, Mike was ready! And today I ask myself the same, am I ready?

"Ms. Jackson, will you please do us the honor of singing Mike's song, 'On Eagle's Wings.'"

Coming from behind the pulpit, a very lovely lady appears dressed in a beautiful long black gown ready to perform. She opens her arms, looking skyward. And her voice resounds throughout.

Tears appear from young and old, but only Ethel sits near the casket, smiling with pleasure.

She finishes her powerful song and Brad tells the biblical story how the prodigal son came home to his father and began his life anew. He tells of personal things and their friendship.

"Mike and I talked about what heaven might be, and I remember his statement well. He said, 'Well, Brad, it's time for me to confess.'"

Silence again throughout, while all eyes stay fixed upon Brad, waiting.

God Help Us

"I asked him what he must confess. And I'll never forget his answer. He looked me in the eye and said, 'Well, it's like this, my friend: if my day should come before yours, this is my wish. Keep my eulogy short and sweet. Sing no sad songs for me. But more than anything, tell them how He removed my sin as far as the east to the west at a place called Calvary.'"

And Ethel's eyes sparkle as never before, satisfied.

"Today, I will therefore honor Mike's request telling you, good-bye, God bless you till we meet again tomorrow."

Mike's family moves slowly to the casket with Brad leading the way. One after one, they touch his casket. And suddenly, a young man dressed in white linen stands next to Ethel. They hold hands, touching his casket. A sound of taps from an honor guard, and Ethel stands alone, looking upward smiling.

She moves close to Ailene, looking up into her eyes pleasantly. "Please, darling, stop the crying. Don't you know he's just around the corner?" she says, giggling.

And Ailene is looking at her puzzled. "But where around the corner?" she asks.

Ethel looks up into her eyes in disbelief. Everyone should know the answer, she assumes.

"The New Jerusalem, darling, the place Jesus built for people like us. Mike and I have it all planned to meet there, but please don't worry, sweetheart, you'll be there, too," she says, giggling again.

Ailene wants to say something, but it's hard saying anything to someone like Ethel.

"But there's something else I must tell you, Ethel…"

"What is it, my darling?" she asks, ever so pleased, waiting.

Arthur (Mac) Mc Caffry

And with a huge smile crossing her face, Ailene says, "You're one foxy old gal for sure, Ethel—no wonder Mike loved you as his mother."

"I know! I know! I loved him too, darling," she says, ever so pleased, giggling again.

The funeral is over and Doug and Martha return home. They see the message light flashing. A voice says, "Doug, this is Colonel Robert Poindexter with Military Intelligence in DC. I know this isn't a good time to talk business, but I need you in my office soon as possible. Bring Martha with you if she desires."

Doug glances toward Martha and she gives him the nod.

He dials Poindexter and he's still at his office.

"This is Doug, sir. Got your message and we'll be at your office at one p.m. tomorrow.

"But hold on a moment, Doug, another matter needs to be discussed."

"Yes, Colonel."

"Well, it's like this, Doug, we've been trying to locate our friend Joshua Bernstein, but so far, no luck. He could be in hiding, without friends, but always welcome with us. He's a good man, a trustworthy man."

"He is, sir, no doubt about it; we'll talk about it tomorrow."

The following morning, Martha and Doug leave for Washington, wondering what's so important. They arrive at Poindexter's office on time, anxious to begin.

Colonel Poindexter greets them cordially, pointing to a couple chairs across from him.

"I believe I have some news for you, Doug, good news for a change."

Doug looks at Poindexter and back to Martha, waiting.

God Help Us

"But I haven't the slightest idea what you mean, Colonel, but good news is welcome anytime."

"Pull your chairs up closer in front of me. I want to see your eyes."

And they're interested, moving quickly, sitting across the desk, staring at him.

And he begins to smile. "You, Doug Cutler, are the designated heir to Mr. Roberts's entire estate! I talked to him before you left Bali, and he sent me his last will and testament. He explained how you and he were like father and son, not only friends, but cared for one another. He cared for you deeply, worried about your safety delivering the tapes. And today, we know he had good reason to worry."

And Doug sits listening, motionless. He's over-whelmed, searching for words. Martha sits listening, surprised, saying nothing.

"But this is really hard for me to understand, Colonel. I knew him only a short time, but we confided with each other, sparing nothing. I knew he trusted me, and I did the same. He taught me things, made me think and understand life," Doug tries to explain.

"You've just given a good description of Roberts, Doug. He was truly a man for all seasons," Poindexter adds.

And Doug moves closer to him wanting to say something, something he believes important.

"But when I look back and add it all up, there was one thing I'll always remember him for," Doug says in dead seriousness.

"Explain it to me, Doug."

Doug looks across to Martha and back to Poindexter, wanting to make it right.

| 369 |

"I found his inner feelings, sir, his heart and soul. He was guided by his faith in God and country, the two most important things in his life. He was like a father I never knew. But there was something else…"

"Tell me about it."

"It's something I'm sure about, sir, for Roberts and me, it isn't over. We talked about the hereafter…the hereafter and then… what?"

"And what does 'then what' mean, Doug?"

Doug looks him over again. "I don't need telling you the answer, sir, I can see it upon your face, your words…you're one of us waiting hear the sound…"

And instantly, Poindexter looks at him again, asking, "The sound of what, Doug?"

"You know what I'm talking about, the sound of a bugle high in the sky…and Him, riding a white horse ready to take us home!" Doug responds without waiting.

And he looks at him again, thinking seriously, admiringly. He sees him as a young, vigorous, challenging young man for the first time. And with trouble coming for sure, he needs his kind.

Poindexter moves closer, glaring at him from across the table.

"There's more, Doug. This isn't the end of our relationship, we're on the same side, there's a lot more of this kind of talk coming later. Roberts was smart, real smart. He let me know a couple of months ago you're informed about everything, everything true Americans fight for. And that's the way I am too, Doug, standing before you, telling you the same," he says, strong and powerful, causing Doug to look again at him giving orders, sounding like Roberts.

Poindexter rises slowly from the table, walks around where Doug sits next to Martha, and grasps his hand.

God Help Us

"Would you like to carry on the same policy Nate did, Doug, the same way he did beginning this very day?" he asks, bluntly.

And Doug looks up at him, grinning. "I told him my feelings then, my commitment hasn't changed. Nothing could please me better, sir."

Poindexter places his left hand upon his shoulder, shaking his hand, smiling.

"You've met the test, Doug, from this moment forward, you're one of us."

Doug studies his words looking pleased. "It's an honor and a pleasure, sir, I'll give it my best, believe me I will."

"Later you'll meet our group here in Washington. Go visit his grave at Arlington and come back when you're settled. There's a lot going on...trouble brewing across the globe, never letting up."

"Roberts stated the same to me before his death, sir."

"But there's another matter, Doug..."

"Another matter, sir?" he asks surprised, waiting.

"What do you know about, Joshua...Joshua Bernstein? He's missing and it bothers me...bothers all of us."

"Joshua met us at the airport during the exchange. He said he and his followers in Israel were waiting to see what takes place after the seven year treaty is signed. He seemed to be okay, but I could tell he was worried."

Poindexter looks up at him, shaking his head. "I don't blame him for being worried! He has a lot to be worried about once the Palestinians move beside them as a nation in Jerusalem."

The meeting is over, and Doug and Martha waste no time heading for Roberts grave at Arlington National Cemetery. They stand gazing upon the headstone. An inscription in big letters reads:

> Nathaniel P. Roberts, Colonel, US Army
> West Point, Sergeant Major, Class of 1965"
> Member of "The Long Grey-Line: Lover of God and Country"

Next to his grave is his father's grave, another West Point cadet. Next to his father's grave is his grandfather's grave—all West Point.

Martha becomes emotional, and for the first time, a tear appears.

"Three generations of Roberts served our country, heroes all. And today, they rest with God," Martha says somberly, walking slowly away, leaving Doug alone.

Moments of sorrow remembering their time together, and suddenly, he comes to attention, saluting before his grave respectfully.

And he turns away, pondering again, thinking back to their conversation before arriving at Kennedy. With tears in his eyes, he walks slowly away, hanging his head. Finally, tears cease, his face begins to glow, and a smile returns. He remembers his friend's proudest moment, telling him his name is written in the Book of Life forever...his worries are over!

—⁂—

Six weeks go by, and Doug and Martha sit at home having breakfast. The phone rings, he picks it up, and a business-only type of voice says, "This is the law firm of Johnson and Pratt. I wish to speak to Mr. Doug Cutler."

"This is Doug, sir," he answers.

"We're ready to read you the settlement as stated in Nathaniel P. Robert's last will and testament. Can you be here tomorrow at ten a. m., Mr. Cutler?"

God Help Us

"My wife and I will be with you at ten tomorrow, sir," he replies, wondering what's in store ahead.

They leave early the next morning, and ten minutes till ten, they're seated in the attorney's office. An elderly well-dressed gentleman versed in law introduces himself.

"I'm Robert Johnson, attorney for your late friend, Nathaniel P. Roberts. Suppose we get down to business immediately with facts and figures. Okay with you, Mr. Cutler?" he asks, smiling friendly.

"It is fine with me, sir."

"I'll proceed with the reading of Mr. Roberts's last will and testament. My secretary will make note of our meeting in detail, and within a week, you will receive a complete report of this entire meeting. Are there questions before we begin, Mr. Cutler?"

Martha and Doug look at one another, wondering what's taking place.

"No questions needed."

"Good! Now we can move on. His will is a very plain and simple will, easy to understand. You, Mr. Cutler, are the sole heir to all assets bearing the name Nathaniel P. Roberts. The 6,000-acre ranch in Montana is yours, Mr. Cutler. That includes cattle, barns, any type of structures, etc. The only remaining thing not yours is the air above," he says, chuckling.

"And the last notation of the will reads as follows: Doug only will understand the case."

Doug looks over at Martha, wondering, and back to his attorney, glaring at him, waiting, and finally continuing, "But yet today, we're still trying to determine his intentions with the case. But it's yours, Mr. Cutler, it's yours!"

Arthur (Mac) Mc Caffry

And there's a flare of mystery when they gaze upon a small case lying in the middle of the large desk before them. Doug opens the case and enclosed in fine silver wrapping is the biggest blackest Cuban cigar he has ever seen. He wants to laugh all out but remembers where he's at, so he holds back. Lying beside the cigar is another small package with two musical recordings. They read, "Julie Andrews sings 'The Sound of Music.'" And the other reads, "Judy Garland sings 'Somewhere Over the Rainbow.'"

Doug lowers his head thinking back, fighting tears. He alone knew the colonel and all his earthly pleasures. Long moments of reminiscing again, and he turns away, beginning to laugh. And with a final good-bye, another glance back to the big Cuban cigar sitting next to the recording, he mutters low, tenderly, "And thanks again, Mr. Roberts…thanks again for being the father I longed for, but never knew."

And as our Lord and Savior once said while hanging from a cross looking up at his father at a place called Calvary, "It is finished!"

CPSIA information can be obtained
at www.ICGtesting.com
Printed in the USA
FFOW03n0653070616
24805FF

9 781681 642246